4. 1. 21
22. 1. 21
29/11/21

D0512435

Please renew or return items by the date
shown on your receipt

www.hertfordshire.gov.uk/libraries

Renewals and enquiries: 0300 123 4049

Textphone for hearing or 0300 123 4041
speech impaired users:

.32 11.16

'Porter gives you everything you want' *Telegraph*

528 633 08 3

Henry Porter was a regular columnist for the *Observer* and now writes about European power and politics for The Hive website in the US. He has written six bestselling thrillers, including *Brandenburg*, which won the CWA Ian Fleming Steel Dagger, *A Spy's Life* and *Empire State*, which were both nominated for the same award. His most recent thriller was the universally praised *Firefly*. Henry Porter is frequently described as the heir to John le Carré. He lives in London.

Also by Henry Porter

Remembrance Day
A Spy's Life
Empire State
The Dying Light
Firefly

FOR CHILDREN

Master of the Fallen Chairs

HENRY PORTER
BRANDENBURG

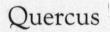

First published in Great Britain in 2005 by Orion
This paperback edition published in 2019 by

Quercus Editions Ltd
Carmelite House
50 Victoria Embankment
London EC4Y 0DZ

An Hachette UK company

A CIP catalogue record for this book is available
from the British Library

PB ISBN 978 1 78747 945 6

10 9 8 7 6 5 4 3 2 1

Typeset by Jouve (UK), Milton Keynes

Printed and bound in Great Britain by Clays Ltd, Elcograf S.p.A.

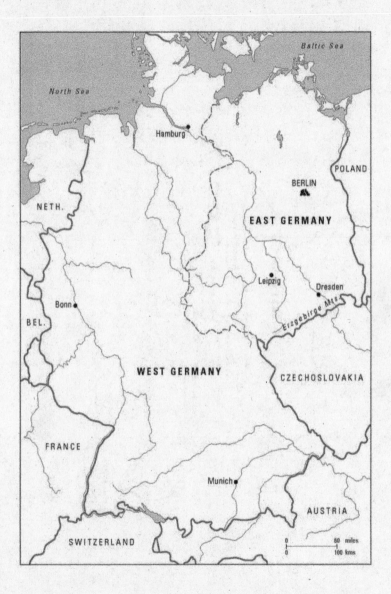

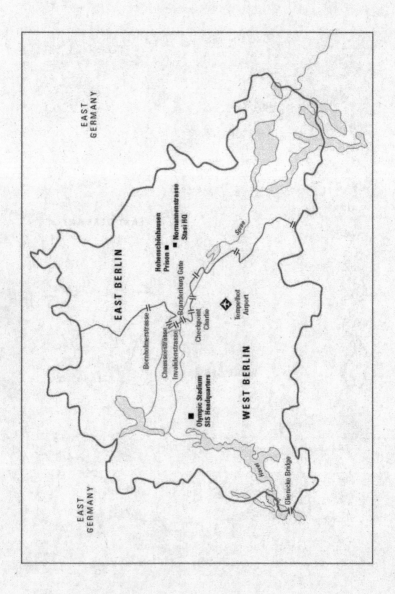

PART ONE

ONE

Edge of the Void

The man in the straw hat dogged his footsteps from the first, keeping his distance, yet never bothering to hide himself. Rosenharte saw him loitering outside the hotel when he checked in, then at the conference centre and later sitting at a cafe in Piazza dell'Unità, a mournful fellow with a washed-out face, who wore the hat unconvincingly on the back of his head as though he'd just won it in a shooting gallery.

At times he got so close that Rosenharte could see the ventilation holes in the side of the hat and a mark on the narrow brim. He wanted to be seen – that much was clear – and once or twice Rosenharte thought he was going to approach, but then he seemed to decide against it and darted away into a side street.

He wondered if the man was the visible part of the Stasi's surveillance operation in Trieste, put on his tail to remind him of their presence. Though he didn't need it; they had made it clear to him that the city would be saturated with officers. Everything he did would be watched.

Perhaps the man was being fielded by a Western agency as some kind of ploy to draw out the Stasi surveillance. But that didn't make sense either. If the Americans or British were watching – which surely they were – they would know about the Stasi and include them in their calculations. Eventually he concluded that the straw hat was a detail, a side issue to something far more menacing.

He ignored the man and threw himself into the conference on the rise of artistic conscience in the late Renaissance, a theme that had drawn 150 academics from all over Europe. Between lectures and discussion groups, Dr Rudi Rosenharte explored the streets of the hot, carefree city that was so beautifully drenched in summer light. He took himself to the bars around the main square for cognac and espresso and watched the passing parade, marvelling at the unbelievable fullness and plenty of Italian life and – naturally – at the women. Even now his eyes were not dead to their charms, or to the contrast with life in East Germany where beauty was scorned as a bourgeois obsession and you couldn't buy a lemon from one month to the next.

Yet never for a moment did he forget that he had been brought to Trieste to rendezvous with an old lover – a lover who he knew had been dead for the best part of fifteen years but who the Stasi believed was alive.

On his third day in Trieste she made contact. Inside an envelope containing the daily conference bulletin was a handwritten note from Annalise Schering, which instructed him to walk unaccompanied to the end of 'Molo IV' – Pier Number Four – in the Old Port, where she would be waiting in the early evening with chilled champagne. There was much to admire about the letter: the handwriting was perfect, the romantic urgency of the sentiments just right and the location exactly the sort of desolate, neglected place Annalise would have chosen. It was as if the authors had bottled and preserved her essence. He read it several times before using the house phone in the hotel lobby to call Colonel Biermeier of the Stasi Main Directorate for Foreign

Intelligence, the HVA, who was running the operation in Trieste. Biermeier came to his hotel room to examine the letter just after three that afternoon.

'It's an obvious fake,' Rosenharte insisted to the back of Biermeier's head as he read it on the little balcony. 'It's a trap. They're trying to trick us. We should go back and forget the whole thing.'

The colonel shook his head and turned to him, his unhealthy white face and brilliantined dark-grey hair shining in the sunlight. He blew out his cheeks and flapped the front of his jacket against the heat. Rosenharte wasn't in the least fooled by these diversionary tactics. He returned a steady gaze, purposefully expelling the anxiety in his mind. Every pore of Biermeier leaked the Stasi odour, and Rosenharte briefly wondered how he had carried out so many operations in the West without being apprehended. 'No, Comrade Doktor, this is no fake. The handwriting matches our samples exactly. We will go ahead as Brigadier-General Schwarzmeer has ordered.'

'But if anything goes wrong, I'll be held responsible. You've got my brother in jail and he'll be punished. What justice is that?'

Biermeier smiled, came over to him and put an arm around his shoulder. 'Go, Rosenharte. See what the woman has to say. We believe there's much she can tell us.' He paused. 'Look, what's the problem? You give her dinner, win her affections as only you know how, and bring her back to us. Take her to bed, Rosenharte. Make her yours again.'

Rosenharte let out a bitter laugh, momentarily recalling the 'love tutorials' of the Stasi spy school. 'Make her yours again! You're still living in the fifties, Colonel.'

'You know what I mean. You were one of us before the Firm decided your talents lay elsewhere. You did this for a living. You, above anyone, know what to do with this woman. I don't have to

5

remind you that you have an obligation to the state equal to that of a serving officer.'

Rosenharte lit a Marlboro and inwardly grimaced. He hated the way the Stasi called themselves the Firm in imitation of the way the CIA used the word Company. 'Then you'll keep to our agreement and allow my brother Konrad and his family to go free if I meet her?'

Biermeier didn't respond.

'You *will* release them?' Rosenharte persisted.

The colonel turned and permitted himself a nod – a deniable nod.

'That's a yes?'

Biermeier closed his eyes and nodded again.

'I don't want your people following me. Pier Four is deserted and very exposed. I went there earlier. She'll spot anyone on my tail.'

'That's doubtless why she chose it. No, we won't follow you. We're relying on you to bring her to us. It's all on your shoulders.'

There was a gentle knock at the door. Biermeier opened it to a young officer carrying a plastic bag. 'This is Schaub. He will show you how to operate the listening device. We've got better equipment since you were in the service. You'll be impressed how small it is.'

Rosenharte sat down on the bed heavily. 'You expect me to seduce this woman wired up to Normannenstrasse?'

'I'll be the only one listening. Anyway, when it comes to that part of the evening you go to the bathroom and take it off. It's the conversation before that interests me, not your lovemaking, Rosenharte.'

Schaub tested the microphone and transmitter, then Rosenharte removed his shirt and submitted with mild protests as Schaub towelled the perspiration from his skin and taped the equipment to his chest and back.

'Some part of you must feel pride,' Biermeier told him. 'After all, you're going back into harness for the state.'

'Nothing could be further from the truth,' said Rosenharte. 'I was never any good at this kind of work.'

The colonel exhaled impatiently. 'Ah well, of course now you count yourself a member of the intelligentsia. You speak fancily and affect an air of superiority, but remember, I know the man behind the façade. I read your file. What was it one of your many girlfriends said? "A clever, selfish bastard."'

Schaub smirked then got up and left.

'You mean she didn't mention my lovable sense of humour?' said Rosenharte. 'My skills as a cook, my steadfastness, my sobriety, my modesty . . .'

Biermeier shook his head disdainfully.

'Well,' said Rosenharte, 'at least I'm a clever bastard who knows himself. How many of us can say that, Colonel?'

Biermeier shook his head and sat down.

'I'd like a shower before I meet her.' God, he was talking as if she was actually going to be there.

'Not possible,' the colonel said. 'Use that queer aftershave you bought for yourself.'

Before leaving Biermeier looked over the transmitter once more and fiddled with some tiny wires at the back of the microphone while Rosenharte held his arms up and looked out on the veranda. 'Remember to press the button at the side once you see her,' he said. 'It's easily forgotten.'

Just before six Rosenharte dressed, checked himself in the mirror and then left the hotel. He crossed the Piazza dell'Unità feeling the heat of the day still pulse from the stones beneath him and noticing the wheel of swifts in the sky. Did the Stasi know? Had they faked the letters from Annalise Schering to expose his great lie? No, no one in the GDR could possibly know that she had killed herself fifteen years before; that he was as likely to find her at the end of Molo IV that evening as Greta Garbo.

He saw Annalise now, as he walked. The little apartment in Brussels on a winter's evening, he picking his way through the plants and the clutter of holiday trophies, finding her in the bath surrounded by candles and roses, her head resting on one arm lying along the side of the tub. Dead. Bloodied water. Vodka bottle. Pills. Needle of the overheated stereo clicking round the centre of Mahler's Fifth. His feelings then, as now, were guilt and a kind of horror at the operatic bathos of her death scene. Annalise always overdid things, that was for sure.

He passed through a series of parallel streets that led down to the sea, and reached Via Machiavelli where he paused, mopped his forehead and unstuck the back and front of his shirt from his skin. He set off again, never obviously glancing back, and made for the deserted quays where the big-hearted seaport opened its arms to the steamers of another century. There he looked at his watch – he was early – and, laying his jacket across the back of a bench, sat down to smoke a cigarette and stare across the flat calm of the Gulf of Trieste. Some way out to sea a ship lay at anchor, the only point of reference in the haze that had been building up through the long, hot afternoon. As he absently tried to determine where sea and sky met, it came to him that he had reached the edge of the void that separated East and West, a decorous no man's land of grand cafes and squares that looked like ballrooms, which was every bit as treacherous as the killing zone between the two Germanys.

Konrad would relish the ambiguity of Trieste, a frontier town that tried to forget the communist world at its back; and he'd shake with laughter at the idea of his brother's tryst with a dead woman. Rosenharte allowed himself a quick, rueful smile, as though his brother was sitting on the bench beside him. It had the effect of briefly lessening his agitation but then he thought of his twin's plight as the Stasi's hostage. To ensure his cooperation and that he wouldn't defect, they were holding Konrad in prison. For good measure, they'd taken his wife Else in for questioning and placed Konnie's two boys in the care of the state. He wondered what Konrad would do in his situation and knew his brother would proceed with all caution and wait to see how things unfolded. There were always openings, he had said once. Even in the GDR no situation was ever hopeless.

He took a last drag on the cigarette and flicked it across the paving stones into the sea. A fish rose to the butt then darted away beneath the oily film of the harbour water. From the rear of the opera house behind him came the sound of a soprano warming up for the evening's performance. Rosenharte turned and listened with his head cocked and recognized Violetta's part from the first act of *La Traviata*. He looked up to the mountains that pressed Trieste to the sea and noticed columns of white cloud quite distinct from the haze that veiled the city.

His attention moved to a German-speaking couple, stout and sunburnt, who were sitting on a bench not far away swinging their legs like happy children. Stasi officers? He thought not: too well fed, too content. Austrian tourists, most likely. He watched them openly and the woman smiled back with a hint of admiration in her eyes. Then he rose and, hooking the jacket over his shoulder, he walked past, nodding to them both.

Ahead of him was Molo IV, a broad stone structure that protruded into the harbour with quays on both sides and a huge single-storey warehouse along its spine. He passed through a gate near the old seaplane terminal, lifting a hand to a man reading a paper in a little cabin, and turned left to walk up the pier. On the way, he noted the few people around – two workmen stripping something from a roof, a man rigging a fishing rod, and some teenagers kicking a ball in the vast abandoned marshalling yard. They all looked plausibly engrossed. He walked on twenty yards, rounded a temporary fence that protected some pumping machinery and trudged up the pier, picking his way through the rusting iron debris and tufts of dead weeds that grew in cracks between the stones.

'Here he is,' said Macy Harp, nudging Robert Harland with his elbow. 'Bang on schedule like the bleeding Berlin Express.'

They both moved back from the doorway that led onto one of the heavy iron walkways running along outside the disused warehouse. This huge nineteenth-century complex lay at a right angle to Molo IV. They were about 200 yards from Rosenharte, who was moving away from them. Harland trained his binoculars on Rosenharte and reflected that both he and his quarry had much to lose if this went wrong. He had only been British Secret Intelligence Service station chief in Berlin for a year, and he was still on probation. This operation was one hell of a risk to take when he knew that most of the senior people at Century House regarded him as a field man without the necessary reserves of prudence. They couldn't deny he always got results but these were attributed to flair and boldness, two characteristics less favoured in MI6 than either the public or the intelligence service imagined. The head of the European desk had given him a certain amount of support together with Macy Harp – the best odd-job man and, when required, all-round creator of mayhem that the service had to offer – but Harland knew as well as anyone that many in Century House were actively hoping for the operation to fail. Harebrained, wild, impetuous – those would be the words murmured by his superiors across the lunch table at the Travellers Club – and his career would effectively be over.

He shook himself and concentrated on Rosenharte. He was every bit the specimen that the Stasi had deployed in Brussels all those years ago. At the time of the Schering operation his fake passport had put him at thirty-two, which would make him about forty-seven now. He had looked after himself: he was tanned, still slim and there wasn't a trace of grey in the sandy hair. But he betrayed a certain edginess and Harland could see he was moving without enthusiasm to the rendezvous point, glancing back and to his side every few paces. 'How many Stasi have we got?' he asked quietly.

Harp's habitually cheerful face squinted into a notebook. 'About a dozen. Our Italian friends think there are more, as many as twenty, but that's based on the crossings from Yugoslavia over the last forty-eight hours, not on observation in Trieste.'

'And what do we make of the character with the straw hat?'

'At first we thought he was Stasi because we've seen him a couple of times. Jamie Jay took a look at him this morning, followed him to a fleapit hotel in the New Port.'

'But how does he manage to be here ten minutes before Rosenharte?'

Macy Harp withdrew one of a ration of five cigarettes from a slender silver case and lit up. 'It's simple. He saw Rosenharte out here when he did his recce this morning, realized he had started off on the same route this evening and decided to get here ahead of him.'

'Right,' said Harland doubtfully. 'But what the hell's he doing here?'

'Steady on, old chap. All will be revealed soon enough.'

'Where's Cuth?'

'Having a drink over there on the seafront. He can see everything from where he is. The Italians have taken pictures, so we've got a complete gallery back at his place.'

'He's too far away. Get him nearer.' Harland couldn't help showing his irritation.

Harp turned to him. 'Come on, Bobby, we're all doing this for the love of it – and you. Jay's taken leave to help out and Cuth Avocet's given up a week on the Tweed.'

'It's an official operation.'

'I know, I know. Still, you can't deny that the Office hasn't exactly given you all the support you need.'

Harland said nothing. Was it that obvious?

'Ah, I've got Jay,' said Harp a few moments later. 'He's lurking in one of the ruined sheds in the centre of the pier. You see him?'

'Right . . . look, I appreciate you giving your time, Macy, but I want you to understand that this does have the chief's blessing. It's very important. Could save a lot of lives.'

'I'm sure you're right, Bobby,' said Harp amenably. He looked around and sniffed the air. 'Christ, this place smells. What the hell was stored in here?'

'Hides. Uncured leather, I imagine.'

Harp looked around. 'You know the port machinery was entirely powered by water? Every crane, pulley, lift was powered by compressed water. Hydrodynamic power. Bloody amazing what they got up to in the nineteenth century.'

'Yes,' said Harland without interest. 'Are we certain Rosenharte didn't make any calls from his hotel phone once he had found the note?'

'Can't be sure,' said Harp. 'We know the place is crawling with

Stasi and they're likely to have set up a way of communicating with him without us knowing. The hotel is not the easiest place to watch.'

'I bloody well hope they don't think we're here. The idea is that it's just Annalise. If they get any hint of us we're finished.'

Harp nodded. 'Tell me about chummy down there. How come he's going to meet a woman he knows is dead?'

'Because the Stasi have forced him.'

'But why didn't he tell them she was dead?'

'Because he couldn't – not back in 1974 and especially not now. Suffice to say we put him in—'

'An impossible position. I see that, but how – the girl's death? Was he compromised? Has he been working for you?'

Harland remained motionless behind his binoculars.

'There's something I'm not getting,' said Harp.

'That's right, Macy.' He wasn't about to tell him everything, and anyway it was far too complicated.

Harp nodded. He knew better than to press the point. 'Christ, I'm not sure how long I can take this smell.'

Rosenharte caught sight of the man with the straw hat issuing from a ruined building on his right and coming down the pier towards him. Rosenharte slowed, then stopped and pressed the little button on the side of the device taped to his chest. The man was weaving like a drunk. As he got closer Rosenharte was able to get a measure of him. The little round beer paunch and poorly cut suit jacket unambiguously announced a citizen of the German Democratic Republic. His gaze was fixed on Rosenharte and there was little doubt that he was making straight for him.

For a few seconds he expected some kind of violence, but then the man seemed to stumble, clutched at his thorax and cursed before brushing off the hat and rushing the few feet to where Rosenharte was standing. At the last moment he tried to dodge out of his path, but the man lunged to the right, snatched at his shirt and gripped it with such force that Rosenharte instinctively lashed out. The man looked aghast, and only then did Rosenharte understand that the face below him was contorted with pain and fear. He kept putting one hand to his throat and was searching wildly about him. A part of Rosenharte registered disgust at his breath and the foam that had gathered at the corners of his mouth, but he gripped him by the shoulders and told him in German to be still and he would try and find him some help. As he said it, he took in a lined brow beaded with sweat, two indentations on the nose where a pair of spectacles habitually rested, a filthy, frayed shirt collar and a day's growth of stubble. He shook him, looked into his eyes – there was no malevolence in the expression, merely panic – and told him again that he must help himself by calming down. He tried his halting Italian, but reverted to German and lowered his voice.

In Dresden he had once seen a man's eye poked out with an umbrella. People stood around as the blood gushed from the socket and the young man went into shock. A woman knelt down and held him and he calmed down almost immediately. So Rosenharte touched the man on the cheek and held him gently. This seemed to work for a little while, but then his eyes began to stare and his body shook with a series of convulsions that forced them both towards the edge of the quay. They staggered in a drunken waltz for a few seconds, kicking up swirls of dust and snapping the dried weeds around them, until the man suddenly collapsed into his arms and pushed him against a large iron mooring bollard.

Now some words came from him. 'Rye . . . Ryszard . . . Rye . . . Kusimiak.' Rosenharte's backside came down involuntarily on the shiny warm surface of the bollard.

'Be still, for God's sake, or . . .' At that moment he lost his footing and found he had no purchase to stop the momentum of the other man. For a second he was suspended over the water, then he toppled from the bollard. Falling the four or five feet, he was certain he saw the man's hand reach to his pocket before he dropped forward and rolled down the quay wall into the water like a weighted sack.

More angry than shocked, Rosenharte surfaced and struck out to a chain that was hanging down from the top of the quay. He grabbed it, placed both feet against the barnacle-encrusted stone and began to haul himself up, pulling the chain through his hands. As he cleared the water line he heard a voice and looked up to see a man holding out his hand. He was yelling something in Italian. Rosenharte wrapped the slimy chain around one hand and took a few more steps, but at this point his angle to the quay made it impossible for him to proceed further. He moved to the left, then swung back in the opposite direction and reached out to grab hold of the Italian's hand. A few desperate moments of scrambling ensued before he was kneeling on the quay, hacking the seawater from his throat.

He wiped his eyes and looked up. Around them stood a semi-circle of teenage boys with fishing rods. Rosenharte gazed into a broad young face and a pair of intelligent blue eyes and nodded to show he was okay. The man put a hand on his shoulder and said, 'You're okay; just stay there for a bit.' Rosenharte knew this was no Italian.

Then one of the boys caught sight of the body in the water and started shouting. All five stripped off and dived in, apparently unconcerned about what they might find. One unceremoniously yanked the man's head up by the hair while the others shoaled round and pushed the body towards the chain.

'Perhaps it's better that I speak German,' hissed the man after he'd instructed the boys in Italian to loop the chain under the body's arms and tie a knot.

It was the last thing Rosenharte wanted. He shook his head furiously, put his hand in his shirt and ripped the wire from his chest.

The man showed little surprise. 'Don't worry, it won't work after that soaking.'

'Who are you?'

'A friend of Annalise.' The man was looking back up the pier at the people who had materialized from nowhere.

'You're English?' said Rosenharte.

He nodded. 'Is he one of your people?' he asked, pointing to the water.

'My people? No.'

'Look, we're about to be joined by the police.' The Englishman gestured with his chin. Rosenharte turned to see a navy-blue Alfa Romeo threading its way through the scrap iron. 'Be at the Ristorante Grand Canale by nine thirty. Take a table outside, on the canal pontoon. Just make it seem as though you happened on the restaurant by chance. You got that?' He punched him lightly on the shoulder. 'Good fellow – everything will be okay.'

Rosenharte had seen the restaurant on the canal and thought that it looked expensive. He was about to protest, when one of the boys shouted at them to take up the slack on the chain and begin hauling the body out of the water. They both looked over the quay to see that it had snagged on a protruding stone. At that moment two policemen jogged from their car to help pull the man over the edge. The Englishman knelt down and began rhythmically pumping at the man's back. Water began to dribble from the mouth but when the cough he was hoping for didn't come, he rolled the man over, felt his pulse and listened to his chest. His hands moved expertly around the body, at one point slipping inside his jacket. Then he took hold of the nose and chin and pushed the head back slightly. No sooner had he touched the man's lips with his own than he recoiled, wiping his mouth furiously on his shirt and spitting on the ground. One of the policemen attempted to take over, but the Englishman pulled him back saying there was something wrong. '*Attenzione, Signore, non e buono.*'

A sense of contagion swept the boys who had just clambered out of the water and they all began to back away from the body. Rosenharte looked down with a candid lack of emotion at first but then bafflement and shock hit him. He wondered what the sudden extinction of this ordinary human being meant for him. Things like this didn't just happen.

From the warehouse, Robert Harland watched the police car with Rosenharte inside disappear through the Old Port gates, followed by the ambulance carrying the body, and considered whether his operation was compromised. He too was certain that the struggle with the man on the pier and the death were significant. He turned to Cuth Avocet – the gaunt figure known throughout British SIS as the Bird – who had slipped up a back stairway to join them in the dusk of the old leather store. 'What the hell was that about?' he asked.

'Search me,' said the Bird. 'I guess we'll know a bit more when Jamie reports back.'

'At least he was in position,' Harp said.

'Point taken,' said Harland. He looked out over the water. 'We'd better get back to the van and start preparing the watch on the restaurant.'

'The fellow's hardly going to feel like meat and two veg after someone's just tried to do him in,' said the Bird lazily.

'It didn't look as though he was trying to kill him,' said

Harland. 'I watched the whole thing. At the end Rosenharte was trying to help him. Let's be going.'

The Bird put out an arm. 'Perhaps you should wait for the area to clear first. There's a couple of bogies down there.' He pointed to two men who'd materialized from beneath them and were making for the dock gates.

'That makes . . .'

'Fourteen,' said Harp.

'So now we know what we're up against,' said Harland.

Half an hour later, Harland sat in the back of the black Volkswagen van with Jamie Jay, sorting through the contents of the black leather wallet that was still swollen from immersion in the Adriatic. Harland held up an identity card to the light and read out the name Franciscek Grycko. 'What's a bloody Pole doing here? The Stasi and the Polish spooks are barely on speaking terms. Normannenstrasse wouldn't involve them in something like this. They're considered far too insecure.'

Jay read one of the business cards, which had fallen out in a little wad. 'It says Grycko is a sales representative of a shoe business – International Quality Shoes, Wrocław.'

'Shoe business!' said Harland contemptuously.

'There's no business like . . .' Seeing Harland's face Jay stifled the joke.

'It's a pity you didn't get his passport,' Harland said.

Jay looked offended. 'You try kissing a dead shoe salesman with vomit in his mouth and see how long you can stand feeling him up at the same time. As things are, I probably established some kind of record out there.'

'You think they knew each other?'

Jay shook his head. 'Rosenharte said the man had an attack of some sort – practically fell into his arms foaming at the mouth.'

'We saw it from the warehouse. I got the impression he was just trying to speak to him. What about the taste you mentioned? You think it was poison?'

Jay wrinkled his nose. 'Dunno. *I* feel okay.'

'Good. So who's monitoring his phone at the hotel?'

'Cuth has gone to take over from Jessie.'

'Christ, I hope Jessie's changed by now.'

'Of course. She'll look just the part. Rosenharte's going to fall in love all over again.'

'We don't need him to. All that matters is that the Stasi believe she really is Annalise.' Harland noticed the doubt in Jay's eyes. 'What?' he demanded.

'Well, there's so much that is out of our control.'

'It's an intelligence operation, for Pete's sake, Jamie, not a bloody garden party.'

'Well, we've done our best with the letters and Jessie, but in the end it all depends on Rosenharte's reaction.'

'Right,' said Harland. 'If for one moment he looks like he doesn't recognize her, or gives the slightest hint she isn't Annalise, he's lost and might as well defect tonight. He won't last a minute under Schwarzmeer's interrogation.'

'Schwarzmeer?'

'Yes, Brigadier-General Julius Schwarzmeer, director of the Hauptverwaltung Aufklärung.' He paused and looked at Jay's eager face. 'Sorry, I forget that you're rather rusty on all this. Still, it's good of you to give your time like this.'

'The HVA is the foreign arm of the Stasi – a subsection, right?'

'Yes, they're in the same building in Normannenstrasse and the HVA has officers in all the Stasi regional headquarters.'

'The same people, then?'

'The HVA are better trained, better paid and allowed to travel to the West. The ordinary Stasi officer has to make do with the occasional holiday in Bulgaria.'

'And the purpose of all this? I mean, I get the immediate aim, but what's the bigger picture?'

'If it comes off, you'll see. It may even help in your patch.'

'With all respect I very much doubt Oman is going to benefit from this.'

'You'd be surprised. Shake the sand out of your boots, Jamie. There's a lot to connect the problems in your part of the world with the Stasi. That's what this operation is about. That's why I have the chief's blessing and why the Joint Intelligence Committee so eagerly await the results of our efforts here tonight.' He stopped. 'Look, I'd better be getting along. I want to give the wallet to the Italians and I'm interested to hear what they've got to say about Rosenharte's state of mind after that business out on the pier.'

They climbed out the back of the van together. It was almost dark by now. Harland noticed that huge thunderclouds had formed and trapped the heat in the city. The last light from the west touched their summits and gave each a rosy peak.

Jay set off in the direction of the Grand Canal while Harland turned from the sea and headed for an old insurance building near the Carabinieri headquarters, where Ludovico Prelli was running the Italian surveillance operation as a personal favour to Harland.

On reaching the building he passed a security check at the door and leapt up the echoing stairway to the first floor, where two men inspected his diplomatic passport. He was directed through a wide passage that was filled with some of Prelli's team of watchers. From within Prelli's office, a little way along the passage, Harland heard the low, humorous growl of Alan Griswald, his CIA counterpart in Berlin, who had excused himself from a family holiday in Venice to be in Trieste for the next twenty-four hours.

'Hey there,' said Harland. 'What news from the Rialto?'

'Nothing, 'cept I doted on your very absence, Bobby,' replied Griswald.

'It's good to have you here. Thanks for coming.'

'It was wonderful but I couldn't look at another Tintoretto ceiling.'

'Has Ludo filled you in on what just happened in the Old Port?' Harland shook Prelli's hand and gave him the wallet. 'He was a Pole named Grycko. A shoe salesman. Does that mean anything to you?'

Griswald shook his head. 'What did he die of?'

'Heart attack, maybe. He had a lot of saliva around his mouth. Maybe poison was involved, but my man tried to give him the kiss of life and he seems to be okay. Anyway, we'll have the post-mortem results by tomorrow. Right, Ludo?'

'No, by this evening, I think,' said the Italian.

Harland sat down. 'What did the police think of Rosenharte? What was his mood like when they took him back to the hotel?'

The Italian pressed his fingertips together and looked thoughtful. 'The police say they thought that he did not want to show what he was thinking. He was shocked but he controlled himself, like you English.' He smiled at Harland.

Harland nodded, picked up the straw hat, which had been retrieved from Molo IV, and examined the inside rim. 'I wonder who the hell he was,' he said.

TWO

Blackout

Rosenharte arrived at the restaurant with his hair damp and his shirt still showing signs of compression from the small plastic suitcase that he'd brought from Dresden. He was led to a table at the far end of the pontoon, where he sat down and ordered a bottle of local white wine. He turned his face towards the sea breeze that was beginning to tug at the corner of the pink tablecloth and, feeling a little conspicuous among these chic Italians, lit a cigarette.

All but two of the ten tables on the pontoon were occupied, mostly with young couples leaning into each other with unforced intimacy. He slipped down in his chair a little and watched the people drift along the banks of the canal. Some Latin-American music struck up in one of the alleys leading towards the centre of town. On hearing this, a couple strolling by paused, took each other's arms and executed a few perfect steps of dance under the cone of a street light before fading into the shadows like phantoms.

It was still hot but the breeze was cooling him down and he was able to log the men and women strolling along the canal who seemed to have no particular object in view and yet were curiously attracted to this stretch of the water. He noted with a certain relief that the old muscles were beginning to flex; the instincts that he had been taught to use at an almost subliminal speed in Stasi training school were coming back. If the beginning of the evening was anything to go by, he would need them.

He was there ten minutes before he became aware of a woman standing on the gangway leading to the pontoon. Her gaze came to rest on him and she gave a shy little wave. For a moment he stared dumbly at her, unable to think of what to do, then gave a half-hearted wave himself. She was heavier than Annalise but the difference could easily be due to the passage of time. Her hair was about right, too – dark and pulled back by a clip, and her outfit – the white linen skirt, loose jacket, canvas shoes and sagging shoulder bag – was exactly what the middle-aged Annalise would have worn. But, to be frank, she was nothing like as beautiful as Annalise and had none of her lightness of movement and grace. She was now beside the table, wreathed in smiles and holding out both hands, palms outward.

'For Christ's sake stand up,' she hissed in English without losing the pleasure in her face. 'Stand up and take hold of my hands. Look into my eyes, then give me a hug and kiss me.'

He did as instructed, feeling rather foolish and then came to grief when she offered her right cheek and he went for her left. He apologized. The situation was too bizarre and he felt anyone watching would immediately see beneath this phony reunion.

'Hey,' she exclaimed, perhaps a little too loudly, 'I remember you always did that. Rudi darling, it's so wonderful to see you.' She clasped him to her one more time and he smelt her perfume. Then she let him go and stepped away, seemingly to absorb her first sight of him for fifteen years. 'Well, are you going to give me dinner, or what?'

Rosenharte mimed what he hoped was a charming admission of his clumsiness, then, realizing that she was waiting for him to pull out her chair, scurried round to help her. As he left her side, he touched her on both shoulders.

'You're getting the hang of this,' she said, looking up and flashing her teeth at him. 'I think we both need a drink, don't you? I'll have some of that wine.'

He filled her glass.

'Did they give you another transmitter?'

He shook his head.

'Good. My people can hear us, but it's just one way.'

'You're not Annalise,' he said. He had to put on record that this was not her because a vague suspicion that he had been set up by his own side still lurked in his mind. His microphone may have been dead but there was always the possibility that the Stasi were listening through another.

'Of course I'm not her. You surely didn't expect her?'

He said nothing and she produced a puzzled look. 'Oh, I see what you want. Christ, this *is* complicated, isn't it? You think you're being set up by your own side?'

At least the woman was quick. 'Where did Annalise's parents meet?' he asked. He knew the Stasi didn't have this on their files because he had never told them.

'Her father was a Belgian missionary in the Congo. Her Irish mother was a young nun. Annalise was the result of a scandalous affair, which forced the couple out of the church. They lived in Ireland until Michel Schering died, at which point both mother and daughter returned to Belgium. Is that okay?'

'What was the characteristic that distinguished Annalise from ninety-nine per cent of humanity?'

The flame in the candle shuddered. She brushed the hair from her eye and thought. 'Her ability at languages. She could speak seven or eight and was reputed to be able to learn a new language in under a month.'

'Yes,' said Rosenharte. 'But everyone knew that. I was looking for something else.'

'Her blood group. She had one of the most rare blood groups known to mankind. Okay?'

He nodded, still unsure, but now he had to make the gamble – accept this woman or not.

'Put your hand on mine,' she said, gazing into his eyes so effectively that something stirred in Rosenharte. 'We're being watched. There're about a dozen Stasi. That's good, because we want them to see us getting along and then in due course you beginning to seduce me.' She gave him a mischievous smile.

He smiled and offered her a breadstick. 'I hope I'm up to it,' he said playfully.

'Of course you are,' she returned. 'You like women, Rudi, and even if you don't fancy me, you're going to look as though you do. Now, light my cigarette.' She exhaled the first drag. 'The wind's getting up. It's a relief after the heat.' She clasped her hands together and let her shoulders tremble like a small girl. She was pretty good at this.

'You English always have something to say about the weather.' He paused and glanced across the canal. 'I don't know your real name and I cannot call you Annalise, but—'

'Then use a pet name.'

'I called her Anna.'

'Then use that,' she said with a laugh.

'Your people – British intelligence – can hear me now?'

She nodded.

'They should know there are people's lives at risk.'

'If anything goes wrong, you can defect. We've got enough people here to help you at the first sign of trouble.'

He looked at her without bothering to mask his feelings. 'My brother Konrad is in jail. They will hold him there until I return to the GDR.'

She absorbed this without changing her expression. 'All the more reason to make this work without raising their suspicions.'

'You talk of suspicion. Already your operation is compromised. That man dying out at the pier: the Stasi will know that something is wrong. Why did you ask me to go there?'

'We wanted to see how many people were following you and identify them.' She smiled again and brushed the back of her hand against his cheek. 'Let's order, shall we?'

'The man who died – who was he?'

'We don't know yet. Look, it would be a lot safer if you were to leave all this to later; these questions are showing in your face. Just keep to the script and begin sweet-talking me, honey bun.' She winked at him and her hand moved to touch his leg under the table. 'Relax, Rudi, and tell me about your work.'

Almost directly above the restaurant there was an ornate first-floor balcony, which ran along four shuttered window bays. Behind these was an exceptionally well-appointed drawing room where Harland had set up his forward observation point. In the room with him were Harp, Griswald and Prelli with two of his assistants. From here they monitored the movement of the Stasi team that had followed Rosenharte from the hotel. Harland listened to the reports coming in. They were now aware of a pair loitering on the bridge nearby, three men in a car parked a little distance from the canal, a couple disguised as tourists who had been sighted on the corniche and two men who had just taken a table at the other end of the pontoon. There were about five others moving up and down the banks of the canal. In short, the area was crawling with East German intelligence officers. Harland knew this kind of close-quarter surveillance was a Stasi speciality. It'd be a miracle if so many eyes did not spot that Jessie and Rosenharte were faking it. Still, as far as he could tell they were responding to each other with a fairly convincing mixture of warmth and wariness. And if it looked good from where he was, then it might just fool others.

Something attracted his attention to the awning immediately below the apartment and he cursed. 'Those men – who are they?'

'Which men?' asked Prelli.

'The men who're waiting at the maître d's lectern.'

Prelli nodded and said something under his breath. A few moments later his watchers confirmed that they were part of the team that had come over the border. 'It's a damned shame you don't have a two-way with the woman,' said Griswald. 'You could tell her about those goons.'

'She knows they're there,' replied Harland. 'Rosenharte's just told her. He's doing pretty well given the circumstances.'

There was silence in the room while he listened to the couple talk. He watched the waiter take their order, then turned to Griswald. 'So what do you make of this thing about his brother being in jail?'

Griswald's bulk shifted so that Harland saw his rubbery features and fine blond hair in the small amount of light coming from Prelli's equipment. 'They must suspect he's going to run.'

'They suspect everyone the whole time. That's the point about the Stasi.'

'And yet it may be to your advantage, Bobby. It means your fellow's gotta go back East if his brother is in the slammer. And if he *does* go back, he's gotta work for you. There's no way out for him.'

'Yes, but he won't just be risking his own life. Could be his brother's too, which will add to the pressure. That way people make mistakes.'

'To me, he looks like the kind of man who can take it. A lot of bearing. A lot of poise. He looks like a damned prince sitting down there.'

'Yes, that's why they used him as an agent in the seventies.'

Finally the two Germans had gained the attention of the maître d' and were being shown to the only free table, the one nearest the gangway.

'Shit,' said Harland. 'That means they have to pass them on the way out.'

'It's going to be okay,' murmured Griswald. 'They're doing fine.' He paused. 'Tell me about the brother.'

'They're identical twins. Our friend has made something of a name for himself as an art historian. He's kept his nose clean, apart from the odd scandal – other men's wives, that sort of thing. The brother is a dissident. In and out of jail, including spells in Bautzen and Hohenschönhausen.'

'*The high pretty houses*,' said Griswald. 'What was his crime?'

'Consorting with demagogic and hostile elements – something of that nature. He's a filmmaker. When he was released after a sentence served in Rostock, his membership of the union of filmmakers was revoked. We don't know much else about him.'

A quarter of an hour elapsed during which they heard Rosenharte describe his life commuting between Leipzig and Dresden and tell Jessie about the lecture he was due to give the following day. The conversation was moving along quite well now. A radio crackled and Cuth Avocet, hidden in the van a little distance from the side of the canal, said, 'Are you watching up there? One of those bogies is walking over to them.'

Harland moved his face up and down the slats. He saw a slim, middle-aged man in an open-necked shirt walking towards the table.

'Jesus,' said Griswald.

*

Rosenharte placed his hand on top of hers. 'We're about to be joined.' Then he cupped her chin in his hand and leaned over to kiss her.

'That's good,' she said, looking him straight in the eye and smiling. 'You are rather good at that.'

'Thank you.' She was not the first to say it.

The man was within a few feet of them. He hesitated and craned his head as though not quite sure that he had recognized her then, seemingly satisfied that he had been right all along, he approached the table. 'Annalise!' he exclaimed, performing an embarrassed bow. 'Annalise Schering, is this really you?' He spoke in English. 'It can't be!'

She stared at him with a look of open bemusement. 'I'm sorry . . . do we know each other?'

'The Commission in Brussels! Yes, it *is* you. Don't you remember me? Hans Heise from Bonn. We worked in the same Unit in DG8, the Directorate General for Development. My office was down the hall from you.' He gave her an indulgent look.

She studied him, then glanced at Rosenharte, who smiled politely. 'I'm sorry, I simply can't place you. Which office did you say?'

'The Development Directorate, under the Dutchman – Jan van Ostade. Surely you remember?'

'I certainly remember him, but forgive me I . . .' she shook her head. 'I'm sorry, it must seem rude, but I don't remember your face.'

He looked troubled. 'But you remember my name, surely. Heise – Hans Heise. We used to meet at parties held by the English couple, the Russell-Smiths. I was married then. My wife's name was Martha. Perhaps you recall her. In the summer we attended a horse show in the country with the Russell-Smiths.'

'His name wasn't Jan van Ostade,' she said. 'It was—'

'Ugo van Ostade,' said Rosenharte, shooting a firm smile in

Heise's direction. 'You introduced me to him in a restaurant. I think it was at *Le Tabernacle*. He was drunk, I seem to recall.'

She turned from Heise to Rosenharte, a look of relief beneath her smile. 'Yes, exactly. And Ugo was replaced by Pierre Laboulaye.'

'Laboulaye?' said the man, now resting his hand on the back of her chair and looking up as though casually searching his memory for Laboulaye. 'Wasn't he the one who played the field with all the women in the Commission?'

Exactly, thought Rosenharte. He himself had filed the report to his superiors suggesting that Laboulaye was wide open to blackmail. Now this Stasi scumbag was playing it back to him, using his report to test the woman's identity.

'You know,' she said, folding her fingers under her chin, 'I remember everyone in that office. I can see them all now. Where did you sit? Not on the right, because the Italian and Spaniard were there. What were their names? Perhaps you remember. Carlo and . . . ?'

She was playing him at his own game. Heise opened his arms as though to say that he couldn't be expected to remember everything.

'Then on the left,' she continued, 'were the secretaries and the research group. Perhaps you were part of the research group?'

Heise hesitated. 'No . . . I did not have my desk exactly there.'

'But where then?' she said. 'Not in the Director's office, surely?'

'No, down the hall.'

She frowned and shook her head. 'That's not possible.'

'Well, perhaps she will remember you later,' said Rosenharte helpfully. 'I should explain that we are seeing each other for the first time in fifteen years. Maybe one ghost from the past is enough this evening, eh?'

The man straightened. 'You will excuse me for interrupting.

Bon appetit.' He nodded to both of them before retreating to his own table, where he acted perplexity and awkwardness to his dining companion, a younger man with a conspicuously pallid face and heavy spectacles.

'Thanks,' she said. 'I know what this means to you now.'

'Do you?' asked Rosenharte under his breath. 'Do you really know what has just taken place? I mean really?'

'Yes. You supported my identity as Annalise, so you are now committed.'

'You understand it intellectually.' He put his hand up to her face again, a gesture that had the advantage of hiding his own expression from the men at the other end of the pontoon. 'I will listen to what your side have to say, but they must give me an assurance that they will do nothing to endanger my brother's life. That's the condition of my cooperation. He has two children. If anything goes wrong, the children will be taken from him and their mother for good. Is that all clear to you . . . and to your associates?'

She nodded. 'I have children of my own,' she said.

'Yes, but unless you have lived in the East, you cannot appreciate the cruelty of the Stasi. An enemy of the state – a dissident or spy or just some punk in Prenzlauer Berg – must be overcome by hatred. And this is not just a matter of sentiment, you see, but a duty that requires each officer to destroy the enemy of the state in the way that is calculated to hurt them most. You know about the Chekists in Russia?'

'As a matter of fact I do; I did Soviet studies at university. The Cheka – Commission to Combat Counterrevolution Sabotage and Speculation. I always liked the idea of combating speculation.'

'Well you'll know that the Stasi follow the Cheka. They specialize in an institutional vindictiveness, formalized hatred of an order that even you cannot comprehend. If it means taking the children from a woman who has already had one nervous break-down, then they'll do it. If it means causing my brother to suffer further heart problems, then they'll do it.' He brought his hand down and looked at her. 'There can be no mistakes. Until we get out of this restaurant you must do what I say. Remember, I knew Annalise. I know the way she would have behaved in this situation. You must be guided by me.'

'I hear what you're saying, but you really must stop showing it in your expression.'

They continued with their meal, drinking more than was good for them and occasionally managing uproarious laughter. Just after eleven the wind changed. Instead of the sea breeze, much cooler air came straight from the mountains and made the little skiffs and dinghies moored along the side of the canal bump into each other. The pontoon began to shudder and strain at the chains that anchored it to the side and bottom of the canal. Rosenharte noticed the first flash of lightning way off in the mountains. 'Here's some real weather for you to talk about,' he said.

She turned to catch the second strike, which lit a landscape of thunderclouds. At this, Rosenharte moved his chair closer so that he could put his arm on her shoulder. He brushed the hair from her ear, whispered urgently and looked into her eyes to check that she'd understood. Then he pushed the chair back and took up his glass of wine, still smiling.

'Your friends will understand what's happening,' he said. 'They must not show themselves.'

She nodded and spoke into her lapel. 'Hope you heard all that. We're going to have a row and I'm leaving.'

Half a minute later she straightened in her chair and brought down her glass. 'You haven't changed, Rudi. You used me and left me all those years ago, without a thought for my feelings or how

I would cope when you'd gone. And now you want me to do your dirty work for you again. What guarantee do I have that you won't leave me when you've got what you want? I'm a human being with feelings. That didn't ever occur to you, did it? I can't be used again like this. I won't be. I'm telling you I won't be!' She had begun quietly but now her voice was rising.

Rosenharte patted the air in front of him to calm her. 'Hey, hey. Do you want the whole restaurant to hear?' He swept the tables on the pontoon with an embarrassed smile. 'Look, I'm sorry. You knew the circumstances were difficult. It wasn't possible for me to act in any other way. Please, Anna, be reasonable.'

'Not until you admit that you ran away instead of behaving like a man.' By now she had the complete attention of the diners, who had all stopped worrying about the impending storm and were staring in their direction with unconcealed pleasure. She looked away, trembling and evidently fighting back tears of anger, then, seeming to settle something in her mind, she leaned forward and slapped him. Rosenharte's glass fell from his hand and drenched his lap. She turned on her heels and, flinging a final insult over her shoulder, marched indignantly towards the gangway.

A few seconds later the storm announced its arrival over the centre of the city with a thunderclap that added greatly to the melodrama of the scene. The electricity supply struggled with the power surge, the lights coming on twice before extinguishing in relay as though a series of switches had been thrown. Whoops of delight came from a side street now cast in medieval darkness. Rosenharte felt for his glass and filled it with the remains of the wine, soaking his hand in the process.

About five minutes later a figure slid into the chair opposite him. 'You screwed that one up, Rosenharte. The General will not be happy.' It was Heise, hissing at him in the dark.

Rosenharte set down his glass and tried to light the candle, which had blown out. 'What could I do after you scared her with all that crap about the Commission? She knew you were checking her out and she accused me of being involved in an operation to trap her. Where the hell's Colonel Biermeier, anyway?'

'Where's your microphone? Why isn't it working?'

'It may have escaped your notice but I was thrown in the water. It's back at the hotel. You should have realized it would be ruined and I would be out of contact.'

The candle flickered into life. Rosenharte saw Heise throw himself back in the chair. 'The police were in the hotel. Naturally we couldn't approach you. Anyway, never mind that now. The colonel says you must go after her.'

'How? I don't even know where she's staying.'

'You didn't think to ask her the name of her hotel?'

'Well, she was hardly going to tell me after you'd announced your presence. You gave the game away, Heise, or whatever your name is. She knew you were testing her. She accused me of bringing you here. She's devastated. Says I've betrayed her.'

'What did you say?'

'I said I didn't know who the hell you were, but she didn't believe me. You screwed up, not me.'

'You will show more respect if you know what's good for you. Now, go and make it up with her. This is an order.'

Rosenharte leaned forward. 'Look, you little piece of shit, I tell Biermeier what you just did and you'll be steaming open letters in Rostock for the rest of your miserable career.'

Heise's eyes glinted in the candlelight. 'Who was that man who died on the pier?'

'I don't know. I've never seen him before. At first I assumed he was part of your operation.'

'What did he say to you? Did he give you a message?'

Rosenharte withdrew the napkin from his lap where he had been drying the spilt wine and threw it on the table.

'No, he couldn't speak. He was dying. He was dead before he even hit the water.' The first drops of rain began to splatter around them. Then he said, mollifyingly, 'Look, I don't understand any of this. I don't understand why you're interested in this woman. She's a drunk. She's crazy. You saw.'

Heise got up. 'These are judgements you're not competent to make, Rosenharte. Go. You'll find Knef, the man dining with me, at the entrance of the restaurant. He'll lead you to her.'

'Wouldn't it be better to do this in the morning? She's upset now.'

'Go.'

'Do I have your assurance that you will keep your men back?'

Heise said nothing.

'You do it my way or it won't work. Call General Schwarzmeer and tell him this is what I said. Call Biermeier. He'll say that I'm right.'

The man seemed to accept this. 'You have until tomorrow afternoon. We'll contact you in your hotel at two.'

Rosenharte turned and moved across the empty pontoon to find Knef.

From the apartment, Harland watched the exchange between Rosenharte and the Stasi agent. Although he couldn't hear what was being said and could see little because of the blackout, he had the feeling that Rosenharte had risen to the occasion. Fifteen minutes had elapsed since Jessie's departure. It was plain to all of them in the room that she was buying them time to get into position. Prelli's team reported that she had already stopped at a cafe and downed a cognac before setting off for the hotel by an elaborately circuitous route that betrayed a certain drunken panic.

THREE

Kafka's Message

The Stasi followed Jessie to a bar that was doing brisk business in the spectacular downpour, the storm having rumbled round Trieste loosing bolts of lightning at its highest points before the rain came. Quickly the streets were awash and Rosenharte and Knef were forced to take shelter in a doorway. At length, word came from the Stasi that she had arrived at the Hotel Sistiana soaked and definitely the worse for wear. Knef and Rosenharte followed about twenty minutes behind and arrived just as the lights came on, at which point Knef fell back to let Rosenharte go on alone.

She was sitting in the hotel bar near the entrance, a picture of alcoholic deflation. The barman looked up at Rosenharte as he wearily filled the glass in front of her. A blackout candle still flickered between them.

'Maybe it's time for you to have some rest,' said Rosenharte gently, sliding onto the stool next to her.

She nodded. 'Yes . . . look, I'm sorry about the restaurant. It was stupid of me. I just wanted to . . .' Her head lolled forward while she made a hash of stubbing out a cigarette.

'I didn't know you smoked.'

'Only in times like these.'

'We'll talk about it in the morning. Now what you need is sleep.' He paid off the barman and guided her to the door, then to the lift, where she made a very credible display of needing his support. As they waited, Rosenharte heard a couple come into the hotel and ask for a double room. '*Tutti sono occupati*,' said the manager crisply, before signalling the doorman to lock up for the night. Rosenharte turned to see the couple that had sat down near him on the seafront.

In the lift, she moved away from him, straightened and smiled.

'What's your real name?' he asked.

She shook her head. 'Sorry, can't say. We're in suites four-one-five to four-one-seven. They're waiting for us there. You'll find three rooms and two bedrooms if you need to rest at some stage. I'll be on hand in the morning should we need to convince anyone else that we're lovers.' They got out of the lift and walked quickly to the south side of the building, where she paused outside the door to suite 415. 'The floor is secured,' she told him. 'There are no other guests here. As you'll appreciate, the Stasi could not have anticipated your arrival here but the rooms have been swept for listening devices anyway. No one will be able to take the lift up to this floor and the fire exit has also been barred. Everything's been done with the maximum of discretion.'

'They'll already be watching the building,' he said.

'Let them. The place is totally secure. The Italians are cooperating.'

'They know about me?'

'How else do you imagine you weren't held for questioning over that man's death?' She touched him on the arm. 'Everything's going to be fine. Really, you did very well out there.'

She turned the key in the lock and opened the door. 'Dr Rosenharte,' she announced, and without waiting, walked through the suite and left by another door. There were just two men. A tall, well-built Englishman with a shy smile stepped forward and offered his hand. 'I'm Robert Harland. This gentleman is from the CIA.'

Declining Harland's hand, Rosenharte took time to appraise the American: a large, shrewd-looking individual with possible German ancestry. 'And your name?' asked Rosenharte.

'Maybe later,' said the American.

'Can I give you a drink?' asked Harland.

'Scotch on the rocks,' he replied, looking round the suite. It was several degrees more luxurious than his room at the Hotel Svevo.

'You handled that very well out there,' ventured the CIA man.

Rosenharte took the drink and regarded him. 'Whereas you don't impress me at all. You start out on an operation with only a vague idea of how it will be executed. A wing and a prayer – isn't that your expression? And with this empty craziness you risk my family's security.'

'Why don't you hear what we have to propose?' suggested Harland, gesturing to a chair.

Rosenharte shrugged as though he wouldn't be staying long, though he knew he was locked up with these men for the night and had no choice but to listen to them. 'Who was the man who died?' he asked quietly.

Harland sat down. 'His name was Grycko. A Polish national. Does the name mean anything to you?'

'No.'

'Not ours, and not yours – are you certain you didn't recognize him?'

'Quite certain. Why should I?'

'He didn't say anything to you?'

'A name. He mumbled a name, but I forget what it was. The man was dying. He made no sense.'

There was silence in the room. 'Look, we understand the risks, and if you're not willing to help us, well, you still have time to get out. It's a simple matter to arrange for Annalise to behave so unreliably that even the Stasi won't think of touching her. You can go back and tell them you gave it your best shot and that the stuff in the letters hinting at NATO secrets was just a come-on to entice you to Trieste.'

'Letters?' said Rosenharte. 'I saw only one. There was no hint of secrets in that.'

'There were three – one in late July, the other two in August – sent a week apart.'

August was when the Stasi picked up Konrad. 'You knew they would be intercepted by the Stasi before they reached me, because they open everything from abroad. You were relying on that.'

Harland looked up at him. 'I'm afraid that's exactly right. But now . . .'

'And you don't have any idea of . . . ?'

'Of what?' asked the American.

'Of the damage you've done? My brother is in prison.'

The American nodded. Rosenharte had noticed that he never seemed to lose his smile. 'He's saying you've fucked up, Bobby. His brother was arrested *because* of the letters. They've taken him as some kind of hostage to make sure Dr Rosenharte does what they want.'

'Yes, that's what you were saying over dinner.'

'And then they took his wife,' said Rosenharte, 'and put the two children into a care home a week ago just to make sure.' He circled the room and stopped to face Harland. 'What seems an ingenious game to you spies in the West is life and death to us in the East. A mother and father are in prison and being interrogated. Because of those letters a family is snatched from their home and separated.'

The American stroked his chin then loosened his tie. 'Personally, I think you're right. We should focus on the conditions in your country more than we do. We should always remember that.' He paused. 'But the only course now is to decide how to proceed.'

'You have a duty to my family.'

'I think Mr Harland appreciates that,' said the American. 'But we're in this situation now. We have to keep our heads and move on with caution.'

'Caution.' Rosenharte spat the word out. He was too angry to express his contempt properly. They had shown no caution whatsoever. He sank to the chair and picked up his glass. 'I'm an art historian now. I don't have access to the sorts of things that you want. Why pick me?'

'We have a particular and limited task in mind,' said Harland. 'And you are the only person who can do it for us.'

'I can do nothing for you until we have certain things straight. For you this operation contains no risks at all. If it goes wrong, you go home and think of another little game. I get a bullet in the back of the head or, if I'm lucky, twenty years in jail. My brother and his family will also be punished.'

'I understand,' said Harland.

Rosenharte undid a couple of buttons on his shirt. Despite the rain the night was still oppressively hot. 'What is it that you want?'

Harland exchanged looks with the American. 'We believe that you may be able to help us gain some information on the whereabouts and intentions of a man named Abu Jamal.'

'I've never heard of him,' said Rosenharte. The American sat down at the polished mahogany table and leant on it with two heavy arms, causing it to tip slightly. 'Abu Jamal is also known as Mohammed Ubayd, a Syrian terrorist who is financed and given safe haven by the Stasi in East Germany. We know he's been receiving medical treatment for a kidney complaint, maybe even a transplant. He pays regular visits to the Leipzig area.'

'You brought me here for this! I have no knowledge of these things. I haven't had any contact with the Stasi for a decade and a half, apart from the usual requests to act as an informer on my colleagues.'

'Yes,' said Harland patiently. 'We know who you are, Dr Rosenharte. We know about you.'

'There's another man we're interested in,' continued the American. 'He moves between Dresden and Leipzig, like you, and he is a professor of international relations. His name is Michael Lomieko, known to his friends as "Misha" because he spent much of his career in Moscow. Misha and Abu Jamal are very close associates indeed and have developed a policy of revolutionary intervention, which, put simply, is to attack Western targets and cause chaos and terror. Misha has added know-how and ambition to the projects of what was a run-of-the-mill Mid East terrorist operation. It's the apparent scale of the plans that's worrying us. Both men have the tacit support of the Party high command – Schwarzmeer and the head of the Stasi, Erich Mielke. And maybe even the first secretary is involved. Jamal and Misha are allowed to dream up their plans together in the comfort of the Stasi safe houses.' He paused. 'So you see, we're eager to catch Jamal and, if possible, Misha, but we would also like to prove the state sponsorship of terrorism. Have you heard of this man Misha? Professor Lomieko?'

'Yes,' said Rosenharte. 'I know him.'

'Then, with your cooperation we could do this,' said the American.

'Don't assume that. I know him only because we sometimes travel on the same train between Dresden and Leipzig. That's the only experience I have of him. I have exchanged only two dozen words with him in my life.'

'I think that's a good thing,' said Harland, moving the bottle towards him. 'Have another drink. We've got a long night ahead of us.'

Rosenharte studied him. He seemed likeable and intelligent

but it was unthinkable that such a man could occupy a similar position in the Stasi. 'Tell me, Mr Harland, how old are you?'

'Forty this year.'

'Yes, I thought so. You see, my brother and I were born in 1939, just after the outbreak of war. We will both be fifty in December. At that age you lose the taste for intrigue and adventure.'

'You look five to seven years younger,' said the CIA man.

'Thank you,' said Rosenharte, acknowledging the obvious flattery with a slightly world-weary expression. 'Has it occurred to you that the point of these operations is only to show your superiors that you're busy – to justify your role as intelligence officers? How much work do you generate for yourself with these operations?'

The American shook his head. 'You're wrong about that, Dr Rosenharte. We're trying to prevent people being killed. Your government has a record of supporting Libyan and Palestinian terrorists. Abu Jamal is just the latest manifestation of this. Misha is the interface of that relationship, passing information, help, inspiration, money, from the Stasi to Abu Jamal. Even by the peculiar standards of East Germany this is criminal behaviour.'

Harland leaned forward, his arms resting on his knees. 'What he's saying is that working to bring these men to justice, or at least to the attention of the Western media, should not be regarded as treasonable behaviour by you and it is certainly not some frivolous work creation by us. Believe me, we are desperately concerned about this man and we're in deadly earnest.'

'So where are we?' asked the American. 'Should we move forward on this? It seems the best way out for you, Dr Rosenharte.'

'If I help you, I want an agreement that you will bring me, my brother and his family out to the West, find us homes, jobs and medical treatment for Konrad. These are my conditions.'

'To get your brother out of prison is a tall order,' said Harland.

'We're not going to promise something that we can't deliver. But if our plan works, you stand every chance of getting your brother released because we're going to give you something they really want.'

They were right, Rosenharte conceded, there was only one way to go. 'But I have your agreement on the other things. I want them to be given a home. I want treatment for my brother and help to find him useful employment. He's a gifted filmmaker but he'll need support – contacts and introductions. I'll need help to leave the country. I demand less for myself because I have my own career.'

'You have international renown,' said Harland.

'That's true in my field for the few papers that have been published in the West. But my work is not published in the GDR because of my brother's conviction.' He stopped. 'Do I have your agreement?'

'Yes, you do. We will meet all your demands.'

'Then I'll help you. But there is one further condition. When I go back I must take something to convince them that Annalise is an important source.'

'A sample of what she may be able to acquire in the future,' suggested Harland.

'Then I may be able to persuade Schwarzmeer to release my brother.' He paused, looking at the eager faces. 'You are aware who Schwarzmeer is?'

Harland nodded. 'Of course, and we already had something like this in mind. In fact it's extremely good material.' He nodded to the American. Presumably he had supplied it.

'And whatever happens, you'll bring my brother's family out as soon as possible, regardless of whether my brother is still in Hohenschönhausen.'

'That shouldn't be a problem,' said Harland. 'The Hungarians took down their border with Austria in May. Thousands are

43

leaving the GDR and going through Czechoslovakia to Hungary every day. We've already got people out that way.'

Rosenharte shook his head. 'You heard Honecker say last January that the Wall will be standing in a hundred years' time if the reason for its existence is not removed. The reason for its existence is to stop people going to the West! If they allow people to leave through Hungary it makes a mockery of their Wall. So it follows they'll stop that route.'

'Still,' said Harland, 'it shouldn't present too many problems. How old are the children?'

'Eight and six years old . . . I think.'

'Then no problem at all.'

'So what am I taking back?'

'The only things they care about,' said the American, 'are computers, software, programs. Defence programs from NATO would push all their buttons at once. We have something very special – very new – in this line. We'll give you a disk we have had prepared with the help of Langley and colleagues of mine at NATO.'

'Who's running this operation?' asked Rosenharte. 'The CIA or British Intelligence? Who am I doing a deal with?'

'Me,' said Harland. 'The CIA is helping and will benefit from the information that you provide.'

'How many people know about it?'

'As few as possible.'

'It's well known that the Stasi have penetrated your services, in particular the British. I insist that if I agree to this plan you never refer to me by name or give other information that may yield my identity. This is my principal condition.'

'Naturally, we'll give you a code name – what about Prince?'

'Whatever you like. Now I want you to order up from room service. A bottle of champagne, two glasses and caviar.'

44

'You don't have to do this now. The hotel is secure. The management is well aware of the need for discretion.'

'But not every member of the staff is. There are always mistakes. The Stasi will come back here in six weeks' time and ask questions. That's the way they work. They'll find one person who remembers something.'

Having taken some money from Harland, Rosenharte moved to the bedroom next door and, with the woman, began creating a scene of abandoned love. They undressed – she to a slip and he to underpants – then lay on the bed until the doorbell rang, at which Anna, as he now called her, gave him a final check, tousled his hair and chucked him the white bathrobe provided by the hotel. An elderly waiter brought in a tray and smiled benignly at the scene of middle-aged passion. Rosenharte gave him a 30,000 lira tip and patted him on the shoulder as he left.

Whatever the oddness and difficulties of the situation, they were now operating as an effective team. 'You know,' she said, her eyes dancing, 'in other circumstances and if I wasn't a happily married woman, I'd be very content to be in a hotel room with you, Rudi.'

This made him smile. She may not have been the beauty that Annalise was, but she was attractive and intelligent, and she was beginning to grow on him.

'But there are just one or two touches I think we should add for purposes of authenticity.' She reached up, removed the robe from his shoulder and kissed his bare skin twice, each time biting a little.

He cleared his throat. Things were beginning to stir in him.

'Right, that's enough of that,' she said briskly. 'That's an old teenage skill of mine. They should come up nicely by the morning.'

Five minutes later he returned to the sitting room.

'Okay,' said Harland, rising. 'Let's get some air in here. It's stuffy as hell.' He walked over to a French window, which led onto a little terrace that was hidden from the street by a wall. Rosenharte noted that the room wasn't overlooked from the buildings on the other side of the road. Large pools of water lay on the terrace.

Harland returned, sat down and smiled apologetically. These English mannerisms of modesty and self-effacement were profoundly irritating to Rosenharte because they obviously meant so little. But in other respects he seemed genuine and Rosenharte surmised that they were alike in some ways. He guessed Harland was a bachelor, as well as a loner.

'This is what we know about Misha,' Harland said. 'He has a room in a Leipzig university building and he meets with Abu Jamal in a safe house in Leipzig, probably an apartment normally used by the Stasi for meetings with the Inoffizielle Mitarbeiter – the Stasi's civilian collaborators.'

Rosenharte didn't need a lecture about IMs. He raised his eyes to the ceiling.

Harland ignored him. 'He has also visited Abu Jamal in hospital three times over the summer. The last visit was a few weeks ago. We know that he spends about twelve days a month in Leipzig. The rest of the time he's on the campus at the Technical University at Dresden, researching explosives and so forth. He visits Berlin only occasionally.'

'That's more information than I could ever have acquired,' said Rosenharte. 'Why do you need me?'

'We want you to make contact with someone who has more evidence to pass to us – proof of the involvement of Abu Jamal and Misha in at least one bombing. More important, this contact may have information about plans for future attacks.'

'Who's the individual who can give you this information?'

'We don't know. All we have is a code name: Kafka.'

'Then how will I find this person?'

There was silence. He looked at Harland and noticed that one of his eyelids was flickering involuntarily. Harland tried to still it with his fingertip. 'You are not going to find them,' he replied at length. 'He or she will find you.'

'If this arrangement means that you have to give them my name, I can't allow it. What will happen if this person is questioned by the Stasi? They break people. They broke my brother in Bautzen. He was a strong man, very fit, but Bautzen wrecked his health.' He paused. 'I think it would be better if you told me everything, don't you?'

Harland inhaled deeply. 'We wouldn't dream of giving your name to anyone. Besides, how could we give your name to someone whose identity we don't know?' He stopped and leaned back in his chair. 'We want this evidence very badly, but we are equally concerned for your safety.'

Rosenharte shook his head sceptically.

'I mean it.'

'Go on, please.'

'A month ago, a woman was visiting Leipzig as part of a Christian Fellowship group. This person has done some work for us, mostly as a courier. Before leaving Leipzig to travel to West Berlin she carried out the usual checks on her luggage to make sure nothing incriminating had been planted on her. She didn't find anything until she reached a hotel in the West. She had received a message telling her to look again. What she found were some very interesting documents and a letter to us.'

'And you believed this?' asked Rosenharte incredulously.

'At first we were inclined to think that this was one of the Stasi's little pranks, but then the names in the documents proved very useful. In fact, the US government was able to make an arrest of one man and to begin tracking another. Both are connected with

Abu Jamal. It turned out to be very valuable intelligence indeed – but you see we had no idea who had given it to us. The documents were wiped of fingerprints, there was no handwriting – nothing to betray the identity of the donor.'

'So why didn't you send your courier back to Leipzig?'

'We did. She came back with a message delivered the same way. Kafka wanted a German, someone with good cover who could travel to Leipzig as often as they liked without raising suspicion. Then a senior member of our outfit remembered you and we did some research and found that everything fitted perfectly.'

Rosenharte did not hide his bafflement. 'Why did he remember me?'

'He was in Brussels in 1974.'

'You recalled that you had something on me and thought you could force me to do this?'

'No,' said Harland. 'We are not going to force you. We need you to be committed because you *want* to be. In exchange we will do as you ask as regards your brother and his family.'

'I need to think about this, but first I want to know how this person will make contact.'

'We must have a decision by morning. If you're not going to do this, we'll have to make certain arrangements in order to protect you and your story. To answer your question about the contact, there are procedures for you to follow in a specified order. I cannot tell you these until I know that you're coming on board.'

Rosenharte nodded. 'I'll take some rest now.'

'Go ahead,' said Harland. 'We'll make ourselves scarce until about seven – does that suit you?'

Rosenharte slept little. By dawn he understood that cooperation was the only way, because at least it offered some hope of freeing

Konrad and slightly better odds of bringing Else and the two children to the West. He had to do it, even though Harland's operation seemed vague and a little crude. He had no expectation of success, but by the time he had tried and failed to make contact with this person in Leipzig, Else, the boys and – with much luck – Konrad would be in the West.

At six thirty he gave Harland his decision. By seven he and Anna had played their role for the benefit of the young man who brought them breakfast, which they consumed like a married couple, saying little.

He returned to the room to find Harland and the American bent over coffee and a basket of pastries.

He did not return their greeting but instead lit a cigarette and launched into the thing he had been turning in his mind. 'When the real Annalise died you decided to keep her alive. I can easily imagine that was an extensive operation. Why? What purpose did it serve?'

Harland picked the crumbs from his chinos. 'She transferred to NATO in the early part of 1975 to the Department of Defence Policy and Planning, where she was mostly involved in the translation of documents and preparation of papers for summits.'

'And some you fed to the Stasi through a new controller?'

'Yes, as a matter of fact a man named Kurt Segler, a gardener at NATO headquarters. It proved a very reliable arrangement.'

'But the Stasi are not fools. They'd have suspected something when the substitute Annalise gave them false information.'

'That was the whole point.' He stopped and gave Rosenharte an oddly apologetic look, indicating the seriousness of the secret. 'It never was false information. We used her as a truth channel.'

FOUR

The Song Bird

Rosenharte understood the function of a truth channel immediately but Harland went ahead and explained it anyway. 'Everything she predicted did in fact take place. She was the most accurate source they had ever had. You see, we needed a way of telling the Russians what our actual intentions were. We knew that if they trusted Annalise as a spy, we could feed them stuff that was unambiguous about the Western position.'

Rosenharte's attention had wandered during Harland's exegesis to a black and white bird that was calling from the corner of a roof opposite the hotel. The American had followed his gaze. 'Are you a birder, Dr Rosenharte?'

'A birder? Ah, yes, I like to know what I'm seeing. Birds were a passion of ours when my brother and I were boys. I was just reminding myself that Trieste is on one of the major migration routes for nightingales in the spring. Did you know that?'

'What's that bird over there?'

'In German it is called a *Mittelmeersteinschmätzer.*'

They both laughed.

'In Latin it is *Oenanthe hispanica.* A wheatear is I believe its name in English. It has its own call but sometimes it imitates the song of other species.'

'Can you still imitate a song?' asked the American. 'Because that is what we need you to do when you get back into East Germany. Or have you been out of the business too long?'

Rosenharte nodded slowly. 'I have no other option if I am to get my brother's family out. You should understand that that is all I care about. So, yes, I will sing the tune of another bird.' In that moment Konrad came to his mind and he thought how this encounter would benefit from his brother's gift of witty encapsulation. It was after all a very bizarre situation.

'But you look concerned.'

He got up and poured himself some coffee from the breakfast flask – even lukewarm it was unlike anything in the GDR – and stirred a lump of unrefined sugar into the liquid. 'You bring me here to dine with a woman who has been dead for a decade and a half; I'm given fake love-bites by her substitute. You inform me that the entire operation was originally set up not to deceive my side, but to tell us the truth. You ask me to meet a source in Leipzig whom you have never met and cannot vouch for. Now I find myself talking metaphorically about bird calls. I was thinking that life doesn't get much stranger than this.' He stopped and examined each of them in turn. 'And I was asking myself if I need to be insane to put my trust in you.'

Harland nodded sympathetically but Rosenharte saw his eyes hadn't lost their purpose. 'For instance,' he continued, 'on the truth channel everyone knows that the Stasi does not simply accept what it's given. They make tasks for their agents to gain specific intelligence. They wanted me to test Annalise in that way during the autumn of 1974, just before she died.'

'You're right,' said Harland. 'Similar demands were made on Annalise's substitute and in the spring of '75 we orchestrated appropriate responses which seemed to satisfy the Stasi. It was a collaborative effort, involving several nations.'

'Then I should know what other information she gave them.'

'In outline, yes, but let's face it this isn't exactly pillow talk. You wouldn't have spent the night discussing these things. But I'll give one or two examples of the way we used her. During the Strategic Arms Limitation Treaty talks, cables, handwritten notes and letters between heads of NATO states, even one from Reagan, were leaked. On 15 March 1985 when Chernenko died she supplied them with documents and telegrams between the US government and NATO and the agenda of meetings between defence ministers held by the new British Secretary General Lord Carrington. That was her last job for us. But this had been going on for a long time. Back in December 1979, for instance, an exchange between Jimmy Carter and the Secretary General of NATO concerning the Russian invasion of Afghanistan was made available so the other side knew that the West's protestations were deeply felt and that they would act if there were any further territorial incursions. But all this only worked because they *believed* she was their spy.'

Rosenharte leaned forward and asked: 'In '75, how did you explain her disappearance? One moment she was working for the Commission, the next she was in NATO handing over secrets to a gardener. It doesn't seem a very natural progression.'

'After the suicide, we had to work very hard,' said Harland. 'When Annalise Schering went off the radar screen we put it about that she had suffered some personal loss and a suspected break-down. A few months went by and she eventually resigned from the Commission to take the job at NATO. She was, as you know, a fairly solitary person and had few friends. Her mother was dead by then and she had no other family. The Belgian authorities were helpful because at that time Brussels was full of Stasi Romeos trying to bed every bloody secretary in town. What worked for us was that the only East German agent who knew her was you. There had not been time for them to do the usual background checks and place other agents around her. That all happened later, when she went to NATO, where – incidentally – it was explained that her collapse had been brought about by a thyroid imbalance and an unsuitable affair. You were that unsuitable affair. She told her new controller that she had lost her heart to you, but that you drank too much and were therefore a security risk. They were impressed by her sense of mission and the self-sacrifice entailed in dropping you.' He stopped and looked Rosenharte in the eye. 'It was all very neat . . . though . . . I do appreciate it was painful for you.'

'Indeed,' said Rosenharte, not letting them see his anger. Just after he had left Annalise's apartment on that dreary evening, he was picked by the Belgian police. Two days of interrogation followed, at the end of which they told him he was to be charged for the murder of Annalise Schering. They said he had faked her suicide by forcing her to take an overdose of sleeping pills and then cutting her wrists as she lay asleep. Evidence of her blood was found in the bedroom, which they said supported the theory that she had been placed in the bath after she was drugged and had become unconscious. It would be difficult to contest in court, particularly as they'd show that Rosenharte was a Stasi agent who'd been trying to make Annalise Schering work for East Germany. He was reminded by a senior police officer that Belgium had not yet abolished the death penalty and that at the very least he would face a minimum of twenty years in jail. Then two British spies and a Belgian intelligence officer came to the police station cell and put a proposition to him. He would be released without charge, as long as he remained in Brussels and filed regular reports of his contact with Annalise. Thereafter they would provide the pretext for his return to East Germany. If for one moment they suspected that he had told the truth to the Stasi they would release tapes proving his cooperation with the West, including pictures of his taking what appeared to be an envelope containing money. He had no choice. For the first three months of 1975 he maintained the fiction of his affair with Annalise in his messages to the East, all recorded on the mid-section of a conventional Frank Sinatra music cassette and then sent to an address in Berlin.

He looked at Harland squinting through the smoke of his cigarette. 'I have always wondered what your side said about me to the Stasi through the substitute Annalise. They would have nothing to do with me when I got back to Normannenstrasse.'

Harland coughed awkwardly. 'I'm afraid there may have been some allegations of a sexual nature, it being well understood by us at the time that the Stasi had a horror of that kind of deviance in its own ranks. But of course I was not directly involved.'

Rosenharte had always suspected this but again decided to keep his anger to himself. 'When did the arrangement with the replacement finish?'

'When the woman became pregnant by her real husband. We couldn't have her meeting her controller with a bump. He'd want too many explanations. The thing had come to a natural end. Security measures were increased in NATO headquarters, with several people being investigated and questioned. When the gardener was arrested, Annalise sent word to the Stasi that she risked being exposed and could not continue. Soon afterwards it was put about that she had left to marry a Canadian businessman. End of story.'

'When was this?'

'Late spring, 1985.'

'And in all that time, you like to think that they did not take photographs of her? What if they took pictures last night? All they have to do is compare the two.'

'We hope they did.' Harland looked at Griswald and grinned. 'She worked for us in NATO. She was the second Annalise. She came out of retirement for this job. As far as they're concerned, it *is* Annalise. That's why I believe you'll be safe for as long as it's necessary. Then we will get you out.'

Rosenharte got up, walked to the window and looked down into the street, which was now beginning to fill with people. It was Sunday 10 September and church bells were tolling across the city. He was suddenly taken by the colour and animation of Italian life again. Bar umbrellas were being erected, flowers watered and pavements being swept outside one or two stores by trim, fastidious women. Immediately below them was a fruit stall where baskets of produce were laid in a perfectly balanced pattern. It seemed to him that no decision was made about the centre of Trieste without someone first asking what effect it would have on the appearance of the city. He watched a few people making their way to early morning mass and brought to mind a black and white film written by Billy Wilder, *Menschen am Sonntag* – People on Sunday. Konnie had found a rare print and shown it to him on a projector that kept breaking down. While he fiddled with the machine, he gave a commentary on the film, a brilliant discourse on the way the little masterpiece from the time of Weimar captured the unknowability of each person. 'Cinema doesn't have to be explicit,' he had said. 'It can let a mystery hang in the air and each person makes of it what he or she will, according to their character.' Dear, brave Konnie. He had to get him out soon.

'So,' said Harland, trying to gain his attention.

Rosenharte turned.

'You know,' continued the American, 'you guys are screwed in the East. The economy is in meltdown, the young people are all leaving, nothing works, the factories are forty years behind the West. Everything's up the Swanee.'

'The Swanee?'

'*Kaput. Alles ist kaput.*'

'Is the West any better? Until last year you had a President who only made decisions when he had consulted his wife's astrologer. We read about these things in the East, you know. And what about last year, when every economy in the West nearly failed because of the greed of investors on Wall Street?'

'You can't compare that with what's going on in your country,' returned the American amiably. 'Literally nothing works in East Germany. There's no food, the transport system is shit, the manufacturing base is thirty years out of date. Every time someone has a new idea it goes before a dozen committees before it can be implemented. And when things break down all the effort is put into investigating possible sabotage rather than fixing the problem. Sabotage is the alibi of every dud factory manager. But the Party bosses care not one jot about this because they have all the comfort and luxury goods they need. Way off in the hidden compounds, the Party hierarchy have every luxury and all the best medical treatment. We know what's going on, Rosenharte. Nothing works unless you're a Party boss.'

'Some things do,' said Rosenharte slowly, conceding to himself the accuracy of the American's picture. 'Everyone is in work; they are provided for; they are guaranteed a place to live and their children are well educated – even most Western experts agree on that.'

'Yes, but what a corrupt version of paternalism that is,' he said, truly warming to his theme. 'The Communist Party – the Social-ist Unity Party, as you call it – expects a man to stifle all his ambition, all his views and tastes. The Party decides everything for him, from cradle to grave. And if he doesn't go along with it, he's put in jail. That's hardly a healthy society.'

'You're right about many things in the GDR,' said Rosenharte. 'But you must never underestimate the Stasi. It is a state within a state. And that state has never been healthier. Nothing happens in the GDR without the Stasi knowing about it.' He paused. 'Three months ago, my brother's elder son was interrogated by an officer because of an essay he wrote for his school. The teacher had passed it to them because it contained "unpatriotic and anti-social ten-dencies". You know what this essay was about? The migration of birds! An eight-year-old cannot write about a bird flying over our national border without the Stasi seeing it as a threat. I repeat, do not underestimate them. Now, tell me what you want me to do. Where must I go in Leipzig? How do I communicate with you?'

'Are you a religious man, Dr Rosenharte?' asked Harland.

'No.'

'Well, we need you to be converted to the cause of Christian brotherhood and peace. It is in this context that Annalise has offered to help East Germany. As she explained in the letters she sent you in the summer, she wants to help rectify the technological imbalance between West and East. That much the Stasi know, though of course you don't because you haven't seen those letters. It's the old argu-ment about preserving peace by equalizing military power. You must put some time into thinking about this before you go back. Flesh out a story in your own words.'

Rosenharte made a mental note to do so and realized in the same moment that he would have to hone the old skills of decep-tion and providing impromptu but convincing explanations. 'I have very little time now. I must give my paper to the conference and make contact with my side before that.'

'There'll be time for everything,' said Harland. 'First we need to discuss how you're going to meet Kafka.'

Harland and Griswald said goodbye to Rosenharte at the hotel, having drilled him in the procedures to be followed for contacting the West and for making himself known to Kafka in Leipzig. They waited for an hour before leaving by the service entrance and making their way to the conference centre. After the first lecture started they slipped in and joined Prelli in the projection box at the back of the lecture hall. Prelli pointed out the two Stasi agents that had been hurriedly planted in the audience. Harland watched as Jessie entered and took a seat two rows from the front. Rosenharte turned and nodded discreetly to her, at which a man on the aisle leaned forward and showed interest.

At three, Rosenharte rose and walked to the podium. An effusive Italian academic introduced him as the premier authority on early seventeenth-century drawings in East Germany and added that from the work published in the West — sadly still so limited — it was clear that as a thinker Rosenharte was breaking new ground. His work at the Gemäldegalerie in Dresden, said the man, proved that the dialogue between art historians would continue to exist whatever the differences between states. Rosenharte replied with a bow, the lights dimmed and he began speaking without notes and in English.

Harland now saw an entirely different man from the wary individual he had been dealing with. He spoke fluently and addressed his audience with the charm of a politician. Five minutes into the lecture, Rosenharte pressed a button on the slide projector and on the screen there appeared a drawing in rust-coloured chalk of a cripple boy. He stared at it for a moment, then silently ran the pointing stick around the distortion of the boy's back, hunched shoulders and empty, elfin face.

'Ten years after this was made by the young Annibale Carracci, some words were written by William Shakespeare: "Cheated of feature by dissembling nature, deformed, unfinished, sent before my time into this breathing world scarce half made up."' He paused. 'Beautiful words. And a beautiful drawing to describe deformity, wouldn't you say? But this sketch before you is also revolutionary in its compassion, a work that breaks free of the controlling taste of the patrons of the time. In his own hand the artist has written beside the boy's head, "*No so se Dio m'aiuta*" – I don't know if God will help me. And so the artist, like a photo-journalist today, witnesses the injustice of the young boy's condition, and provides a challenge to God and therefore to the religious authorities. Why? Why are people born like this? Why do men shrink from them and dogs bark at them in the street? These are the questions of a revolutionary conscience and I maintain a socialist conscience. Carracci calls God and the Church to account.'

Over the next forty minutes he developed the theme of artistic conscience. When he reached the end he opened his hands to the audience. 'No,' he said. 'God does not help this man. But we must. That was Carracci's message.' With a tip of the head he thanked them for their attention.

The hall burst into spontaneous applause.

'It's the same lecture he gave in Leipzig. It's why he was chosen by Kafka.'

'He was chosen by Kafka!' said Griswald.

Harland nodded. 'And now I understand why.'

Griswald, no slouch when it came to reading the subtext,

59

puckered his brow. 'What are you talking about, Harland? What haven't you told me?'

'Just that. Rosenharte gave that lecture in the early summer in Leipzig. It seems that Kafka – whoever that is – liked the look of him. You see the lecture can be read two ways. If you are an unimaginative commie it appears to comply to the usual Marxist theories about the suppression of the masses and the rise of capitalism et cetera, et cetera. It can also be seen as an argument against persecution by the state and the stifling of free expression.'

'A bird who can sing several tunes at once,' said Griswald. 'Hey, look, Jessie's on the move.'

She had left her chair and was on the edge of a group of admiring academics gathered round Rosenharte, waving her arms comically over the heads of the others. Rosenharte got up to greet her. They kissed and she gave him a light congratulatory hug. Then she broke free and tapped her wristwatch to say that she had to leave. As she went she blew him a kiss. Harland spotted the small padded envelope that she had slipped into his hand.

'The ball's in play and our man's on his way,' said Harland, noting the two Stasi agents hurrying down the central aisle to be near Rosenharte.

'So there goes our agent. Sent before his time, scarce half made up,' said Griswald.

FIVE

A House in the Forest

The lights of fireflies were pulsing on the fringes of the airfield near Ljubljana, Slovenia, when the Stasi convoy pulled up beside an old Antonov 26 which stood with its props gently revolving in the warm night air. Rosenharte watched them fleetingly before the party clambered up a retractable stairway and dispersed through the aircraft. It smelled of fuel and tired upholstery.

Biermeier appeared in the cockpit door looking self-satisfied, walked up the aisle nodding to his men and sat down heavily next to Rosenharte.

'Which airport are we flying into?' asked Rosenharte.

'It's enough for you to know that you're returning to your homeland,' he replied.

'I hope there's something to drink. Anything will do – a beer or some water.'

Biermeier gave him a long-suffering look and barked the order to one of the Stasi officers who had accompanied them from Trieste, then turned to Rosenharte. 'So, you got the first delivery from your friend. That is good. But what interests me is the dead man. Who was he?'

'I told Heise. I don't know – some drunk who had a heart attack.'

Biermeier nodded and frowned at the same time. Rosenharte examined his profile with interest. His runaway chin and sloping forehead meant that his face ran to a bulbous point at his nose. He had several moles on his neck, which evidently presented problems when he was shaving, and a little red rash had appeared at the top of his cheeks. He was unprepossessing and oafish, yet he was far from stupid. He gave the impression of a man with a large character who'd consciously forced his personality into the Stasi norms of merciless reliability.

'We'll have to look into it further. You must understand that this seems very suspicious. We know he was following you in Trieste.'

Rosenharte shrugged. 'Look, I don't know who the hell he was. I didn't want to go to Trieste in the first place. Schwarzmeer forced me. Frankly, I don't want anything to do with this business.'

'You have no choice. Now tell me what was in that package she gave you.'

'I have no idea. You have the package.'

'But she must have told you what was in it. She must have made a hint or two.'

Rosenharte recoiled from his garlic breath. 'I know nothing except that it concerns NATO defence programs. Why don't you open it for yourself?'

'She must have told you more.'

'Is this an official debrief, or should I wait until I see General Schwarzmeer?'

'This is my operation – I have security clearance.'

'As I understand it, this operation concerns the gravest issues of national security. Open the package but don't compromise me. I've done my job.' He turned away and looked out on the flashing light at the end of the wing. Eventually Biermeier gave up on him and moved to be with the other members of his team. An unexplained delay kept them there for an hour before the engines started up and the plane rumbled down the tarmac, causing the fittings of the interior to squeak and the lockers to crash open. Once they were airborne, Rosenharte moved to the port side of the cabin to look out over the Alps with a certain boyish glee, as they took a course that skirted Austria and flew northeast towards Hungary and Czechoslovakia. The landscape was pretty well illuminated by the half moon and he could just make out the ridges along the tops of the mountains. He thought of walking the valleys below with his brother, a thing they had promised they would do once Konnie's health improved. He always insisted it was simply a matter of time but two years had passed without him being able to raise the energy. He needed treatment in the West and that was what Rosenharte was going to get for him.

After two hours, with first light beginning to show in the east, the plane circled three times then landed on a runway at a military base somewhere in the south of the GDR. They taxied past the humps of fortified aircraft hangars where men in overalls could be seen moving about beneath naked lights.

Two Ladas and a military truck awaited them, but only Biermeier and three officers got off the plane with Rosenharte. Then the Antonov, emitting a good deal of black exhaust from its starboard engine, turned and prepared to take off again, he assumed for Berlin-Schönefeld, where Annalise's material would be examined.

Now back on German soil, the Stasi had become a degree more officious and, as they walked to the cars, the largest of the men took hold of his upper arm. Rosenharte shook himself free and spun round. 'Understand this: I am not your prisoner!' Biermeier nodded to the man, who dropped back a couple of paces, but Rosenharte knew that this didn't bode well. In their eyes he was more suspect than helper.

He had to reverse that.

They set off through what he knew must be a restricted zone. On several occasions the empty road swung by large compounds of apartment blocks and stores that had been flung down in the great beech forests to accommodate the Russian military, massive buildings quite out of character with their surroundings. About forty-five minutes on, as the road began to climb, they reached a gateway and two men appeared from a hut behind some bushes. After checking their credentials and scanning the faces in the cars, they opened the gates. A long drive led to a clearing in the woods where there were four well-tended, single-storey summer-houses, all with verandas. The model for these was the Russian dacha, though there was a defended, sinister air about them. All the windows and doors were fitted with grilles. Despite the rustic setting, the place had somehow been impregnated with the Stasi's dismal paranoia.

He was led to the furthest house and down some steps to a base-ment, which was so soundly built that it might have served as a bomb shelter. He was shown to a large room with a bed, table, chairs and a glass bowl in which there rested a solitary apple. The light came in through four horizontal windows along the ceiling. 'You will remain here until they call for you,' said Biermeier. 'Everything you need is here and food will be brought to you.'

'I have commitments in Dresden tomorrow,' Rosenharte said.

Biermeier regarded him as though he were a child. 'The only commitments you have are to the state, Herr Doktor.'

For three days Rosenharte saw no one apart from the men who brought his meals and escorted him for a daily turn in the grounds. When he asked for something to read, he was given two old copies of *Neues Deutschland* and *Wochenpost*, and a translation of stories by

Jack London. It took all his self-discipline to avoid worrying. He told himself that he was being held while Annalise's material was assessed and they decided whether to proceed further. But he also understood they would be checking on every detail concerning Annalise's position at NATO, her life in Canada and her present circumstances in Brussels. He could be expected to know little of this, but they would look for inconsistencies between what they'd discovered and his account. He went over and over everything that Harland and the American had told him, praying at the same time that they had given Annalise's new life convincing depth. A single error, the slightest hint of incongruity or a sense that Annalise's existence was just too two-dimensional to be real, and he would be done for.

The glimpse of life in the West – the first since he'd left Brussels – had sharpened his outrage at the way the Stasi had incarcerated him but also his fear of what they could do with him and Konrad. The brilliance of the Italian day accentuated the German night. He wished Harland and his American friend could have one day of his experience, sweating in a noiseless white cell, schooling himself in answers to an interrogation that he could only hope to predict, knowing that if things went wrong, he would be destroyed. Westerners would never understand the reality of the Stasi's power and their dogged, almost surreal pursuit of the ordinary man.

By the morning of the third day – Thursday 14 September he noted – he was ready to start kicking up a fuss in the belief that too much compliance indicated some kind of guilt. When the man brought him breakfast, he demanded to see someone in authority and told him that this was a shameful way to treat a person who was seeking only to serve his country. He returned a couple of hours later, picked up the tray and silently indicated that Rosenharte should follow him.

It was no more than a hundred yards to the first house, and the moment after Rosenharte reached the top of the steps from the basement and took in the day, he saw a figure on the veranda, lounging in wading boots that had been rolled down to his shins. The face was hidden in shadow, but he knew it belonged to Schwarzmeer.

'How do you like our little retreat, Dr Rosenharte?' he called out as Rosenharte approached. 'A lover's paradise, no? It's a tragedy that Miss Schering could not be here with you. There are some splendid walks through the forests.'

He reached the veranda and looked up. 'Why are you holding me prisoner, General?'

'You know the drill, we have to make certain checks. I could not allow you to wander around Dresden with all that knowledge.'

'I don't have any knowledge. I took delivery of a package, that's all. I don't know what it contains.' He noticed two of the bodyguard detail lurking in the house. Biermeier was nowhere to be seen.

'But you know who gave it to you *and* where she works *and* what she does. That is knowledge of a very interesting kind to the spies that seek to destroy our country.' He pushed himself out of the wicker chair and gazed down a path cut through the beeches to a lake. 'Perfect conditions for angling,' he said with a sigh, then rubbed his hip. 'It's good for the soul to spend time out here, eh? In nature, among the trees with nothing but the fish to try your patience.' Rosenharte recalled that Schwarzmeer fondly viewed himself as a countryman who wanted only a good hearth, a plate of meat and a stein or two; a hayseed who was ill-at-ease in the big city and mistrusted its ways. It was all fantasy. He was the son of a clerk and a milliner. For generations the Schwarzmeers had died with Berlin's soot in their lungs.

He had changed little since the seventies, when Rosenharte had twice encountered the then Stasi Lieutenant Colonel before leaving for Brussels. He had the same equable presence: the lips slightly parted ready to laugh; the eyes that smiled with comprehension; and the ingratiating manner which was all the more nauseating for his insistence that he was the sort of man who could only speak his mind. This, he insisted, was the reason that he would never rise higher in the Ministerium. But he had, having been promoted to the top post in the HVA on the retirement of the great spymaster Dieter Fuchs three years before.

He had put on weight around his middle; his neck had thickened and his cheeks had filled, making his eyes more hooded at the corners. Yet his face was essentially unchanged: he had the same waxy pallor, well-shaped nose and full, almost sensuous lips. Back in the seventies, someone had told him that he looked like a Roman Caesar, which evidently pleased Schwarzmeer because he constantly drew attention to the similarity, with archly self-deprecating remarks about his weight in middle age. On drawing near, Rosenharte had immediately noticed the General's most distinctive feature – the forehead that bulged above his eyebrows. It reminded him of Schwarzmeer's prodigious powers of calculation.

'You made love to the English woman, Doktor?' he said, stamping his right foot on the wooden decking, apparently to stop his hip from hurting.

'Is that any of your business?'

'Everything is my business. That is my motto. Everything is Schwarzmeer's business. Did you make love to her? Did she taste the fire of your passion?'

Rosenharte shrugged and looked away.

'And yet she let you go so easily enough the first time. Your performance cannot have been so good then.' Schwarzmeer chuckled to himself.

'I cannot say.'

'Come, Comrade Doktor. I have some people that wish to meet you.'

Rosenharte climbed the four wooden steps to the decking and entered a gloomy interior. Three men in suits and a starchy blonde woman in her early forties were seated at an olive-green table. Schwarzmeer gestured to another wicker chair in front of the table, taking one to the side himself and resting his leg on a little stool. There he began idly examining a hunting hat that bristled with fishing flies. 'So, Rosenharte, you will tell my colleagues what you found in Trieste?'

'How do you mean?'

'What you saw. What you found. Don't be a fool now.'

'I found Annalise Schering and we dined together, as Biermeier will tell you.'

'Yes, Colonel Biermeier,' said Schwarzmeer.

'She told me that she was willing to hand over certain information about some new computer systems used in NATO. Communication systems, I think. She didn't tell me what these were because she said I wouldn't understand.'

'You say you *found* her.' It was the woman, whose hands were nipping at the file in front of her. 'That's not true, is it? Unless you have failed to tell us something, you had no instructions to go to that restaurant by the canal. Only to go out on the pier?'

'Yes, you're right.'

'Then she found you?' said the man next to her, a clerkish individual with receding hair brushed forward. 'Are you suggesting that in all Trieste she happened upon the right restaurant?'

'No. I made a point of asking the hotel staff if they could recommend somewhere. Annalise knew where I was staying and I realized that she would check with them to find out where I was that evening. I told them to tell anyone who asked for me.' It was a poor lie because the Stasi could easily check his story.

'That seems a rather vague way of making an important contact. Why didn't you stay in the hotel?'

'To tell you the truth I was rather shocked by that man dying. I decided to have a drink or two and get some air.'

'Yes, we wondered about the man. We didn't find out who he was because the authorities in Trieste did not release any information about him. A man dies in the port and not one Italian policeman can say who he is. There is no record of his death. No inquest. Nothing. Does that not strike you as strange? Perhaps he didn't really die. Perhaps he passed you information about the meeting place and was miraculously revived in the ambulance.'

Rosenharte lifted his shoulders and opened his hands. 'He was having some kind of convulsion when he approached me on the quay. He said nothing that I understood. I assumed he was one of your people.'

'But we have it that he mentioned a name to you.'

'That's true, but I can't remember it exactly – Kusimack; Kusi-something.'

'And he said this word before he entered the water.'

'Yes.'

'Perhaps you would then explain why the microphone picked up nothing. In fact no sounds were heard from the scuffle, which suggests that you hadn't switched it on.'

'That's not true. In fact I switched it on as I went up the pier, even though Biermeier told me to do so only when I saw Annalise.' The four of them consulted each other with nods and a murmur or two.

'It's interesting, is it not, that you were required to meet Annalise Schering on the pier but that at no time was she actually present there? None of our officers saw her enter or leave the dockyard that day. How do you explain that?'

Rosenharte inwardly cursed himself for not thinking of an answer to this obvious question. 'She told me she was aware of the surveillance from the start; it nearly scared her off completely.'

'That doesn't seem very convincing,' said a man who hadn't spoken before.

'Look, I can't comment on these things,' said Rosenharte. 'I'm not part of your world. All I know is that I made contact as you required and I brought back a package, which you were not expecting. So, by any standards the operation was a success. Have you examined the material? Is it helpful?'

'Of course we have,' said Schwarzmeer. 'But that's not our concern here.'

He realized that this was at least a tacit admission of their interest. 'Then what is?' he asked calmly.

'To find out if you are in league with the forces that wish to disrupt the security of the state.'

He shook his head incredulously. 'You compelled me to make the journey against my will, saying that it would be bad for my brother if I refused. I did what you told me. I saw this woman again. I had relations with her. I did all this because you asked me. Yet now you hold me here against my will and accuse me of treasonable activities. This was not my plan. It was yours.' The expressions in front of him remained unmoved.

'Tell us about Schering,' said Schwarzmeer. 'It's some time since we were in contact with her.'

'She told me that she had worked for you at NATO until '85. You must know much more about her than I do. I only saw her for twelve hours. And she was pretty drunk for much of that time.'

Schwarzmeer did not respond. There was a silence in the room.

The light had shifted and he could see the people in front of him better. Collectively they presented a study of his country's blank, heartless interior.

'She also told me about the gardener who was arrested and the security checks at NATO that made her work for you difficult.'

'This is something that puzzles us,' said the man who had made most of the running so far. 'If she was worried about being discovered, why return to NATO headquarters? Or put it the other way round, if she had left in a hurry, why did NATO not suspect that she was the source, and at the very least refuse to employ her in such a sensitive position? You must see it doesn't make any sense.'

'These things are not my area. I was suspicious about her letter – I said so at the time. I told you to have nothing to do with it, but you went ahead. Now you expect me to vouch for Annalise's good motives towards the state. That's not my responsibility, surely? And it isn't just that you make me answer for her; now my loyalty to the state is called into question. If you felt I was unreliable, why send me to Trieste?'

'Don't get heated,' said Schwarzmeer. 'Did she say anything about the reason for contacting us, apart from seeing you again?'

'She is passionate about the cause for peace, to the point that she is a bore on the subject. She has made certain requests.'

'What are they?'

'She wants to make contact with the peace groups in Leipzig and Berlin – confidentially of course – in exchange for handing over the material.'

'That will be easily arranged,' said Schwarzmeer. 'We will have our own people represent them.'

'She says that she wants to do it through me. She trusts me.' He wanted to provide himself with more cover for his trips to Leipzig but he regretted saying this as soon as it was out. Schwarzmeer's eyes darted to the table.

'And yet in 1974,' he said, 'she refused to deal with you any longer because you were a security risk. What has occurred to change her mind?'

'I don't know,' said Rosenharte.

'So this is another thing that doesn't make sense,' said the lead inquisitor. 'There are too many inconsistencies in this story of yours for us to believe you.'

'It's not my story!' he was almost shouting. 'That's the point. I refuse to be put in a position where I'm defending Annalise Schering's story to you. If you don't trust her motives, don't deal with her. It's as simple as that. Ignore what she gave you. Believe me, if you weren't holding my brother I'd have had nothing to do with this operation.' He got up and walked around. He could tell that they were surprised, but what did it matter if they saw he was agitated? He stopped in his tracks, turned to them and shook his head silently, then looked out of the window. The midday light was diffused through the forest, drenching and flattening the forms. One or two leaves had turned brown. Autumn was not far away.

'Sit down,' said Schwarzmeer, 'and we'll complete our interview.'

'Why should I? Why should I continue? The more you insist I answer for Annalise Schering, the more responsibility I shall have to bear when things go wrong. Better that I cut my losses now. I know you will lock me up – you've already done that. What do I have to lose?'

'Sit down and stop being such a damned hysteric,' said Schwarzmeer quietly.

Rosenharte returned to the chair. 'I have never shown anything but loyalty to the state. All I want is to be treated with respect.' Again he saw that look pass through their faces, patronizing and at the same time brutal – the expression of people used to absolute power.

'It's not true,' started the woman. Rosenharte fixed her with a look. It was remarkable how women like her consciously expunged all traces of sexuality and softness from their appearance. 'It's not true that you are always loyal to the German Democratic Republic. We have reports of your criticism of the Secretary of the Dresden Party.' She looked down at a piece of paper. 'You were heard to say in response to his speech at the May Day celebrations that it was pious drivel. A donkey could make a better speech, was what you said.'

Rosenharte smiled. 'I deal with words, with the exact meaning of words. That's what scholarship is about, accuracy and the weighing of evidence. Comrade Kresler's speech was vapid, empty rhetoric. What we want from our leaders is truth and inspiration. What we get in Dresden is food queues and broken trains.'

The woman looked along the table triumphantly.

'The people are not stupid,' continued Rosenharte. 'They want to believe in socialism, but they cannot accept lies that insult their intelligence. They think less of the Party because of it. I was only expressing the common view.'

'A disloyal view none the less,' observed Schwarzmeer.

'To the Party, or the ideals of socialism?'

'Both,' said Schwarzmeer. 'They are the same thing. You would do well to remember that.' He clasped his knees and got up, which seemed to be a sign for one of the men and the woman to leave the room. Then, after giving Rosenharte a weary look, he pulled the wader straps up to his belt, fastened them and left.

'I am Laurentz,' said the older of the two men that had remained. He was in his forties and had the air of a practical man – a construction engineer or a factory administrator. 'This is Richter.' Richter was pallid with wispy blond hair that curled at the collar.

'At last, some names,' said Rosenharte. 'Are they real?'

'We are archival specialists. We deal with the past and we have real names.'

Rosenharte knew that that meant they scurried about in the filing system at Normannenstrasse, picking up trails from long ago and applying them to current intelligence problems. It was this pair who must have supplied Hans Heise with the information about the Commission so that he could test Annalise.

'We specialize in people's lives,' said the younger one, whom Rosenharte realized had barely moved since he'd been in the room. 'We construct a biography of a life, any life, in order to identify certain psychological traits, certain patterns.'

'And we have been looking into your life,' said Laurentz. He glanced down. 'Actually, a lot of work was done back in the seventies and then more recently, in connection with your brother Konrad's crimes.'

'And through this analysis,' said Rosenharte, 'you will decide whether I have the right psychological profile to make a traitor?'

'That is a little crude but yes, it is certainly one of our aims. We also suggest ways of addressing a problem with, say, an interview subject or someone who is harbouring a secret.'

The little shit was happy to sit there and admit that his speciality was suggesting ways of breaking people. 'Are you threatening me?' asked Rosenharte.

'No, what makes you say that?'

'Because I have heard of these techniques and know that you wouldn't hesitate to use them on me.'

'We are not threatening you,' said Laurentz. 'We just want to confirm a few things about your background and your career.'

'Right, the old stuff about my parentage.' His eyes drifted to the window and then a room next door. He noticed through the open door a man sitting in a chair with his legs crossed and his hands folded in his lap. Rosenharte's subconscious had interpreted the man as a shadow. Who the hell was he? He turned with an enquiring look to Laurentz and Richter but they ignored him.

'You and your brother Konrad were born on 15 December 1939,' Richter intoned, 'to Manfred and Isobel von Huth, both of them early members of the National Socialist Party. Your father joined the Second SS Panzerdivision, "Das Reich", in 1939. He rose to become Obergruppenführer and saw action in Russia in 1942 and 1943 when he was linked with the massacres of several thousand civilians in Ukraine. In 1944 he became Brigadeführer und General of the Thirty-second SS Panzergrenadierdivision, "30 Januar", and again saw action in Russia and in the defence of Berlin. Your mother, Isobel, was an aristocrat, a von Clausnitz, and it was at her family estates that your parents settled before the war. Your mother died in the bombing of Dresden on 13 February 1945 at which point it seems Marie Theresa Rosenharte, a housekeeper in the family home, took charge of you and your brother. In March 1945 your father died in mysterious circumstances and it is now generally assumed that he was either executed on orders of the high command, or that he was simply murdered by his own troops. Some time in that spring Frau Rosenharte took you to her farmhouse south of Dresden. She and her husband, an invalid from World War I, Hermann Rosenharte, adopted you. There were no other children.'

'Is this necessary?' asked Rosenharte. 'Am I still to be held responsible for the actions of my parents?'

'Naturally, this is a sensitive matter for you,' said Richter. 'Fascist tendencies of that order are still an embarrassment.'

'They say the apple never falls far from the tree,' chimed Laurentz.

'I don't think of my natural parents from one year to the next. I cannot even remember them.' This was not quite true. He held one image of his mother – a neat, slender woman, sitting in the window bay of a great house. She was looking down at a book. When they entered the room with their nurse she turned and smiled with a look of remote interest. Rosenharte supposed that this must have been shortly before she was killed in Dresden. He and Konnie would have been five years old. From then on the only woman whom he had called mother – and loved as a mother – was Marie Theresa Rosenharte.

'Perhaps you have subconsciously eliminated these memories,' said Laurentz. 'It would be perfectly understandable, given the nature of your father's crimes.'

Rosenharte shook his head.

'You did well at your studies,' continued Richter. 'The Rosenharte boys were the best students ever recalled at the small country school, which I don't suppose is saying much in a community of cowhands and woodsmen. You both attended Humboldt University in Berlin, where your talent for languages displayed itself. Your brother studied political theory. You went on to gain a doctorate in history and taught at Humboldt. You were aged twenty-eight when you were approached by the Ministerium für Staatssicherheit.' He stopped and consulted a thin blue folder. Rosenharte's eyes came to rest on the Stasi seal, a hand holding a rifle aloft beneath a fluttering banner. 'You were trained at the MfS school at Potsdam-Eiche. Your record as an officer with the MfS was well below expectations; you had little natural ability and were on several occasions reported to be in breach of disciplinary and security rules. Finally, you were deployed in the West – your file states as a last chance – first in Bonn then in Brussels. It was here that you met the woman known as Annalise Schering – the only successful attachment of this nature that you made. But within a few months it was reported to us that you had mishandled the situation. When approached by another officer, the woman said that she could not trust you with the delicacy of the task ahead. Then, rather than activating the agreed procedure to return to the GDR, you waited to be recalled and showed some signs of reluctance to leave the West.'

'It was at this time,' said Laurentz, 'that your brother Konrad got into trouble with the authorities and was first arrested.'

'To ensure that I returned,' said Rosenharte.

They ignored him and peered into a file together.

'You were married in 1980,' continued Richter, 'to Helga Goelkel. There were no children and you were divorced in 1982, just sixteen months later. Since then there have been a number of unsuccessful relationships which have all foundered because of your . . .' he stopped and looked up from the file, 'because of your philandering, Rosenharte.'

'For a man of your gifts,' said Laurentz, 'it is not an impressive career.'

Rosenharte smiled at them ironically. 'You missed all the good bits: my work at the Gemäldegalerie Alte Meister in Dresden and my studies on the restoration of the Dresden collection carried out by the Soviets, the papers on Dutch realism and the drawings of the collection. The essays and papers published in the West. They're modest achievements, I agree, but I am proud of them.'

'Let's face it, all this could have been carried out in the West. There's nothing in your work which distinguishes it as the product of a socialist living in a socialist state.'

'And my lectures? You dismiss those as well?'

'A hobby,' said Laurentz, 'to entertain the idle members of the so-called modern intelligentsia – individualists who have

77

forgotten the meaning of duty and loyalty to ideals of socialism. What I see here is a complete absence of the selfless contribution to the state required of every responsible citizen.'

'I do my best,' said Rosenharte hopelessly. 'But not everyone is equipped for a life devoted to the socialist cause. It's a special gift. I believe, however, that my lectures develop some themes that have not been considered before.'

Laurentz ignored this and looked at his companion. 'And there's the matter of your failure to help your MfS colleagues in Dresden,' said Richter.

'What? You mean my refusal to take money in exchange for information about my colleagues at the Gemäldegalerie?'

'Three times you were asked, and three times you refused. That is not exactly devotion to the state. The picture emerges of someone who is set against the state and does not mind deceiving it,' said Laurentz.

'A psychological predisposition to defy the state's authority,' said Richter. 'A pattern, which manifests itself in the anti-social stance of your brother's persistent offending.'

Rosenharte got up again because he was in danger of hitting the little bastard. He walked away from the table and took another look out of the window, ignoring the man he had spotted listening next door. It was clear to him that he was not just in the hands of the Main Directorate. A whole range of Stasi specialists had been brought to bear on his case. Schwarzmeer was plainly going to cover all the ground before making a recommendation to the head of the Stasi, Erich Mielke.

'It's most impolite to get up like that,' said Richter petulantly. 'We're dealing here with matters of the utmost importance.'

Rosenharte exhaled heavily. Play it cool, he told himself. Let them have their fun.

'You haven't had a drink now for nearly four days,' observed Laurentz. 'Are you missing alcohol? Is that a problem for you?'

'I haven't given it a thought. I drink for pleasure. I don't need it and don't miss it.'

'That is not the feeling of your colleagues at the gallery. They think you drink to escape. They say you drink too much.'

'If that's all they've got to say about me I should feel relieved.'

Then they asked him about the women, naming one after the other with a prudish exactitude; the wives of friends, two students, a librarian, the girl who picked him up on the train from Berlin – although they had it the other way round – a netball instructor, and an assistant at the Dresden Intershop named Lottie, who gave him *Südfrüchte* – the fruits of the southern hemisphere, bananas, pineapples and, once, a mango, which were impossible to acquire in any quantity. They wanted him to know there was nothing they could not find in their files. They told him plainly that they were even acquainted with his sexual preferences. Rosenharte smiled at this. 'By *preferences* you mean that I prefer women to men.'

'You know what we mean,' snapped Richter. 'What you like to do in bed.'

'I like to fool around a bit, talk, drink, make love and go to sleep. What about you? Perhaps you can suggest more interesting activities, Richter. Boys, poodles, leather – tell me.'

'You're being frivolous, Rosenharte.'

'I didn't raise the subject of relationships. You did. Anyway, I would like to know what these women reported my preferences to be. What else did they say? Does the Stasi have a rating system of sexual prowess? Perhaps you've developed a secret scale of performance? Did you talk to my ex-wife, Helga? Well, of course you would hardly get the most flattering portrait of me from her.' She had been a bleakly beautiful woman: tall, fine-boned and in some ways like a Flemish Madonna with her white skin and tranquillity, which he had mistaken for a kind of inner grace. But after a year or so there was never any real conversation and the sex had faded. What she liked to do most was to clean and sweep wearing a pressed pinafore with the strings tied tightly around her waist. She watched television incessantly without comment or the slightest particle of curiosity. Why on earth had he married her? Well, she'd seduced him and he had been blinded by her extraordinary love-making. And of course he loved to see her in the flesh, rising in the morning, drying herself after a shower. She was exquisite and he wanted her as his. What a damned fool he had been.

'It is understood that she left you because of your unreasonable demands and habitual intoxication.'

In a way they were right. After a period trying to find out what was wrong he gave up and spent his evenings with friends or reading and drinking in any bar that stayed open late enough. A year into their marriage, Konrad gently asked that she should not be brought out to the farmhouse where he lived with Else. One of the group of people who met there had good reason to believe that she had reported what he had said to the Stasi. Nothing was ever proved but this was the beginning of the end. Rosenharte almost wondered whether she had been instructed to marry him to keep an eye on Konrad's circle.

The survey of his life moved to Marie Theresa Rosenharte's death of untreatable cancer three years before. It was said, by Richter's nameless sources, that Rosenharte had shown the poor woman not the slightest help or support. He laughed at them because the lie was so preposterous. He and Konnie had not left her bedside for three weeks and they had been devastated when she died.

Richter implied that on the occasions Rosenharte did help Else, when Konrad was in Bautzen prison, he had an ulterior motive: to seduce her.

He let them see that he was troubled and hurt by these accusations, but all the time he watched them with a grim detachment, recognizing that when used during the full Stasi custody, in which a prisoner was skilfully disorientated from the outset, the technique would become very corrosive indeed. Konnie had told him that they had repeatedly said that Else had been unfaithful to him, an allegation that ironically allowed him to cling to his sanity because he knew it to be untrue. The lie had been his saviour.

What Rosenharte was seeing now was an overture to the methodical dismantling of his personality that would take place if he made a mistake. Konnie had also told him what they did in Bautzen to consolidate the work done in Hohenschönhausen – the beatings and confinement in a space measuring twelve by fourteen inches, the backbreaking labour, the stomach and chest infections that spread like pollen in summer through the place they called the 'Yellow Misery'.

But why threaten him now? If they were eager to get their hands on more of Annalise's material – and he was sure they were – what good did it do? Maybe it had something to do with their twisted obsession with the control and ownership of people. They were giving him a sense of their omniscience, their ability to reach inside someone's head and destroy whatever they wanted to.

The leaden deprecation of everything about him and all he held dear was dragged on until evening, when the interview suddenly ended as though the pair were meeting a pre-arranged timetable. They closed their files, got up and walked out, leaving Rosenharte gazing through the grilles of the window. He turned to see if the silent observer was still there, but he had left also, and Rosenharte wondered if this man would be his eventual nemesis, a shadow of a person ready to materialize when his fate was sealed.

SIX

Night Enquiry

Five minutes elapsed before two of the resident guards came and led him back to the basement. There was food – bread, sausage-meat, cheese and another solitary apple – waiting for him, together with a packet of Cabinet cigarettes. He ate the apple, deciding to save the rest for later, and settled down to a new batch of old magazines and newspapers.

He read until ten, without hearing a sound outside or in his own building, then ate and smoked a couple of cigarettes. A little later on he lay down on his bed without undressing.

As he expected, they came for him again. In the dead of night, two men rushed him, still drowsy, across the damp grass to a low concrete tumulus surrounded by lights. He had the impression of a fortified storehouse; inside there was a lot of equipment – hoses, protective suits, helmets and implements. He was roughly placed on a stool in front of three dazzling lights.

A voice came from behind them. For some reason, Rosenharte was certain that it belonged to the man who had sat so quietly through the first interrogation in the adjacent room.

'I'm sorry?' he said.

'You met the woman known as Schering in August 1974,' said the voice more loudly.

'About then,' said Rosenharte, straightening his clothes. 'I had picked her up in a bar. At the time, I was working as a guide in the Musée des Beaux Arts. She came to one of my tours about a week later and things developed from there. You know all this: it was in my reports at the time.'

'And you became lovers. How would you characterize her feelings towards you?'

'I believe that soon afterwards she became very attached to me.'

'She fell in love with you.'

'If you put it that way, yes.'

'When did you discuss working for the GDR?'

'I left it for about four weeks, then introduced the subject one evening.'

'She wasn't shocked?'

'No, but she said there was very little of interest for us in the Commission. She was hoping to land a job at NATO.'

'This was not mentioned in your reports.'

'I didn't want to say anything to Colonel Neusel – my controller at the time – until she'd definitely got the job. Besides, she wouldn't tell me which department she'd applied for.'

'But when she did receive news of the job, she dumped you. Is that what happened?'

'I don't know. Some time that winter she seemed to lose her enthusiasm for our relationship. She said it had come at the wrong time for her: she wished that we had met five years later. Then she refused to see me. I tried to get in touch but she wouldn't answer her phone or the messages I left at her apartment.'

'She cut you out of her life?'

'Yes. Look, why are we going over this again?'

'Please just answer the questions. Did she leave you immediately?'

'Yes, but I had hopes of renewing the relationship, which is why I was unhappy to be recalled. Now I understand that she had offered to work for you through another channel and that my attempts to get back on good terms with her were pointless.'

'But this great love of yours had disappeared overnight? It evaporated. Is that a fair statement?'

'Yes, I suppose so.'

'Then how do you account for the sentiments that she expressed in her letter to you this summer? They were somewhat passionate, were they not?'

'She told me she had written more than one letter. If I had been able to see the others I might have understood her motives better. But now, having talked to her, I realize that the time we spent together all those years ago meant a lot to her . . . and in retrospect, to me also.'

'How did she know where to contact you? You're an obscure art historian, not the conductor of a famous orchestra or a film star. How did she know where to write?'

He coughed. 'This is difficult.'

'Go on,' said the voice, patiently encouraging Rosenharte to ensnare himself.

'Five or six years ago I sent her a couple of notes. They were posted abroad by a friend who is now dead. I told her what I was doing and said that I would give her a tour of the collection of old masters in Dresden if she came to the city. It was a light-hearted message, I suppose. To my surprise, she replied by the same means – she got someone to post the letter in the GDR. I don't know who that was. She told me that she was going to marry and leave Europe, but her tone was affectionate and, well, wistful.'

'You have the letter now?'

'I've got it somewhere, I'm sure.'

'Why did you not say you'd been in communication with Annalise Schering before we took you to Trieste?'

'I didn't want to admit that I had been in touch with a foreign national, which I well appreciate could be interpreted as a crime. The other reason is that I didn't want to be involved. I thought if you knew that we had corresponded it would encourage you to send me. And I had my doubts – doubts about the project and doubts about my feelings for her. A lot of water had passed under the bridge.'

There was silence behind the lights. The voice was taking its time. Rosenharte coughed again and wished he could have a cigarette. He peered beyond the glare and made out the shapes of at least four people.

'So you say that Schering was familiar with the techniques of posting a letter in our country so as to avoid the vigilance of the state security?'

'Yes,' said Rosenharte, seeing the trap but unable to avoid it.

'Then why did she not arrange for the letters she wrote you this summer to be mailed from within the GDR?'

'I don't know. She didn't say. Perhaps she didn't have someone she could trust to do it for her.'

'Or perhaps she knew that this correspondence would not escape the notice of Department M, the postal control services. In other words, she knew that her letters from abroad would be opened. She was making the offer to us, not you.'

'That has occurred to me, but it doesn't necessarily mean that she is trying to deceive you.'

'You have heard the phrase, "beware of Greeks bearing gifts"?'

'Yes.'

'And you have considered the possibility that the gift she proposes to make the GDR could damage state security.'

'That possibility is implicit,' said Rosenharte. 'I myself pointed this out when you first proposed it to me. All along I have said she could be used by the Western intelligence service.'

'So now we must decide on the nature of the person who is making this gift.'

'Yes, I suppose—'

'And we have reached the conclusion that this person is remarkably inconsistent. In some circumstances, she demonstrates prudence and foresight, for instance when she got rid of you in favour of a more reliable means of communicating with us. Indeed, all through the years of dealing with her she showed detachment and good judgement – a model agent. But there's another Schering, who can also be hot-headed, given to emotional outbursts and to excessive drinking. When she left you in the restaurant in Trieste, that was most unlike the woman we knew.' The voice stopped. 'Although it was entirely like the woman that you wrote about in your first reports. It's almost as if we are dealing with two different people.'

They were so close. Rosenharte felt his pulse race. He inhaled and put his hands on his knees. 'But your people saw her in Trieste,' he said at length. 'It *is* the same woman.'

'We know that. But how would you explain the difference in her behaviour?'

Rosenharte leapt in the only direction he could. 'Maybe,' he started thoughtfully, 'it has something to do with the way we respond to each other. We get under each other's skin, though we are still attracted to each other.'

There was a murmur behind the lights. 'It is odd that she refused to meet any of our people in Trieste – she specified as much in her letter to you – and yet for ten years she worked with us and had no problem meeting different officers from the MfS. Why has she suddenly developed this phobia for the very people that she wishes to help?'

'She did tell me that she had been scared by the lax security in your people at NATO. She didn't want to expose herself to the same risks, and when Heise approached us in the restaurant she expressed the same fears.' Again it was the only answer he could give. Rosenharte felt his stomach constrict. Just two sessions and he had been forced into a space where it was impossible to manoeuvre. Then the inevitable question came hurtling from behind the lights.

'Which foreign intelligence agency are you working for, Rosenharte?'

'I am working for no one except the Gemäldegalerie in Dresden.'

At this, a large man appeared from behind the lights and walked to Rosenharte, took his face roughly in his hands and peered into his eyes. Rosenharte felt his gaze oscillate nervously between the shadows of the man's eye sockets.

'You are working for the Americans,' he said. 'I can see it in your face.'

'Maybe I am,' Rosenharte said and pulled back, out of the man's shadow. 'Maybe I am working for the Americans . . . Or the British or even the West Germans.'

This brought silence to the room. Rosenharte held the man's eyes. 'But if I am, I don't know it. Only you can tell if I am being used.'

The man let go.

'What makes you think that you're being used?'

'I have repeatedly said that this could be a trap. It's for you to decide. I have told you everything I know.'

The man looked down at him steadily, without giving the slightest hint of his feelings. It occurred to Rosenharte that he was at that moment fighting for his life. 'Look,' he said, 'this isn't a problem. You know what Annalise gave you before. Judge her on her past performance; judge her on what your people are analysing in Berlin. But don't judge her on me. That isn't logical.'

The voice came from behind the lights again. 'What do you know about her past work for us?'

'Nothing. But she did tell me to ask you a question.' He stopped, as though he was making sure he was getting something right. 'Why no thanks for her news on the Ides of March in 1985?'

'The fifteenth of March?' asked the voice. 'What happened on the fifteenth of March?'

Someone cleared their throat. Schwarzmeer. 'It refers to the death of Konstantin Chernenko and the succession of General Secretary Gorbachev four days before.'

'Yes,' said Rosenharte. 'On the fifteenth, everything changed in the Geneva arms limitation talks and she told you about it. She gave you the updated briefing documents, the telegrams between Washington and Brussels, and the agenda of a meeting between defence ministers held by the new Secretary General, Lord Carrington. What she couldn't copy, she memorized. It was her last job for you. And you never thanked her.'

'There were other things on our minds, I expect,' said Schwarzmeer.

'Well, she hasn't forgotten it. That's why she wants to run this operation on her own terms. She will decide what to give you and when . . .'

'It's not for you to dictate terms to us,' said the voice behind the lights.

'I'm not. She is, and whether you choose to believe her is your responsibility, not mine. I have no interest in this matter, other than seeing that you complete your side of the deal.' He paused. 'Now you must free Konrad as you promised you would.'

'You have not told us about the arrangements for taking delivery of the material,' said the voice.

'No, I haven't,' said Rosenharte.

'Well?'

'I will tell you when you have allowed Konrad to return to his family.'

The big man's expression didn't change as he stepped back and delivered a powerful blow to the side of Rosenharte's head, sending him sprawling from the stool on to the compacted earth that served as the floor of the bunker. There was a scuffle as another came forward to help beat him. Rosenharte received several kicks to his back and kidneys and a pistol-whipping across the nape of the neck. Even in that moment he understood that each blow confirmed that the Stasi was, in its brutal way, showing interest in the material that Annalise Schering had to offer them.

He supposed that he had been carried from the shelter unconscious, but that didn't explain the taste in his mouth, the heaviness in his limbs or the sense that a long time had elapsed. He readied himself for the shock of being in prison, but when he cracked open his eyes he saw that he was wrong. He was in a very light place, which was pleasantly warm; there was a smell of dust in the air. He moved his head and found that he was lying on a bare wooden floor. He shut his eyes against the brightness and became aware of someone beside him urging him to raise his head. This woman kept on saying 'water' to him. 'Drink, Comrade.'

And he drank, cup after cup, before lying back and allowing his eyes to focus on a plaster ceiling that had holes punched into it so it was possible to see the timber that supported the floor above. He was directly beneath a plaster roundel of a hunting scene – men with muskets and dogs pursuing a stag. It seemed familiar to him but he could not for the life of him think why.

'In this very room.' It was Schwarzmeer's voice, low and casual from behind his head. 'In this very room your father said farewell to your mother for the last time. They drank champagne, brought up from the cellar on 1 January 1945. It was noon on a very, very cold day. The Red Army was a few hundred miles away, but they still thought that the Führer would perform a miracle. Your mother had less than six weeks to live; your father would be dead before spring came. This is where they last saw each other – General Manfred von Huth and his fascist wife, Isobel von Clausnitz. The young men of Germany were being slaughtered on the Eastern front, running backwards, starving, dying in the snow. One last toast to the Third Reich. Here, in this room.' He spoke as though setting a scene for a drama.

Rosenharte raised his head and blinked the sleep from his eyes. His neck hurt dreadfully, but he turned to see Schwarzmeer sitting on a lone chair, dressed in a dapper light-grey suit with matching grey socks.

'Did they stand over there by the window, looking across the schlosspark to the hills, and raise their glasses to 1945? Or did they gaze into each other's souls and see that the end was near? It's interesting to speculate what they were thinking then, no? Did they know it was all over, or did they still believe the Führer?'

'Why have you brought me here?' asked Rosenharte.

'It's part of the SVP. As you know, we like to do research: prepare ourselves by entering the minds of our subjects, absorb their experiences and learn to predict their reactions.' Rosenharte recalled that SVP was Stasi shorthand for *Sachverhaltsprüfung* – a check on the facts of the case.

'This place has nothing to do with my life.'

'Oh but it does, Herr Doktor. It was also in this room that you last saw your mother. It's all in your file, even those tiny experiences. Have a look at this.'

Schwarzmeer moved in his direction. With the woman's help Rosenharte struggled to a sitting position.

'That is all,' said Schwarzmeer. 'He'll be all right.' He paused to allow her to go, then placed a clear envelope in Rosenharte's hand. 'Take them out.'

Three very small, square photographs slipped into his lap. Each one showed a man in a black uniform sitting on a grand run of steps. Standing uncertainly in front of him were blond twins in the uniform of the Hitler Youth: khaki shirts, lederhosen, white socks, tiny swastika armbands.

'That's you and your brother,' said Schwarzmeer triumphantly. 'You see, he was already making you part of the Nazi state. Unbelievable that someone would dress a three-year-old in a fascist uniform.'

Rosenharte returned them to the envelope thinking that there were still plenty of young people dressed in uniform in the GDR.

'These were found when the place was cleared out after the war and they came to us. Imagine the diligence and foresight which preserved these for the future. One of our people knew they would be useful one day.'

Rosenharte sighed. 'I am glad they've made you happy.'

'Let me tell you who furnished us with the rest of the information about this household.'

'You don't need to,' said Rosenharte.

'It was Marie Theresa Rosenharte, the woman you called mother. She was the one who brought you here that day – but your real mother was pining for her Manfred and paid little attention to you. Although she had only been in service here for six months, Frau Rosenharte had already formed the opinion that your mother

91

was a cold and ruthless woman, without much feeling for anyone or anything apart from your father and the Nazi party.'

'All the more reason for me to see them as irrelevant to my life.' Rosenharte didn't show he was shocked that they had talked to Marie Theresa. She had been a chatty woman of limitless good nature, who almost certainly thought she was helping her sons in their careers by talking to the Stasi. She would have been as open to them as she would be to her priest. That would have certainly remained her position until Konrad was arrested. After that she had freely likened the Stasi to the Nazis.

Rosenharte had got to his feet and was looking through the broken glass to a line of garden statuary – beasts from classical mythology, most of them now decapitated. The gardens were overgrown and the grass was tall, but the design was still visible from the raised saloon. He looked at the lake, choked with weed around its perimeter, and the bridge. Then he caught sight of the grotto, actually just a niche in a high wall that had been fashioned to look like a ruin. He distinctly remembered the word 'grotto' from his childhood and the fun of playing at the foot of a fountain, where water trickled from the mouths of fantastic sea creatures over slippery green boulders. The wall had mostly crumbled into the garden and the fountain was gone.

'So, it begins to return to you,' said Schwarzmeer. 'The last summer of the fascists.'

Rosenharte shook his head. 'I remember nothing of this place.'

'That's a shame because it represents your debt to the state, the state that overlooked the monstrous crimes of your family and gave you the advantages of a socialist upbringing, the best education in the world.'

Rosenharte looked at him, unable to express anything but disbelief. 'You criticize the Nazis. What about Bautzen, where you held and tortured my brother without even telling his family what he had been found guilty of?'

'He was convicted of distributing fascist propaganda that endangered the peace.'

'And what does that mean? How can making a private film and showing it to a few colleagues endanger the peace? How is that fascist propaganda? And for this, you sent him to a prison used by the Nazis. Whatever you say about the West, they don't fill old Nazi jails with their own people.'

'Those observations alone are enough to earn you a sentence in the political section of Bautzen.'

'No,' said Rosenharte, louder than he intended. 'You will not threaten me any longer. I have done nothing but comply with your wishes. I will not be treated like an enemy of the state.' He paused to collect himself, aware that he was straying over the line of what the Stasi would tolerate. He had to paint himself as a man with an independent mind, with his own views, but one whose basic loyalty could not be doubted. That way they would believe him.

'Look,' he said, 'I understand that you have to do your business. But Konrad has had enough. He is a good man and a good socialist. All he has ever been guilty of is bad judgement. Let him go.'

'That's not possible.'

Rosenharte waited a few moments then said, 'I know you are interested in what Annalise has to offer. Otherwise you would not be wasting your time with me. She will only play if I am involved. Her position at NATO is so sensitive that your officers won't get within a mile of her, and if they do try to contact her, she will simply report the approach. You work with me, or nobody. And if you work with me, you free Konrad.'

Schwarzmeer's face hardened. 'That's not possible. Your brother is suspected of criminal activities.'

'I don't believe that. He's a sick man, incapable of presenting the slightest threat to you. Let him return to his wife and children. Let him find the treatment he needs for his heart and his teeth.'

'Nothing stopped him when he was free before.'

'No doctor or dentist would see him.'

'Well, he must wait his turn like everyone else. No one can receive special treatment.'

'His teeth became rotten in Bautzen because of the beatings and the diet. When he got out, your people stopped him seeing a dentist. He couldn't even get an appointment with a veterinary surgeon. Let him go home. He's suffered enough.' Rosenharte was aware that a pleading note had entered his voice.

Schwarzmeer moved from the bay window on the east side of the house, the place where his mother had sat so erect and untouchable that last time, and walked to the centre of the room.

'Who will look after him? His wife is helping with enquiries.'

The drab, brutal efficiency of it appalled him. 'Okay,' he said at length, 'you win. If you return Else and the children to their home and give me an assurance that you will not abuse them any further, I will cooperate. Then we will talk about Konrad.'

'You do not make deals with us,' snapped Schwarzmeer. 'As I have demonstrated by bringing you here to Schloss Clausnitz, your family owes the people of East Germany for their tolerance. The very least you can do in return is to act in the interests of the security of the state.'

'But I have,' replied Rosenharte. 'You promised to release Konrad if I went to Trieste. I did what you wanted. Now . . .' He stopped to control the sense of helplessness that rose in him. 'You cannot do this thing without me, and don't think I haven't got an idea of what she has to offer. The security of the state is in your hands, not mine.'

'I warn you, this—'

'No, I warn *you*, General,' he said, raising his voice. 'If you don't free Else and the children, Annalise will never help you. And before you interrupt me again, there is one other condition of my cooperation. In order to facilitate the next stage of this operation I must be free and allowed to move without surveillance wherever I choose.' He knew that to be impossible, but he could see that Schwarzmeer was about to concede something. And behind that, Rosenharte reasoned, was the certainty that the first secretary and the head of the Stasi had already been told of what Annalise Schering could bring from NATO. Schwarzmeer had to get it for them.

'Now,' he said, moving his aching limbs towards the door. 'I'd like to be taken back to Dresden. I've lost several days already. I have work to do.'

Schwarzmeer blocked his way. 'Trick me, Rosenharte, and I will see your Nazi brains crushed from your head in a vice.'

Rosenharte smiled at the grotesque image and knew that Schwarzmeer regretted saying something so crude. 'I just want to live in peace, General, and see my brother restored to health. That's all I want. And if I can help you in the process, then I will feel I've done my duty. May I now return to my home?'

'How will she contact you?'

'I don't know. But I know that she's already made arrangements. She will contact me near the end of the month.'

Schwarzmeer said nothing, but stepped out of the way. Rosenharte walked to the open French windows where he knew there was a flight of stone steps that splayed into the garden. There were three men waiting for him at the bottom.

'We will be in touch,' said Schwarzmeer.

All Rosenharte heard was the birdsong coming from the great deserted garden that had been his childhood playground.

SEVEN

Dresden

He was returned to Dresden in an unmarked delivery van late that Friday. Over the weekend he bought some food, slept a great deal and made one visit to a bar nearby, but had no contact with anyone he knew. Then, as the working week began, he set about making an unvarying routine for himself. Whereas before he'd taken any number of routes into the centre of the city, stopping off at different places for coffee on the way, he now stuck to the same road, arriving at precisely 8.50 a.m. each day in the Zwinger, the huge baroque palace that housed among other things the Gemälde-galerie's collection of Old Masters. He ate his lunch on the same bench, looking across to the restored Semper Opera House, and then returned to his apartment near the Technical University at about 8.30 p.m., after a drink or two in the same bar.

His purpose was to lull the Stasi surveillance teams as well as to get an idea of their strength. Very soon, he became used to the men and women around him touching their noses, changing folded newspapers from one hand to the other, sweeping off dark glasses and flourishing handkerchiefs. He saw two different men with what looked like the same metal camera case on consecutive mornings. This he knew contained a change of clothing – probably a hard hat, glasses, wig and false moustache, and boots with thick rubber soles to alter the individual's height. He was aware of the watchers following him on both sides of the street, one almost parallel to him, another about thirty yards behind and a third about the same distance ahead of him. He understood how they changed positions and were replaced by other individuals in an endlessly adapting choreography. He noted the fixed observation posts on the way to work – the men loitering on street corners reading magazines, or looking at bus timetables. And he saw how the watchers slowed or changed direction when he unexpectedly stopped off to buy a packet of cigarettes; how the white or dark green Lada trailing him in the traffic would drift to the kerb.

Had they forgotten that he'd received precisely the same training as they? Surely his file mentioned he'd taken surveillance and counter-surveillance courses, studied the use of dead letter drops, target pattern analysis, surveillance detection points and the use of disguise both to outwit surveillance and enhance it. They must know that their secret craft was also his: a bit rusty, maybe, but getting better by the day.

At spy school he had not particularly excelled at the basics of his new trade, but this hadn't been a deterrent to his eventual deployment abroad – the reason he'd agreed to join the Stasi in the first place. Misgivings about his height – he was several inches over the norm for a spy – his political dedication and what was termed his moral fibre were overcome by his skill at languages and his powers of reasoning. In truth, it hadn't been difficult to shine in a class of dullards and thugs and he'd sailed through the selection board for the HVA.

Rosenharte had much time to think and to see his city anew. The life he led in Dresden now seemed utterly cheerless and he felt ashamed at the threadbare world around him. With irritation he noticed the broken stones on a footpath that ran along his street. They'd been that way as long as he could remember, like the missing tiles from the roof of his building and the street light that had been knocked over by a truck a year or two before and was left at an angle of forty-five degrees. It was surely not beyond the city authorities to tidy up the place, yet even with the GDR's fortieth anniversary celebrations a few weeks away it hadn't occurred to them to try to live up to the slogans that proclaimed on every public building the wonders of living in a socialist state.

There was almost a purpose to the drabness, he felt, as though it had been decided in principle that any improvements, any relief from the joylessness, would concede too much to the bourgeois values of the West. Compared to the carefree population of Trieste, his fellow citizens appeared scratchy, rude and disengaged from life. They were simply existing. After nine in the evening the streets were empty, the people too bored, broke or tired from work and the business of finding the essentials of life to do anything other than slump in front of the TV and watch life in the parallel universe of West Germany. What a very strange opiate that was for the popular masses of a communist state approaching its glorious anniversary!

Of course there were those who still possessed surplus energy. He saw them out training for sports or throwing themselves into various activities organized by Party and factory. Others became obsessed with their damned correspondence courses, although the qualifications did little to improve their lives in the impersonal apartment blocks that rose around Dresden; the diplomas and certificates didn't put food on the table or reduce the waiting list for a Trabant or allow them a foreign holiday or get them a phone or a new jacket. It was pointless work designed to keep people occupied and vaguely in the service of the state, the theory being that self-improvement added to the collective strength of the GDR.

He knew that it was part of the accommodation people had to reach with the Party. They went through the motions of loyalty, making occasional acts of obeisance and paying lip service to the idea of socialist progress. Konrad had captured it in a script called *The Sleep Walkers,* which was his most overtly political work. It had come from a conversation they had had about the oddities of Rosenharte's neighbours. There was fat Willi Ludz who dealt in auto spare parts from an apartment where he kept bits of car engines wrapped in oily rags and catalogued like the precious finds of an archaeological dig. Old Klemm from Number 74 spent most of his time in the library plumbing the mysteries of Marxism-Leninism and reading *Neues Deutschland* in a private quest to reconcile what he saw around him with the texts of the political faith. And in Number 22 there was an unmarried mother named Letitia who Rosenharte had learned occasionally worked as a prostitute at the Bellevue Hotel to make ends meet.

These characters were woven into a tale inspired by a book Konrad had read about a tribe living on the Amazon which believed that their waking hours were all a dream while their real lives were led when they slept. All that was significant in the stories of the characters based on Ludz, Klemm and Letitia occurred in the boundless and borderless freedom of their dream world. It was a rather moving idea and he wished his brother had been able to shoot more than a few minutes of *The Sleep Walkers.*

He too moved as though in a trance and completed his rounds in the Gemäldegalerie with unusually leaden diligence, attending the daily meeting with the director, Professor Lichtenberg, visiting the restoration department where he kept an eye on works by Titian, Parmigiano and Wouvermans and writing one of the endless reports about bringing high art to the people with a socialist message. The gallery was not free from the East German addiction to paperwork, the mountains of reports, commentaries and analyses – or *Papierwulst* – that clogged every office in the country. He knew no one would read it but this was simply a requirement of his job, a piece of protocol that he would have been foolish to neglect.

On Wednesday 20 September he decided to take his first risk. He made a detour on his round through the galleries and arrived outside Lichtenberg's office where he found the professor's assistant, Sonja Weiss, alone. She was perched on the edge of a desk buffing her nails while reading an old Hungarian travel brochure. Sonja and he had once had a short, uncomplicated affair lasting six or seven months, which had ended without rancour when she found someone she preferred. Her attitude to sex and the manner of departure were equally straightforward. Two years later, they were still firm allies and, because the Stasi hadn't named her during his interrogation a week before, he assumed she was not one of their informers.

Sonja hopped off the desk, gave him a mischievous smile and popped a kiss on his cheek. She had a taste for cheap costume jewellery and jarring combinations of styles in her dress. She experimented uninhibitedly with different hair colours. At the moment it was jet black with blonde streaks. Vulgar perhaps, but nothing she did detracted from the natural prettiness which lay underneath and her neat, well-proportioned figure.

They talked for a little while, then he cleared his throat. 'Sonja, can I ask you a favour?'

'And here I was getting all nostalgic. You want to use the phone in his office? Right? Go ahead. We think it's clean. Oh, by the way, I forgot to mention that some man came looking for you when you were away. A weird guy – gawky. He didn't leave a name, but said he'd be back.'

'You don't have any more information then?'

'I think he was a foreigner, maybe Czech or Polish. But he spoke quite good German. The professor told me to get rid of him and wanted to find out how he had got in here.'

'One of our *friends*?'

She shook her head. 'No, a country boy. You could see by his clothes.'

'I suppose we'll find out when he shows up again.' He paused. 'How's Sebastian – that's your man's name, isn't it?'

'Good but busy.' He thought he caught a significant raise of her eyebrows to emphasize the last word, indicating that Sebastian was involved in political agitation.

'I see. Well . . . tell him to be careful. Now, you make yourself scarce for the next few minutes, okay?'

He went into the office and closed the door, praying that the place wasn't bugged. He dialled the number in East Berlin that he'd memorized in front of Harland and the American in Trieste and was put through to an answerphone which clicked on without a recorded message. 'It's Prince,' he said, his eyes straying to a small landscape by Salomon van Ruysdael on the professor's wall. 'I need a delivery of material within the next week. Good material.' He hung up and slipped out of the office.

Sonja gave him a conspiratorial look in the corridor. 'Good luck – and *you* be careful, my handsome Doktor.'

'Thanks,' he said. 'I will.'

At this time of year, Rosenharte would normally head out of the city on a Friday to spend a couple of days walking in the hills around Marienberg, near where he had been brought up and where Konnie and Else now lived. But with all the family in one sort of custody or another, he didn't feel like it and, besides, he knew he should remain visible and available in the city. He spent Friday evening in his apartment, restlessly arranging books and fiddling with three tomato plants on the ledge outside his window.

The place was not ideal – nothing ever was – but he still thanked his luck that he had managed to find it so soon after his divorce from Helga. He had left everything with her and the flat was still pretty sparse. Basically it was one long room, equally divided between sleeping and living areas by a thick red curtain. The bed was an old pre-war affair, with sagging springs and squeaking iron joints, from which Rosenharte could see out of the window across the roofs of the Technical University. Along the wall were a small bookcase and a wardrobe whose legs had been wedged to stop it toppling over on the uneven wooden floor. Over the years Rosenharte's lovers had introduced touches of decoration and comfort to the living room – vases, the odd cushion, a rug and a reproduction of the battle of San Romano by Paolo Uccello. When they moved on, the place quickly surrendered to his work. Books accumulated in neat columns and the old sixties typewriter, which he had such difficulty finding ribbons for, resumed its position at the centre of the table. There were a few framed black and white snapshots along the bookshelves: one of himself and Konnie on a cross-country skiing trip in 1972 and another of them standing either side of Marie Theresa after university graduation. The largest photograph was of Rosenharte in profile, taken by Sonja three years before. He kept it because it made him look young and reminded him of a spectacular walk in the frosted woods near a village called Cunnersdorf; but he had his doubts about the leather and steel photo frame, which Sonja had made for him.

This picture was the only sign of vanity in Rosenharte's home, which in its concentration on study and exercise – a corner was devoted to walking boots, rucksack, ski poles and climbing ropes – resembled a college student's rooms. There was no television set, no record player – he did not have the money to replace the one Helga took with her – and only minimal cooking facilities. Like many a student, he was used to making the trip to another floor to take a bath, but he did have his own lavatory and a large old-fashioned basin with pre-war taps that occasionally sputtered hot water.

He was ambivalent about the place. He liked the solitude it gave him but, after a prolonged occupation, he began to feel his life had somehow become suspended, which was why sometimes late at night he fled and went drinking, then brought a girl back.

That Friday evening he remained in the apartment, cooked a meal and shared it with a cat that came across the roofs from a neighbour's apartment, read the final draft of the lecture he was to give in Leipzig, despaired at the long-winded title – 'The Evolutionary Purpose of Representational Art' – then dropped it in favour of 'The Bull in the Cave'.

In the evening he began to notice tiny discrepancies between the way he'd left the apartment and its present state. He assumed as a matter of course that they'd searched it when he was picked up before going to Trieste. But also, it seemed, since he had been back. Three books habitually placed beside the typewriter, on top of each other and always opened at pages 102, 203 and 304, had been moved. The middle volume about Gothic art, which he never consulted, was now open at page 210. On the shelf, a matchbox containing a pen nib and some paper clips placed exactly in front of the letters GEN of a book entitled *Der Jugendstil* now stood in front of the letters NDS. The shade of the table lamp was angled differently and some papers had been moved on the windowsill: beside them was a narrow band that was free of dust. He realized that the rooms must have been bugged and marvelled at the wasted effort. He had no phone, because he was on a list of thousands waiting to be connected, and it had been months since anyone else had been there with him. The only human voice heard in the apartment was the sound of him sleep-talking. He imagined some milk-faced technician up all night, straining to interpret the slightest murmur, and when he eventually got into bed at midnight he muttered a few incomprehensible sentences to the dark.

Next day, he went out early to buy a packet of cigarettes at the local Konsum store, and immediately noticed that there were far fewer Stasi on his tail. He guessed that this was because there was so much talk of demonstrations and meetings. Sonja had mentioned it in a stage whisper as she skittered past him in the Dutch collection on Friday afternoon. And now, as he walked through the Technical University campus with the idea of putting in an appearance in the gallery, he was approached by an old acquaintance, a good sort named Heinz Kube, who taught fluid mechanics and was now full of the burgeoning democratic movements that were challenging the state.

Before Kube could go on about the manifesto released by the New Forum two weeks earlier, Rosenharte put both hands on his shoulders and cut him off in mid flow. 'My friend, I think I'm being followed. I don't want to get you into trouble. Just shake my hand and congratulate me on my lectures. When they ask you what passed between us, tell them that.' Poor Kube, thought Rosenharte, they'll have him in overnight and give him the third degree.

He went to the park and read *Neues Deutschland*, mentally grimacing at its pieties, then turned to an Austrian academic periodical he had brought with him. He was sick of being watched and had just about decided to move on to the gallery, where he would at least find some privacy, when about a dozen punks entered the park from his left. At the same moment, another group materialized from beneath the shade of some poplar trees – skinheads with laced boots reaching to the top of their calves and tight denims held up with braces. Very soon a bottle arced through the air towards the punks and broke on the path in front of them. One of the punks picked up the broken neck and flung it back at them, catching a skinhead on the forearm. The youth looked down and yelled out, '*Scheisse – Punkscheisse*.' Stones and more bottles started flying and the two groups closed in.

Rosenharte put down his periodical and watched, bemused, then he noted that the Stasi team were consulting each other. One broke cover to use a radio, while the other two moved hesitantly towards the edge of the fray.

'You'd better stop those louts before someone gets hurt,' shouted a man in a checked shirt and a cream-coloured cap. 'Today's youth!' he said despairingly to Rosenharte. 'You'd think they'd got better things to do.'

Rosenharte nodded and then with astonishment saw that the man was winking at him. It was Harp, the British intelligence officer he'd met briefly at the hotel with Harland. With the cane and clothes, he looked fifteen years older. The accent was good too; exactly right for the region.

'Time to get going, Dr Rosenharte,' he murmured. 'Ditch this lot and find your way to the Neustadt Bahnhof by five this afternoon. There's an old building opposite the station that was a restaurant before the war. You'll see the sign. To the right of the sign there's a door, which you can push open. I'll see you in there after five. Mind how you go. The place is in a terrible state. Got all that? Good. Make sure you're not followed.' With this, he strolled away to talk to three or four onlookers who were shaking their heads.

Rosenharte moved quickly to the side of the park and, spotting a bus going to the centre of town, ran to catch it. As the doors closed he saw one of the Stasi men frantically looking round. He rode the bus for two stops, then boarded another bound for the suburb of Weisser Hirsch, across the River Elbe to the east of the city. At the last stop before the bus turned round he got off and set out across the Dresdener Heide, the great heath to the north of Weisser Hirsch. He lay in the sun and ate the meagre lunch that he had kept in his pocket since leaving the apartment. At four, he made for the outskirts and then picked his way through the sleepy streets until he reached an almost entirely ruined block that lay between Königsbrücker Strasse and the railway line. There were very few people about, but Rosenharte moved cautiously, waiting and watching at every turn. When he found the burnt-out restaurant near the station he sidled up to the door, placed his back against it and lit a cigarette. Satisfied that no one was watching, he pushed the door with his backside and slipped through to find he was in a large space that was open to the sky. The roof had fallen in several years before and charred timbers hung down from the floors above. A profusion of shrubs and weeds had taken root in the rubble.

'Thanks for being so prompt.' The voice came from the gloom of the rooms further back, which had evidently been untouched by the British incendiary bombs.

Harp was now in blue overalls and was accompanied by a much taller man with a thin face, red complexion and a prominent broken nose.

'This is my associate Cuth Avocet, known by all as the Bird.' Both men were grinning inanely.

'Where's Harland?'

'In Berlin,' said Harp. 'It's not possible for him to get away at the moment.' He paused. 'So, we picked up your message from the Medium and came across as soon as we could.'

'The Medium?'

'Yes – the technology that puts you in touch with the other side.' He smiled. 'You see! Like a medium.'

Rosenharte did see and smiled politely.

'Cuth Avocet,' said the tall one, stepping forward and offering his hand. Rosenharte thought they had got past the introductions but took his hand. 'How do you do? I've heard a lot about you, but sadly we missed meeting in Italy.'

They moved back to the dark area where there were three collapsible fishing stools, a bottle of wine and a candle. 'Rather festive, don't you think?' said Avocet. 'Would you like a drop of this lovely stuff before Macy polishes it off?'

Rosenharte accepted, thinking he had entered some bizarre British film. 'You understood my message?'

'Absolutely,' said Macy Harp. 'Absolutely. We've fixed a rendezvous in West Berlin for a few days' time. It's flexible. "Annalise" will give you some material. I take it you'll need your side to witness all that?'

'They will, whether you want it or not. I was questioned for four days when I came back. This material has to settle all their doubts.'

'Have you begun to make contact with Kafka yet?'

'How could I? I'm followed everywhere.'

'You think this new stuff will get them off your back? Current estimates put Stasi strength at about eighty thousand, which means they have the capacity to watch pretty much anyone that interests them. Maybe we have to face the possibility that this isn't going to work. Maybe you're never going to shake them off.'

'It will work,' said Rosenharte. 'They've got a lot to occupy them at the moment. People are very restive. They'll be watching everyone who has ever criticized the Party and there are a lot of those.'

'Is it going to spread?' asked Harp.

'Difficult to say. People understand that nothing's working and the economy is in trouble. They're tired of queueing for everything.'

'I don't know how you've all stood it for so long,' said Avocet. 'Nearly forty years.'

'*Überwintern*,' said Rosenharte. 'We are hibernating.' That was exactly it. Everyone was waiting for spring but had no idea whether they would live to enjoy it. Rosenharte always understood he was better off than most because of his job at the Gemäldegalerie. The quiet of the galleries, the peace he found there and the experience of his daily contact with the pictures allowed him to lead a completely fulfilled intellectual life. He poured his energy into the contemplation of great works of art and to some extent regarded the paintings – the Rembrandts and Van Eycks and Vermeers – as his companions in the long dark winter, each of them as estranged in spirit from East German society as he was.

Harp smiled. 'But maybe the thaw will come one day soon.'

Rosenharte shook his head. 'Maybe,' he said. He didn't particularly like the pleasure they took in their own amateurism, their ignorance of German life, their insouciance. But they were all he had. 'I've told the Stasi that I will continue to work with Annalise on condition that they release Else and the children. I think they'll go along with this, because the envelope you gave me in Trieste contains things that clearly interest them. Once Else has been freed, I want to get all of them out.'

'And leave your brother at their mercy?'

'Konrad would want this. I know it. He won't be able to stand the idea that the boys have been taken away from Else. You can be sure the Stasi have told him that she's in custody and they are in a home because it will add to his sense of powerlessness. That's what they do in Hohenschönhausen.'

'It's not going to be easy to get him out,' said Harp. 'I don't want you to go away with any false hopes.'

'I understand. We'll concentrate on Else first.'

'How quickly will they release them?'

'Soon after I come back from the meeting with Annalise,' said Rosenharte. 'Then we need to move them as soon as possible.'

Harp's face did not change, but his tone did. 'I'm afraid we won't be able to move them until there has been some progress on contact with Kafka. You must understand that this is very important to us.'

'You don't trust me?'

'No, it's just the way it is, old chap. Besides, if Else and the kids just disappear to the West, they're hardly going to let you alone, are they? We need Else to sit tight at home until the Bird is ready to take them out and we're firmly in contact with Kafka.'

'And when they get to the West they will be looked after?'

'You have Bobby Harland's word on that, which means it *will* happen,' said Harp.

'How will you get them out?'

'What do you think, Cuth?'

'I'm inclined to a crossing of the Czech border, a swift journey by car to Hungary, which they will enter on false passports as my family, and then Bob's your uncle: two large cream buns for the lads in Vienna and a double brandy for your brother's missus.'

'How will I contact you?'

'You've got the number of the Medium and they can't trace that. It's a relay system – phone to phone to phone which transfers to the West by a secret means. They may be jolly good at beating people up in jail, but when it comes to electronics your chaps are positively Neolithic.'

'That's not true. Phones are tapped at my end and the calls I make can easily be traced. I need another means.'

'We'll try to sort out something.'

'How's *Annalise* going to contact me?'

'By mail, naturally. The letter was posted yesterday and the Stasi should intercept it tomorrow. Of course, you *don't* know anything about the trip to Berlin.'

Rosenharte couldn't subdue his impatience. 'They suspect that method of communication. They think it's been used to attract their attention.'

'Don't worry. What we're giving them is good enough for them to ignore any minor doubts they've got.'

'Can you tell me what it is?'

'No, because I don't know. But we've had some help from the Americans so it's going to be good and very much up to date. Once we've got Else out, things may become difficult for you and we have got to come up with something to deal with that.'

Rosenharte looked up through the ceiling to the sky. The questioning by Schwarzmeer's people had exposed so many flaws and false assumptions in the British planning that he had no confidence whatsoever. 'Do you have any ideas?'

'We'll have to wait and see how things turn out,' said Avocet. 'There's no point in planning anything now.'

'I'm afraid I agree with the Bird,' said Harp. 'Now, I think we'd all better bugger off, don't you? We'll see you in Berlin. All the instructions will be in the letters. You can make your way out the back,' he said, gesturing behind him. 'It's a bit more discreet. We'll follow in a few minutes.'

Rosenharte said goodbye and groped his way into a yard, which had served a number of buildings at the back of the restaurant. A few minutes later he was heading for Augustus Bridge, wondering how long it would be before the Stasi picked up his trail.

EIGHT

By the Elbe

The afternoon was still warm when he reached the Augustus Bridge, which crossed the sluggish waters of the Elbe. It was only when he had passed the figure standing midway across that he recognized Sonja. She had her back to a group of young men wearing the blue shirts of the Free German Youth Movement and was looking downstream.

He hesitated, wondering whether to disturb her, then called out. She didn't turn so he crossed over to her side of the bridge. 'Sonja? Is there something the matter?'

She shook her head.

'Is there anything I can do?' He placed a hand lightly on her shoulder.

'No,' she said. 'I . . .'

'Sonja . . . ?' At this point he felt he'd done the wrong thing. He was also uncomfortably aware of a squeak of desire for her. 'Can I take you for a drink?'

'Where would we go in this Godforsaken shit heap? Where?'

'I know places. Look, you'll be doing me a favour. I could really use the company myself.'

She turned to him for the first time. 'They arrested Sebastian. This morning.' She stopped. 'You don't look that good yourself.'

'Difficult times,' he said. 'Look, maybe they've only taken him for a short spell. They arrest a lot of people, hold them for questioning then let them go. They take people out of circulation when they think there's going to be a demonstration. You said yourself that you thought something was going to happen. If you knew that, they did too. He'll be back with you next week.'

'How can I be sure?'

'Because it happened to me last week. I wasn't in Italy all that time: I was being questioned.'

'That's not the point.'

'Come on, tell me all about it over a drink.'

She shook her head. 'I can't talk about this in public. It's too sensitive. It's really private . . . there are things . . .' She took out a handkerchief to dab her eyes and wipe her sunglasses.

'Come on,' he said. 'We'll buy some beers and go and see an old friend of mine. We can talk there.'

'I'm not going back to your place.'

He looked down into a tear-stained, freckled face and brushed the hair away from her eyes. Sonja was in her late twenties, but she seemed like a child now. The desire left him.

'Even if I wanted to, which I *don't*, it would be impossible. Come along.'

He took her by the arm and led her back over the bridge towards Neustadt. Half an hour later, having got hold of some beer, they walked on a deserted path along the riverbank. Tiny insects swarmed in clouds above the water; a few swallows and house martins dived and stalled around them. Sonja remained silent. At length they came to a *Schrebergartenkolonie*, an area of small allotments where Dresdeners were allowed to grow their own produce and set up sheds. The gardens were well established and some included two or three fruit trees now weighed down by plums and ripening pears and apples. The people fortunate enough to acquire one of these gardens gained privacy and some small sense that they were masters of their own environment. In the summer, many decamped to the gardens more or less permanently, sleeping in the huts and cooking their meals in the open. Down here, away from the impersonal apartment blocks and the demands of the state, people could be themselves.

Rosenharte noticed Idris's old Diamant bicycle roped to the fence and called out softly over a clump of bamboo. A rustle was followed by a black face appearing between the canes. 'Rudi, my friend, what pleasure is this! It has been many months since we have seen each other. Too long for good friends.'

The head disappeared, then popped out a few feet away above a little white gate. Before opening it he reached out, clasped Rosenharte's neck and kissed him three times. Rosenharte introduced Sonja and watched the conjecture and awe dance in Idris's eyes. It must have been a long time since he had had any real contact with a woman. Like all foreign workers, he suffered terribly from the racism of the GDR, and had been beaten up and knocked off his bicycle more than a few times. It was during one of these incidents that they had met, Rosenharte having intervened to stop a gang of youths wrenching the bicycle from under him.

Idris Muzaffar Muhammad, part Arab and part Dinka, had then invited him to his plot by the river. He told Rosenharte that he was the son of a wealthy Sudanese landowner who had come to the GDR in some kind of exchange programme and was then stranded after his family fell from grace in Khartoum. Idris now lectured about irrigation and water conservation at the Technical University, but he was also a highly cultivated man and over many hours sitting by the Elbe had told Rosenharte about the early kingdoms of the Nile. He was now in his early forties.

Idris didn't know what to say to Sonja and he hopped from one bare foot to the other in his white robe, clapping his hands gently. 'Is this to be Frau Rosenharte?'

'She can speak for herself,' said Rosenharte, grinning, 'but I think you'll find that marrying me is the very last thing on her mind.'

This made Sonja smile.

'I'm so sad,' said Idris. 'This man is the very, very best man. It is pity.'

He led them into the little garden, divided into three vegetable patches and a larger piece of ground, which was spilling over with flowers. Between these ran immaculate paths made from stones and pebbles taken from the riverbank. Idris was a dedicated scavenger: anything of use that was borne down the Elbe or thrown out at the university was strapped to the Diamant and wheeled back to his garden where it was pressed into service.

'We've brought beer for you,' said Rosenharte.

Idris flashed his white and gold teeth, showed them to a table made from salvaged planks and found stools for them. They sat down and opened the beer and looked at the river. Idris told them that sometimes he fooled himself that he was sitting by the Nile, surrounded by the noises and smells of his childhood.

'Her boyfriend has been arrested,' said Rosenharte when there was a lull in the conversation. 'Can we have a few moments alone?'

'I shall cook a meal for us,' said Idris. He went off to busy himself with a little iron stove in the shed and soon a stream of smoke appeared from a pipe that protruded from the roof.

'So, what happened?' asked Rosenharte.

'They took him this morning. Early. I was there. They told

him that he was under suspicion of "rowdyism and incitement hostile to the state". They mentioned something to do with anti-state propaganda.'

'What did he do?'

'He made some posters calling for freedom of expression and stuck them up at night. Someone ratted him to the Stasi.'

'Do you know why?'

She shrugged. 'No. Have you got another cigarette?'

He handed her the packet and his lighter.

'Rudi, Sebastian's crazy – he's got no sense of danger. He needs someone to watch out for him.'

An idea occurred to him. 'Did they have you in and ask you to work for them in exchange for letting him go?'

'Yes, they implied it would be better for Sebastian if I started helping them.'

'Me too. You see, my brother's in prison. That's the way they do things.'

'Really, your brother?'

'Did you tell them about that phone call I made the other day?'

'No.'

'And what about . . . ?'

She saw what he was thinking. 'No, I didn't tell them about us. Look, I wasn't going to admit to sleeping with an old guy like you.'

'Thanks,' he said, remembering being ambushed by Sonja's bluntness so often before.

'It didn't seem so strange when we were doing it because I adored being with you, Rudi. But it does seem odd now.'

'Okay, okay! Let's talk about something else, shall we?'

She leaned forward and put a hand on his knee. 'I didn't mean to hurt you, Rudi. You're a wonderful man and very funny. The best talker I know. By the way, where's all that gone? You don't laugh like you used to – the drinking and the humour. You've become so serious.'

Rosenharte gave her a bleak smile. 'Things on my mind, you know? My brother . . .'

'Yes.' She paused to drink some beer and looked away. 'Anyway, I love Sebastian. For the first time I understand what people are talking about. You know, I *really* love him. *Love* him!'

Rosenharte nodded. For a brief moment he saw an image of Annalise sitting on a bench in the centre of Brussels saying much the same thing.

'When they take you in again, I don't want you to tell them about me at all. Do you understand? Say I'm a bore – whatever you need to.'

'Some people came before that. Different people from the ones I've just seen. I had to tell them about the guy who was looking for you.' She touched her chin with her middle finger and pressed it. 'They took down an exact description of him and asked me to phone a special number if he came back. They also wanted to know if I'd seen you with another man. He was older – a short, plump guy in his fifties.'

'Who wore a straw hat?' said Rosenharte, thinking of the dead Pole.

'Yes, that one. So who are these men?'

'I don't know. When did they ask you about him?'

'Just last week. When they searched your office.' She looked down and revolved a plain silver ring on her right hand. 'I'm sorry, I should have told you, I know. They may have put a microphone in there too.'

'Thank you.' He glanced at Idris, who was feeding small pieces of driftwood into an opening at the front of the stove and revolving a number of pans around the heated plate on top. He whisked and stirred and mopped his forehead with increasing urgency.

'And you're sure that the professor's phone isn't tapped?'

'I can't be sure. But they ask me who he calls, so maybe not.'

'Or maybe they're testing you. Look, it's very important that you don't tell them about that call, Sonja. My freedom depends on it.'

'Sounds like you're in worse trouble than Sebastian.'

'If they find out about that call, I will be. I'm relying on you.'

She put up her hand as though taking an oath. 'I won't tell them.' And then she produced that broad, shy smile he had always loved. It was quite distinct from the mischief that played on her face most of the time and was reserved for moments of intimacy or when she found something really funny.

'Thank you. I won't tell them anything.'

Idris emerged from the shed and hung four small brass lanterns on the trees around them. 'Now we have a feast,' he said. 'And this lady must reconsider her decision not to become Frau Rosenharte.'

'Why are you persisting with this?' asked Rosenharte, laughing.

'Because you need wife. Your life means little without the children.'

'I've been married!'

'But no children,' said Idris.

He started ferrying small dishes of food from the shed, giving their Arabic names and describing their ingredients: *adas*, a lentil stew with garlic which he had reheated; *fule*, dried broad beans, cooked and served cold; *tamia*, deep-fried chick peas; and *tabika aly-oum*, a mutton dish. There were salads of mint and lettuce and hot breads baked on top of the oven. After the meal, Sonja moved, without saying anything, to a dilapidated chair in the shed and curled up. Idris threw a large piece of white cloth over her like a fisherman casting a net, and returned to finish the beer with Rosenharte.

'Where do you get all this food from?' asked Rosenharte idly. 'I've never seen any of these things on sale in Konsum. How do you do it, Idris?'

'People brings it for me. Anyone who goes to Middle Eastern countries knows to bring back Idris foods.'

'But this is all so fresh.'

'Yes, a friend of mine he return from Yemen a few days ago. He bring me the meats. I am happy to share it with you, Rudi.'

'Do you hope to go back to Sudan sometime soon?'

'Even now I can go in my homeland, I am not paying for the airplane ticket. Ticket very, very expensive.'

'That's a shame. If I had the money I'd give it to you.'

Idris smiled enigmatically – gratitude for the unhoped-for kindness, mixed with regret. Not for the first time, Rosenharte wondered what went on behind his obliging eyes. Then something occurred to him. 'This man who went to Yemen and brought you the food, is he the man at the university? Michael Lomieko? His friends call him Misha.'

'Yes, of course,' answered Idris, as though it was the only answer that Rosenharte could have expected. 'He has many, many Arab friends also and he goes to many, many Arab countries. He visit Sudan and he come back and tell me in July that I can go in Sudan. It is safe for me there now.'

'I've travelled on the train to Leipzig with Misha. He seems a good man.'

'Yes, he is a good man,' said Idris. He was plainly thinking about something else.

Rosenharte decided to take a risk. 'He knows an Arab gentleman called Abu Jamal. Have you heard of him? I think he stays in Leipzig sometimes.'

This gained all Idris's attention. He turned to Rosenharte so that his face was lit by the lantern. 'Why do you ask these questions? You do not want to know this man. He is very, very dangerous, this man.'

'In what way is he dangerous?'

'You could die even for knowing his name in this country.'

'But how do you know him, Idris? You're a lecturer in irrigation. Why would you know these things? Has Misha asked for your help?'

'I can ask the same question to you, Rudi. How do you know this man? All day you look at pictures in your gallery. This is not your business.' He lowered his voice. 'This is business of terrorist and killers. Do not say his name again.'

Rosenharte poured the last of the beer into the glasses. 'I need to find out where he is.'

'That is why you come here?'

Rosenharte shook his head. 'I didn't come seeking your help. It was only when you mentioned Yemen that I thought of asking your advice. It was a shot in the dark.'

There was a long silence while Idris turned from him and cupped one hand over the other to pick his teeth. A few minutes later he said to the night, 'The woman – Sonja – is she part of this enquiry that you make?'

'No, she just let me use a phone the other day.'

'I am no donkey. Flies do not sit on me.'

'Sorry?' said Rosenharte smiling.

'She will tell them.'

'Did you overhear what she was saying?'

Idris gave him a furtive look.

'Then you will understand that she was put in an impossible position. She had to do what they asked.'

Idris shook his head as though hearing of a great disaster. 'But you must not tell her anything more. This woman loves another man and she will do anything to save him. Beware of this woman, Rudi.'

'You're probably right.' He wished that the light allowed him to see Idris's face properly. He was now aware that something had altered in Idris's manner: his tone was more deliberate, and the subtlety, which Rosenharte always knew was there, began to display itself. 'You seem preoccupied, Idris. Have I offended you?'

'Everything is very, very good. Do not worry, dear Rudi.' His attention had moved to some moths that were batting into one of the lanterns.

'Can you help me on this man Abu Jamal?'

Instead of replying, Idris got up and crept to the shed to look at Sonja. Satisfied that she was genuinely asleep, he came back and pulled his stool towards Rosenharte, so that his face was just a few inches away. 'When you help me, Rudi, you expect nothing in return. So now I will help you. But first you must tell me why you need to find this man.'

Rosenharte explained about his brother and his family and said he had a chance of freeing them if he acquired some information about Abu Jamal, who was suspected of terrorist acts in the West. He left out all mention of the trip to Trieste and the Stasi 'debriefing' and did not specify the interest of the British and American intelligence services, although he assumed that Idris would suspect their involvement. When he finished, Idris stroked his chin and asked, 'Are you a Marxist, Rudi?'

'I am a socialist, yes, but not like Lenin or Stalin or Honecker.'

'Herr Gorbachev – you think he is a good man?'

'He seems a decent man, yes. I think he is doing the right sort of things in the Soviet Union. Reform is needed everywhere in the East, not least in the GDR.'

'I am a Marxist and a Muslim,' said Idris. 'Does a man do the will of God or of the state? This is very, very difficult question.'

'It is,' said Rosenharte, feeling chilled through and stiff after sitting for so long in the same position. 'Tell me, Idris, why are we having this conversation?'

'Because there are other people like you and me who want reform in communist countries, but remain socialist. They do not believe in terrorism either. It hurts us in the East and it hurts Arab countries.'

'Can you help me with hard information?'

'I will send someone, a younger man. His name is Vladimir. He will help you.'

'A Russian?'

'He's a good man and very, very clever man,' said Idris, tapping his forehead.

'Is he a Russian?' Rosenharte repeated.

Idris conceded a nod.

'Has this Vladimir been trying to find me before?'

'How is that possible?' asked Idris, as though Rosenharte was being incredibly stupid. 'I have not told him about you, so how can he look for you?'

Rosenharte got up and thanked him. Idris snatched at the air and found Rosenharte's hand, held it loosely for several seconds and looked up at him. Rosenharte thought how much he liked the man – a true affection that bridged every possible cultural and ethnic difference. He grinned.

Idris acknowledged the sentiment with a wink. 'The Russian will find you and he will help you soon, Rudi. Soon.'

NINE

An Axe to the Frozen Sea

He drifted back to the city with Sonja clinging on to him, drowsily insisting that he should kiss her, which he eventually did, experiencing the familiar pleasure. Then she wanted to make love and pulled him behind some bushes, feeling him and squirming in his arms. He reminded her of Sebastian, she said.

'It's you I want now,' she said, folding her arms around his neck and looking up at him with petulant need. 'And I will make you do it.'

'No,' he said, pulling away. 'I can't. I'd love to but I just can't.' He wanted her and it would be so easy but something was holding him back: the sense that he had to stay focused.

'Come on. I need you.'

'You don't,' he said, shaking his head. 'Please understand this would be wrong for both of us.' He was surprised at himself.

She scowled at him but seemed to accept that it wasn't going to happen.

They walked to a large, desolate apartment block on the south side of town, where he left with a murmured apology and kiss of genuine tenderness. She shook her head and without a word slipped through a door that banged behind her. Feeling lousy he hurried off to a dive he knew in the crypt of a bombed-out church and sat alone at a table, methodically draining one beer after another among half a dozen Dresdener nighthawks. His mind moved through his predicament more frantically than he liked.

By one o'clock he reckoned that he looked drunk enough to persuade his Stasi surveillance that he had been on a bender all day. He downed the last of his beer and prepared to leave. As he made his way to the door of Die Krypta, two men slipped from a table in the shadows, took hold of his arms and moved him expertly through the narrow entrance and up the flight of steps. Rosenharte allowed himself to be borne along and only when they emerged into the dimly lit street did he protest. Neither of the men spoke until they reached a car, where there was a third man waiting at the wheel. 'Good evening, comrade. My name is Vladimir. We want to talk to you. Can you come with us to a safe place?'

'You're the man my friend spoke of?'

'Yes,' said Vladimir. 'We found you soon after you left your girl at her apartment. We had to make sure you weren't being followed.' His German was good but his accent heavy. The car moved without haste, as if making for the Stasi headquarters in Bautznerstrasse, but then veered off to a building in Angelikastrasse, the KGB residence in Dresden, which stood just a hundred metres away from the Stasi. The three men took him to a basement where Vladimir offered him a drink. Rosenharte asked for coffee.

'You were quick to find me,' said Rosenharte, thinking that Idris must have sped to a phone on his bicycle soon after he'd left.

The Russian smiled. 'It was a coincidence: we already knew about you. When the Stasi mounts this kind of operation we take an interest. But there's something we don't understand: why are you so important to them?'

'It's a long story.' He paused to examine him. 'Idris said you could help me. Is that true?'

'It depends how,' said Vladimir. He had an interesting face, pale and unmistakably Slav, with a good deal of authority in his expression. He took his time to respond and had a rather expressionless young voice. The other two men plainly deferred to him.

'I want news of my brother. He and his family have been arrested.'

'And your brother is?'

'A man who makes films – a broken man who was once a dissident. His name is Konrad Rosenharte. My twin.'

'And they took his family as well. That's unusual.'

'His wife Else is under investigation for violations of emigration laws.'

'And yet the whole of East Germany seems to be travelling to Czechoslovakia to apply for visas at the West German Embassy in Prague. It's not difficult to leave. You can even go via Poland if you wish. The GDR is like a sieve at the moment.'

'She wasn't even trying to leave the GDR. They're using her detention to gain a hold over me.'

'Why would they do that? Your brother is the troublemaker, not you.'

'I cannot say. But I'll tell you everything I know if you help me.'

'Do you have a lot to tell us, Doktor?'

'Yes.'

Vladimir circled him, with his hands thrust forward in the pockets of his leather bomber jacket. Rosenharte took him to be completely ruthless yet also someone whom he might be able to deal with. The KGB could be very useful to him. It was the second intelligence power in the land with a vast station in Berlin and satellites in every major city. Theoretically there to watch over the

Soviet Union's interests, particularly the 400,000 military personnel stationed in the GDR, the KGB also still had something of a supervisory role which had been established after the war when Stalin's men constructed the East German state. During Rosenharte's time in the Stasi, Normannenstrasse deferred to the KGB in everything from training to the broad strategy of intelligence gathering in the West. To some extent the Stasi still looked for inspiration from one of the KGB's earliest antecedents, the Cheka. But while the Chekist spirit was still very much alive in the Stasi, the KGB had moved on from its obsessions with fascists, class enemies and imperialist agents to make a reluctant accommodation with the new Russia of *glasnost* and *perestroika*.

At length Vladimir spoke. 'Idris is a friend of ours and I trust his judgement, but it's difficult to see how I can help you. We have no access to people in Stasi jails and they don't share information with us like they used to before Herr Gorbachev came to the Kremlin. But maybe we can open up some avenues. We'll see what we can do for you.' He looked at Rosenharte thoughtfully. 'Idris said you were interested in a man named Abu Jamal. Now why would you ask him about that?'

'I wanted to know his relationship with Michael Lomieko – Misha.'

'Ah, Misha!' said Vladimir. 'Everything always comes back to Misha. I repeat the question: why do you want to know about him?'

'I travel on the train with him to Leipzig, that's all.'

Vladimir gave him a broad grin and shook his head. 'Don't take me for a fool, Rosenharte. I know that you went to Italy a week or two ago because we have done our research on you. I cannot guess at the relationship you have with the Western intelligence services, or whether the Main Directorate for Foreign Intelligence knows what you are up to, but that is why you want to know about Abu Jamal and Misha, is it not? Come on, let's be straight with one another.'

Rosenharte felt out of his depth, but he did have a glimmer of an insight. Idris must be watching Misha for the KGB. That meant the KGB were interested in Misha's relationship with Abu Jamal and the Stasi for exactly the same reasons as the British. That could mean the KGB disapproved of East Germany's support for terrorism.

Vladimir stood with a look of deep contemplation. Then he nodded encouragingly. 'Tell me your problem, Rosenharte.'

'This is difficult,' he started. 'I have been given hope that if I gain information about Abu Jamal I may be able to get my brother released. The slightest information could help.'

The calculation was visible behind the Russian's eyes. 'Abu Jamal is not in the GDR, but we understand that he is returning for consultations at a villa in Leipzig. Is that any help to you?'

'A villa? Why are you telling me this?'

'Because I expect an exchange of information. I want you to tell me everything that you pass to your friends in the West.'

'What is the villa's name?'

Vladimir approached one of his men and whispered to him. The man left the room.

'Are you a reformer?' Rosenharte asked him after a few moments' silence.

'Everyone is a reformer today. It is the only way. But the Party in East Germany hasn't understood this and won't implement the necessary modernization programme. The writing's on the wall. Isn't that the way the Bible puts it?'

'Not on the Berlin Wall. Honecker says it will last another hundred years.'

Vladimir turned to him. 'Yes, and the president of the Volks-kammer, he agrees with him; the secretaries of the Central

Committee, the Minister for State Security and the first secretaries of all the districts, including Dresden, all say the Wall will last for ever. We must take their word for it.' When a Russian spoke with this sarcastic tone, one could only conclude that the KGB understood that things were changing or had to change. It made him wonder how much of the KGB's time was spent watching the leaders of the GDR.

The other man came back with a folder. Vladimir spent a few moments leafing through it before flourishing a map, spreading it on a table in the corner and summoning Rosenharte to look him squarely in the face. 'I am a loyal communist, Rosenharte, and a loyal citizen of the Soviet Union. Understand that. You should know also that I value loyalty in all my associations.'

Rosenharte nodded and looked down at the city map of Leipzig. It was covered with about sixty round black stickers. Some were accompanied by notes in Cyrillic handwriting, others by blank labels. 'These are the Stasi safe houses in Leipzig. There are seventy-eight in all.'

'Seventy-eight!'

'They increase every year. But we no longer have access to the latest information. We have three addresses.' He pointed to dots around the city centre. Then he turned and gripped Rosenharte's shoulder with one hand. He was much smaller than Rosenharte and had to look up into his eyes. 'No matter what complications and intrigues you experience, our help must be kept secret. I will not tolerate you keeping anything back from us. I want to know everything. That is the price of my help.'

'I understood the first time you said it,' said Rosenharte amenably. 'I'm here only to help you any way that I can. I will keep to my side of the bargain.'

'Good. The girl you were with earlier this evening, have

nothing more to do with her. She's working for the Stasi. I don't want the slightest hint that you and I are collaborating.'

'I work with her.'

'Then keep your distance. And no more episodes like this evening.'

'There wasn't an episode this evening.'

'Good.' He paused. 'Make love to that woman again and you'll regret it.'

Rosenharte nodded.

'I'm glad we've got these things straight. I will find out about your brother, if I can.'

Rosenharte stood for a moment. 'Sometimes I feel this is like a novel by Kafka.' He watched Vladimir's face for a reaction.

'I don't read Kafka,' he said indifferently.

'So Kafka means nothing to you?'

'I read him when I was a young man. It seemed juvenile stuff to me even then.'

Rosenharte tried another tack. 'Have you had me followed? Did you send someone to meet me in Trieste?'

'Herr Doktor! I didn't hear your name before last week. How could I send someone to Trieste to watch you?'

'And you didn't send anyone to the gallery where I work?'

'Of course not. Why would I do such a thing? We don't operate like that.'

The interview was coming to an end. 'How will I contact you?'

'You won't. We will make contact with you in a week or so.' He paused. 'If you want to free your family, you must make sure that you keep everything that has passed between us secret. Now go off and read some good Russian authors. Forget the Czechs; they're too dark for these times of light.'

'Times of light?'

'Oh yes, times of light, Herr Doktor, times of light.' He appraised Rosenharte openly then put out his hand. 'I will see what I can do for you. Goodbye.'

One of the men gave him a piece of paper and he memorized the three addresses in Leipzig. Then they took him to within a kilometre of his apartment and left him in a wasteland between three huge blocks. It was past four o'clock when he turned the corner into Lotzenstrasse and saw a car waiting for him. He ignored it and kept moving towards his building with the unsteady purpose of a drunk. Before he reached the door, two Stasi leapt from the car and approached him.

'Identity card please,' shouted one.

As the man examined it, the other asked where he had been.

'Trying to get laid,' Rosenharte mumbled.

'You should be in bed, old man. No woman would look at you in your state.'

Rosenharte asked if he could go. They returned the card and he shuffled to his door.

He slept much of Sunday and read through his lecture in the evening, making one or two cuts. Very early on Monday he packed a case and made his way to the Hauptbahnhof to catch the first service to Leipzig. As far as he could tell, there was no one following him. The train was late and he drank several cups of coffee while he watched a group of disconsolate Volkspolizei standing round a stack of riot shields. An officer came over to buy coffee.

'Why are you here?' asked Rosenharte pleasantly.

'Negative hostile elements have threatened to disrupt the order of the station.'

'Don't negative hostile elements ever sleep?'

'We have to be vigilant at all times,' said the officer disagreeably. 'Anyway, what's it to you?'

'Nothing. I am just pleased we are in such safe hands.'

'Thanks,' said the man without a trace of irony. 'Good day to you.'

Rosenharte climbed up to one of the elevated platforms where trains passing through the city stopped. About a dozen people boarded the train. Having secured a seat, he went straight to the lavatory where he washed his face in a trickle of cold water and stared at his reflection. The mirror was scratched with some words which he had to stoop to read: *Glasnost in Staat und Kirche. Keine Gewalt!* – Freedom in church and state. No violence! On the wall the same hand had etched: *Wir sind das VOLK!* – We are the PEOPLE!

Noble sentiments for a piece of vandalism. It was interesting how more graffiti was appearing everywhere.

Dawn came with a chilly, autumnal light that picked out patches of mist lingering over the rivers and lakes. Everywhere summer was in retreat: the trees were on the turn and weeds along the rail track were dead and broken, ready to collapse into the winter earth. Oddly, the coming of autumn always made Rosenharte feel invigorated and full of possibility and, as he looked out on the cows grazing in the heavily dewed pastures of Saxony, a sudden optimism surged in him. Somehow he would free Konnie, Else and the boys.

They reached Leipzig just after nine, having been delayed twice by unspecified engineering problems. At the station there were scores of Vopos in summer uniform and the familiar huddles of men in civilian clothes with no obvious purpose to hand. But no one seemed to be interested in him, and he was able to walk unobserved from the entrance and head towards Karl-Marx-Platz, the place where he had once watched First Secretary Honecker preside over a festival by the Freie Deutsche Jugend – the Free German

Youth. He had recoiled from the sight of the dapper little old man in a grey suit, blue tie and red rosette feeding on the youth beneath him, leaching their energy and creativity.

He went to a newspaper stand and bought a copy of *Das Magazin*. Holding it in his free hand, he walked a couple of hundred yards to the Nikolaikirche and entered by a side door, the main door being blocked by construction work. He stood for a few moments in the back row of pews, gazing up at the plaster palm fronds that sprouted from the columns, then moved to a small office at the back of the church where a few religious books and postcards were for sale. As instructed by Harland and the American in their last hour together in Trieste, he bought three cards, all views of the church, signed a visitors' book with the name Gehlert and wrote, 'Mine eyes have seen the coming of the glory.'

The first postcard was posted in the door of Number 34 Burgstrasse, bearing the same quotation; the second was left blank between two pilasters under the clock of the old town hall; and the third, inscribed with the words 'To Martha with love', was deposited with an unwelcoming manageress at a café nearby.

This done, he walked to the Thomaskirche, the imposing church where J.S. Bach once led the choir, and repeated his remarks in a second visitors' book, signing as Harry Schmidt. Outside, in the thin autumn sunshine, he lit up and read *Das Magazin*. A young couple came up to him wanting cigarettes and the price of a beer. He gave them cigarettes but told them he was broke, which was true.

Harland had told him not to expect Kafka to make contact immediately because this initial procedure was simply a way of announcing himself, and more important, a sign that he had been briefed by MI6. Kafka would make his move only when he was sure it was safe. After about an hour, Rosenharte made his way to the university canteen, for which he'd been sent a meal ticket by the organizers of the lecture series, and ate an early lunch of stew and dumplings. It transpired that he had hit the place at the same time as various university sports teams, all on high-protein diets. He sat among the rowers and their trainers and got himself a second helping, some cheese and a cup of coffee.

By two thirty he was standing at the front of a full lecture hall, with students and university staff crowding the aisles, slightly regretting the meal. He was always nervous before speaking, which was why he took such pains, rewriting and rereading his papers so often that when he came to give them he had memorized the entire text. A long introduction by a professor of philosophy did little to calm him, but then the lights dimmed and an image of a bull from the prehistoric caves of Lascaux in central France appeared on the screen. Rosenharte let his audience gaze at the bull for a few moments then began to speak, the words that had seemed so stale on the page now coming to life. He talked of the technique, the limited palette of prehistoric man, the conditions in which he painted and the use of such modern ideas as composition, perspective and foreshortening. He felt invigorated, totally in charge of his material and his audience.

'This was probably painted by a young man some eighteen thousand years ago. In the same cave there are other animals, which we know from radiocarbon dating were painted by other people much later. To us they seem all of a piece, the same period, but in fact two thousand years separate the artists. They probably didn't even speak the same language.' He looked up from his paper. 'Those two men were as far apart as Karl Marx and Jesus Christ.' There was a nervous shifting among the staff and some of the students smirked. 'Not in their nature, I hasten to add, but in time.'

He couldn't think what had got into him to make this aside, which would only weaken the message of his text. He asked for the next slide, which was of galloping bison from the Altamira caves in northern Spain. He sensed the effect it was having on his audience. Someone in the front clapped his hands in delight. 'If the bull was a great work of art,' he continued, 'this one, painted about seventeen thousand years ago, is a masterpiece without parallel. Through the subtle application of tones and shading, and the skilful use of colour, the image reaches a perfection unequalled by any modern artist. There is volume, mass and energy in this creature and it emerges alive and concrete from the rough surface of the rock, almost as if the rock has given birth to the bull. The hair, beard and fur of the animal have an almost tangible reality. This beast *lives*, my friends, and it is as great a work of art as any of you will see during your lifetimes.'

The foundations had been laid. Rosenharte now moved to his theory. If the height of art had been 7,000 years before man planted seeds, millennia before he mounted a horse or invented the wheel, how was it possible to think of art in terms of evolution? Evolution implied a gradual improvement over time, an accumulation of qualities and a discarding of flaws. 'But in no area,' he said, turning from the bison to the audience, 'has this painting been equalled in all the history of art – not in the simplicity of technique, the overall harmony of design or the expressive animation of form. This man observed and analysed with all the speed and confidence of modern man. In fact he was better at it than us.'

He continued on this theme for twenty minutes, showing paintings from different eras, but before he could move to the final section of the lecture, a voice boomed from the middle of the auditorium. Rosenharte shaded his eyes and looked up to see a large man on his feet, plucking at his chin with hopeful authority. 'But what purpose did these paintings serve society, Dr Rosenharte?'

'None, because there was no society,' Rosenharte shot back.

'That's my point,' said the man. 'That's exactly my point. We must all agree that the principal function of art is to serve society by expressing that society's aspirations and reflecting its qualities and achievements. If these primitive decorations, these doodles and daubs, bear no relation to any recognizable society, then they must be disqualified from the realm of art.'

Rosenharte shifted to his right so he could see the man. 'Why *must* we all agree? Do you really believe that all art, no matter from what period, is dependent on our views about what is and what is not a society? I have to tell you that it is a very old-fashioned view.'

There was a murmur of approval among the students, who were clearly excited by this rare exchange of convictions. The man was having none of it. 'Is it old-fashioned to favour works of art produced by an advanced state like the German Democratic Republic – perhaps the most sophisticated society ever known on earth – over the graffiti of primitive tribesmen?'

Rosenharte's blood began to rise. He went to the front of the stage and addressed the man personally. 'The problem in the GDR is that we don't know what art this society has produced. Why is that? Because most of the artists who have anything to say are banned. They have been gagged and, ironically enough, work in conditions similar to the primitive tribesmen you disdain – alone, in the dark and without a public. They paint for themselves and for the future because our society cannot or will not hear its own voice, will not listen to its own heart.'

The man could stand it no longer and started pushing along the row towards the aisle.

'Oh come on, why don't you stay and argue this one out?' said Rosenharte.

'I will not listen to any more nonsense, and if people know what's good for them they will follow me from this hall.' One or two made to move, but the majority cried for them to stay and began a slow handclap. This was not at all what Rosenharte wanted. He put his hands in the air and appealed for silence. 'I did not come here to embarrass the university authorities, but merely to talk about the destructive idea that all art must be seen in terms of evolutionary progress.'

'The only person you have embarrassed is yourself,' cried the man from the door.

He resumed his lecture, which was heard respectfully but without enthusiasm because it was clear that all anyone wanted to talk about was the exchange between him and the anonymous academic. When he reached the end there was silence, then a deafening round of applause. The philosophy professor who had introduced him did not get up to the platform to offer formal thanks, as was the custom, but slunk away with a colleague, shaking his head. Rosenharte busied himself with his papers and reluctantly accepted the congratulations of the students, then stepped down from the platform and joined the crowd filing through the door.

'Well, Doktor, I guess that's the last time we'll hear one of your stimulating talks here.' He glanced to his left. A woman in her mid to late thirties was looking ahead of them, smiling. 'I'm glad I came. It was easily the best so far.'

'Thank you,' he said, wishing she would turn her face to him. 'But I screwed up with that crack about Marx and Jesus Christ. I think that's what annoyed my critic. Do you know who he was?'

'Manfred Böhme, professor of political science and a senior figure in the local Party.'

'Böhme! Yes, I've heard of him. What was he doing here?'

'Checking up on you. Your last lecture – the one about the drawing by . . .'

'Carracci.'

'Yes, Carracci. It was excellent. However, one or two people suspected that you were criticizing the Party in a sly way. No one had a text, so it couldn't be checked.'

They reached the corridor. He lit a cigarette and looked around. 'I always feel a sense of anti-climax after these things. Would you like to go for a drink somewhere?' He noticed a very confident face, full lips and an acute but well-defended expression in her eyes.

'Why?'

'What do you mean, why?' he said.

'I mean what is your motive?'

'I haven't known you long enough to form a motive.'

'You will soon.'

'Know you, or form a motive?'

'The second,' she said.

'Do you want a drink, or not?'

She gave him a long-suffering look. 'Okay, I will take you to a place I know. We can talk there. My name is Ulrike. Ulrike Klaar.'

He hooked his bag over one arm and they walked a little self-consciously to a place on a quiet street not far from the station, where they sat across from each other at a small round table. Rosenharte was able to study her properly. The arch of her eyebrows made him think he should watch what he said but there was also a humorous glint in her eyes. He noticed that she was pale for the time of year, that she was slightly built despite her height and had a habit of smiling at the end of a sentence. He had the sense that she was the opposite of Sonja; that she underplayed her looks and wasn't particularly interested in appearing attractive. He liked this about her, too.

'We can't be long,' she said, after they had stumbled through some awkward pleasantries. 'I have an appointment at five.'

'Anything important?'

'Yes, as a matter of fact, it's very important, Herr Doktor.'

'Rudi – my name's Rudi.'

'I prefer Rudolf. It suits you better. But I will call you Rudi, if you like.'

'I have to go soon, too. I want to take a walk before I leave, maybe to the Clara Zetkin Park.'

'Why?'

'I need the exercise.'

She shrugged. 'It's okay. But why do you *have* to go?'

'I don't *have* to go. I just want to stretch my legs.'

'But you said you *had* to go.'

This was not going well. He took a mouthful of beer and watched three police trucks that were disgorging Vopos.

'What's going on?' he asked. 'There were riot police at Dresden station at five thirty this morning. Do they think something's going to happen?'

'Monday evening prayers at the Nikolaikirche. That's where I'm going after this. We meet every Monday to pray for peace. The authorities don't like it because other groups come – the environmentalists, people who want to leave the GDR, people who want free speech and reform, people protesting about prisoners of conscience. Some day the Stasi are going to break into the church and take everybody. They've already arrested many of my friends.' Her eyes flared, then she looked out of the window and suddenly straightened. 'Were you followed here?'

'I don't think so. Why?'

'There was a man looking at us from the other side of the street. You can't see him now because of the trucks. I think he was at the lecture.'

'It was open to the public. Perhaps he's an admirer of yours.'

She gave him a withering look. 'You shouldn't smoke so much at your age. You're in the danger zone.'

He stubbed out his cigarette. 'What did he look like?'

'Tall, thin, russet-coloured hair almost like yours. He looks strong – maybe he works with his hands – but nervous, unsure of himself. Someone who is out of place in this town.'

'You're very observant,' he said.

'But does it mean anything to you?' she asked.

He shook his head. 'No, I don't think so. Tell me more about these prayer meetings.'

'They started last year. Last January we tried to advertise them by leaving leaflets in people's letterboxes. But one man went along to the police and, before everyone got up the next morning, the Stasi and the police had removed the leaflets from the letterboxes with long tweezers. Somewhere, the Stasi had a supply of specially long tweezers for this exact purpose. That's the most amazing part of the story.'

'So no one came?'

'No, about five hundred people showed up in the end. That was really the start of it.' She smiled and stirred her tea. Rosenharte watched her.

'Of course,' she continued, 'a lot of people took the leaflets to the police out of fear. Still, they *are* beginning to understand. In the summer there was a man who organized a festival of street musicians. I remember the date because it was my birthday, June the tenth. Musicians came from all over the GDR and began playing in the centre, but because it was not officially sanctioned, the police moved in and arrested anyone with a musical instrument – they even rounded up members of the city's orchestra because they were carrying violin cases.' She suppressed a giggle but her eyes began to water. 'Can you imagine? They arrested players from the orchestra *in the city of Bach*.' She placed a knuckle at the corner of her eye to stop a tear.

'They're frightened of their own shadows,' he murmured.

'No, they're frightened of us. We, the people.'

'We, the people,' he mused.

There was a silence, a good silence, he thought, because neither felt the need to say anything.

'A friend of mine,' she started, 'thought you might be the brother of Konrad Rosenharte, the filmmaker. Are you?'

'He's my twin.' He paused and looked away. 'He's in prison.'

'What for?'

'The usual . . .' He stopped, suddenly overwhelmed by the thought of Konnie. 'You see, he can't take any more. They broke him last time.'

Her hand fidgeted indecisively on the surface of the table. 'I'm sorry. It's nearly as bad for those on the outside,' she said, 'the help-lessness, the not knowing. That's the way they designed it, to hurt as many people connected with their target as possible.'

'You sound as if you know about it.'

She nodded. 'Everyone knows something. The best anyone can do is support loved ones. That draws some of the poison.'

'What a country,' he said under his breath. 'They've got Konrad's wife, too. The children have been taken away.'

She shook her head in disbelief. 'Then why did you take such a risk today? It won't be ignored. Believe me. Not with your brother in jail.'

'I didn't intend to say anything,' said Rosenharte. 'But then I made that stupid remark about Christ and Marx and when that fool started spouting, I . . .'

'I had the impression that you were cooler than that.' Her rather critical demeanour had returned.

'Maybe I should have been, but the attitudes of that man are the ones that imprisoned Konrad. You know every formal act of expression has to be checked by a committee of nincompoops. The entries in the catalogue I have written for the Gemäldegalerie are being checked by five people. And each one thinks he should weigh in with a correction or some simple-minded observation. I have to tell them that Rembrandt *wasn't* a Party member. Konrad's only crime was to make a private film that displeased the authorities – and for this they put a block on his career and jailed him. They destroyed his health because they didn't like his film.'

She nodded in the direction of a couple that had sat down near them. It was a warning to him that he could be overheard. 'When will you return to Dresden?'

'This evening, probably – I'm not sure. I'm hoping to meet someone.'

'Oh?'

'It's not important. It's related to work.'

'You'll see this person after your walk in the park?'

He nodded.

'And in Dresden, what will you do when you go back?'

'My life is taken up with Konrad at the moment. It's a pretty complicated business.' He paused. 'Then I suppose I'll eventually get down to writing a book from these talks – a book that will never be published, of course.'

'But a book that will be read,' she said brightly.

'I hope so.'

'It will be your life's work. A great book. A book that will be an axe to the frozen sea inside us.'

'That's a wonderful phrase,' he said. 'I'd like to use it.'

'Then you must give credit to the author.' She looked up from her tea enigmatically.

'I'm sorry, I don't recognize it. Who said it?'

'Kafka,' she said very quietly. 'Franz Kafka.'

TEN

Clara Zetkin Park

Outside the cafe Ulrike brushed stray wisps of her dark-brown hair away from her face with a gesture of irritation. 'We don't have much time. I need you to listen very closely to everything I say. But first, I must know how you heard about the villa in Clara Zetkin Park.'

Rosenharte had prepared his answer for when he met Kafka. 'I did my own investigations in Dresden. I found out from Misha's colleague in the Technical University. It was by chance that I heard that Abu Jamal stays there.'

She frowned doubtfully. 'Nothing like that comes by chance. And please don't use names.'

'Trust me, it's not important how I know.'

'It *is* important,' she said, 'but I'm going to ignore it. Now listen. We'll walk to the park. We'll go the long way to avoid the traffic cameras. They use them to track people's movements. It won't take long. I'll show you the villa, but don't be obvious. Remember, in this city one in four of everyone you see is working for the Stasi in some way or other.'

They set off to the southeast of the city. 'I am a fluent Arabic speaker.' She walked quickly and spoke with head down. 'I spent most of my childhood in Arab countries. I studied European languages at university and I was employed by the government as an interpreter and translator of documents. I also worked at the university doing the same thing, though my position now is much less sensitive than it was. I am at the Central Institute for Youth Research, which in itself requires some security clearance.'

'Why would you need it there? They're just another group of people adding to the paper mountain, writing reports that no one reads.'

She stopped and smiled firmly. 'And you're about to write a book that won't be published. At least my work provides me with a living. I don't want to be rude, but would you just let me talk? I need to tell you a lot in a very short time.' He nodded and they continued. 'We have to be vetted to work at the institute because of what we're finding out in our surveys. Disaffection has been growing among young people. Your audience today was an example of that. Ten years ago they'd have all got up and left when Böhme told them to.' She stopped speaking as they passed a group of Vopos and flashed them a supportive smile that was returned by their officer. 'But this isn't the point. I still have access to the Department of International Relations and I have a friend there.'

'And this friend has shown you proof that the GDR is supporting Middle Eastern terrorism? That doesn't seem very likely.'

'Please, everything will be clear, if you listen. The bombing of the nightclub in Berlin – they knew about that though it was Libyans who carried out the attack. What I know for certain is that they're going to do something big at Christmas in the Federal Republic and that there'll be attacks on Western interests next year in the Middle East. The Arab has a list – the American embassies in Jordan and Egypt. Jordan will be in January, Egypt some time in March. There's something planned for Vienna and maybe Paris, but we don't have details.'

'I can't believe the Stasi would leave this kind of material lying around for you to read. They wouldn't put anything like this in writing.'

'Of course they didn't put it in writing. These attacks will be enormous – as big as the truck bomb that hit the American embassy in Beirut. A lot of lives are going to be lost unless you listen carefully and then get this information to the West.'

Rosenharte stopped. 'Why me? Why have I been chosen for this job? I'm just an academic.'

'Like me. But we have a duty.'

'Exactly why would an academic doing youth research know about these things? The other side will need to know how you got this information.'

'The Arab drinks heavily. That's why he has problems with his kidneys and liver. My friend is the woman they have assigned to look after him while he stays here in Leipzig. She has already got clearance to work with the professor and she's a valued employee. She was the natural choice.'

'You mean the GDR supplies a woman for him?'

'Yes, of course! A woman who speaks Arabic.'

'And he gets drunk and tells her everything?'

'That was true until his operation. He's become fond of her and she was with him in the hospital when he had a kidney transplant. He needed an interpreter. He was on drugs and it was then that she began to learn the details. We acquired two names of his associates in the Middle East and these were passed to the West in the summer.'

'Yes, those names are what convinced them that your information was good.'

She nodded. 'The rest we have deduced by the telexes and the movements of the professor.' She avoided Misha's name.

'You're sure that the authorities are involved?'

'Yes, but they keep their distance from the planning, which is why the Arab is not guarded as closely as he should be. Everything goes through the professor. That's the weak point. We know when the professor comes to Leipzig, when he goes to the villa, when he travels abroad to Yemen or Libya or Sudan. We know about his money, which all comes from the Party.'

'Is the Arab here now?'

'He comes next week, or the week after. We're not sure.'

'And he'll stay at the villa?'

'Maybe. There are other places he uses. We won't know until he's here.'

They had skirted the centre of town and now reached the park. Some children were trying to get a kite airborne and one or two couples sat on the grass. Rosenharte noticed that a number of the trees had died from pollution. It was the same everywhere, but in Leipzig the lignite smoke that was responsible seemed even worse that day. A slight taste of sulphur hadn't left his mouth since he stepped off the train.

'We all cough from November to the spring here,' Ulrike said when he mentioned it to her. 'In winter many people have respiratory problems. Is it as bad in Dresden?'

'Nothing like this,' he said. They had stopped at a path. She turned to face him. 'Take me in an embrace and look over my shoulder.' Rosenharte held her lightly by the waist and shoulder. 'There is a large, dark green building on the far side of the park,' she said to his right ear. 'Next to that is the villa, but you can only see a little of it because of the high fence.'

'I see,' he said, thinking that it would be entirely feasible for someone to remove Abu Jamal at night. He let her go, after looking down at her face and noticing that her skin was almost translucent.

'There's something I don't understand,' he said. 'Why didn't you give all this information to the British woman who was here in the summer? Why wait?'

'It was too dangerous for her to take this out. And anyway it wasn't until the Arab's medical operation in August that we had hard evidence of the plans and dates for these attacks.'

'Why do you think I stand any better chance of getting this out?' She looked at him. 'You can handle this. I know it.'

'Did you know they were going to send me? Did you choose me?'

'You were a candidate. We knew you travelled on the train with the professor because he complained about seeing you one morning to his secretary. He said that you were just the kind of unproductive member of the intelligentsia that he despised.'

'But you suggested me to the British. They wouldn't have thought of me otherwise.'

'Among other people, yes.'

'What made you think of me?'

'We knew you came here quite often to teach your classes and lecture. You have a pretext for being here. You seemed perfect.'

Rosenharte didn't buy any of this, but decided not to press it. He was shooting the rapids, he thought, and it was crazy to question the only other person with a paddle. 'What other information can I take to them?'

'That's all. The likely timing for the actions in Jordan and Egypt are surely enough for you.' They had turned and were moving out of the park. She was looking down at the path ahead of them. 'You understand we're bound together now,' she said. 'We're dependent on each other in a way that's dangerous for us both. If you are caught, you will tell them in the end. So will I. We know that. You have to be very careful.'

She glanced up, real fear in her eyes. He had made much the same speech in Trieste to Annalise's stand-in.

'There's one other thing I don't understand,' he said. 'Why don't you leave? If you took this information out yourself they'd give you a place to live and a job.'

'Leave!' She hissed the word. 'I will not leave. That's the problem at my church: the tensions between those who want the freedom to go to the West and those who want to stay and build a country where people can speak freely and meet without thinking there's an informer in the room. They're the true democrats. The others just want a new car and a better standard of living. I want to rid the GDR of these stinking old men who steal everything from us and give us platitudes about sacrifice in return.'

'If you go on like that, you *will* be arrested.'

'The time has come when everyone has to take risks, Rudolf – Rudi. You know that.'

'But if we're going to work together on this thing, I have to know you're not going to put yourself in an exposed position.'

'We're already exposed. We've reached the stage when it's no longer enough for an intellectual like you to make clever points that you hope one group of people will understand while the others don't. We have to occupy the streets and take possession of our city.'

'Well that's for sure,' he said, looking round him. They had reached a very run-down quarter where the cobblestones were loose in the road and the plaster had dropped from the nineteenth-century façades on both sides of the street. Drains had become detached and were ruptured. Bands of damp had spread three or four feet on either side of them and moss flourished in the cracks. Further down the street, one of the houses had collapsed and the two neighbouring properties were hopefully shored up with a few poles of scaffolding.

'Ulrike.' It was the first time he had used her name. 'I want you to listen to me. You saw the number of police we passed on the way here.

They will never let you simply take the state from them. You saw what happened in China. You read reports of Politburo members making threats about repeating Tiananmen Square in Germany. They will do it here, I promise you. You must leave. I can't, but you can.'

'We have to take risks. We will fight violence with non-violence. They can't massacre us in the middle of Europe. We're not living under Adolf Hitler.'

He shook his head. 'It's a pity we can't take a proper walk out in the country,' he said. 'Somewhere clean and without pollution.'

She frowned, then stopped in her tracks and turned to face him. 'We're both old enough to know that you want two things – to sleep with me and for me to fall in love with you – the double triumph.'

He grinned. 'I mentioned a walk. That was all.'

She returned his gaze, her eyes shining with defiance. 'You do understand that it's not going to be possible?'

'I wasn't thinking of that. I was—'

'I have watched you in those lectures. You want people to love that elegant intellect of yours, your passion for art, your eloquence, the sense that you're above it all. You need to seduce people.'

'My lightness of being,' he said, trying to humour her.

'No, it's much more dangerous than that.'

He smiled at her mischievously. 'So you won't be the axe to my frozen sea?'

She shook her head and pointed to a chimney that was leaking a trail of heavy smoke across the city. 'I'd rather work in that factory over there or in the gravel pits outside the city. I'd rather be detained by the Stasi for a night's questioning than lose my freedom to you.'

'Don't be so extreme. More than you can imagine depends on *both* of us remaining free.'

She gave him a look of surprise, letting him know that she hadn't expected his reaction. 'Don't worry. Keep your cool and we shall both get through this.'

'I will keep my cool, as you put it, but it's not just us. My brother and his family are involved. I have a lot to lose.'

She nodded.

'How will I get in touch with you?' he asked.

'By the same means as before, but don't go to the Nikolaikirche. Sign the book at the Thomaskirche, leave any postcard at the cafe, or one wedged between those two pilasters. Then wait outside the Thomaskirche. I will find you.'

He gave her the address in Dresden, but left out the apartment number. 'If you want to contact me, send a postcard to Lotha Frankel. Frankel used to live in my apartment. Sign it *Ruth* if you're in trouble, *Sarah* if you need me to come to Leipzig. I will see it without it being delivered to my apartment.'

'I'll see you then,' she said, turning away.

'Be careful.'

'I will. Now go, before you make yourself conspicuous.' She set off down the street that would take her to the centre of town. Rosenharte watched her go. About fifty yards down the road she suddenly turned and smiled at him.

No, he said to himself firmly, he would not be swayed from his task of getting Konrad and Else and the boys out of the country. That was all that mattered.

ELEVEN

Berlin

He made his way to the station, unable to decide about Kafka. She certainly wasn't what he'd been expecting, but the more important thing was that her story didn't hang straight at all. No more than a handful of senior officers would be allowed to know that the GDR sponsored terrorism. It was simply unbelievable that this provincial university worker had acquired such significant knowledge from a friend.

But what did it matter to him? He'd made contact with Kafka, and she had coughed some very startling information. That was all he needed for the British. When he told them that there would be more information, and that they would have the precise location for Abu Jamal in a couple of weeks' time, they'd have to start moving on Konrad and Else.

He crossed Dresdnerstrasse and came to a man standing by a suitcase of trinkets for sale: a watch with Karl Marx on the face, a pair of men's shoes, a small communion bell, a flag holder and an empty photograph frame. Rosenharte nodded to him, lifted his shoulders and opened his hands, as though to say he was broke too. He moved on towards Karl-Marx-Platz. As he turned to the traffic in order to cross the road he caught sight of a man about fifty yards away who had been looking at him, but who now jerked his interest in the opposite direction. He was a big, rangy fellow in a checked shirt of orange and green and tight stone-washed jeans, all of which rendered him useless as a surveillance officer. This was certainly no Stasi footpad intent on merging into the general drabness of Leipzig. Rosenharte knew it must be the same character who had turned up at the gallery and who had watched him with Ulrike at the cafe. He wondered whether he had followed them to the park, and if so whether he had drawn any conclusions about their visit. Now the man was looking at him directly and seemed to signal that he wanted to talk. Rosenharte was curious, but decided he wanted nothing to do with him and quickened his pace. The man broke into an effortless jog to keep in touch and waved a couple of times. Rosenharte thought he heard him call out. In very little time they reached the square where the Volkspolizei were mustered in their thousands. A good number of Stasi were hanging around in civilian dress, some with side arms in the back of their waistbands, others with radios and cameras. As he walked along the east side of the square towards the station, he heard a voice shout his name.

It was Colonel Biermeier, who had burst from the mêlée of police and was pursuing him with four plainclothes Stasi officers. 'Stop, Rosenharte. Stop now!'

He turned round.

'Where are you going?' demanded Biermeier. 'Where have you been?'

'I'm late for the train,' he said.

'The train to Dresden does not leave until five forty-five. You have thirty minutes. Why are you hurrying?'

Rosenharte looked over Biermeier's shoulder; the lanky pursuer had vanished. 'I'm a nervous traveller.'

'You didn't answer my question. Where have you been?'

'For a walk in the park. I needed to calm down after my lecture.'

'Yes, I heard about that. You seem to have offended the locals.' Biermeier folded his jacket over his arm and wiped his brow. 'Why did you evade your protective surveillance in Dresden?'

'Protective surveillance! Is that what you call it? I simply left my apartment early this morning. I can't help it if your men were asleep. That wasn't my fault.'

'You should have indicated to them that you were leaving.'

Rosenharte shook his head in disbelief. A young man with a bad case of acne, who had been walking towards the line of police, suddenly produced a white sheet from under his denim jacket and held it between outstretched arms. On it was the slogan *Freiheit für die Gefangenen 12/9* – Freedom for the prisoners of 12 September. For several seconds, the youth marched along the line of police in a comic goosestep. No one moved until Biermeier bellowed, 'Detain that man!' The sheet was wrenched from his hands and he was hustled into the back of a military vehicle with a canvas top. At this point he turned and pulled down his jeans to show part of the word *Freiheit* written across his backside.

Biermeier bellowed, 'Cover that man, you idiots!' and then turned to Rosenharte, who did not bother to suppress his amusement.

'Now you've found me, can I go back to Dresden?' he asked.

Biermeier shook his head. 'No, you're going to Berlin.'

'Why?'

'It's enough to know that we have need of you there.' He looked at his watch. 'We'll take the train; it will be quicker.'

Forty-five minutes later they were on the Berlin train. Biermeier sat across the aisle from Rosenharte, trying to ignore him.

'You should take some time off, Colonel,' said Rosenharte

good-naturedly. 'You look stressed. Find yourself a nice young mistress. Have a few drinks. Live a little.'

'I don't drink.'

'But you make love, don't you? Or is that forbidden under article one thousand and two of the Ministry's code?'

Biermeier did not answer.

'Biermeier – a brewer who doesn't drink. It's odd how inappropriate some names are and the journeys they make. Do you know the story of Joachim Neander?'

'No, and nor do I want to.'

'Joachim Neander was a pastor in the seventeenth century who was banned by the church because he refused to celebrate communion.'

'What's a damned priest to me?'

'Nothing, I imagine. But the story is interesting. Joachim retired to the country, grew his vegetables, made love to his dear wife and walked in the valley near his house. The people loved him so much that when he died they named the valley after him – Neanderthal. A hundred or so years later some workmen were mining a limestone cave and came across some very strange remains indeed – half human, half ape.'

'The priest?'

'No, the bones turned out to belong to an entirely unknown human species and, naturally, they were given the name Neanderthal. And so Pastor Joachim's name lives on.'

'Is that what you spend your time learning in your gallery? Useless information that is no good to anybody?'

'All information is useful. Isn't that what General Schwarzmeer says: everything eventually finds its use?'

Biermeier examined him for a moment. Rosenharte noticed that the whites of his eyes were tinted yellow.

'You're an arrogant bastard, Rosenharte. So damned sure of yourself on everything, aren't you? Well, they won't be hearing from you in Leipzig again. You've blown that one.'

Rosenharte shook his head. 'Whatever you have heard was taken out of context. The man wanted to be offended; he came for that purpose. Besides, I need to make contacts with the church community there as agreed with our friend in Trieste. So I must return whether they want to hear my lectures or not.'

They said nothing more for the next hour or so but as night fell and the train dragged itself north to Berlin, then through Alders Hof and Karlshorst – the bleak suburb where the KGB maintained its headquarters – Rosenharte decided to make things plain to Biermeier. He leaned across to him and said, 'I won't cooperate until I have a deal.'

Biermeier shook his head contemptuously. 'If you know what's good for you, you won't say that again. You have no idea how bad they can make your life.'

'Nevertheless, I want one.'

At the Ostbahnhof they were met by three cars, one of which contained a trim man in his early forties who introduced himself as Colonel Zank from HA II, which Rosenharte recalled was the main department for counter intelligence. Zank took them to the Interhotel where they ate tasteless white fish in an empty dining room. Zank watched them with a bloodless smile. Then Rosenharte began to recognize something of this man's stillness and reserve and he understood that the shadow that had observed him as he was interviewed by the archivists in the forest hideaway had moved into the world of substance.

They drove to Karl-Marx-Allee, then headed east to the Lichtenberg district where they turned left on Mollendorf. As Rosenharte knew well, the short and unremarkable Normannenstrasse was the first right. It was nearly fifteen years since he had been there, but apart from the increased number of security cameras and one or two new apartment blocks, no doubt occupied by Stasi families, little had changed. They passed the stadium, the home of the minister's personal football team, Dynamo, and he recalled a story about the referee who awarded one too many decisions against Erich Mielke's Stasi team and was threatened with jail. They turned sharp right and reached a barrier. A camera to their right swivelled in their direction. And here he had to clasp his knees to stop his hands shaking. He would get through this for Konnie's sake. That was his mission – his life's mission – and if he held on to that thought, he'd handle everything well.

The guards took their time checking each man's credentials, then waved the cars through to the main entrance, hidden from the courtyard by a canopy and a screen of ugly concrete lattice work. One or two lights were on in the large courtyard. The car carrying Rosenharte pulled up just beyond the covered area. He got out and looked up at the seven-storey building that contained the minister's suite of offices. Most of the lights were on.

The escort peeled off and just one other man, apart from Biermeier and Zank, entered the building with Rosenharte. Zank nodded to the desk on the right and gestured to a paternoster lift, indicating that Biermeier should go first, followed by Rosenharte. They stepped off the moving platforms at the fourth floor and were shown to a characterless antechamber without windows.

And there they waited.

Zank went off and came back several times, but said nothing. Biermeier seemed to enter a deep official torpor. The place was slightly overheated and there was a staleness to the air that was so strong that Rosenharte was sure it wouldn't be shifted if the windows were opened for a month. When eventually Zank returned for the fourth or fifth time and summoned Biermeier and Rosenharte into a dark passage, he noticed the curious odour intensify. It was as if he was moving through a gassy medium of suspicion and terror that had saturated everything in the building. They passed through an office with three secretaries and came to a door, which Zank eased open. On entering, Rosenharte saw a long, panelled room with a conference table on the right and a seating area, consisting of four armchairs upholstered in blue, on the left. At the far end, there was an island of red carpet on the parquet floor. At the centre of this stood two upright chairs, a large desk and a blue armchair.

From the way Zank and Biermeier were touching their tie knots and smoothing their hair in the corridor, Rosenharte had known they were about to enter Mielke's presence.

They came to a halt halfway along the conference table, but it was only after a few seconds that he saw a diminutive figure in uniform standing by the window, holding the net curtains apart – a little old man staring into the night. He threw a testy look in their direction and then returned to whatever was absorbing him outside. They waited. No one spoke. Rosenharte stared at the man who had run the Stasi for thirty years, causing untold misery to untold numbers. The monster was hardly impressive, and for a fleeting and foolhardy moment all Rosenharte could think of was the Wizard of Oz.

Then he remembered Konrad.

Zank spoke. 'This is Rosenharte, Minister.'

'I know it's Rosenharte. What do you take me for?' He moved away from the window and went behind his desk with short, quick steps, his arms held slightly in front of him. He shuffled some papers together and looked up at them. 'Do you expect me to shout? Come over here.'

They moved forward into a pool of light at the edge of the carpet where the minister surveyed them disagreeably.

'Where's Schwarzmeer? He was told to be here.'

'I believe he is on his way,' said Zank diplomatically.

'That's not good enough. I don't have time for delays.'

Rosenharte took in the man in detail: the snaggled front teeth in his lower jaw, a permanently down-turned mouth, pointed, protruding ears, bristling grey hair and eyes that seethed with offence and hatred. Every kind of medal ribbon was stitched to the breast of his summer uniform, which was tailored from a vulgar, shiny material, and various decorations had been plastered to its front, almost randomly, like labels on a parcel. Rosenharte assumed he had been attending a formal function, although there was no sense that he had been mellowed by drink or good conversation. It was well known, even when Rosenharte briefly served the MfS, that he neither smoked nor drank, and that his conversation did not extend beyond the affairs of state, sport and hunting.

Rosenharte was an inch or two taller than Biermeier and Zank and this worried him because the minister was under five foot five. He sank a little into himself and looked ahead, the precise opposite of the minister's habitual struggle against the stoop of old age. No one said anything. On the desk was a death mask of Lenin in a Perspex case, to the right a shredder, an ordinary black telephone and a switchboard with a white handset that connected the minister with other members of the Politburo. Immediately behind the desk were two panelled doors, which Rosenharte assumed hid a safe because the doors stopped four inches from the floor.

The minister looked up. 'In Leipzig, what are they doing, Biermeier?'

'Everything appears to be under control, Minister. It looks like they have put the lid on these demonstrations for good. But we must remain vigilant, of course.'

Mielke shook his head and shot him a derisive look.

'They are traitors. They should be locked up. Shot, if necessary. It's the only language these people understand. There were five thousand of them on the streets tonight in Leipzig. They bring disgrace to the GDR and undermine the efforts of all loyal socialists. What do you say about these people, Rosenharte? Are they your people? Are you a member of the hostile forces ranged against the socialist state?'

'No, Minister.'

'But it's people like you, isn't it? People who don't know what hard work is. People who want to read books all day while the state provides for them.'

He was picking a fight. Rosenharte wasn't going to rise to the bait. 'I think the important thing to realize, Minister, is that the demonstrators are not from one group. There are a number of minority interests that have coalesced to cause this trouble.'

'How do you know so much about it?'

Biermeier fidgeted beside him, as though he was going to have to answer for what Rosenharte was saying.

'I don't know much. I simply observe that there is very little homogeneity among the demonstrators. They all seem to want different things.'

The little goblin clapped his hands. 'Exactly right. There, you see! I have to go to an outsider to tell me these things. Every type of anti-social element is using this excuse to cause trouble on the fortieth anniversary of the GDR, knowing that the world's attention will be focused on us. They're nothing but opportunists and they should be shot like vermin.'

'Quite so,' said Zank.

'But in the summary of all the reports I've received this evening, there is no analysis that underlines this lack of an overall ideology among the demonstrators.' He banged his desk with a small clenched fist. 'That is our opportunity, comrades: to drive a wedge between these groups, compel them to tear each other apart. Zank, I want your proposals on a strategy.'

'Certainly. I think it is an exceptional insight of yours.'

Biermeier risked an incredulous glance in Zank's direction.

'Have you got anything to add, Colonel Biermeier?'

'This is not my area, Minister, but I think there's every reason to believe that the demonstrators have been inspired, and in some cases supported, by capitalist interests in the West.'

'Exactly,' said the minister. 'I want a breakdown of all the different factions: where they get their money from, their links to the West, the names and backgrounds of the hardcore. Colonel Biermeier, give everything you have on this to Zank here. This paper has top priority.' He looked at a calendar on his desk. 'Today is Monday twenty-fifth September. I want it on my desk by early morning Wednesday. We need to implement these political-operational tasks by next week, when we will show them what we are made of. I want a list of every active dissident in the country, and an analysis of where all these people are coming from.'

'Of course, Minister,' said Zank.

'We have a fight on our hands. It's going to get worse before it gets better. But that is the struggle of socialism and as good Chekists we will do everything that is necessary to maintain order and security. We must put the whole strength of this service to overcoming the political-moral weakness that threatens our socialist state. We *will* prevail. We *must* prevail, comrades.' Spittle had burst from his mouth as he spoke, and each emphasis was accompanied by a chopping motion. Rosenharte was transfixed by the energy of the man's hatred. Could this creature ever have been a babe in arms, a child running through the grass?

They heard a door open softly behind them. 'Where have you been?' the minister shouted.

Schwarzmeer greeted him formally but without apology, then moved to the other side of the desk so that he could whisper to the minister. Rosenharte caught the words 'briefing for the general secretary . . . from hospital'. Zank looked at Rosenharte and silently shook his head to indicate that he should forget what he had just heard. Rosenharte could not forget. He had read nothing in the papers about Erich Honecker being ill. Honecker ill: that was news.

As he watched the two men, he wondered at their relationship. The minister was a vulgarian through and through, a cunning, crude, brutal man who saw no percentage in hiding his nature. Schwarzmeer, on the other hand, possessed a kind of sophistication, or at least the desire to appear other than he was. Yet despite the difference it was clear that they understood each other. As Schwarzmeer finished what he was saying, Mielke looked up into his deputy's face, nodded vigorously and said 'good' several times.

Then he gestured to the conference table behind them, and told them all to sit down. He took the chair at the end, Schwarzmeer sat to his right, Zank to his left. When Rosenharte sat down next to Biermeier to face the windows, he was told to move two places so that the minister could see him. He placed both hands on the table, splayed his fingers on the cool, oak veneer, then brought them together.

Mielke looked at him. 'So, Dr Rosenharte, we must decide whether we believe you, or whether to throw you in jail with your brother. That is simply the task before us tonight. You have failed our service once. We will not let that happen again.'

Rosenharte knew that he had to take the initiative. 'Minister, I have said nothing that can be believed or disbelieved. As General Schwarzmeer will tell you, I never wanted anything to do with this operation because I didn't want to be held responsible for things outside my control.' He saw a flicker of worry pass through Biermeier's eyes. 'But the general has persuaded me that this is my duty and I am therefore happy to serve as a tool, as an implement of your policy. But, Minister, I cannot answer for the truth of what has been passed to us by Annalise Schering. I don't know whether she is genuine in her desire to help the state, or is working against us.'

'That's a clever answer,' said Mielke. 'But it's not a convincing one.'

'I can't give any other. I cannot vouch for her motives.'

'You are to be sent to the West to make contact with her again and receive more material. But before you leave, I want to know more about you.'

'But I have received no word from her.'

He dismissed this with a wave of the hand. 'She has made contact, but I suspect you knew that would happen. You probably even knew the date.'

Rosenharte shook his head. 'No, Minister. I knew nothing.'

'My view, Rosenharte, is that you're a gifted wastrel. I find no evidence of your commitment to the state in your files. You are a man who has allowed his weaknesses for alcohol, smoking and women to rule his life. You once had a chance to serve us and you screwed up on the job. As I understand it Schering herself suggested you be replaced.'

'I try my—'

'You have never shown a willingness to sacrifice your pleasure or convenience to the interests of those around you. You are the son of an SS general who has inherited a degenerate and selfish character. Isn't that true? You failed the service because of this congenital weakness.'

Rosenharte said nothing.

Zank moved, but did not take his eyes from Mielke. 'The minister is concerned by something which we in Main Department Two have brought to his attention,' he said. 'The first is the man who died in Trieste. He was a Pole named Grycko. We believe that he was working for Western intelligence and was about to make contact with you.'

Rosenharte let his hands move for the first time since they had sat down. He knew the Stasi hadn't got the first idea who Grycko was, or what he wanted. 'I can honestly say that I have no knowledge of this man. He said nothing that meant anything to me before he died. I had never seen him before in my life. The whole thing was a mystery to me.'

'We believe he may have passed something to you,' said Zank.

Rosenharte shook his head solemnly. 'Colonel, you only have to ask yourself, what could he possibly want to pass to me? As someone said, I am an obscure art historian. What would be the purpose in contacting me? I have nothing. I know that; you know that. It doesn't matter if you disapprove of the way I've led my life – believe me, I have my own regrets. And, well, it doesn't even matter whether you trust me, because neither my character nor my actions are at issue here. It's whether you believe that what you're getting from Annalise Schering is true. That's all that matters to you. Speaking for myself, I wouldn't trust something that comes to you so easily. But that's just my suspicious nature.'

To his surprise, the minister nodded. 'We'll go ahead with the plan tomorrow. See to it that I'm kept informed throughout.' He shifted with a little wiggle in his chair. 'If you're playing a game with us, Rosenharte, you will pay for it with your life. Understand that.'

The room seemed to have got darker, the atmosphere closer. It occurred to Rosenharte that the smell, which seemed not to affect the others at all, came from a gradual seepage of the little man's essence – a pungent concentrate of evil.

The others began to move, but Rosenharte remained seated, looking ahead of him at the curtains. Now. He had to say it now.

'You want something?' said the minister.

'You expect me to retrieve more material from the woman. Is that right?'

'Naturally,' said Schwarzmeer brusquely. 'You heard what the minister said.'

'If you want me to go to the West, I have conditions.' He turned his head to face the terrifying old man squarely. 'I want Else and the two boys returned to their home immediately. And I want to see my brother.'

The minister looked at him as though he was mad. Then he waved his hand again and got up. 'You deal with it, Schwarzmeer. This is an operational detail.' With this, he moved from the conference table and walked to a door in the corner of the room and disappeared.

They took Rosenharte to another, less well-furnished room in the labyrinth of Normannenstrasse where they had to open windows because of the heat from the radiators.

The three officers sat opposite him with Schwarzmeer in the middle.

Rosenharte wasn't going to wait for them to speak. 'If you want this material, you must release Konrad and undertake to allow him to regain his health in peace. That is what I want in return.'

Schwarzmeer's face resembled a clay mask in the half-light of the room. The bags under his eyes seemed to have filled. 'You do not come here and make deals, Rosenharte.'

'Well, that's what I am doing. In Trieste I was authorized by Annalise to use her as a bargaining position. I told her that my brother was in your prison. I told her the state he was in when he came out last time.'

'We can make you do what we want,' said Schwarzmeer. 'You *will* go and you *will* return with the intelligence. And that is all there is to it.'

'No,' said Rosenharte quietly. 'I am prepared to suffer anything. Unless I have what I want, I will not go. And if I don't go, you won't have what you want. She will not help you without me.'

Schwarzmeer looked at Zank.

'These difficulties you face now with demonstrations,' Rosenharte continued, 'are nothing compared to the perils represented by the technical advances in the West. You will crush the people on the street eventually, but then you still have the problem of the West's technical superiority. They progress by leaps and bounds every month. I have an idea what Annalise's material means to you, because she told me how important it was.' He paused. 'Besides, what's the point of keeping Konrad and Else in jail? They're harmless people. Konrad is a shadow of himself; Else is a simple, loving mother.' He stopped for a beat or two. 'This is about humanity; and it's about showing good faith to a woman in the West who appears to be risking everything in the cause of technological parity.'

'So what exactly do you want?' asked Zank.

'Before I leave, I want half an hour with Konrad in private. I will tell him that he is to be released, because that's what you are going to do. When I'm in West Berlin, I'll make a call to the neighbour of my brother at six in the evening – Else does not have a phone. I will bring the material back with me only if she answers and tells me that she and the two boys are home.'

Schwarzmeer moved to protest.

Rosenharte put up a hand. 'Then I shall request a second collection from Annalise in two weeks,' he continued. 'By that time, Konrad must be with Else and receiving medical and dental care. During the period before and after my second visit to the West, my brother's family will be left in peace, unmolested by surveillance or any form of harassment. They are to be treated with respect.'

Schwarzmeer glanced at Zank again. This interested Rosenharte because Schwarzmeer was the ranking officer and the HVA carried far more prestige than Main Department II in the ministry. Maybe Zank was more than he said. Maybe Zank was running things.

'And if there are problems with the material,' said Schwarzmeer, 'then we revert to the status quo as of tonight.'

'There won't be.' It had been almost as though someone else was speaking for the last twenty minutes. But now he heard his voice falter and he coughed to cover it. Zank's anaemic features twitched with understanding.

Nothing more was said. Rosenharte was taken to another part of the building and placed in a holding cell, which was little more than the end of a passage fitted with bars. A crude iron bed was swung to the horizontal position by a lever outside the cell. All except one light was switched off. A man coughed down the corridor. He sat down on the bed and, to the embarrassment of his rational self, prayed to Ulrike's God.

PART TWO

TWELVE

The West

Harland poured a second sachet of sugar into his coffee and looked round at the surge of passengers filling the departure lounge bar at Tempelhof airport. It was the third trip he'd made that day from the SIS offices at the Olympic stadium to Tempelhof. This time he met Alan Griswald in the bar.

'What time's her flight?' asked Griswald, looking down with admiration at his new mobile phone.

'There's a half-hour delay. She should land in twenty minutes – if she's on it.'

'How's she doing?' asked Griswald. He began to buff the display of the phone with his sleeve.

'Well, I think. London's impressed. The worry now is how long her story will last under Schwarzmeer's scrutiny. They're being very thorough indeed.' Griswald gazed at the arrivals board as Harland told him how the Stasi's inquiry had taken them to western Canada – Vancouver and Sylvan Lake, a town south of Edmonton, Alberta – where Annalise was supposed to have lived with her husband Raymond Knox before their divorce. The Canadian Security Intelligence Service were being more than helpful, shoring up parts of the hastily assembled background that looked likely to collapse, and improvising a set of deeds to a property north of Sylvan Lake, bank accounts, life insurance policies and share deals in her married name of Knox.

The Canadian end of the story appeared to be holding up for the moment, but in Brussels the Stasi's operation to track and watch NATO's new employee was so extensive that SIS had to call on help from the CIA and from the French, West German and Belgian intelligence services. Outside the NATO building, Harland's worry was that the East Germans would short-circuit the process by kidnapping Jessie for interrogation behind the Iron Curtain. SIS had to ensure that this didn't happen, but at the same time make certain their protection was discreet as hell. Inside NATO there was every possibility that East German agents, who had been planted by the Stasi, or turned while working there, would unearth discrepancies that gave the game away. Again, records were adjusted and people who had known Annalise Schering in her previous role at NATO were squared.

Harland confessed that the operation had sprawled in a way that he simply hadn't envisaged. At SIS headquarters in Century House it was openly said to be taking up too much money when the clear priority of the moment was Gorbachev's visit to the GDR and the need to acquire intelligence about the Soviet Union's intentions in the event of widescale upheaval in the East.

Griswald's response to this was to blow out his cheeks and lift his shoulders. 'Yeah, well, we all have that problem. Believe me, every jackass at Langley thinks he knows better than I do what I should be doing in Berlin. Don't worry, Bobby. I have a real good feeling about this operation of yours.' He looked up at the board again. 'You're certain she's coming?'

'Yep. Talked to her yesterday. We're assuming the letter was intercepted and they will act on its instructions.'

'You know, they aren't total jerks, Bobby. And Rosenharte, well, he's not one of your natural good guys. Remind me why you didn't insert someone more reliable than Rosenharte in Leipzig and forget this rigmarole with Annalise. It makes the whole operation so goddamn complex.'

'This way we get the chance to feed them information from an impeccable source that's going to cause them years, well, at least months, of barking up the wrong tree.' He stopped and revolved his spoon in the sugar at the bottom of the coffee cup. 'It's too good an opportunity to pass by, Al. Besides, Kafka chose him. Rosenharte was the only person Kafka would work with. You know I had to do it this way.'

'Does that bother you?'

'Everything bothers me.'

'You don't worry that we're being used?'

Harland thought for a moment. 'Could be, but all I know is the first material proved damned helpful. On that basis I am happy to proceed. Are your people getting hot under the collar?'

'No, they just raised the usual issues. They're cool for the moment.'

They waited a further twenty minutes. Flights from Dusseldorf, Cologne and Brussels all landed without a sign of Jessie.

'Doesn't look like she's coming,' Griswald said.

'Of course she's coming,' said Harland. 'She's got to make it look as though she's taking precautions to cover her movements from NATO.'

Griswald sighed again. 'You know what? I'm gonna go to the Blue Fish and have some goulash. It's quarter of nine already. Why don't you meet me there later?'

'Hold on!' said Harland. 'Look, it's her.'

Jessie was marching along a glass-covered walkway carrying a shoulder bag.

'Where the fuck's she been? Nothing's landed in the last half-hour.'

'Sitting it out in the Ladies, I imagine, and so disguising which flight she came in on. She did exactly the right thing. She's a bloody good operator, Al.' Harland spoke into a radio mike inside his coat. 'Macy, you ready? She's here. Cuth, did you get that?' He pressed the earpiece home, listened and turned to Griswald.

'Have they seen any familiar faces?' asked Griswald.

'They're not sure,' replied Harland. 'Let's move.'

They went down to the main arrivals hall and waited at a discreet distance from customs fifty yards apart, Griswald using his new phone rather ostentatiously. It was only a few minutes before Jessie walked out of customs and searched for signs for the taxi rank. She was wearing a well-cut, dark-blue business suit that was perhaps a little conservative for Annalise Schering's taste but was in keeping with someone who wanted to go unnoticed. She had walked a few paces from the barrier when Harland heard the Bird's voice. 'Bobby, there're a couple of bogies moving in from your left. One's in a light-grey suit, the other a leather jacket.'

Before he had time to reply he saw another two men come in through a revolving door and look in Jessie's direction.

She kept on towards the exit for buses and taxis without seeming to notice the men.

'They're going to take her when she gets outside,' Harp whispered in the radio. 'Tudor says two of them have just left a blue Merc. Another is still at the wheel.'

Harland swore. He was still far enough away to see the situation as a whole. If Jessie left the building she could be bundled into a car without difficulty and be carried over the border within the hour. There was nothing for it but to move. 'We're going to stop them. The whole bloody thing's blown. Okay, go!'

At this, the Bird appeared from a queue at the hotel information desk and started towards Jessie. Macy Harp walked from the entrance to a washroom, while Tudor Williams moved rapidly into position behind the two men who had just entered the terminal building.

Jessie pushed on apparently oblivious, yet seemed drawn to Griswald's bulk. Griswald took the hint and swivelled round to face her. He was still on the phone, but all his body language indicated that he wanted to end the call and approach the woman that he had just noticed moving in his direction. Not for the first time, Harland briefly noted his friend's acting skills. Griswald dropped his newspaper, fumbled with the phone then opened his arms.

'Wait.' Harland spat out the word and, without missing a beat, the Bird, Macy Harp and Tudor Williams dispersed, two of them losing themselves in a tour group that had just exited customs, the members of which were all swapping telephone numbers and saying their goodbyes.

'Hey there,' Griswald cried. He had lowered the phone and was simulating disbelief and pleasure. 'For Chrissake, what are you doing here? Jesus, Annalise. I'll be damned.'

Jessie looked taken aback, but smiled bravely and approached to offer him her hand. Griswald bent down and planted a kiss on both her cheeks. 'Jesus, I thought you were living in Canada, sweetheart. What the hell brings you to Berlin? You'll have dinner with me. Promise.'

These were the last words that Harland heard before he too plunged into the crowd and started calling out, 'Car for Neumann, car for Herr Neumann.' He reached the other side of the mêlée and turned to see the man in the grey suit standing about twenty feet from Griswald. The young tough in the leather jacket had walked over to the car hire desk and was watching Griswald and Jessie with open interest. The other two men had disappeared.

He turned and spoke into the microphone. 'Tell me what you see.'

'I'm outside,' said the Bird. 'They've definitely got a team here, but they're not going to try anything while she's talking to Alan. Tudor's gone to get one of the cars in case we need to pursue.'

'Tudor,' hissed Harland, 'make sure you pick up the black Merc and park it right outside entrance C. Then go in and make as though you're Griswald's driver. Leave the rest to him. Now get a bloody move on. Cuth, stick by their car in case anything goes wrong. You're responsible for her safety. Do anything you need to protect her.' Harland slunk away, briefly registering that the Stasi's effort to mount one of the first abductions in Berlin for many years meant that while they had doubts about Annalise's story, they were still genuinely interested in what she might have. If it had all been a put-up job, as Griswald suggested, they wouldn't be risking a snatch in the view of Tempelhof's new CCTV system.

By now Griswald had put an arm round Jessie and was steering her gently towards the exit. He couldn't know that Tudor would be outside when he got there, but at least he and Jessie were working a good double act. Even from where Harland stood, he could see she was protesting and at one stage pulled the bag from Griswald's chivalrous grasp. He lifted his lapel and spoke. 'Everyone except Tudor back off. Macy and Cuth, you get the other car and follow Tudor. He'll drive to the Avalon Hotel on Emser Strasse. Macy, find a phone and book a room for two nights in the name of Annalise Schering. Tell Markus on the front desk that we won't be using the room and that I will sort things out later. We want them to see her going to the hotel and having a drink with Griswald. Convey all this to Griswald, Tudor.'

'Then what?' This came from Macy Harp.

'We're going to have to improvise things from the Avalon, but

I'm working on the assumption that they're here because they really are interested. That means the betting is on Rosenharte coming over. We're just going to have to keep her out of their clutches until then.'

'But what then?' Macy Harp again. 'They're not going to give up tomorrow just because Rosenharte is in the West. In fact the likelihood is that they'll try harder.'

'Later, Macy. We'll cross that bridge when—' He stopped. Griswald had come to a halt at exit C and was gesturing outside. Jessie shook her head. Harland thought they were both overdoing it a bit, and for one moment it looked as though the East Germans were going to intervene, but Tudor came through the door and spoke to Griswald.

'What the hell are they doing?' asked the Bird, who could see everything from the car.

'Quiet! I'm trying to listen to Tudor's mike,' said Harland. He heard Griswald say, 'Well, my car's outside, Annalise. At least let me give you a ride to the hotel. Maybe we can have a drink at the Avalon – it's my favourite bar in Berlin.'

She replied: 'We'll have a drink, then I really must have an early night.' She allowed Tudor to take her bag and was ushered through the door by Griswald. It was then that Harland understood. Griswald was playing himself, an inquisitive CIA officer who had happened upon someone working at NATO with no obvious reason to be in Berlin. He was giving Jessie the once over and in so doing, providing her a story for the following day. And Jessie, being no slouch in these matters, had grasped the tactic immediately and was responding with a combination of reluctance and guilty compliance that the Stasi could not mistake.

This might just work, thought Harland.

*

173

In the early hours of Tuesday 26 September, as Rosenharte lay on the narrow iron bed, one leg on the cell floor, an arm folded over his eyes against the light, it occurred to him that the Stasi headquarters possessed a kind of organic life of its own. The walls sweated condensation; the smell he'd found so unsettling in the minister's suite was just as present on the lower floors although it included new elements which he approximated to disinfectant and decay; and there was a queer noise – a distant clicking followed by a long sigh, which suggested an enormous ventilator keeping the place filled with just the amount of oxygen necessary to sustain life. In his half-dreaming state, he remembered Konrad talking about the earth's largest living organism, a giant underground fungus, which had spread over hundreds of years through a forest in Michigan. Konrad had gone on and on about it, explaining that the DNA of the fungus taken from one end of the forest was exactly the same as at the other end, which proved that it was the same organism. Trees had lived and died, but the fungus continued silently occupying the forest inch by inch, either as a parasite or saprophyte – he wasn't sure which. Rosenharte had asked him what the difference was. 'The first draws life from the living, the second from death and decay,' he replied, giving his brother a meaningful glance over the top of his round spectacle frames. 'I suspect this is parasitic, which is why I would like to make a film about that giant fungus in Michigan.' It was a few moments before Rosenharte realized Konrad saw the fungus in the forest as a metaphor for the Stasi and the GDR.

He smiled to himself. At times Konrad could be slightly priggish and superior yet he also had a mind so oblique, so gentle in its dissent that it was truly surprising that his work had ever offended the authorities. He often said the Stasi had only persecuted him because although they didn't understand his work they suspected criticism lurked in it. That was why the charges at his secret trial in Rostock had been vague and the prosecution case so blustering and inept. They didn't possess the sophistication to pin anything on him, and so had relied on the catch-all charge of anti-state propaganda, which no court official felt it necessary to substantiate before sentencing him to three years' hard labour in Bautzen.

Rosenharte also knew, and reminded himself as a matter of course every once in a while, that his failure to return from Brussels in 1975 had first prompted the Stasi to investigate Konrad, who until that moment had lived his life pretty well below the parapet. They had become interested in him and later investigated his work for hidden meanings, an investigation that ended with his trial. Konrad had never even so much as hinted at his brother's responsibility and always took pains to blame the totalitarian state, but then he understood that Rosenharte had joined the HVA primarily to get out of East Germany and organize Konrad's escape so that they could both live in the West. It was an irony – or something worse – that the delayed return had resulted in Konrad's detention.

And now they were both behind bars in Stasi cells.

He swung his other leg to the floor and rested there with his head in his hands for a few seconds before springing up, taking a leak and washing his face in the basin. He would neither sit nor lie any longer because it indicated submission – an acceptance that locking him up was reasonable.

A few hours passed. He prowled his cell until the daylight began to show on the reflection in the lino beyond the bars. Then sounds of the workforce entering the Stasi citadel came to him as though he was hearing the footsteps and the slamming doors from one end of a long tube. A uniformed orderly arrived and placed some bread and tea on a small flat surface outside the cell, then worked the lever so the bed slammed up to the vertical position. Rosenharte was told to stand back as a small table together with a fixed stool were swung into the cell by means of a kind of turnstile. He did not move. 'Take it away,' he said quietly. 'I won't eat until I'm let out of here.'

The man shrugged, revolved the table out of the cell and walked off down the passage carrying the tin tray. Another hour passed.

He knew the deliberation that would decide his and Konnie's fate was still going on and he had now given up all idea of predicting which way the decision would fall. He distracted himself by trying to remember the thirty paintings by Giorgione in order of their likely execution, then the thirty-five works by Johannes Vermeer with similarly demanding conditions. He daydreamed about a visit to the Mauritshaus in The Hague where three of his favourite Vermeers hung. There was much to see and much to do in his life yet.

Then three men came, unlocked the door, pulled him from the cell and frogmarched him along the empty corridor, down a flight of stairs to a loading bay where a white van waited. Three steps led up to an open door in the side. Rosenharte saw the tiny compartments and a row of key hooks by the door. He demanded to be told where he was being taken, but they said nothing, forced him up the steps and into the nearest cubicle and slammed the door. There was a ledge, which for a smaller man could act as a seat, a steel bar that ran from floor to ceiling and a ring at his feet. At least he hadn't been manacled to the bar, which was the way that he guessed most prisoners travelled.

Someone banged the side of the truck and shouted, and it moved out of the bay into the open. Soon he could hear the light morning traffic around them. He sensed that they were going north but after a few minutes gave up trying to keep track. There was no point, and – frankly – his terror had got the better of him. Konrad had told him about these vans, and how the Stasi took suspects on long journeys before depositing them at an interrogation centre or prison having achieved the first requirement of dominance and control over a subject – disorientation. It had been weeks before Konrad knew that he was in Berlin, not Karl-Marx-Stadt. And only the brief sighting of an arrowhead of migrating geese had told him he had been taken to Rostock for his trial. There were tales of men being driven for days, manacled to bars in the cubicles so that they could not sit, stand, or move to keep themselves warm in winter.

Rosenharte's journey lasted just twenty minutes. After a series of abrupt turns the truck slowed and entered another enclosed space where the engine was shut off. There was silence for a few seconds: no shouting, no banging. The door to his cubicle was opened and he was beckoned into the gloom of a large garage, where an identical white lorry stood. A little way from the bottom of the steps, Colonel Zank stood with his hands clasped behind his back. He glanced down as he screwed a cigarette butt into the ground with his shoe, then looked up with a grin. Perhaps Zank knew Rosenharte was out of cigarettes.

'Never say that we do not keep our word,' he said. 'Welcome to Hohenschönhausen.'

THIRTEEN

Konrad

A metal door rolled back with a low rumble. Zank gestured Rosenharte out into a large courtyard at the centre of which there was a square of grass and one or two shrubs. Three sides were occupied by uniform blocks rising five storeys high. Nowhere in the GDR was there a building more expressive of the state's ponderous brutality.

'This is our main facility,' said Zank. 'We have every convenience here.'

Rosenharte looked around at the barred windows – hundreds of them, behind which he knew lay identical cells and interrogation rooms. 'Every convenience?' he said.

'Yes,' said Zank, lighting a cigarette. 'We can take pride in the work that's done here. Without Hohenschönhausen where would we be? The hostile negative forces would have overrun the state years ago. It's important to remember such things during this fortieth anniversary year.'

They turned right to walk away from the interrogation blocks along a stretch of the perimeter wall. Zank threw out an arm to a long, low, red brick building to his left. 'This was constructed by the Nazis as a kitchen and feeding station. The Soviets used it to detain objectors to the de-Nazification programme in the years after the war. There were cells in the basement, named the U-boats by prisoners. Perhaps you've heard of them?'

Rosenharte nodded. Hunched over Marie Theresa's hearth and a bottle of Goldbrand, Konrad had whispered the secrets of the U-boats, the warren of cells, flooded with freezing cold water, where men were left to rot in the dark. He hinted at unspeakable tortures practised by people who proclaimed liberation from Nazi barbarity yet employed the Gestapo's methods. Hundreds, maybe thousands, of martyrs had been destroyed in the U-boats, their spirits broken and robbed in the underground hell.

'Of course we have no need for this place now,' said Zank, as though talking of some distant historic curiosity. 'Our methods today, well, let us say they are more humane and sophisticated. We work *with* our subjects to show them how their actions have jeopardized the collective security of the state. Naturally, inquiries into criminal activities are still the basis of the work at Hohenschönhausen, but we all understand that punishment *and* reform are the twin pillars of the judicial system.' On the word reform he had raised his index finger in the air.

'I'm sure,' said Rosenharte leadenly. He wondered whether Zank was in fact with Department XIV which ran the Stasi's chain of penal and interrogation institutions. Hohenschönhausen was in his jurisdiction; Konrad was his prisoner.

They took a left turn and came to the main entrance where there were two electronically operated gates for vehicles, a small gatehouse and a side entrance for pedestrians. Except for the men in the watchtowers at each corner of the compound, and three men visible in the gatehouse at the front, no one was about. That was the striking thing about Zank's 'facility'. It was past eight thirty, but they had seen less than a dozen people since their arrival. There was a monastic hush about the place, a profound, internalized concentration, which signified to Rosenharte that the business of crushing and breaking souls began at an early hour each day.

'And over here, beyond the reception centre, we have the prison hospital. Oh yes, we have a hospital here, too.'

Was this genuine pride, or Zank's idea of humour? Rosenharte felt dread in his stomach. He understood that the journey in the prison truck from Normannenstrasse and Zank's little tour had been designed to intimidate him, but this was nothing compared to the news that Konrad was in the hospital. It would take a genuine medical emergency for the interrogators to relinquish one of their subjects to the dubious care of the Hohenschönhausen medical staff. Konrad had often told him that most sickness here and at Bautzen was regarded as malingering.

They reached a door at the centre of a long, narrow building with a tiled roof, which Zank informed him was the oldest in the compound. He pressed a bell and a tall, cadaverous attendant in a white coat appeared behind the glass, drew several bolts and turned a key.

'Security, security!' Zank said, with mock dismay. 'Still, we can never be too careful, can we? After you, please.'

The man Rosenharte had taken for an attendant turned out to be a Dr Streffer, a Stasi officer with the rank of lieutenant-colonel. He led them along a corridor, which stank in equal parts of urine and a coarse cleaning fluid he remembered from his school days. They reached a glazed door that was covered with an iron mesh. The glass was grimy and there were smears of dirt on the doorframe and along the skirting board on either side. Rosenharte tried, but could see nothing through the glass.

Streffer turned and, avoiding Rosenharte's eyes, fixed his gaze to a spot over his shoulder. 'It is forbidden to have physical contact with the prisoner. It is forbidden to exchange articles with the prisoner. It is forbidden to give information to the prisoner that is not strictly of a personal nature. It is forbidden to talk of release dates or any part of the legal security process that has brought him here. You may not refer to the inquiries that he is subject to or the conditions of this facility. These are state secrets. Is that understood?'

Rosenharte nodded.

'If any of these conditions are not met, the interview will be terminated immediately. Prisoner 122 is—'

'Konrad!' said Rosenharte fiercely. 'His name is Konrad Rosenharte.'

'Prisoner 122 is a very sick man and he will tire easily. You would be well-advised not to place any further strain on his heart.'

He turned the handle and pushed the door open. Konrad was seated at a table in filthy pyjamas. His hands were crossed in front of him and his head was drooping. It was clear he had no idea what was going on. When he looked up, his expression remained blank, as though he was struggling with some kind of delusion.

'Konnie. It's me – Rudi.'

A smile began to shine in his eyes as he took in Rosenharte's features. 'Is it really you?' he asked. 'Good Lord, it is you, Rudi. How did you get in here? They don't allow visitors.' His voice was lifeless; every word was an effort. 'Am I going to die? Is that why they let you in?'

'No Konnie, you're not going to die. I have done a deal to see you. I'm doing all I can to bring you home. They know you're too ill to cause any trouble. They understand that.' As he spoke, Rosenharte took in the shell of his twin. Since his first imprisonment, Konrad had looked five or six years older than Rosenharte.

His hair had thinned and, owing to the loss of several teeth, his cheeks were a little sunken. But up until that summer they were still unmistakably identical twins. They stood at the same height and were within a few pounds of each other's weight.

Nothing could have prepared Rosenharte for the sight of his brother in that room. He had lost twenty to thirty pounds; his eyes had retreated into his skull; the veins stood out on his hands and neck; his forearms were like an old man's. The slightest action, as when he brushed his cheek with the back of his bony hand, caused what remained of his vitality to drain.

'What deal have you done, Rudi?' He smiled – that old sceptical smile that he used to tease Rosenharte when he was being dogmatic or pompous. 'What deal can you do with these people?' His eyes moved to Zank, who was standing behind Rosenharte, and then to the doctor. 'You can't deal with them, because all they want is to finish me off. That is their only objective.'

'That's enough,' said Zank. 'You may not speculate on the motives of this institution. You may not utter defamations against the state.'

Konrad shrugged like a drunk and bowed his head. 'I'm sick, Rudi. I know that. Maybe I don't have long.'

Rosenharte shook his head desperately. 'I'll get you out of here and find you proper treatment, Konnie. Else and the boys will be free by this time tomorrow.'

Konrad's eyes rose to meet his, a look of hope gleaming through the pain. 'How did . . . ?

'Don't tire yourself, dear brother.' Before Zank or Streffer could intervene, he moved forward, grasped Konrad's shoulder and looked down into his expression.

'Unhand the prisoner. Step away now,' Streffer commanded.

Rosenharte did as he was told. 'I am rendering certain services that are important to the state.' He glanced at Zank. 'Look, they know Else is a loyal citizen; they understand the boys deserve to be with their mother at home. This will happen. I'm telling you this will happen!' He looked at Zank again, but got no response.

'That's good, Rudi; you've done well.' He smiled again. Rosenharte noted that even now he enjoyed the warmth of his brother's approval. It had always been like that. However much he had achieved, Konnie's praise was the only thing that mattered, and that was because Konnie's standards were high. He knew what they were both capable of, knew when Rosenharte was coasting. It had always been Konnie that kept them up to the mark, whether in cross-country skiing competitions or mastering a new subject at school. Now, as his brother suffered for his beliefs, it made Rosenharte feel shallow and inadequate. In his *Überwinterung* – his hibernation – he had shirked his moral and intellectual responsibilities, and instead retreated to an inner sphere, taking his pleasures when he could, with women and drink and the exquisite proximity to the work of great artists. He had let the banners and the slogans, the repression and coercion, wash over him, convinced that he was following a higher calling and leading the only authentic life he could. But he was wrong. Konnie's protest may have been subtle and puzzling, but at least he had remained true to himself.

They looked at each other for a moment. The presence of Streffer and Zank was no obstacle to their ability to communicate. Konrad understood what his brother was thinking, saw the fear and guilt in his eyes and assuaged it with a humorous wink. These messages passed so quickly that they barely noted or articulated them. Just a few minutes into the meeting, they were in each other's minds – back on the old wooden jetty near the Rosenharte farm, looking at their identical reflections in the water of the lake and watching sticklebacks glide between the weeds.

'We'll have a picnic on the jetty yet,' said Rosenharte. 'Next summer we'll take the boys and Else there and show them how to catch trout. And when you're feeling stronger, we'll do some hiking. Just you and me, like old times. Maybe a little cross-country skiing.'

'Yes,' said Konrad. 'We shall certainly do that.'

Zank moved to the door and Streffer averted his gaze to the window.

'I *will* get you out of here, Konnie. Just hold on for me.'

'Good,' said Konnie. 'That's good. I'll do my best.'

Streffer opened the door. 'The interview is terminated. The prisoner is too weak.'

Before Rosenharte could say anything more, he had been guided out of the door by Zank. In the passage he shouted out: 'Hold on, Konnie. Just hold on!'

Outside, Zank escorted him to the main gate, where they found Biermeier waiting with a car. As they reached him, Rosenharte suddenly turned and gripped Zank's shoulder at the collarbone. For a moment he thought he would kill him. 'You'd better make sure that my brother receives the proper treatment, because I am holding you personally responsible for his wellbeing.' Zank shook himself free. 'Remember Zank,' he hissed, 'you can never be sure of the cards you're dealt in life.'

He didn't know what he had meant, other than that the system from which Zank drew his power was no longer an eternal monolithic certainty. Zank's features hardened and a chilly, sadistic mediocrity was momentarily revealed. Maybe he understood better than his masters that times were dangerous for the Party and the Stasi. He was, after all, still a young man, and he knew as well as any member of his generation that the subterranean forces might one day prove too strong for the Party apparatus.

Zank glanced at Biermeier with a look of contempt – either for Biermeier or Rosenharte, it was not clear – spun on his heels and walked off in the direction of the administration block.

Biermeier let Rosenharte watch him go and in that moment, Rosenharte knew of his own deep conversion. If ever there was a 'hostile negative element', it was him. He would oppose these people, their prisons and their muffled brutality with everything in his power. Something had happened in that room, when he saw the husk of his twin's once proud physique and bearing: Konrad's defiance had passed to him and in the process metabolized into something potentially far more violent. He looked up at the rippled cloud coming in from the north and composed himself.

'Come on,' said Biermeier quietly. 'Let's get in the car. We've got work to do.' Then, as he opened the door, he added, 'This place gives me the creeps.'

Ten minutes passed before Rosenharte absorbed that remark and turned to look at Biermeier with interest.

FOURTEEN

A Picnic

Rosenharte crossed the Berlin Wall for the first time in his life two hours later. It took about half an hour, while the border police on the eastern side looked over his credentials and exit visa. Then he followed the trickle of old people who were allowed to visit relatives in the West, through the Death Zone carved across Berlin, which they couldn't see because of the high boards either side of the road. He carried a case and a copy of *Neues Deutschland* tucked under his right arm, as instructed by Annalise in the intercepted letter. In his wallet were 600 German Marks, for which he had signed several forms at Normannenstrasse and had undertaken to give a complete account of his expenditure on his return to East Berlin.

He reached the point where three traffic lanes converged at the western part of the Berlin Wall on Zimmerstrasse, then walked over the white line painted across Friedrichstrasse, noting a sign that declared, 'You are entering the American sector. Carrying weapons off-duty is forbidden. Obey traffic rules.' A few yards on, he came to a modest hut in the middle of the road, and showed his passport and waited while an American major examined it. The officer looked down at him intently and checked his face against the photo again. 'Welcome to Checkpoint Charlie, Dr Rosenharte; I understand you speak English. Is that correct?'

Rosenharte nodded.

'I've been told to tell you that the arrangement at the Cafe Adler stands: your friend will be waiting there as you expected, but she is going to ask for a meeting with your side as soon as possible. Do you understand? She won't have time to explain. You're just going to have to take the lead from her.'

Rosenharte nodded. The officer made a final check against a clipboard, and without looking up said: 'And by the way sir, several of your people have been through at other crossing points and are in the cafe now. Mr Harland and Mr Griswald say everything's under control. Everything's gonna be fine, just so long as you let things happen. Okay?' He handed back the passport. 'Have a good day, sir.'

Rosenharte walked round the back of the hut pleased that the Americans were involved. He entered the Adler by the side entrance, just under the letter C of Cafe. To his left hung a rack of newspapers, each fixed to a rod, and a small counter, where a cashier stood talking to two waitresses, one of whom lazily looked him up and down. The cafe was full, but Annalise's stand-in had a table to herself by the window on Zimmerstrasse so that she could see when he crossed. She lowered a newspaper and waved. Rosenharte glanced around the tables as he walked over, furiously kick-starting the pleasure in his face and thinking that he must find out this woman's real name. She rose from the chair and hooked her arm round his neck, looked at him with myopic joy and kissed him most tenderly. 'It's just marvellous to see you,' she whispered. 'We have a lot of company in here. It's all going to be okay.' He smiled back at her. She was so damned good at this that all sorts of automatic responses stirred in him.

'It's good to see *you*,' he said. She saw his look, noted the emphasis. Now they were communicating, as they needed to.

She drew back from him and placed the back of her hand against his cheek. 'You're tired, Rudi. Are you okay?'

'I'm fine.' He nuzzled her. 'They've just let me see my brother. It's not good news; he's very sick.'

She nodded, her eyes registering concern, and then stepped away. 'But you have other admirers here,' she said, flashing a look at the waitress. 'Well, I want them to know you're all mine.' She gave him another playful kiss, then signalled for another beer and they sat down. 'You want something to eat?' Rosenharte shook his head, noticing that she used the construction *you want*, rather than *do you want*, just the sort of idiom that someone who had lived the other side of the Atlantic would pick up. She was formidable, this woman. Very cool, very self-possessed. He liked what she was wearing, too – jeans and a dark-brown suede jacket.

'We have a problem,' she said, lowering her voice and her head at the same time. 'It's dangerous for me to be here in Berlin. I was spotted at the airport last night. A man I knew a long time ago in Brussels, an American who is something in the military. Well, that's what he says.'

Rosenharte said nothing. He had no idea what she was talking about but understood it was for the benefit of the Stasi.

She glanced left and right. 'I want to talk to your side directly. I have to make new arrangements.'

He nodded, crossed his hands on the table and looked at the case on the chair next to him. He had packed it in Dresden on the off-chance that he would have to stay over in Leipzig. It had been taken away from him at Leipzig station by Biermeier, then one of his men had handed it back just before he crossed the Wall, saying his clothes had been laundered. There were one or two slight differences in its appearance – the handle had been tampered with, and the plastic trim around the edge of the case seemed new. He had immediately guessed that it had been fitted with a microphone and a transmitter. He waggled his thumb in its direction. She gave him an imperceptible nod.

'I'm sure they would like to talk to you,' he said quietly, 'but we should go somewhere more discreet. I will have to make a call.'

She leaned forward and rested her hand on his. 'You know I've never been to the Tiergarten. They have boats on the canal there, don't they? We could take a trip, or have a picnic. The weather's not too bad; at least it's not raining.'

Rosenharte glanced out of the window at the grey sky and said yes, that would be a splendid idea. Then his eye caught their reflection in the glass ceiling of the Adler and he was struck by how natural they looked. They had managed to close the distance that had been so marked in Trieste.

'I need to get some cigarettes,' he said.

She beamed. 'As a matter of fact I bought you some duty free. Marlboro, right?' She dug into a shoulder bag and produced a carton of two hundred.

'Thank God,' said Rosenharte. 'I was going a little crazy.' He tore open a pack and lit up.

'You know, Rudi, your English seems to get better and better. Your accent is so good. Soon you'll sound like an Oxford professor.'

'Thanks,' he said, feeling the rush of nicotine. 'Look, why don't we go to the park and eat in one of the restaurants? It would be more convenient.'

'No, let's buy some food and make a picnic. It'll be easier to talk.'

A few minutes later they left the Adler and stood outside waiting for a cab to come. She put her arm in his and squeezed his bicep with her other hand. A few tourists were taking pictures and looking across into the East with binoculars. Rosenharte stared at Checkpoint Charlie and realized that this little hut made a point: it didn't recognize the white line painted across Friedrichstrasse as a border. 'Why Charlie?' he asked suddenly. 'Who was Charlie?'

'Oh come on,' she said, 'I thought everyone knew that. Alpha, Bravo, Charlie. This is crossing C.'

They hailed a beige Mercedes cab that was turning to go back down Friedrichstrasse, away from the border. The driver got out and, without asking, took Rosenharte's bag and put it in the boot.

The moment the car moved off, she snuggled up to Rosenharte and began to feel his chest. 'Are you wired?' she mouthed.

'No, but I think the suitcase is.'

'Yes, I thought that was what you meant. It won't pick up anything in the boot.'

Rosenharte darted a look at the driver.

'It's okay,' she said, 'he's one of us.' She leaned forward. 'Is the radio on, Tudor?' The man nodded. 'Bobby, can you hear me?' she asked.

'Yes, go ahead,' came Robert Harland's voice over the cab radio.

'We're going to get some food and then make for the Tiergarten for a picnic. Got any suggestions where?'

'They won't like it – it's too open.'

'They'll have to put up with it.'

There was a pause.

'Where are you?' she asked.

'Ahead of you,' he replied. 'Tudor, drop them to the north of the Neuer See in the Tiergarten. You two can cross to the south by one of the bridges. There's plenty of cover there. We'll have Griswald's people all around. How are you going to make sure they know to approach you there?'

'They already know. The suitcase has a microphone,' said Rosenharte.

'Fine,' said Harland. 'But it's important you keep on demonstrating that you are relative innocents in this business.'

'I have a number,' said Rosenharte. 'A number to call in an emergency.'

'Right,' said Harland, 'so, when Annalise stops to get the food, you find a phone and make that call and tell them she wants to talk. Now, tell me what you've got for us, Dr Rosenharte.'

Rosenharte lit another cigarette. 'I've made contact with Kafka and I have important information. But now you must keep your side of the bargain. My brother's family will be released by this afternoon. I want to hear your proposals for freeing my brother from the hospital wing of the Hohenschönhausen. He's very sick.'

'But you want to get Else and the children out of the GDR first, is that right?'

'Yes. I was allowed to see Konrad for a few minutes this morning.' He stopped, looked out of the window and prepared to say the thing that he'd barely articulated to himself. 'If he doesn't receive the proper medical treatment soon, it's going to be too late. I think he will die.'

'We'll start working on that right away. But you have to realize that this is a very tall order, Dr Rosenharte. We can get his family out, but your brother is a different matter entirely. We'll work on this, but now we need to concentrate on the few hours ahead of us. Is that okay?'

Rosenharte said yes, reluctantly.

'Right, basically Jessie . . . I mean Annalise is going to make a proposal to them and she will hand over certain items today. You will take the more important material back with you tonight or tomorrow. She's got to do a lot of bullshitting. All you have to do is stay on your toes and we will get through this. Is there anything else we need to discuss?'

Rosenharte noted Harland's slip. So her name was Jessie. He mouthed 'Hello Jessie' to her. She smiled.

'What're you going to do if they make a move?' she asked, a knot in her brow appearing. 'You saw them at the airport last night. Their intentions were obvious.'

'We're going to be there. All the roads from that immediate area in the park will be watched.'

'But I don't have a wire. How are you going to know if we're in trouble?'

'We'll have one forward observation post who will never lose sight of you. They're not going to do anything in such a public place.'

'I'm glad you're so confident,' she said, rubbing at a spot on her suede jacket.

'Look, you make the delivery and tell them the rest of it's somewhere else.'

She didn't look convinced.

'One other thing,' said Harland. 'What about the Arab gentleman? Have you got anything more for us, Rosenharte?'

'This is for later,' he said firmly. 'But I can tell you that the material you have given to my side caused the Minister for State Security to interview me last night. So they are interested. I think they believe in this.'

'Good, we'll talk later.' Harland paused. 'Oh, Tudor, that was good thinking with the suitcase. Well done.'

They stopped at a grocery store. Rosenharte walked across the road to a payphone and dialled the number in West Berlin he had been given by the Stasi. A woman answered, and after a few seconds he was put through to Biermeier, who expressed himself satisfied. He said there wouldn't be a problem finding them in the

Tiergarten. His men would follow and wait for half an hour – they could see Rosenharte now, as he was making the call.

Less than ten minutes later, Tudor dropped them on the Grosse Weg, the road that meanders through the park, and they took a secluded path to a large, irregular lake known as the Neuer See. Rosenharte was carrying his bag, so they kept the conversation to a minimum until they found a spot beneath some beech trees overlooking the lake.

He perched on a rough wooden bench, opened the bottle of wine and filled two paper cups. She crouched nearby and expertly set about slitting bread rolls and filling them with ham and cheese. 'You're good at that,' he said. 'I like to eat in the open, too. I do a lot of this when I'm out walking.'

'Yes, you always liked to walk. Some day we should go to the Alps in spring or the Pyrenees.'

Rosenharte caught sight of a yellow bird flitting in some saplings about thirty feet away. 'It's a young bird,' he said. 'This year's young bird – *eine Grasmücke*. I think you call it a werbler. Something like this.'

'A warbler!'

They smiled.

He handed her a cup of wine. 'You know, I have never seen a *Stieglitz* – in English it is called a goldfinch. There is an exceptional painting of the bird in the Mauritshuis – a tiny bird chained by a ring around its leg to a perch. It's a beautiful but very sad painting. Captivity.' He thought of Konrad.

'I don't remember you telling me that you had been to The Hague,' she said.

'I didn't tell you,' he said. 'I took the train one day from Brussels. It's not so far. Maybe a two-hour journey. That museum has one of the greatest collections in the world. I will go again one day.'

'I hope you do,' she said. Her eyes had moved to the path behind them. Rosenharte turned to see three men approaching them. He got up when they were twenty yards away and called out. 'Can we help you?'

'We were sent by Biermeier,' said the one in a fawn mackintosh. 'Miss Schering, it is a pleasure to meet you. An honour.' The man had a studious air about him. He took off his spectacles, held them up to the light and then cleaned them vigorously with a white cloth. Rosenharte examined the other two. In their double-breasted business suits and loud ties, they were indistinguishable from West Berliners. He assumed they were armed.

Jessie placed the paper cup on the bench beside her but did not get up or take the hand that he had offered. 'I have asked to see you because I'm not satisfied with the way you're treating me.' Her German was perfect and there was no mistaking the flinty edge to it.

'Fleischhauer. My name is Fleischhauer,' said the man in the mackintosh, returning his hand to his pocket. 'May I?' He sat down beside her. 'We don't want everyone in the Tiergarten to hear this, do we? I'm sure we can settle any problems you have.'

'I have given you so much over the years,' said Jessie exasperatedly, 'and yet I learn you are making enquiries about me. Two weeks ago, a friend of mine from Canada called to say there had been a man snooping about in my past, trying to dig up things. Only the Stasi, it would seem, treats one of its most loyal informers like this. I can't walk down the street in Brussels without being followed, and last night at Tempelhof your men were swarming all over the place. I saw them. It was fortunate the American didn't notice.'

'Who was he?' said Fleischhauer with interest.

A wind came and sent a little shimmer across the water and blew the beech leaves of the previous winter into eddies. Jessie brushed the hair from her face. There was no mistaking her anger. Rosenharte was full of admiration for her performance. 'He's something to do with military intelligence. He recognized me from NATO headquarters. His name is Colonel Nathan Barrett. But he could be something else for all I know. Your men were about to approach me when he saw me. What the hell were they doing? A few seconds later and I would have been in trouble, this whole operation would have been blown.' She stopped. 'I take it that you have examined the material I gave Dr Rosenharte in Italy. You understand its importance?'

Fleischhauer nodded. 'It's useful, as far as we can tell.'

'Useful! Is that all you have to say? Do you people understand what's going on? Have you any notion of the technological revolution in the West? You're being left behind.'

Fleischhauer removed his glasses again to deal with one final smear. 'We have a good idea of certain advances.'

She shook her head. 'I doubt it. In March, two scientists working at CERN in Switzerland produced a paper. They have not published it yet, but they propose a way of managing information in a network of computers, a way of keeping track of the vast flows of data that is generated at CERN. You see, the problem they faced was the constant turnover of staff and the resultant loss of knowledge.'

'We know of that problem in our organization,' said Fleischhauer pleasantly. He didn't seem especially interested.

'Exactly! Information is not leaked, but it *is* lost. It haemorrhages or evaporates when people die or leave or are assigned to other duties. What these two scientists suggest is a way of pooling the information so that everyone in the organization has access to it.' She was warming to her theme. 'The two scientists call it a web. I've got you a copy of a NATO paper on this, which draws heavily on their work. You should read it because we're on the threshold of a revolution.'

'We know about these things already.'

'The very fact that you dismiss what I'm saying means you don't have the first idea about them.' Jessie picked up her cup and threw back the remains of the wine.

'Fräulein Schering.' Fleischhauer folded his arms and leaned forward. 'Since 1969 we have known about such networks – the Advanced Research Projects Agency Network. This is being closed down by the US military right now. ARPANet does not even have funding. If you say these networks are so important why would the US military abandon them?'

'Because they're idiots. Remember that NATO is in Europe. It's not the prisoner of US military thinking. The people I work with realize the importance of networks, and they understand CERN's information management problems are minute compared to NATO's. Just think of the advantages of an internal network with an ability to connect people who need each other's information. It'll transform the military planning of the West. The Warsaw Pact countries will be left in the dust.'

'Don't be so sure about that,' said Fleischhauer.

She got up. 'Well, if you're not interested, there's really no point in continuing this conversation. We can all go home.'

'I didn't say we weren't interested. It's just—'

'It's just that you don't want to admit to me how far behind you are. Look, I understand that. But that's why I'm here. I am a pacifist and the only way to ensure peace between East and West is to make certain that your side keeps pace with ours.'

'We understand that, Miss Schering.' He glanced in Rosenharte's direction. Plainly he did not want to be having this conversation in front of him. 'My government would like to arrange a full briefing by you in the GDR. If you will come with us now, we can have you back in West Berlin by tomorrow afternoon without anyone knowing.'

She stared down at him. 'And lose my bargaining position over Rudi's brother? I'm a pacifist, Herr Fleischhauer, but I'm not a bloody fool. I want Rudi's brother released and until that happens I will limit my cooperation.'

'These arrangements are already in hand. Anyway, spending a day in the East talking to people who appreciate all that you have done doesn't make your position any weaker, surely?'

This was Rosenharte's cue. 'I saw Konrad in the prison hospital at Hohenschönhausen less than six hours ago. There was no preparation for his departure.'

'That's not true,' said Fleischhauer, looking into Jessie's eyes. 'Your friend cannot possibly be acquainted with all the ministry's intentions.'

'I saw the minister himself last night with General Schwarzmeer,' said Rosenharte. 'Nothing certain was agreed about Konrad.'

'And Konrad's family?' asked Annalise. 'Why were they arrested? You took the children too, I understand.'

'They have already been released and are on their way home at this very moment. We keep our word, Miss Schering.' He swung round to Rosenharte. 'Tell her, Rosenharte. Tell her about your arrangement to call Else this evening.'

Rosenharte nodded. 'It's true.'

'Still, there's no need for me to go to the East,' said Jessie with a reasonable smile. 'I am telling you everything I know. If your technicians need a briefing, I'm not the right person. While I grasp the implications of these innovations, the technological aspects are beyond me.' She delved into the bag, then flourished a sheaf of paper. 'I have this for you. It's the paper I mentioned, plus a diagram of the network. This has all the information you need about NATO's proposed non-linear text system. It originates from a man named Berners-Lee at CERN and is known as hypertext. The paper is called "The Hypertext Revolution in Information Management at NATO". It couldn't be more secret. If you know how the information is managed you know how to read the information.'

Rosenharte caught a glimpse of an elaborate diagram before Fleischhauer slipped the document inside his raincoat. 'This is not a good place for passing such information. We should go to a safe house.'

'Look, to be quite honest,' she said, breaking into English, 'I want to spend as much time as I can with Rudi. That's why I came to Berlin. There's a package in my bag. It contains six floppy disks with a third of the source code for the proposed NATO network. When Rudi returns to the East he will bring six more disks.'

Fleischhauer hesitated, and in that look Rosenharte saw the essence of GDR's secret officialdom – the cunning, the greed and brutality, but also the fear. Fleischhauer was plainly under orders to convey Annalise back to the GDR, but she had been smart enough to bring only a portion of the secrets with her. A third of the disks were in her bag, a third were presumably in her hotel and the last third were in Brussels. Fleischhauer could probably guarantee to retrieve those that were in the hotel, but now he had to calculate whether to remove her forcibly to the East and risk losing the final delivery of disks, or leave her in the West and so earn the considerable displeasure of his masters. Rosenharte was pretty certain which way Fleischhauer had come down.

'This arrangement is surely agreeable to you?' said Rosenharte.

'This *arrangement* is nothing to do with you,' said Fleischhauer, not bothering to hide his irritation. 'What you know about, Dr Rosenharte, are pictures and little birds in the woods. So please leave us to discuss this matter . . . in fact I suggest that it will help your brother's situation if you keep silent in these negotiations.'

Rosenharte grinned. 'There's surely no need to pull rank here. We're in the West. Let's have a drink for God's sake.'

Jessie looked at Fleischhauer. 'You mention Rudi's interest in ornithology: *little birds*. How would you know that if you weren't listening to our conversation before you arrived? You've got us bugged, haven't you? Rudi, are you wired with a microphone?'

Rosenharte opened his arms, then patted himself all over and made much of emptying his pockets out.

'Then it must be in your case,' she said with fierce indignation. She picked it up and tossed it twenty feet away, then turned to Fleischhauer. 'If this is the way you treat me, I can hardly accept your invitation to the East. Have you any sense of the risks I've taken for the GDR? Have I ever asked for money? In nearly fifteen years, what did I demand of the GDR? I'll tell you – nothing. And this is how you repay me.' She was trembling with indignation.

Fleischhauer was unmoved. 'As you say, these are important matters. And what you are doing for us now could be of the *utmost* importance to the state. That is why we must take all precautions: maybe it explains our haste and lack of gratitude. But deep down, you know that the state, the ministry and the first secretary himself appreciate your devotion and loyalty. That is one reason why they want to see you in person. You have never been to the East? You should come.'

'Let's drink to that,' said Rosenharte, seizing the tube of paper cups and prising three from the top. He lined them up precariously along the edge of the seat, together with his and Jessie's cups. Then he seemed to think better of it and handed two to each of Fleischhauer's heavies and began to pour the wine, making a great song and dance about the bouquet of the modest red that Jessie had bought at the mini market. When the cups were filled he made a bow, bent down to his own cup and set the bottle down, all of which caused Fleischhauer to stare with irritation at a distant part of the lake.

Fleischhauer had a schedule to meet; Fleischhauer was wondering how long he was going to have to put up with Rosenharte bleating about his damned brother. Rosenharte understood that. Rosenharte knew Fleischhauer inside out. He stepped back, chucked a wild look of pleasure at Jessie and prepared to make his toast. 'Hey, come on boys, hand the drinks around.' He could see that the two men felt a little silly, but the one nearest to him leaned forward to give his boss a drink. At this, Rosenharte dropped his own cup and plunged his hand into the man's left-hand jacket pocket where he had seen the weight lying and pulled out a compact handgun. He flourished the gun, before pointing it at the other man, who was reaching to the back of his waistband.

'No,' he said, wagging his finger at him. 'Put your hand in your trouser pocket.' He paused, and examined the gun. 'Now, what are you doing with this? The PSM – the Pistolet Samozaryadnya Malogabaritniy – the handgun of choice for the quiet assassin. This little Russian devil, I seem to remember from the Stasi fire-arms course, uses a bottleneck cartridge that will penetrate something like fifty layers of Kevlar. Isn't that right? The shell was designed by a woman called Denisova.' He turned to Fleischhauer. 'You see, it's not just old masters and little birds that Rudi Rosenharte knows about. He knows that the magazine release is in the butt and that the safety catch is let into the side and can only be operated from the rear.' He demonstrated. 'He knows about this nasty fellow, though he would prefer not to. What are you doing here with this thing? You're talking to a friend, a hero of the state – not some criminal element pushing drugs in Prenzlauer

Berg! This woman has risked her life for a decade and a half and you have the gall to come here with weapons and threaten her.'

'It's obvious to any sane mind that we were not threatening her,' said Fleischhauer, shaking his head in disbelief. 'We were issuing an invitation.'

Rosenharte demanded the second man's gun and threw it into the lake, then told him to pick up the suitcase and hand it to Fleischhauer. 'Working on the assumption that you *have* bugged this case, I am going to ask you to hold it up while I speak to Biermeier.' Jessie's eyes sparkled with amusement.

'Biermeier, are you hearing me? Good. I'm sending Fleischhauer back with the first delivery. I will bring the second instalment tomorrow, as long as I find Else and the kids safely at home when I call this evening. The third delivery will be made when Konrad is free and receiving treatment. I will call you by telephone to make sure you got this message, but in the meantime I'm going to send these idiots back to you. Annalise is prepared to forget the whole matter as long as we are left in peace for the next twenty-four hours.' He paused and turned to Jessie. 'Would you like to speak to Colonel Biermeier?'

'No, I think you've said everything,' she said.

'Then why don't you put the disks in the case, my darling, and these gentlemen can go home.'

Fleischhauer unzipped the top slightly and Jessie gave him the package. 'I hope you possess the hardware to run these,' she said.

'Be sure that we have,' said Fleischhauer.

'Now, be off with you,' said Rosenharte. 'Otherwise I'll start firing these bottleneck rounds in your direction.'

They watched them go.

'That's a high-risk strategy you're following there, Rudi.'

'Yes, but if they had forced us into a car and driven us over the border, we'd both be lost.'

'It wouldn't have come to that. They would have been intercepted by our side.'

'And then where would I have been?'

'I take your point. How did you know the gun was on his left side?'

He smiled. 'Although these guns are very light, the pocket sagged a little. When he took the first cup with his left hand I knew it would be in that pocket.' He handled the gun and examined the side of the barrel. 'Perhaps one of your people could use this.'

'We very rarely carry weapons,' she said. 'Look, they wouldn't know what to do with it.'

'I'll dump it before we leave the Tiergarten.'

FIFTEEN

The Men from London

Later that afternoon, flanked by Robert Harland and the Bird, Rosenharte walked to another payphone on the street and dialled the number for Biermeier. A couple of minutes elapsed before he was put through. Biermeier seemed guarded. Rosenharte guessed there were others in the room with him – Schwarzmeer? Zank? The minister himself?

'Did you get the message that I will be coming tomorrow with the complete set of new tyres?'

'Yes, but we were wondering why you didn't use the opportunity to complete the delivery today. Our representatives weren't pleased.'

'Your representatives frightened her. But, look, you have the material now and the delivery will be completed tomorrow as long as Else is home. Nothing has changed from this morning when I left to do this job. Nothing. I am completing the plan agreed by you.'

'Where are you now?'

'I can't tell you that.'

'Let me speak to her.'

Rosenharte held the handset away from him and said: 'They

want to speak with you.' Then he returned it to his ear. 'She's shaking her head. There is nothing she wants to say to you at this moment.'

'I hope you're not playing any games with us, Rosenharte. The boss is keeping abreast of developments hour by hour.'

'Tell him I am fully aware of that. All I want is to get my family mobile. I hope that these tyres will help and that the delivery tomorrow will further establish my good faith.'

Harland made a slashing sign across his throat. Rosenharte nodded. 'We're going now.'

'When will you come tomorrow?' demanded Biermeier.

'Some time near one. Maybe later. It depends on her travel arrangements.'

He hung up. Harland unplugged the sucker mike from the handset and wound the wire round the small tape recorder. 'I'll listen to this later,' he said. They got into the car with Jessie and slipped into the afternoon traffic.

'Tell me about Colonel Biermeier,' she said. 'We think he was in counter-intelligence before this recent posting with HVA.'

'He's a typical Stasi career officer, though he doesn't drink or smoke and he's a bit of a prude. He's not held in high esteem by his fellow officers.'

'Oh, how do you know that?'

'Well, he is treated with disdain by one officer, a young colonel named Zank. It was he that took me to see my brother this morning.'

Harland nodded. 'Peter Zank – the coming man. At least, he was as of July when we last heard of him. Maybe he's watching this case, looking over Biermeier's shoulder, crowding General Schwarzmeer on the minister's order? Does that make sense?'

It did, but Rosenharte said, 'I can't tell you. I know nothing of these things.'

The car plunged into the entrance of an underground car park and an electronically operated gate opened. The Bird dropped them at a lift, which took them to a large, modern apartment on the top storey, with views over a park in Charlottenburg. The American was there along with two men he didn't recognize, and he came to meet him as the elevators opened, laying a big arm round his shoulders and steering him towards a drinks tray. 'My name's Griswald – Alan Griswald – I don't think I told you before. By the way, you did absolutely the right thing in the park.' He turned and looked over his shoulder. 'I hope you said so, Bobby. It was very smart.'

'Yes, very cool thinking.'

'You're damned right it was. They had a car ready and waiting. They were about to take Jessie on a scenic tour of the Eastern sector. No doubt about it. We'd have had to intervene, and then where would we be? What are you going to have, sir – beer, whisky, bourbon?'

Rosenharte said he would have some Johnnie Walker Black Label. 'What was that about a forward observation point? I saw no one who could help us there.' He turned to the room with a smile.

'We were there,' said Griswald, 'it just seemed like you were handling things pretty well for yourself.'

There was an awkward pause. 'What about this place? Is it safe?'

'Absolutely. Swept a couple of times every week. My wife is back in the States with the kids. I've got two boys – like your brother, I believe.' He gave Rosenharte an open smile and turned to Harland. Griswald's bulk and shrewdness were both reassuring. 'So, Bobby, how do you want to handle things?'

'This is Mr Phillips and this is Mr Costelloe,' said Harland. 'They run the German desk in London. They've come to hear about Kafka. Should we sit down?'

Rosenharte could feel his anger rising. First the mess in the park, now these two Englishmen being sprung on him. 'You should have told me about this arrangement. Too many people know this secret.'

'These people are okay,' said Jessie. 'I've worked with them both for twenty years. They're absolutely solid, Rudi.'

He smiled politely. 'I am sure you're right, but I'm the only one in this room at risk. If there is one mistake my entire family is put in danger. After all, it's not unknown for the Stasi to penetrate your ranks. George Blake once lived here in Berlin.'

Costelloe got up and approached Rosenharte. He was a typically anonymous bureaucrat – stout and wearing glasses, a shapeless grey pinstripe suit, blue shirt, button-down collar and burgundy knitted tie. However, when he engaged Rosenharte's eyes, which he did after a brief shy glance to his feet, Rosenharte was startled. This man's true nature could only be seen when he permitted someone to look straight into his eyes and read what was there. 'I have been with our service for twenty-eight years – I joined as a young man in 1961, just before George Blake was arrested on eighteenth April. There's no one who understands better what he did: I know by heart the case histories of the forty or so people who were shot or imprisoned because of him. I had been in the service six months when the Berlin Wall was put up on thirteenth August. Those two dates forged my hatred of communism; you could not meet a more determined Cold War warrior. It's been my life's mission to resist and to do harm to the system that you've had the misfortune to live under.' He paused. 'Now, please understand that I am here as your ally. The undertakings that I give you now, or that have been made to you by my colleague Robert Harland are, sir, the pledges made by a democratic society, by Her Majesty's government. We will indeed try to release your brother and we will certainly bring his wife and children out of the GDR as soon as you require.' He stopped and gave him a smile. 'Now, why don't you have a seat and we'll talk about Abu Jamal, because at bottom we're all here to try to stop that regime destroying more innocent lives.' With this Costelloe took his place on one of Griswald's sofas and resumed his cloak of impenetrable mildness.

Rosenharte sat down by Jessie and placed his drink by some photographic books on a large coffee table in front of him.

'We need to know how solid Kafka is,' said Harland. 'You're the only person in this room to have met him. We want to know your judgement about this source.'

Rosenharte thought for a few moments, then lit a cigarette. Griswald passed him an ashtray. 'Kafka is a woman. She's engaged in the peace movement in Leipzig. As far as I can tell, she is a genuine source.' Their surprise was palpable.

'Name,' said Harland. 'Her name?'

Rosenharte shook his head. 'I will give it to you when Else is out of the country.'

'Let's leave that for the moment,' said Costelloe quickly. 'What did she tell you about Abu Jamal?'

'In August he had a kidney transplant in Leipzig, or at least recuperated there. The woman who has been assigned to look after his needs has spoken to Kafka. Abu Jamal is expected in Leipzig during next week or the week after. I know where he will be. He'll meet Misha Lomieko there and discuss plans for future actions.' Rosenharte had memorized this part of Ulrike Klaar's information. 'Attacks on the American embassies in Jordan and Cairo, planned for January and March next year. There are two more attacks to be staged in Vienna and Paris but she has no details or dates about these. There is one planned for West Germany at Christmas.'

There was a single exhalation around the room. 'Jesus . . .' whispered Griswald. 'Are you talking bomb attacks?'

Rosenharte shrugged. 'That is what I assumed, but she didn't say definitely. I have to be clear about that. There were many questions I wished to ask Kafka myself, but time did not permit it. She's involved in the prayer meetings in Leipzig. She had to leave to attend one. Does this tie in with your information?'

'Yes,' said Costelloe. 'We have sources that confirm parts of the plan. Clearly we need to know much more – numbers of men involved, identities, money supply. And we'll need you to go back and work on this as soon as possible. We could be talking of saving hundreds of lives, here.' He paused. 'How old is Kafka?'

'Between thirty-five and forty. It's not easy to say.'

'And her background?'

'A translator and interpreter.'

'That's interesting,' he said. 'We have the first Annalise, the second Annalise and now Kafka – all of them translators.'

'What languages?' asked Harland.

'Arabic. She speaks all the major European languages fluently. Her father was in the diplomatic service and she spent a lot of her childhood in Arab countries. She worked in the Department of International Relations, the faculty to which Misha Lomieko is attached, though she mentioned that her security clearance has been in some way impaired.'

'And she has this friend, this close female colleague . . . presumably a colleague?' Rosenharte nodded in Costelloe's direction. 'And she is feeding her information about Abu Jamal's intentions?' he continued. Rosenharte nodded again. 'I suppose it has occurred to you that this other woman may not exist; that Kafka may be the companion assigned to Abu Jamal for his stays in Leipzig?'

'Yes.'

'And you think this is likely?'

'A possibility.'

Phillips, a slight, dark man who had not stirred until then, wore the face of a doctor with bad news. 'But if Kafka's security clearance is no longer valid for her to work in the faculty, they would hardly allow her contact with this most secret of the GDR's associates.'

Rosenharte reached for his whisky. 'I couldn't explore these inconsistencies. I had very little time with her.'

'Where's the safe house?' asked Harland. He had moved to a table in the centre of the room and was making notes on a pad.

'A villa on the edge of Clara Zetkin Park. I can show you on a map. There are other addresses, which are less certain. The Stasi has many safe houses in the city.'

'We'll do that later,' he said. 'What plans can Kafka tell us about?'

Griswald stirred. 'This is not making any sense,' he said. 'Why would anyone hoping to pass information of this sensitivity to the West try so hard to be noticed by the Stasi at those weekly prayer meetings? For Chrissake, they're having conniptions about those meetings. There were thousands of police on the streets last night. Why can't she get herself to the West German embassy in Prague and tell them what she has?'

'Let me tell you something.' Wearily Rosenharte prepared to issue the same disclaimer as he had repeatedly given to the Stasi. 'I cannot guarantee this information or the intentions of the source. I act merely as the messenger.'

'We accept that,' said Costelloe emolliently, 'which is why we need to get people in place in Leipzig and relieve you of the burden of being our only means of communicating with Kafka. It would help if we had her name. You see we have to consider the possibility of this being a Stasi operation to put us on the wrong trail, to waste our effort or to entice us into making an allegation about the GDR's support for terrorism, which can then be demonstrated to be untrue.'

Rosenharte swirled the ice around in his glass and took a mouthful of whisky. Very briefly he considered the position.

'We should discuss the other end of the operation,' said Harland. 'Are they buying the story?'

'For the moment, yes,' replied Rosenharte. 'The minister took a look at me last night in the company of Schwarzmeer, Biermeier and Zank.'

'Zank!' said Costelloe. 'What's Zank doing in a meeting like that?'

'I was wondering what that meant,' asked Harland.

'If Zank is in on this, he's watching Schwarzmeer. Zank will find something wrong, because that's what he is programmed to do. It's a process of thesis and antithesis. Zank is empowered to take whatever action he needs to prove the case against Schwarzmeer. The Stasi is testing itself.'

Harland looked frustrated. 'Look, our aim is to discover the Stasi's relationship with Abu Jamal. Whether they believe what we're giving them is ultimately a side issue. The other matter of importance is that we protect Rosenharte as we go along.'

'I agree with that,' said Griswald. 'And so will Langley and the State Department. If these men are planning to blow up American citizens, Bobby's operation becomes a matter of national security for the USG, and very likely for the French, German, Austrian, Jordanian and Egyptian governments too. I don't need to remind any of you people that we have received warnings before. Just over nine months ago we got word of an attack on an American airliner, which only *some* of us took seriously. Then Pan Am 103 blew up over Lockerbie.'

Harland nodded.

'We are straying from the point,' said Costelloe. 'I believe we have—'

'No,' said Griswald. 'This *is* the point. We can't ignore what Rosenharte is telling us.'

'I wasn't suggesting we should. But the assessment of the Kafka product and what action governments take is not our problem at the moment. There are many unknowns – for example what the Stasi make of the material we're feeding them and the motive and reliability of Kafka – but we *do* know that Zank is involved, which I believe means that we can set our stop watches because it's only a matter of time before his doubts are allowed to prevail. As we know he's no ordinary officer. So I would suggest it's wise to decide on a deadline, by which time Rosenharte and his family are brought out and people are placed around Kafka – say four weeks.'

Having defused the problem, Costelloe turned to Rosenharte. 'I want you to think about your decision not to tell us Kafka's true identity. This isn't just a matter of your brother's health and freedom, important though that is to you: the information could save scores of lives. Don't respond now; just think about it over the next twelve hours.' He rose from the sofa. 'Right, you've a lot to get through. We're going back to London. Keep in touch, Bobby.'

He shook hands with Griswald and then turned to Rosenharte and asked him about the democracy and peace movements in the East. 'In your opinion, will it amount to anything?'

Rosenharte replied that he was sure the Stasi would act forcefully to suppress at least one demonstration to send out a message to dissident groups all over the country.

Costelloe nodded. 'But there is a groundswell of opinion?'

'People are coming together, but one determined use of force will end it.'

'I'm afraid you're probably right.' Costelloe moved towards the lift with Phillips in his wake. 'We'd be very interested to hear anything you pick up on this. Remember that when you're next in Leipzig.' He took Rosenharte's hand. 'You're doing a very remarkable job, sir. It's been a pleasure. No doubt we will be seeing you again.'

Rosenharte watched as he ushered Phillips into the lift and nodded to them. Costelloe's eyes came to rest on him before the doors closed and Rosenharte had the impression that he saw right into him. For a brief moment he experienced a vertiginous fright. He was now playing off four intelligence services against each other across the Iron Curtain. With individuals like Zank, Vladimir and Costelloe involved it was not a situation that could continue for very long.

By six thirty they had been joined by Macy Harp, the Bird and Tudor Williams. Griswald showed Rosenharte to a phone in the bedroom and told him that Harland would listen in on the set in the sitting room.

Looking out on the enticing lights of West Berlin Rosenharte dialled the number of Frau Haberl, a Party member who lived near Else but who was well disposed to her and took messages for her. On the third attempt he got through and Else answered.

At the best of times Else was hesitant, but now she sounded cowed – the effects no doubt of her interrogation by the Stasi and then the sudden, baffling release. He realized that she had been told that he would ring, but had no idea of the circumstances of the call.

'How are the boys?' he asked straight away.

'They're better now. Florian says he hasn't been sleeping. Christoph doesn't seem to have taken in what happened. I think they were shocked by the experience of being . . .' She stopped. 'Of being away. They'll be fine after a few days here.'

Rosenharte saw her in his mind: a large woman with surprisingly delicate features and hands. Over the years her expression of lovely, shy amusement had become dominated by anxiety. 'Yes, I understand. Give them a hug from me. Else,' he said. 'I don't want to raise your hopes, but we should see Konrad soon.'

She said nothing.

'It's okay. There are no secrets about this. I saw him this morning. They let me see him. Do you understand?'

'Yes.' The whole tone of her voice changed. 'Thank God! How was he?'

'Well, but very, very tired.'

'Is his health standing up? Tell me.'

'He'll need rest when he comes home – your cooking and seeing the boys will do the trick. Else, I want you to know I'm working very hard to achieve this.'

'Thank you, Rudi . . . we can't thank you enough.'

'Send the boys my love and tell them we'll go on a hike at the lake. I hope to be with you very soon.' He waited to see if she understood. Konrad and he used the word 'lake' as a code to indicate that they couldn't talk and that an explanation would follow later. It was no more than an alert.

'Yes, the lake. That will be fun. Maybe I'll come too.'

'Everything is going to be okay,' he said. 'I'll ring again and leave a message with Frau Haberl.'

'Thank you Rudi – we send our love to you.'

Rosenharte replaced the handset with a sense of his enormous responsibility. Else was not robust: she couldn't tolerate much more worry without succumbing to depression. If this went wrong, what the hell would she do?

He took himself next door to the sitting room and walked to the window, ignoring the others. He looked out and thought what it would be like to explore West Berlin, the other half of the capital he knew so well. The East had the lion's share of the good architecture, such as had been left after the war, but the West had all the life.

He turned. Harland had begun unfolding a large map of Leipzig. 'Well, that's some cause for a small celebration, isn't it? Did everything sound all right to you?' He was evidently pleased to be rid of the pair from London.

Rosenharte poured himself another drink and lit a cigarette. 'It means nothing,' he said.

Harland searched his face.

'It means nothing that the Stasi have kept to their agreement by releasing Else,' he continued. 'Not to release her would have sent a message to me that they did not believe in Annalise's material. Besides, they know they can pick her up any time they want. That's why I want her and the kids out as soon as possible.'

'We're going to talk about that in a minute. Just show me where this house is in Leipzig.'

Rosenharte went to the table and immediately pointed to the spot on Clara Zetkin Park. 'It's not easy to see from the park because there is a high fence and some trees, but access is potentially good, should anyone wish to visit Abu Jamal unannounced. Kafka will tell us the moment he is there. And if he stays at another house she will get this information to me.' He pointed out the addresses given to him by the Russian.

'Good, now we need to talk about your brother and his family. First your brother. Al, have you got those photos?'

Griswald moved to a desk in the window, picked up an envelope and withdrew several large satellite images. 'These come from 1985, but they should be good for our purposes.'

Rosenharte peered at them, moving his head up and down to bring them into focus. 'You need reading glasses,' said Griswald.

'I don't. My eyes are tired.'

'Believe me, you need glasses.'

At any rate, Rosenharte saw enough to put his finger on the main entrances to Hohenschönhausen, the interrogation centre and the hospital building that ran along the inside of the perimeter wall.

Macy Harp and the Bird got down close to the four photographs. 'One thing is immediately obvious,' Harp said. 'We only stand a chance of pulling this off while he's still in the hospital. Once he's been transferred back to the main detention and interrogation centre, there will be little hope of locating him quickly. But the hospital wing does provide opportunities, even though we have no idea where he's being kept in that building. If we knew that we would be in better shape.'

'There is something that I can do to find that out,' said Rosenharte.

'Oh, how?' asked Harland.

'I must be allowed my secrets too,' he said.

'We will need the information fast,' said the Bird.

'I'll try to get it as soon as I can, though how do I communicate with you? That's going to be a problem.'

'Let's concentrate on this problem for a moment,' said Harland. 'How sick is your brother? We need to know whether he can walk or even climb. Up until now we've never cracked open a jail, which I suppose may be one thing in our favour, but if your brother is unable to move, we need to take that into account.'

'He's sick,' said Rosenharte, 'but the moment he realizes he's being freed he'll do everything he can to help. He knows it will be his only chance.'

'Was he in bed when you saw him?' asked Harp.

'No, he was sitting at a table. I think it was a room they use to continue interrogations while prisoners are receiving treatment. And I do not believe he was drugged.'

'Was there any sign of a gurney or a stretcher in the room?'

'No.'

'So, we can assume he walked. That's good to know, but we will need to take some emergency medication for his heart and maybe a tranquillizer or two. We'll get advice on that.'

'What's the earliest you'd be ready to go?' asked Harland.

Harp frowned. 'Seven to ten days. Maybe more. It depends how long we take to exfiltrate Konrad's missus and the boys. Cuth is going to handle that. He shouldn't take more than thirty-six hours from start to finish.'

Harland glanced at Rosenharte, then spoke. 'Clearly, these two operations need to be planned as near as possible to each other. I'm keen for Else and the boys to disappear without being noticed. Maybe they should visit you in Dresden.' He paused. 'But I have to get these ideas sanctioned by London and . . . well. One thing occurs to me straight away. Once we get Konrad and the family out, there's absolutely nothing to keep you in the GDR. We'd lose our contact with Kafka.'

'That's correct,' he told them. It would be pointless to deny he would leave for the West.

Griswald rubbed his hands together. 'Rudi – may I call you that? – you gotta have some faith in us. We're going to a lot of trouble to help you and it doesn't look good to our governments if you continue to hold out on us.' Then he opened his arms in a gesture of appeal. 'This thing goes beyond you and your family. To be brutal, it's five people against the lives of many. The intelligence you have brought to us today could be massively important.

We need to get to work on it straight away. We have to equip ourselves with all the information.'

There was a silence in the room. He felt uncomfortable. All eyes had come to rest on him expectantly. 'I have one good card in this game,' he said pleasantly. 'You all understand that once I give it you, I may condemn my brother to rot in that place.'

Griswald started shaking his head. 'You got it all wrong. We're not communists, Rudi. We're different. I've known Bobby for a long time and he's never welched on a deal. None of us enter an agreement that we can't keep. If we say we're going to get your brother out we'll all do our damnedest to get him out. You know why that is? It's because we're compelled to make the distinction between what your side does and what we do, between a secret police force and an intelligence agency. We're not angels, but you cannot doubt our motives.'

'You forget that I've been in the business. I understand the symmetry of the two sides. And besides, I don't have Kafka's permission to reveal her name.'

'That's crap, Rudi. It's implicit in the information she gave you. No one could say those things and not expect to be named. She understands that. She's put herself on the line.'

'But I still have a responsibility to her. I have to protect her.'

'No, *we* have a responsibility to her and to the people who wind up at the end of one of these terrorist attacks. That's what this is about.'

Rosenharte put his hands up. 'I'll think about it. But if I do give you her name, I'm going to need certain guarantees about her safety.'

'That goes without saying,' said Harland. 'There's just one more area I want to explore before you go off with Cuth and Macy to discuss arrangements for next week.'

'And that is?' Rosenharte had watched Harland closely these past few hours. He was clearly a field man with little taste for office politics, yet he conducted himself well, letting first Costelloe then

Griswald say the things he needed to be said, even if it meant him looking less capable.

Harland looked away. 'When the Bird and Macy came back from Dresden after seeing you, they told me about the surveillance deployed against you. They said it was truly impressive – so heavy that they doubted they would be able to get near you.'

'It was,' said Rosenharte.

Macy Harp produced a grin as confirmation. The Bird nodded sagely.

'What I don't understand is how you were able to slip away to travel to Leipzig and to contact Kafka without being observed.'

'I caught the very earliest service to Leipzig. There was a car in my street, which I assumed was Stasi, but they didn't stir when I left the building.'

'Yes, but given the effort they had mounted in the previous week, it seems downright strange that they did not follow you to Leipzig. Do you see what I'm driving at?'

'No, I don't.'

'Well, that was the one time you needed to be travelling without restriction and unwatched.' He let that thought settle in the room. 'When were you picked up again?'

'In the main square going back to the Bahnhof.'

'How long was it since you had parted company with Kafka?'

'Not long, perhaps twenty or thirty minutes.'

'And up until that time you had not sensed you were being followed?'

Rosenharte shook his head, then remembered the tall man in a checked shirt. 'That's not entirely true. There was one man who appeared after I left Kafka. It seems the same man had presented himself at the Gemäldegalerie. At least the description of my visitor matched.'

'Was this man Stasi?'

'No, I know the type well. He was far too obvious, too big to be a good surveillance officer.'

'Have you any idea who he was?'

'I was puzzled at the time, but then I forgot about it because I had so much on my mind. He spoke to one of the assistants. By his accent, she took him to be Polish or Czech.'

'And that didn't ring any bells?' asked Griswald.

'Of course it did, but even in this affair I cannot believe the man who died in Trieste and this individual were associated.'

'I'd put money on it,' said Harland, 'though I don't know what it means. But let's just get back to the main square in Leipzig, shall we? Who spotted you?'

'It was Colonel Biermeier.'

'Biermeier! Now there's a coincidence.'

'No coincidence. He's in charge of my case for General Schwarzmeer. He needed to find me urgently because they wanted me in Berlin. The Stasi knew I was giving this lecture. That's how they managed to track me down to Leipzig.'

'Certainly,' said Harland. 'But if they were so desperate to apprehend you, why not go to the lecture theatre where you were due to speak at a certain hour, which they would have no difficulty in finding out from the local headquarters. Why wait until so late in the day? It doesn't make sense.'

Rosenharte had to admit that it didn't but he needed food and rest. He was not going to make this his worry.

Harland persisted when he gave no response. 'There's something here that none of us are seeing, Rudi. Both Alan and I feel there's a hidden hand at work. We need to understand who it is and why. Someone is helping us.'

Rosenharte saw Vladimir's elliptical expression in his mind.

SIXTEEN

The Return

Next morning Rosenharte awoke just after nine when Griswald brought him a cup of coffee. He then sat down in a chair at the end of the bed. Rosenharte felt awkward. He liked to be showered, shaved and dressed before facing the world.

'I'm not good at this hour, Mr Griswald,' he said. 'It takes me time to find my . . .'

'Equilibrium,' Griswald offered with a smile. 'Hey, don't worry. I'm the same. It's our age.' He didn't offer to leave but sat there beaming. 'Jessie's gone out to get you some new clothes and shoes,' he said eventually. 'We'll need them to hide some money for you. Bobby is away talking to his people back in London.'

Rosenharte nodded and got out of bed, feeling rather foolish in the pair of oversized pyjamas provided by the American. He carried the cup and saucer over to the window and looked out on the view again.

'We need that name, Rudi. We can't take action unless we're able to confirm your intelligence.'

Rosenharte turned to him. 'But you've already taken action based on what she's told you. You said so last night.'

Griswald conceded a nod. 'Still, it would help my side to commit the necessary resources.'

'I *am* your major resource. I am costing you very little money. You'll have the name, don't worry. When Else is out of the country and safely in the West with Christoph and Florian I will tell you and by that time we will know when the Arab is coming to Leipzig.'

The American shrugged as though he hadn't really been expecting Rosenharte to move on this. He put his hands to his face in a brief attitude of prayer. 'I have a question for you, Rudi.'

'Go ahead.'

'You're an intelligent guy. You must have known you were making a mistake in Brussels. Surely all your training meant you knew the risks of not telling your side immediately about Annalise Schering's death?'

Rosenharte was surprised. He sat down heavily on a covered bench by the window, lit a cigarette and used his saucer as an ashtray. 'Why're you asking about that now?'

'You see, we have to consider the possibility that you did tell them; that they've known all the time and have been playing along realizing that the truth channel was exactly that.' He stopped and leant forward. 'That would explain why you have managed to live in relative peace and obscurity over the last dozen or so years. If this is the case, it would mean this whole damned thing is a Stasi con.'

'There was very little time that night and I was genuinely shocked by her death. She was very young and I felt guilty about using such a trusting person. You see, I already felt bad about asking her to help us.'

Griswald had started shaking his head before Rosenharte finished. 'But you were trained as a Romeo. You were trained to make love to women and use them. That was your sole purpose.'

'No, that was not my sole purpose. I was sent to the West as an illegal with a false identity and background. I was destined for long-term work.' He paused and looked Griswald in the eye. 'And you know why I agreed to do this. Because it seemed the best hope I had of getting to the West. In the right circumstances I would have defected. But I was not just a Romeo.'

'But you were schooled in the art of love back in the East. We know about these things. Your speciality was seducing lonely secretaries.'

'It was not my speciality. It was part of the job of every agent sent as an illegal to the West.'

'Yes, but the training included techniques of seduction, guidance about the right psychological moment to broach the subject of espionage.'

Rosenharte snorted a laugh and stubbed out his cigarette. 'You're like Biermeier. You're exaggerating the effort the Stasi put into this. Do you imagine there was some kind of love school where we were taught about sending flowers and the multiple orgasm? No, there were just a few talks, one to one, on certain techniques and signs.'

Rosenharte almost smiled at the memory of the anonymous man with the air of a black marketeer who came to the spy school at Potsdam-Eiche and gave each member of the class a tutorial. He described it all to Griswald. Watch their feet, the man would say. When a woman's feet are pointing in your direction, she wants you. If she is sitting down opposite you and her legs are crossed with one foot moving, she is already anticipating the rhythmic movements of the act of love. If her gaze shifts from your eyes to your mouth, if she toys with her hair or brushes her chin she is sending out an invitation. If she places her hand on her hips, touches her mouth or even looks down at her own cleavage, she is drawing attention to her most attractive features and is signalling that she is available. On the other hand, if she keeps her arms folded across her breasts, looks away when she speaks or smiles at the wrong moment when you are speaking, she is not interested.

It had all seemed ridiculously literal to Rosenharte but the Stasi treated it no less seriously than the sessions about building the woman's psychological dependence on her agent and introducing the idea of passing the odd piece of intelligence to a friendly agency – usually Sweden or Denmark. Only when sufficient intelligence had been gained and the woman was too compromised to tell her own side would they reveal that the true destination was East Germany. Rosenharte had pretty much done everything by the book and he thought things were going well. Then Annalise had kicked up when he'd asked her about the private lives of three men in the Commission. She knew immediately that he was working for the East Germans. After that, things had deteriorated quickly and before very long he was looking at her body in the bath.

Griswald listened intently to all this, then asked him once more for the name before eventually leaving Rosenharte to get dressed.

It was agreed later when Harland returned that there might be the need for one more meeting with Annalise, though they would wait to see how things went with Konrad before this was arranged. Rosenharte would tell the Stasi the next rendezvous was set for the middle of October in the West. After that he would make it plain that she was willing to undertake the trip to East Germany.

At eleven Jessie returned with a new jacket, a pair of shoes and two shirts. The Bird set about making neat incisions along the line of the front seam and the collar of the short blue overcoat and inserted the $2,000-worth of high denomination Deutschmarks. He dissected the insoles of the new shoes and padded each with five $100 bills. The remaining $2,000 was stitched into the backing of a broad leather belt. While this went on Harland schooled him in the new procedure to make contact with them, which involved a code that changed each week.

At the end of the morning, Rosenharte was introduced to two men and a woman – all citizens of the Federal Republic – who would slip into East Germany and find their way to Leipzig over the coming weeks. They were on loan from the West German intelligence service, the BND. For the moment, the three were known as Red, White and Orange. They were already familiar with the procedure for contacting Kafka. Rosenharte knew it was only a matter of time before they identified her, but he had no choice but to go along with the arrangement.

Before they set off to Checkpoint Charlie, one of the Germans showed him a photograph of a pleasant-looking apartment block in a small town near the BND's headquarters in Pullach. There was a play area for the boys, plenty of room and a view of the Alps from the back of the building. This was where Else would be housed until Konrad arrived. A local school had already agreed to take the boys in, and most of the neighbours worked for the BND and would be able to keep an eye on them.

Just past one o'clock, Tudor drove Jessie and Rosenharte to Friedrichstrasse where they got out and entered the Café Adler. The place was already under surveillance by Griswald's people, but as yet no known Stasi faces had been spotted. Jessie was subdued. He looked at her with an interrogative raise of the eyebrows. She avoided his gaze and looked out at the traffic passing through the checkpoint. Gradually her hands moved across the table to touch his. Their eyes met. 'What I'm going to say now is me,' she whispered.

'The real you?'

'Yes, the person inside Annalise.' She looked down. 'I want you to understand that I wish you all the luck in the world with this, Rudi; I want it to work for you. Really! And I hope your brother recovers when he gets out.' She stopped and stirred her hot chocolate. 'With this information, you never know, they may let him go.'

'They only let people go when they are *gleichgeschaltet*. How do you say that?'

'Pulled into line – straightened out.'

'And he will never be pulled into line.'

'Have you got your story straight? Everything ordered in your head for the other side?'

'Absolutely.'

She raised her head, then bent down even lower. 'Give my regards to the other woman. I feel a connection with her. Be sure to do that when it is appropriate.'

It was an extremely odd request but he nodded. 'I will. Look, I should go.'

'Yes. Got the package?'

'Yes.'

He leant forward and gave her a peck on the cheek. 'Good luck,' she said. 'I won't come out with you.'

He left the Adler, showed his passport at the checkpoint, then began the walk through the Death Zone to the Eastern border control.

The Stasi were full of surprises. On the other side of the eastern checkpoint they were waiting for him – six men in two cars – yet not with the usual sullen superiority. Now they were all grins and murmured congratulations. Even Biermeier's face had cracked to express a rough pleasure. Rosenharte noted that there was no sign of Zank, and gave his hand to Biermeier. 'I've got it in my inside pocket. Do you want it now?'

'Wait until you get in the car. They're very pleased with the material. Very pleased. It's everything we hoped for.' He opened the car door, but Rosenharte didn't climb in.

'What the hell were they playing at, coming to the park armed like that? She thought they were going to abduct her. Were those your orders?'

'Later,' said Biermeier stiffly. 'We'll talk later. You will stay in Berlin tonight for a debriefing, then you will be allowed to go home. We'll talk at your hotel. Nice coat. Did she give you that?'

'No, I bought it with the ministry's money.'

Biermeier looked stricken.

'Relax. It was a present from Annalise, and nothing in the world is going to persuade me to take it off because some bastard will steal it.' Rosenharte was feeling optimistic. If they were pleased with the disks, they might just give Konrad back to him.

Biermeier permitted himself another smile. 'Get in, Rosenharte, we've got a lot to do.'

Twenty-five minutes later the two cars pulled into Normann-enstrasse and drove straight to the HVA block, which Rosenharte took as another good sign. They were shown to a meeting room adjacent to General Schwarzmeer's office, where coffee and cakes were laid out. Five minutes later the general appeared at the head of a group of half a dozen men and one woman.

'Ah, Rosenharte. Welcome back. Good work, good work. These people are from the Department of Cryptology and the Department of Political Espionage Two, which, as you know, deals with NATO, and the rest come from various sections in the armed forces. They are interested in what you have brought with you – very interested.' He was in an ebullient mood; the Caesar in him was to the fore.

Biermeier handed over the second package of disks with a certain amount of ceremony.

'And there is another delivery to be made soon, I understand,' said Schwarzmeer. 'Sit down, sit down, we haven't got all day. These people have questions to ask you. For security purposes, we will not use names in this discussion and I do not have to remind you, Rosenharte, that you should not reveal any operational details.' Rosenharte fleetingly wished Harland and Griswald were as mindful of security. 'Now tell us when we can expect the final delivery.' He placed his hands squarely on the table and leant forward like a fighting dog – shoulders massive and square, chin thrust upwards, eyes consumed with anticipated triumph.

'We can expect the remaining six disks in a few weeks – by mid-October at the latest. Then our informant wishes to come to the East to clear up any matters outstanding. That will be in November. The informant does not believe there is much more that can be passed to you. This is the limit of our access to these secrets. I believe the process of copying these disks places our informant at great risk, but once duplicated there is no trace left on the original. They will never know we have them.'

Schwarzmeer made an encouraging noise.

'And the last six disks will complete the code?'

'As I understand it, you will then have the source code for the whole system.'

There were many questions, chiefly from the armed services – about the costs to NATO, when NATO would go live with the system and the amount of new hardware and training involved. Plainly all that Annalise had said to Fleischhauer in the Tiergarten had sunk in, and there was every sign they understood the grave implications for the Warsaw Pact military, though there was some hopeful conjecture about the chaos of the new system. Rosenharte deferred to their knowledge, but offered his impression that the system would sort out more problems than it would create.

Before the meeting closed they had to endure a political lecture from the lone woman, a starchy zealot who advised the operational technical sector on scientific matters. Even Schwarzmeer betrayed his impatience, but it was a ritual – like the saying of grace at mealtimes – and the men round the table nodded respectfully as she insisted that technical leaps were no substitute for a military instilled with socialist values. Rosenharte wondered whether she believed what she was saying or was just going through the motions for their benefit. He remembered his adoptive father saying that during the fifties the workers used to block their ears to the factory radios during the interminable speeches from the People's Army. For forty years the benighted people of the GDR had been listening to this enervating rhetoric. It meant nothing, everyone knew that, and yet here was a room full of senior officials who tolerated it. No wonder alcoholism was becoming such a problem. Drink was the only true anaesthetic against such bores.

They went away and Rosenharte was left with Biermeier, Schwarzmeer and one of his aides. It was then that he felt his energy suddenly quit. At first, he thought the experience of listening to the woman had made him feel ill, but then the nausea began to come in waves. He clenched his fists and summoned the strength to ask Schwarzmeer about Konrad's release. The general cut him off, saying it would be soon enough after his treatment was completed. They couldn't let him go now, while he was still ill.

Rosenharte slammed his hand heavily but without strength onto the table. 'The deal is that Konrad is sent home now.'

'There is no deal, Rosenharte,' snapped Schwarzmeer. 'He goes when we say he can. What do you want? Your brother's death? For goodness' sake man, understand that he is ill and that he is receiving the best medical attention available in the GDR.'

'Nothing could be better for him than to return to his family. That is what he needs.'

'That is not the opinion of his doctors, Rosenharte. They have a responsibility to him! They can't just put him on the train to Dresden and hope he gets off at the other end. You see that, don't you?'

The skin of Rosenharte's scalp pricked with sweat. He searched fruitlessly for a handkerchief to mop his brow, telling himself he must establish a date for Konrad's release. He mumbled something about this, but Schwarzmeer would hear no more. He waved his hand. 'Colonel Biermeier, get this man out of here. He's ill, or he's been over-exerting himself in the sack with that woman.' A leer spread across his face. 'There are limits to doing your duty for the state. You should remember to conserve your strength, Rosenharte. We all have to come to terms with our age sooner or later.'

Biermeier took him to the hotel near the Ostbahnhof where he had changed earlier that week. Before leaving, he had some tea brought up and asked Rosenharte to return the Deutschmarks given to him the day before by the Stasi.

Rosenharte told him to look in the wallet.

'You have only spent fifteen D-marks,' said Biermeier.

'There's some change in my pockets.'

Biermeier fished it out.

'Can you leave me some money for the hotel and the train?'

'Certainly,' said Biermeier. 'Why don't we agree you spent two hundred and fifty D-marks in the West, entertaining your girlfriend. That means you return three-fifty, right? Now why don't we make ourselves a bit of money and split the difference? That's one hundred and twenty-five D-marks each. I'll tell you what, I'll save you the bother of changing it and give you two hundred Ostmarks now.' He handed him a couple of blue hundred-Ostmark notes.

Rosenharte shook his head on the pillow. 'That isn't the official exchange rate.'

'I have children,' he said, without embarrassment. 'They have needs.' He looked down at Rosenharte as he stuffed the money into his hip pocket. 'I'll do the paperwork on the cash. We'll talk when you're feeling more yourself. The hotel staff will look in on you this evening.'

Rosenharte raised his head. 'Before you go, tell me about the park. Why were Fleischhauer's team preparing to snatch her?'

'It was the general . . . He's a hothead. He couldn't wait, but then reason prevailed and this morning he has forgotten he even gave the order.'

After Biermeier had left, Rosenharte forced himself from the bed, undressed and laid his new overcoat under the mattress. The shoes Jessie had bought were placed beneath the centre of the headboard, together with the plastic bag containing the new shirt and the remaining packets of Marlboro. If Biermeier was prepared to swindle the Stasi, he would certainly help himself to Rosenharte's possessions while he slept. He washed his face, drank several glasses of water and retreated shivering to the bed.

For the next twenty-four hours he knew little. He was unaware of any member of the hotel staff coming in, though at six in the evening he did notice several aspirins left by the bed. He wound his watch, took three pills with several glasses of water, and returned to bed for another delirious night, his mind jumbling the intrigue of the past three days with images of Ulrike Klaar and Konrad. In his lucid moments, he worried that he would blurt out something important and be overheard, so he held between his teeth the towel he had been using to dry off his sweat. His dreams consisted of endless corridors laid with the patterned linoleum he'd seen at Hohenschönhausen and in the headquarters at Normannenstrasse. The Stasi linoleum moved as a conveyor belt carrying him past open cells, but he dared not glance left or right to see who was in them.

SEVENTEEN

Konrad's Words

On the Friday – 29 September – he woke and knew that the worst of the fever had passed. He opened the windows and looked up at the sky, now acutely conscious of his need for food. At eleven, Biermeier appeared with a waitress in tow. She placed a tray on the table with some soup, bread, raw carrots and a triangle of hard cheese. Biermeier had acquired a bottle of vitamin C tablets, which he pressed into Rosenharte's hand, insisting that he take at least four. 'Keep taking them, because you piss out vitamin C as soon as you swallow it.'

He also brought Rosenharte's suitcase.

'I thought you'd need to shave and clean yourself up,' he said. 'You look half dead.'

Rosenharte eyed the case suspiciously. 'Is that still wired?'

Biermeier shook his head. 'You can check it if you want. We haven't the resources to waste a perfectly good transmitter on you now you're back in the GDR. You already wrecked one.'

Rosenharte began to eat. 'Where's Zank?'

Biermeier's eyes came to rest on him. 'Doing his job.'

'What is his job? Beating the shit out of people like Konrad?'

'No, Rosenharte, you mustn't jump to conclusions. Zank does not work at the interrogation centre.'

'What does he do?'

'He's in counter-intelligence. He has his mind on other things at the moment: the implementation of the plan that the minister called for after you made your observations the other night about the disturbances.'

'That's hardly counter-intelligence.'

'Zank will find a way of making it counter-intelligence. He's on his way up, that fellow.' Rosenharte again wondered about Biermeier. Beneath the gruffness a sardonic personality occasionally showed itself.

'But I said nothing that the minister couldn't work out for himself. It's all so obvious.'

'But you crystallized something in the boss's mind. It worked well for you. That's why he let you see your brother.'

'When are they going to let him out?'

'When he's better. Maybe he's suffering from the same virus as you. By the way, you need some fresh air. Go out in the autumn sunshine at the weekend. Take time for yourself.'

'I have to put in an appearance at the museum. I have been away for so long.'

'Don't worry. They understand that you have been working on important matters. It's all been settled.'

'I don't get you. First you hold me prisoner and give me the third degree, then you bring me vitamin C and start sorting out my problems at work.'

'We're pleased with you. That's why. Now you need to look after yourself and do something you enjoy.'

'It's not easy followed by half a dozen men reading newspapers upside down.'

'You won't attract much interest now,' said Biermeier, moving to the door.

'I need to get Konrad out, Colonel. He was arrested to make sure that I worked for you. Now I have done everything that Schwarzmeer asked, why doesn't he let him go?'

He threw him an awkward look. 'I'm sure he will when he can.'

'I want to be able to contact you about my brother.'

'When he's ready to leave, you will hear.'

'What about communicating the requests to Annalise?' He was aware of the desperation in his voice.

'This will be taken care of when the time comes. You're working with the MfS, Rosenharte! We know how to deal with such matters.' With that he slipped through the door.

Rosenharte took his time to wash and dress, then left the hotel and walked to the station, where he bought more food and some brandy, and boarded a train home to Dresden. He was uncomfortably aware of the weakness in his legs, and that his body was still sweating out the infection, but the alcohol did some good, and by the time the train pulled into Dresden's Hauptbahnhof, he was feeling a bit more himself.

The moment he stepped off the train he encountered a vast crowd of travellers milling about the station. Whole families were on the move, with their valuables stuffed into suitcases. Some people wore clothes they didn't have room for – in one woman's case a cardigan, an old overcoat and a mackintosh – and children's pushchairs were padded with spare clothes. He noticed that the travellers were all young, and he could tell that most of them were workers, families from the bottom of the pile who'd decided to remove their energy and youth from the GDR and make a new life for themselves in the West. And they didn't seem concerned to hide their intentions either. Though the Vopos were out in force and the usual contingent of Stasi was evident, they were openly talking about the West German Embassy in Prague and the conditions to be found in the embassy compound now that the rain had come. They were going no matter what the problems and in each face there was a look of hopeful, nervous expectation. They had cut loose their ties in the GDR, and in their minds were already on their way to a new life.

Rosenharte watched fascinated for several minutes. They were leaving the GDR's paranoid society without regret or shame. And there was nothing the Vopos and Stasi could do about it. But how long would they stand by? The state couldn't haemorrhage these kinds of numbers for long without the already stricken economy feeling it.

He went out into the rain and found a taxi that had just dropped a young couple and their baby. Rosenharte told the driver to go to a bar on the far side of town where he knew he could change the 600 D-marks he had taken from his coat on the train. The transaction was completed quickly. He got 2.2 Ostmarks for 1 DM – a good rate – and took the cab on to within a few blocks of a foreigners' hostel where Idris lived in one room once the summer had gone. Because he had exchanged some friendly words with the taxi driver, who expressed his own desire to leave the GDR, he thought it was safe to ask him to wait. He handed him some notes and a packet of Marlboro and said he would be back in half an hour.

Idris was sitting in the communal TV room with some Vietnamese students and an African. He was staring out at the rain with a bag of nuts and a book in his lap. Rosenharte beckoned him out into the corridor and began to speak, but Idris put his hand to his lips and led him to a filthy service area at the back of the building.

'You want to take that flight to Khartoum, Idris?'

He nodded.

'Here's the money for it – three hundred dollars. That'll buy you a seat.'

Idris took the money, shaking his head in disbelief.

'I want you to do something for me this weekend. Are you free?'

'Of course, my friend.'

'Can you travel to my sister-in-law and take a letter from me that no one else must see? Can you do that for me? Her safety and her children's depend on your discretion, Idris.'

He nodded. 'And your brother. Where is he? Is he free?'

Rosenharte shook his head. Idris nodded sadly. 'My sorrow for you,' he said.

'Thank you. I will call her and leave word that you will be coming.' He stopped and smiled at his friend. 'I hope you don't mind me saying this, but she probably hasn't ever met anyone like you before. She is a good person: it's just that she's led a sheltered life and right now she's very fragile because they have only just let her out. Go easy, talk to her gently and tell her everything that I have written in the letter *will* happen; that I'm doing all I can for Konrad. Will you tell her that, Idris?'

'No problem, my friend. Where is letter?'

'I have to write that now. Can we go to your room?'

When he handed it to him ten minutes later, he said: 'This is private – not for Vladimir's eyes. Okay? But I do want to talk to your Russian friend. Can you arrange that for this evening? I will be at the same bar within the next hour.'

Idris agreed. Then Rosenharte hugged him and wished him Godspeed, both of which struck him as strange gestures as he left the hostel.

Instead of returning to the cab, he jogged the few blocks to his street. The rain was slanting in his face, but when he got there he took his time to creep along a wall to see if the Stasi were outside his building. They weren't.

On the table, just inside the front door, lay a postcard addressed to Herr Lotha Frankel in childish block capitals: 'I hope this finds you well. I saw Ruth yesterday, but everything is all right with her now. I thought you would be pleased to know this. With kind regards, Sarah.' From this he understood that Ulrike had experienced some kind of temporary trouble, but was now free of it and needed to see him. The card had been posted two days before, on 27 September, in Halle. She was taking no chances.

In his apartment he tore up the card, burnt it and flushed the ash down the lavatory. He emptied his suitcase but thought better of packing it again and went to wash his face and brush his teeth. Mindful of the problems Konrad had in jail, he had lately become obsessive about his teeth.

It was too early for the nighthawks at Die Krypta. Instead the place was packed with groups of middle-aged men. Rosenharte sat alone at the bar, gathering the strands of his predicament together, and occasionally eavesdropping on their conversation about the rush to the border. To a man they agreed that young people fleeing to the West were workshy and incapable of the productivity levels achieved by an older generation of good, hard-working Germans.

He drank three beers and began to despair of the Russian coming. He also decided that the man in the group of five, right next to him, who wore a blue corduroy cap and who'd uttered the most vitriol about the scenes at the station, was taking too much interest in him for comfort's sake. He sank the last beer, nodded to the group, said goodnight and left by the main entrance.

The rain had been replaced by a thin drizzle that shrouded the city in mist. The beams of the spotlights intended to pick up what architecture remained of Dresden's eighteenth-century glory ended in blunted shafts. He pulled up his collar and set off gloomily in the direction of his home, hoping that a second drenching would not ruin his new coat.

On evenings like this, the ghost of the city as it had been before that night in February 1945 was always alive in his mind. The sense that beneath the hasty repairs carried out after the war and the open spaces made necessary by the annihilation of whole quarters, of which nothing but ash and dust remained, there was a city plan, a kind of subterranean blueprint of Dresden waiting to rise again. It was the gracious city painted by Bernardo Bellotto, Dresden's Canaletto, who'd left an exact record of the eighteenth-century elevations, presciently setting down everything for the people who would need it after the firestorm.

Sometimes he didn't know whether these were his original thoughts or Konrad's. They had shared walks through Dresden together and speculated without any particular emotion where their natural mother had been when she was atomized in the inferno: a hotel perhaps, the local headquarters of the Nazi party or at the reception for high-born fascists that had been the pretext for her journey to Dresden.

It was Konrad who had told him the story of the phantom mason who could be heard at the dead of night, working patiently to restore the lost edifice of the Frauenkirche.

Rosenharte now stopped in his tracks to listen for the chisel clinking on sandstone, but then he became aware of another sound – the dying echo of footsteps that had come to a halt some way behind him. He moved off, but abruptly changed direction to double back along a cobbled street towards the Zwinger and passed between the Hofkirche and the old palace of the Saxon kings. He saw the man once in silhouette: he was wearing a cap and a raincoat tied tightly at the waist. Maybe it was the character from the bar who had shown so much interest in him. He wasn't about to make it easier for him and sprinted alongside the Zwinger complex to the end of the building where he had often sat in the cafe looking across to the opera. There he retreated to the shadows and waited, half his mind fleeing to the art behind the walls behind him, while the rest of him considered how best to knock his pursuer down and disappear into the cover of shrubs and trees beyond the buildings of the Zwinger.

He heard the footsteps slow to a walk, then saw the shadow move into the space in front of the cafe. The man turned; Rosenharte leapt forward, brandishing an unwieldy metal pole, which he had snatched up from an umbrella stand. He felt silly and he had no idea what to do, but there was no going back now. The man turned, crouched and cupped his hands, then grabbed the arm descending on him, ducked to Rosenharte's right and pulled the arm into his chest. The pole clattered onto the stone with a dull ring. He had moved with such impeccable speed and timing that only when Rosenharte's face was an inch or two from the ground and his arm was being forced back excruciatingly, did he understand that he had attacked Vladimir.

The Russian let him go and Rosenharte fell towards the stone.

'You are fortunate, Doktor. I omitted the disabling part of that move – the knee to the groin.'

Rosenharte got up and apologized.

'And the Stasi trained you in this?' Vladimir asked in disbelief.

'There were some basic courses.' He stopped. 'I don't remember telling you that I was in the Stasi.'

'You didn't. I had to find that out for myself. Come. Let's get out of this rain.'

'Why didn't you come to the bar? I was there for all of two hours.'

'Your bar is full of people from Bautznerstrasse. The Stasi drink there, Rosenharte. I would have thought you knew that. We can't be seen there with you.'

'No wonder one of them recognized me.'

'Yes, he's probably been part of the surveillance detail on your case. Let's get to the car. It's over by the Catholic church. My colleagues are waiting.'

As before, they drove to Angelikastrasse and went to the brightly lit cellar. They all sat down round a table; a bottle of vodka was produced with some shot glasses. Rosenharte shook his head and asked for coffee instead, explaining that he had been ill.

'Okay,' said Vladimir. 'This is what I have to say. I have done research on you, my friend, and have found interesting facets to you. Some of these you would not want us to know about. That's natural. But you should understand I'm aware of your background – your Nazi parentage, your history with the Stasi and some interesting contacts you made on behalf of the MfS in Brussels. We shall leave these matters aside for the moment, but I suspect that they are relevant in the complete picture. What we need to concentrate on now is the immediate situation. I want you to be utterly frank with me, Rudi. Time presses. I have demands on me.'

Rosenharte drew breath, then lit a cigarette and offered the pack round the table. 'You know the only thing that matters to me is my brother,' he said. 'When I've got him out, you can have everything.'

'We would like to hear it now.'

'But you haven't helped me yet. I saw him at the beginning of the week. I managed that without your help.'

'Yes, after your interview with Erich Mielke and Schwarzmeer in the Stasi headquarters.'

'You're well informed, so you'll know that I did this myself. I didn't need your help.'

'We gave you the addresses in Leipzig.'

'Yes, but you didn't say which address Abu Jamal would be using. I had to find that out for myself. What I need to hear from you is how you're going to persuade them to let Konrad go. You offer me nothing in this respect.'

Vladimir cleared his throat and withdrew an envelope from his inside pocket and placed it on the table. 'This letter was written by your brother to you the day after you saw him. *We* arranged that. I tried to deliver it before now, but we could not find you. No one has read it.'

Rosenharte reached out, but Vladimir's hand remained on the envelope. 'I'm sorry. I can't let you have this until you begin to tell us what has been going on.' His eyes were not without sympathy, but there was also a pale, immovable resolve in his expression.

Rosenharte glanced at the other two men. 'You're asking me to sign my own execution order. You might as well tie the blindfold.'

'No,' said Vladimir calmly. 'Nothing of what is said in here will go to your authorities. The KGB simply wants to know the truth of the situation so that we can take appropriate action. Why don't you begin by telling us about your arrangements with the British and Americans?'

'Let me read the letter and I will talk to you alone,' he said.

Vladimir nodded and slid the letter across the table. 'We will give you some time with this,' he said. 'I'll be back in a few minutes.' All three left the cellar.

Rosenharte opened the letter and saw that Konrad had filled two sides with his precise, unadorned hand. The letter was dated to the previous Wednesday and at the top he had written in capitals, Hohenschönhausen.

My dear Rudi,

I will be amazed if this finds you, yet since I have nothing to lose by putting down my thoughts and sending my good wishes to you, dear brother, I sit here in these wretched circumstances and write. The sight of you heartened me, though during the last few days I have become convinced that I am nearing the end of my life and that I should, as the doctors say, put my affairs in order and make my peace with the world. Because there is no one you could call a doctor in this godforsaken place, I say it to myself: your time approaches; your struggle is over.

It sounds melodramatic, doesn't it? I can hear you now chiding me, yet the truth is that I do not look forward now, except to think of my sons' future and Else's happiness, both of which I know to be close to your own dear heart, Rudi. In the event of my no longer being here to look after them, I know that you will nourish them with your love and your care. This makes me more easily resigned to my situation than I would otherwise be. You are my dearly beloved twin brother and my companion in life, and now you will become my substitute, more than equal to the task of bringing up Florian and Christoph. This knowledge gives me strength.

I know that you are doing everything in your power to free me, and that being such an optimist you are convinced that you can pull it off. Maybe you will, in which case you will have performed a miracle and we will celebrate. But, Rudi, do not risk your own freedom in this enterprise; do not jeopardize Else and the boys. I beg you to make certain of their safety before you do anything more.

I close now by sending my love and inexpressible gratitude for the comradeship of the last fifty years. Not a day has gone by when you have not been in my thoughts; not a night has passed in places such as this when the memories of our times together have not preserved me in the darkness. Send my love to my beautiful Else, kiss her for me and hug the boys as if they were yours. You are now the channel for my love, Rudi.

Your ever loving brother, Konrad.

Rosenharte folded the letter deliberately along the two creases and replaced it in the unaddressed envelope, then brushed an angry tear from the corner of his eye. He reached for the bottle of vodka automatically and poured two glasses full, which he threw to the back of his throat. This letter was not the Konrad he knew. Though the handwriting and the slightly old-fashioned way of expressing himself on paper were certainly familiar, he didn't recognize the tone of resignation. In a few weeks the Stasi bastards had reached inside him and shrivelled his life force.

He stared at the table and the envelope and repeated the words he had shouted out in the hospital corridor as he was ushered out. 'Hold on, Konnie. Hold on.'

EIGHTEEN

A Deal with the Russian

Vladimir entered with a knock, an oddly courteous gesture, given they were in the KGB's cellars. He placed a notepad on the table and slipped off his watch, which he then aligned with the notepad.

'So, we have much to discuss,' he said. He peered at the face of the watch then glanced up with a brisk, down-turned smile.

'Can you smuggle a letter in, as well as out?' asked Rosenharte.

'Maybe, but not for a few days.'

'Then I'll write before I go from here tonight and leave it with you.'

'If you like.'

'Before I speak of the other matters, I need to outline the problem with Konrad for you. Then I'll ask what you may be able to do to help me. After that I will tell you all I know about this affair.' He was nervous and prayed to God that he had not mistaken Vladimir's intentions. The tale he was about to tell the Russian was certainly enough to earn him a bullet in the back of the head. But he reasoned that without Vladimir's help there would be little hope of releasing Konrad. There was no option but to take one of the greatest risks of his life.

He inhaled deeply and began the story of how Konrad had been arrested when the second letter arrived from Annalise Schering and how the Stasi's repeated promises to release Konrad had been broken on the advice, he believed, of Colonel Zank. He described the deal he'd done with the British and Americans, but said that he now believed that they would not succeed on their own in getting Konrad out. They would need passes and equipment, which they wouldn't be able to get. The KGB, on the other hand, might be able to acquire the necessary release forms and vehicle passes. Rosenharte would give them to the British and the British would never be any the wiser.

'I can see why you were picked by the Stasi,' said Vladimir. 'Underneath it all, you have a very devious mind, though you don't allow the world to see it. You're perfect spy material, Dr Rosenharte: a loss to the profession.' He grinned. 'Maybe there is a way we could help, but you have to make it worth my while.'

Rosenharte gave him a detailed outline of the Anglo-American operation to trace Abu Jamal and Misha, and showed how it was being done under the cover of leaking information from a highly placed source in NATO. He gave no clues whatsoever to the identity of their British source in Leipzig, but he did tell him the nature of the information he had passed to the Main Directorate for Foreign Intelligence and its importance in the future penetration of NATO communication networks. He knew that Vladimir would be able to piece together the history of Annalise Schering, so he told him about the way the West had used her as a truth channel in the seventies and eighties. At this the Russian cocked one eyebrow – the only sign of surprise he permitted himself as Rosenharte spoke. For the most part he probed and wrote notes in a fluent Cyrillic script, which Rosenharte surmised contained elements of shorthand.

At length, when the ashtray was full and the bottle half empty,

Vladimir, now slouching in his chair, flipped through the pages impatiently, looking for other points. 'The operation against the Stasi is clever,' he said, 'because it preys on their sense of technological inferiority. Did the idea of tempting the Stasi with this bait while retrieving information about the MfS relationship with Jamal come from the SIS chief in Berlin, Robert Harland?'

Rosenharte nodded.

'Someone we must watch,' said Vladimir. 'On the other hand, the man *you* have to watch is Colonel Zank. He's the one who stands between Robert Harland and success, and the one who stands in the way of your brother's freedom. Perhaps he senses that it is the only way the Stasi can retain some hold on you.' He pondered the notes for several minutes and repeatedly nodded to himself.

'You're running against three clocks attached to detonators.' He picked up and handled his watch. 'You don't know how much time you have on each one before detonation occurs. The first clock is your brother's failing health. The second is the security of the informant in Leipzig; a source handing secrets like this over to the West won't last long in the GDR. The source is already dangerously exposed because you're the main conduit and *you* are exposed. The third and last clock is the one ticking away in the Stasi headquarters. It's only a matter of time before you're under arrest and being questioned by Zank about the computer program. You won't be free for very long, Rosenharte.'

'The only clock that matters is my brother's failing health. Once he's free, we can all leave the country and to hell with espionage.'

'Yes, I understand your focus on this, but you will appreciate my surprise that you are attempting to get three of the world's major intelligence agencies involved in the release of a prisoner held by a fourth agency. It is an unusual situation to say the least and it cannot be comfortable for you. Perhaps you're beginning to show the strain.'

Rosenharte shook his head. 'I had flu, that was all. I'm fine. I'm going to see this through.'

'You may say that now, but one mistake . . . well, you know the risks. And those risks are to some extent mine too.'

Rosenharte nodded and said that it was all a question of timing.

'But what about the Leipzig connection?' the Russian asked. 'You say you want to leave immediately, but surely you bear some responsibility for this person?'

'Of course, but I'm morally obliged to look after my brother and his family first.'

'Yes, but it would be regrettable if the information this person apparently possesses does not reach the West.'

Rosenharte looked at him intently. 'What do you mean?'

'What I say. It must be against everyone's interests if Abu Jamal is allowed to carry out the attacks you've told me about. You should stay with the case, no matter what. It's your duty. This person is relying on you to pass this vital information. There's no one else. You're the informant's only link to the West. It could take months to find another means of communicating this intelligence to the right people.'

Rosenharte remembered Harland speaking of the unseen force. He studied Vladimir. 'Does your government want this to happen?'

'Who am I to speak for my government? For President Mikhail Gorbachev? But I think it's reasonable to assume that in the new era of the Soviet Union, there are reformers who regard this arrangement with a terrorist as very old-fashioned and very unhelpful to East-West détente.'

'I see.'

It was six thirty in the morning. Rosenharte got up and stretched. He took some of Biermeier's aspirins and vitamin C and asked if the Russian had some coffee and maybe some food. 'There's one other thing I want to ask of you,' he added. 'Well, a couple of things, actually. Can I use the telephone to call my brother's wife to tell her to expect a friend of ours?'

'Who?'

'I have asked Idris to visit her with a note.'

Vladimir smiled. 'Soon we'll all be working for you, Dr Rosenharte. Yes, you may make that call.'

'And I need to make contact with the West.'

'From a phone here?' He paused. 'You're out of your mind.'

'This must be a private call. It will be untraceable but I must be alone to do it.' Rosenharte had no doubt that he would somehow record the outgoing call and the codes used, but he had no choice.

Vladimir shook his head.

'It won't compromise you.'

'I'll think about it. Now, write your letter while I will find us some coffee.'

Vladimir left him with a pen and several sheets of paper. Rosenharte re-read Konrad's letter, then began to write his reply.

My dear Konnie,

There is no one more courageous than you. Several times over the last few days I have had reason to compare myself with you and found myself lacking. You always were the more principled and the more persistent one, and it is these qualities I want you to draw upon over the coming days and weeks. As I fight for your freedom on the outside, I need you to resist on the inside by staying alive and keeping your spirits up. The ultimate victory over the forces that detain and torment you will be to survive, to live to enjoy your freedom and your family's freedom. Now that Else and the boys will soon be safe, you should concentrate all your energies on this act of resistance, because one way or another I will get you out, even if I have to storm that place myself.

You say I am optimistic. I plead guilty, because I know that our time together on this earth and your time with the family is not over. This is not a matter of hopeful opinion, but a fact. I am also certain that your work is not over; that you have many films in you and that these will be made in the freedom of the new circumstances.

I am not alone in the struggle to free you. We will prevail, Konrad. Help us with all your endurance and spirit.

Your ever loving brother, Rudi.

He folded the paper, wondering whether he should have addressed some of the things that Konrad had said. But this would be to acknowledge his brother's farewell and to admit that they had no more time together – an impossibility. Life without Konnie leading and taking responsibility was inconceivable. In that moment, Rosenharte saw it all very clearly. Perhaps that Stasi man had been right: the apple doesn't fall very far from the Nazi tree. But Konnie *was* different from their natural parents – selfless, generous, tolerant, even if he was a little prim sometimes. But he had suffered because of Rudi's mistakes. Arrested for the first time in the winter of 1975 because Rudi failed to show up, he had become a victim of the Stasi's curiosity. They wanted to know about him and they saw something that needed to be trapped and pinned down. Five years later he was in Bautzen having his teeth knocked out. All Konnie's suffering, then and now, could be traced to that one mistake in 1974 when he found the original Annalise Schering in the bath. From that single moment of vacillation stemmed all his brother's troubles. He could say none of this now, but he would make amends one day.

An hour later he made the call to Frau Haberl's house and after a wait of ten minutes spoke to a drowsy Else. In the most coded way he told her to expect Idris later that day and to follow all the instructions that he would bring. She seemed confused. Rosenharte repeated himself.

'I'm sorry,' she stammered. 'Your friend has already been here and I turned him away. I didn't know that you had sent him.'

'The foreigner has already been to see you? It can't be so.'

'I didn't know his name but yes, he came yesterday.'

'That wasn't Idris. I only asked him yesterday evening. Who was this other man?'

'I don't know. He said he wanted to talk to you and Konrad on a personal matter. A tall man, reddish hair, a foreigner. I didn't like the look of him. I told him to go away.'

Rosenharte recognized the description. 'We'll talk about it when I see you. But look, Else, please give my friend a proper welcome. He's a good man.'

'Of course, Rudi,' she said, then hung up.

Vladimir leaned on his desk with his fingertips pressed together. 'You're taking them out this week? You had better be quick about it. Things don't look so good for excursions to Czechoslovakia these days.'

'Do you know something?'

'Look what's happening. There are four or five thousand people camping out in the West German Embassy at the moment. Nobody knows what to do with them. Honecker can't allow this to be all over Western TV while the President of the Soviet Union and the leaders of all the communist world celebrate the fortieth anniversary of the country in Berlin this week. It's not a good advertisement for the GDR.'

'So?'

'So, they will close the borders. We expect it very soon. In fact we are certain it's going to happen.'

'May I make this other call?'

'By all means.'

'But I have to be alone.'

'Whether you are alone or not, we will record the call. So you might as well tell me how it's done. Otherwise, I will not allow you to use the phone again.'

Rosenharte shrugged. 'Okay,' he said.

As he dialled the first number, Vladimir leaned forward and scribbled it on a pad. Then he removed a round earpiece hanging on the side of the set, held it to his head and gestured at one of his men to make sure the tape recorder was picking up everything. There were a number of clicks and the sound of another phone dialling. When this stopped Rosenharte entered an eight-digit number, which Vladimir also copied down.

'Is that the access code?' he asked.

Rosenharte nodded. He saw no reason to tell him that it changed within twenty-four hours and then again in seven days' time.

He heard the answerphone and repeated the sentence Harland had drilled in him. 'This is Mr Prince. I am calling on behalf of my aunt who wants to rearrange her appointment.' He waited.

The voice of a woman, unmistakably English, came on the line. 'Hold on while I connect you,' she said in German.

There were more clicks, then silence. A minute later he heard Robert Harland say hello.

'My aunt wishes to change her appointment to October fourth, early in the day. That's the only day she can make it.'

'I think we can manage that. And what about your uncle?'

'At the end of the week. Everything must happen by the end of the week.'

'But we'll need a name. You must supply a name to make a proper appointment. That's the only way.'

'There's no need to worry about that. You'll have the name. I'll give it to your representative.'

'It's good to get that straight, Mr Prince. Goodbye.'

Rosenharte hung up and looked round the room. There was a bookshelf stocked with a surprising number of technical studies and manuals, at least four of which were about judo and karate, and three piles of well-thumbed catalogues and travel brochures. On the windowsill there were two cacti, a pair of binoculars, a small radio set and a book in German entitled *Models for Restoring Work Capacity and Monitoring the State of Health after Combat*. Rosenharte couldn't help but smile.

'So you're planning to finish everything by the end of next week? That's going to be very hard.' He got up and pointed to the calendar, then nodded to the two men, who left with the tape recorder. 'The end of the week is seventh October – the fortieth anniversary. It's a bad idea. I and most of my colleagues will be in Berlin. Believe me, Rudi, this is going to be a big day. They're expecting trouble.'

'That's the perfect moment, surely?'

'No, the roads will be blocked. There will be more Stasi on the streets than at any time in the last four decades. Use your head.' He tapped his temple.

'I have to think of my brother's health. There's not much time. That's clear from his letter. I was hoping you could arrange release papers that say Konrad has been summoned to the KGB headquarters in Karlshorst on the instructions of the MfS for twenty-four hours of interviewing on Friday night.'

'Why would we want to talk to your brother on that day? Everyone understands we're stretched to the limit guarding the president.'

'What about the next week – the ninth, tenth or eleventh?'

'Yes, that'll be better. But it's still going to be difficult. It's well known that the KGB and the MfS are not as close as they once were. And the guards may have their suspicions when you get inside Hohenschönhausen.'

'Look, it's just to get the vehicle inside the compound. That's all we need it for.'

Vladimir pouted a look of doubt and swept a strand of hair from his forehead. 'This kind of operation will need higher authority. The GDR is still our ally and partner.'

'What do you want in exchange?'

'The name of your contact in Leipzig.'

Rosenharte nodded.

'Full details of what the British and Americans plan to do about Abu Jamal and Misha. If there is an abduction planned, I want to know about it.'

'Yes.'

'And when you go to the West, you will work for us.'

'I can do nothing for you in the West. I will be a marked man.'

'We'll find a use for you. You're good, Rosenharte, and you have already helped us.' He tapped his fingers on the notepad. 'Some of this may be valuable to us.' He paused to write something down. Rosenharte knew that Vladimir knew he hadn't got the slightest intention of working for the Russians in the West. He was making a pass at him because that was his nature, the nature of the spying game. Vladimir looked up. 'Call this number on Monday morning – in nine days' time. I will tell you then whether I have the necessary permission to go ahead with this. The delivery of the release form and pass will follow. They won't be good forgeries, just enough to get you into Hohenschönhausen. I can't guarantee they will get you out.'

'I'm sure they'll work. The people in this operation will also need Stasi ID photo cards with the appropriate coding and department stated.'

'Personally, I would not advise raising your hopes on this. The British may easily double-cross you, because by then they'll have the name of the contact in Leipzig. They won't need you any more.'

'You'll have the name by then too.'

'That's true, but I am risking nothing. This forgery can be knocked up in the building without trouble. I will of course deny all knowledge of you if you are caught. I do not like to be exposed and you should understand that.'

Rosenharte got up. 'And you'll deliver the letter to my brother as soon as possible?'

He nodded.

Rosenharte went to the door, followed by Vladimir. 'There are just two more things.'

'You never stop asking favours, Rosenharte.'

'This one is not a favour. It's a demand. I don't want to be followed. I have enough trouble with the Stasi without your men on my tail. Do I have your agreement?'

He shrugged. 'I have my hands full. I can't afford to deploy anyone on your tail. What's the other thing?'

'I'd like to know the name of the man I have entrusted my life to. You have enough knowledge to have me executed.'

'As I said just now . . .' A smile twitched at the corners of his mouth. 'I do not like to be exposed. However, since you ask, it is V. I. Ussayamov – Major Vladimir Ilyich Ussayamov.'

'Vladimir Ilyich – the name of a loyal communist.'

'Yes, but also the name given to a child by two loyal communists.' He opened the door and gestured into the corridor. 'I will have one of our people drop you near to your home. You look as though you need a long rest, Rudi.'

A few minutes later the car left Angelikastrasse with Rosenharte lying low in the back, wondering why the Russian had told such an obvious lie about his name.

While he had been talking to Harland on the phone, Rosenharte's eyes had strayed to a box upholstered in blue satin, where a silver medal was displayed. He knew enough of the Cyrillic alphabet to see that it was a first prize awarded in a judo tournament to a man with the initials V.V.P.

Ussayamov was his cover name.

NINETEEN

A Little Static

He wanted to leave for Leipzig that day, but he succumbed to the fever again and took to his bed. It was at these times that he most hated being alone, and he tuned his little Grundig radio to a music programme, then the BBC World Service news. That day in Prague, the West German foreign minister, Hans Dietrich Genscher, visited the compound of his country's embassy and announced that the GDR had agreed to allow 5,500 people to travel by train through East Germany to the West. The same report estimated that 25,000 East Germans had crossed from Hungary to Austria during the last month, but this was on the cautious side. Some put the figure at 60,000. Vladimir was right: it was only a matter of time before they would close the border.

Late on Sunday morning he got up, flung the windows open onto a moist autumn day and hurriedly prepared to leave. Instead of his suitcase, he chose an old rucksack that belonged to Konrad, and packed the clothes he'd need over the next few days together with a shabby waterproof anorak. He fastened his walking boots on the top of the rucksack, then put on his new shoes, momentarily taking pleasure from their square, solid comfort: it was a long time since he could remember owning anything that was so well made.

The news from Prague had swelled the numbers at the Haupt-bahnhof. In some parts of the huge, cavernous terminus it was difficult to move for the people travelling south. The Vopos had their fun by dragooning the crowds first one way then the other, forcing families into queues that snaked along the platforms and had no obvious purpose. On the northern side of the station, Rosenharte noticed about a dozen People's Army trucks, ready to bring the atmosphere of nervous carnival to an end.

Although he was planning to flee also, he felt no particular joy at the exodus, and when he arrived in Leipzig he could not help but admire the city's sullen and immovable defiance. A man who had struck up a conversation on the train told him that a court had sat the day before and sentenced eleven protesters from the Nikolai-kirche to six months in prison. They were each fined 5,000 marks. 'Where will they find that kind of cash? Should we all put money aside in case the Stasi arrest us for walking on our own streets?'

This was new. Strangers hadn't spoken like that to each other in East Germany for decades. He said one thing that struck Rosen-harte and echoed something Konrad had once said: 'In the East we do not trust democracy because the last time we had the vote we elected Hitler. But now it's time we gave it another try.'

Rosenharte followed the procedure to contact Ulrike and took up a station outside Bach's church, the Thomaskirche. The concert he had seen advertised was long ended and there were now few people about. As he waited, he realized it had been less than a week since he'd first met Ulrike. He had a very distinct memory of her presence, her voice and the expression in her eyes when he held her for that brief moment in the park, but he couldn't sum-mon an entire mental image of her.

He was there for an hour and a half before he attracted the attention of two plainclothes Stasi officers. He went to the cafe but it was closed, so he ambled back into the centre of town to take up his watch on one of the alleys leading to the Kirchof, the square in front of the Thomaskirche.

Nearing seven, a young couple approached him – the same pair who had come up asking for cigarettes the previous Monday. The boy told Rosenharte to follow them at a distance of thirty yards and to pass them if they were stopped. He explained that every Sunday night the Stasi patrolled the streets to prevent people posting bills for the Monday peace prayers. Twice they had already been forced to submit to a thorough search.

They walked for fifteen minutes until they reached a once prosperous area in the southeast of the city, where there were a number of squat, Alpine-style chalets, each with two or three large trees in their garden, and a flight of steps running up to a first-floor entrance at the front. The girl turned to him, gave him a look of limp curiosity and signalled to her right with an almost imperceptible tip of the head. Then she took her boyfriend's arm and they crossed the road and vanished into the dusk, laughing.

He went on for thirty or so feet and came to a narrow gateway bridged by an ancient wisteria vine. He ducked and walked down a path, which led him to a door at the side of the house. There were no lights on. He knocked tentatively and waited. No one came. He knocked again, louder, and stepped back to look up at the house. The place had been divided into four or five apartments and was run down in the usual way: the brickwork needed repointing; the shutters were broken and suffering from rot; and the paint on the windows was peeling. Just as he decided that he must have got the wrong entrance, a bulb above him came on and the door squeaked open. Ulrike's face appeared. She looked pale, and her eyes seemed larger and fiercer. She beckoned him in, pushed the door to with her foot and bolted it top and bottom.

'Well, I've come,' he said.

'I know. I can see.'

'That's what you wanted. You sent me a postcard. I would have come sooner, but I've had flu and was laid up in Berlin.'

'You must have given it to me. I was in bed for two days.'

'I'm sorry. Is it difficult now? I can always go and find somewhere to eat and come back.' He grinned, hoping to defuse the tension.

'At this time on a Sunday you won't find anywhere open.' She stepped back and looked him up and down. 'You've lost weight. And you have some nice new clothes.'

He nodded. 'They were very impressed with the information.'

She put her hand to her lips. 'Not now. There are people here. I will introduce you as Peter. You're a teacher. We'll talk after they have left.'

Rosenharte followed her into a neat sitting room which looked like a set for a 1930s film – framed photographs on the wall, two porcelain figurines, a pair of tall brass lamps and a worn-looking walnut veneer desk. Around the sofas and chairs were throws and cushions that established a colour scheme of cream and green flecked with orange. It was all very comfortable. Rosenharte liked the place and felt it displayed an elegance he would not have associated with Ulrike's rather worthy activities at the church.

He nodded to the three men who were sitting round a table with cups of tea and a full ashtray in front of them. God, how he knew this scene – the endless circular discussion, the respectful earnestness, the lack of joy or wit. That was another thing the Party was responsible for. People had become so damned boring.

She introduced him as a friend from Dresden. They nodded. One, an intense sort with a wispy brown beard but no moustache, looked doubtful. 'Perhaps we should—' he began, but was cut off by Ulrike.

'No, no,' she said. 'I can vouch for him.'

Rosenharte nodded and placed his rucksack on the ground.

A younger man wearing a shapeless green jacket buttoned up to the neck removed a pipe from his mouth. 'But, friends, we have reached the stage when the movement is so large that we should say the same things in public as we do in private.'

'That's not quite the case,' said the bearded man, 'but I agree with the spirit of what you're saying. Our aim is to take the private deliberations of each individual conscience to the forum of public discourse, yet we must remain conscious of the dangers. There's still a long way to go.'

'How long?' asked the younger man.

'Weeks, months, years. I don't know. But if we continue with this strict policy of peaceful protest, we deprive them of the reason to suppress our demonstrations with violence. What we have to do now is turn the soldiers and policemen that bar our way, and appeal to each man's conscience. That should be our aim tomorrow – to speak with these people and bring them over to our point of view.'

The third man, a stout fellow with a mass of untamed grey hair and popping eyes, leaned back in his chair smiling and shaking his head. 'You don't understand, Carl. We have reached the critical moment *now*. We will either be broken this week or we will be made. There were just a few thousand last Monday; we need many more this week to show that we've got momentum. We know that the Stasi are among us. Let's face it, the Stasi may even have a representative around this table. What no one can argue with are the masses. If the people come out tomorrow and demonstrate peacefully, then they will have to find a way of responding.'

Ulrike turned from the table to where Rosenharte sat on the couch. 'We've learned they are planning to fill the pews of the

Nikolaikirche with Party members and their own people. So we all have to get there early. I hope you will come with us?'

He nodded.

They talked on for an hour, speculating on the unknowable and arguing over the fine points that separated the democracy movements. Carl and the young man drifted off and they were left with the fellow with wild hair who put out his hand to Rosenharte. 'Rainer Frankel. It's good to meet you.'

'Rainer is my ex,' said Ulrike.

'Husband?' asked Rosenharte awkwardly.

Frankel chuckled. 'No, I didn't get that far.'

'And how is Katarina?' Ulrike asked him.

'Well, but we don't get much sleep.'

She winked at Rosenharte. 'He married one of his students and they have just had the baby boy that Rainer always wanted.'

Rainer nodded good-naturedly. 'Well, I must be getting along.' He kissed her on both cheeks and let his hands rest on her shoulders. 'Be careful tomorrow, Uly. And take something for that infection! You don't look well. Look after her, Peter.'

She saw him out and then returned to Rosenharte with an enquiring look. 'You look as if you need something to eat.'

He nodded enthusiastically.

'Let's have some wine. Rainer brought me a bottle as a late birthday present, and some bratwurst too. I'll make us dinner.' She wrapped a shawl around her shoulders and they went into a small, draughty kitchen that was papered with a montage of postcards, recipes and pictures from magazines. Rosenharte opened the bottle of wine, a thick purplish red, and watched her with pleasure. He liked her new hairstyle, which was shorter, with the hair pushed back into a fine, electrified brush. It made her face younger and more dramatic.

'Is it safe to speak here?'

'Yes, Rainer checked the place before our meeting tonight. We meet in a different place each time, and it is Rainer's duty to de-bug the venue beforehand.'

'They *will* infiltrate your group, you must know that.'

'They already have. We know who it is. He wasn't here tonight.'

'Does he find any bugs?'

'All the time. A week ago he discovered two in a colleague's apartment: in a table lamp and an electrical plug.'

'The younger man, who was he?'

'That's Hendrik. Hendrik Deubel. He's just finished a three-month stint in jail. Do you know why?' She turned to him, wagging a wooden spoon in her hand. 'Because he carried a picture of Mikhail Gorbachev at the protest against those elections that were fixed by the Party in Berlin back in the spring. He was going to leave the GDR, but we persuaded him to stay and fight.'

Rosenharte stared at her hard. 'That's exactly the kind of person who ends up working for them.'

'I know Hendrik isn't. Trust me. I know what I'm doing. I know how to survive here. You'll have to be led by me sometimes, Rudi.'

He told her about seeing Konrad in prison as she fried up some potato and onions.

'I know people who've been in there. They're never the same. It destroys a basic faith in humanity and makes them see life in a new way. It's irreversible.'

They ate in the sitting room, opposite each other with three candles between them. Rosenharte talked about his contacts with the Stasi: Mielke, Zank, Schwarzmeer, Fleischhauer and Bier-meier were all defined for her with scientific precision as though he was identifying separate members of a species. Then he came to the point. 'The result of all this is that I must give your name to the British and Russians.'

Her eyes flared. 'No, not my name, Rudi. You give them some other name. Not mine.'

'The British and the CIA are taking your information seriously, which means that they have to know where it's coming from. They will only help me to free Konrad if they have your name.'

She shook her head.

'But without knowing the source, they cannot assess the intelligence.'

'You mean they say they don't know whether to believe it?'

'Yes.'

'There were things I told them in July and August that they can check on, things that no one could make up. So they don't need to know my name, because they already know what I'm saying is true.'

'Then why did you reveal your identity to me?'

'Because I trust your ability to survive, Rudi, though I see that you're in a very difficult position with your brother.'

'Which you put me in.'

She flinched. 'I didn't know that you had a brother until just before you made contact. That's true.'

'The moment I started receiving those letters from the British, they arrested Konrad and locked up his family. I'm sorry to lay this at your feet, but there's no other conclusion to be made. You have to help me out. If I give them a fake name, they will know soon enough. They already have people here who will start checking.'

She thought about this for a while then asked him for a cigarette.

'I thought you didn't smoke.'

She ignored him and puffed the smoke amateurishly from the side of her mouth. He smiled, but she ignored him. 'If I let you give them my name I will have to leave Leipzig. I need to stay here. This is where our struggle is. This is where we will fight Honecker and the Stasi. Rainer's right: this is our moment. This is where the struggle between good and evil is taking place.'

'But there is another contest between good and evil and that is the modern one between terrorism and the free society that you yearn to build here. You acknowledge this yourself because you were responsible for telling the West about Abu Jamal.' She stubbed out the cigarette, shaking her head. 'And what happens if they start shooting? I was in Normannenstrasse last week. I looked into the eyes of the beast. Mielke will do anything to keep his power. The Party won't hesitate to follow the Chinese.'

'They can't do it in the middle of Europe.'

'We might as well be in Albania for all the contact we have with the West. Where are the foreign camera crews? Mielke can do what he likes.'

She stared at her wine for a while. Minutes passed. Rosenharte got up and stretched, then sat down again and studied her. On the surface she was like so many single women trapped in the country's grinding bureaucracy, apparently finding their only fulfilment in a church that everyone knew was full of informers. But deep down she was brave and cunning and original. He admired the way she kept herself so hidden.

'The British have a theory that you're the person assigned to look after the Arab. Is that true?'

'Partly, yes.' She paused. 'But I have a collaborator. If I allow you to use my name, I will endanger that person too.'

'But you're the person who has most contact with Abu Jamal?'

'Yes.'

'Who gave you that assignment?'

'No one. He picked me. We had some contact two or three

years ago. I told you, I speak Arabic and I know some of the places he goes to in the Middle East. I can talk to him. He likes me.'

'And finds you attractive.'

'Naturally, that was part of it. But he's a very sick man now. His kidney problems may have been cured, but there's nothing that can be done for his liver – he has cirrhosis from drinking. I believe these attacks he's planning are his goodbye. The last throw of the dice.'

'When is he due here?'

'After the anniversary. They don't want him anywhere near the GDR when all the other leaders are here. He will be here from Tuesday – the tenth of October.'

'In the villa?'

'Maybe. I will know by the end of next week.' She sprang from her chair to scoop up the dishes and plates. 'Let's go for a walk. I need some air.'

'I'd better find somewhere to stay,' he said, looking at his watch then his rucksack.

'Don't be an idiot. You're staying here.'

She shrugged on a blue duffel-coat and from the pocket took a black woolly hat which she pulled down tightly over her ears.

They walked for about fifteen minutes through the deserted suburbs to the Voelkerschlachtdenkmal – the Battle of Nations memorial marking the defeat of Napoleon at Leipzig – and passed in silence by the oblong reservoir that mirrors the memorial in the daytime. Rosenharte had never seen it before, and was surprised by its scale. In photographs it resembled the stump of an old tree, but now standing directly beneath its vitrified black mass, the memorial reminded him of the core of an extinct volcano.

'It was built in 1913,' Ulrike said, 'a year before the First World War, to commemorate the victory of a century before against

Napoleon. There's a kind of dire eloquence about it, don't you think? They had death on their minds, those people. All the disasters of twentieth-century German history are written in this stone.' She stopped and looked at him. Her eyes were watering in the cold. 'Is this your Germany, Rudi?'

'No.' He looked into the shadow of her face. 'This is not my Germany, nor my brother's.'

'Are you sure this fatalism has not become part of your soul?'

He could feel her gaze in the dark waiting for his response. 'What a question. I think I'll need time to think about it.'

'People know one way or the other. Tell me which way it is with you.'

'No, I'm not prepared to give a glib answer just to please you.' He paused and looked up at the monument. 'You'd find it difficult if I started asking you searching questions about your religion.'

'Not at all,' she said, suddenly taking off down the steps. 'Ask me anything you like.'

'When did you become a believer?'

She stopped and called back, 'When I realized I always had been.'

'What does that mean?'

'It means that it was always in me, but that I didn't know it.'

'You make it sound like diabetes.'

'That's beneath you,' she said. 'It's simple. I always believed, but didn't exactly know what I believed in. Then last year I started going to church because of the peace movement and I began to feel better – happier, more coherent. But it is no big thing.'

'In some ways I envy you,' he said.

They walked back to the house through mounds of damp leaves in untroubled silence. There she gave him mint tea and showed him to a bed that lay behind a thick green curtain in the passageway between the sitting room and her bedroom. At either end of the narrow iron bed were bookshelves crammed with paperbacks in Arabic, French and German. He glanced over their titles, hardly able to keep his eyes open. Within a minute or two of her leaving he had washed, undressed and was falling asleep to the sound of branches scratching at a window somewhere.

He woke at four to find Ulrike had curled into the contours of his body with one leg lying over his, apparently asleep. Her hair touched his cheek and he smelt her quiet, soft scent. For an hour or so he remained awake, feeling her breath on his neck. At some stage she got under the covers and cuddled up to him, but only for a short time. Then, without warning, she hopped from the bed. As her feet touched the ground, tiny snakes of static swarmed inside her nylon shift so that her entire body was revealed in silhouette beneath the material. For a split second before the lights died, her chin and neck were illuminated by the glow. She giggled, then bent down and kissed him on the forehead before leaving for her own bed.

TWENTY

The Nikolaikirche

Lone middle-aged men arriving early at the Nikolaikirche, dressed better than the average citizen, were treated wearily by the two young helpers at the main entrance. 'Welcome,' said one with a sparse little beard and a gift for quick appraisal. 'First time? Yes . . . good. We're pleased to have you with us. Sit anywhere you like.'

Rosenharte went to the upper of two galleries that surrounded the church and chose a place in the front row so he would have a clear view of the congregation and the altar where the service would be conducted. He leaned over the edge and looked down on the men scattered around the pews, all of them studiously ignoring each other, then buried himself in a copy of the prayer book and read contentedly, recalling his long hours in a small Catholic church beside Marie Theresa.

By five the church was filling. A woman with a shopping bag and a harassed air bustled past him, explaining that there would be a rush at any moment because a crowd from Dresden had just been allowed to leave the station. The Vopos were herding them like cattle through Karl-Marx-Platz. Some had already been arrested and taken away. As he listened, his gaze skated across the church, noting the youth of the congregation and the hope on people's faces. A gentle, nervous hubbub rose from the main body of the church, then someone switched on a light, which played across the surface of the six fluted columns and the plaster palm fronds that sprouted from their capitals.

In his mind he ran over the brief conversation he'd had with Harland early that morning on a phone in the institute where Ulrike worked. Harland told him that he planned to move Konrad's family to the Czech border early on Wednesday.

'I'll meet your representative at the place we agreed before,' Rosenharte said.

'Can you give us the name?' Harland asked.

'Of course,' replied Rosenharte without a qualm. 'Everything is in order. I have a new means of taking delivery of the Berlin package next week.'

Harland seemed to understand what this meant and he had hung up without saying any more.

A few moments before the service began, he saw Ulrike appear with two young men and pick her way through the people sitting cross-legged in the main aisle to a place at the front.

Then the pastor, a man named Christian Führer, walked to the altar table and a hush fell on the congregation. He introduced himself and explained that the service took the form of prayers, followed by an open discussion on matters that were relevant to the themes of peace and freedom. At this, the Party hacks – easily distinguished by their age and more conservative dress – shifted in the pews and stared about sullenly.

Someone began to read from St Matthew: 'Blessed are the poor in spirit: for theirs is the kingdom of heaven . . . Blessed are the meek: for they shall inherit the earth.'

The Beatitudes had not run their course before Rosenharte's

eyes came to rest on a familiar profile on the other side of the aisle from him. Biermeier was there. Three rows behind him was a man he had seen on the plane from Ljubljana. Rosenharte sank low and watched them both from beneath his brow. Biermeier had made concessions to the event and was wearing a light blouson jacket and an open-necked shirt; moreover he seemed to know when to make the proper responses. The second man was less familiar with it all, but was not acting in the way of some of his colleagues and the cadre of Party members.

What the hell was Biermeier doing there?

He had hardly had time to speculate when he realized that tucked in behind a column on his side of the church, sitting as still and impassive as a piece of alabaster, was Colonel Zank. This really shook him. He listened to the remaining prayers and the beginning of the discussion. Only when he followed Zank's gaze did he see that Ulrike had risen to her feet and was in the process of upbraiding a man who wished to leave the GDR. 'This is not simply about *your* freedom,' she said, swivelling round to appeal to the whole congregation. 'We're fighting for a new relationship between the state and the people which guarantees *everyone*'s basic civil liberties. The people who are running away now undermine our case. No matter how you look at it, their actions are selfish.'

A man stood up and respectfully waited for her to repeat the point in several different ways. Then he spoke haltingly. It was, he confessed, the first time he had ever addressed a public meeting. 'No man searching for the personal fulfilment that has been denied him all his life and *will* be denied to his children, can be accused of being selfish. It's part of the Lord's message that an individual should seek to make the most of all his talents, as well as to perform His work and take part in the ministry. How can a man like me – a person with no influence or contacts; with nothing to show for his life except a loving family – hope to have any effect on the Party?'

Ulrike shot to her feet again. 'By staying here and adding to the numbers that greet us outside this church every week; by calling on his friends and family to come to the Nikolaikirche and to stand in peaceful defiance of the state. We're not asking you to break the law, sir, merely to assert your right to demand change here in the GDR. Stay with us. Stay here.'

The discussion came to an end, and after the pastor had made an appeal for peaceful behaviour and said a final prayer, the congregation began to make a move towards the main doors. Rosenharte jumped up from his seat, but by the time he reached the stairway leading down from the gallery, it was packed with people who were clearly in no hurry to leave the sanctuary of the church. He pushed his way through them, mumbling apologies, but when he got to the bottom of the stairway he found that most of the congregation had left the main space. He cast around for Ulrike among the few stragglers, then squeezed through the doors to catch a glimpse of her black hat disappearing into a wheeling mass of people on the Nikolaikirchhof, the square beside the church.

Over the next few minutes he saw her several times, before losing her completely and becoming stalled in a group trying to light candles. He worked his way round to the outer limit of the square, where the Vopos stood two or three deep to prevent the demonstration from sprawling into the city. People were keeping their distance from the area immediately in front of their lines, because the police were making random snatches from the throng.

At the centre of the square, the crowd was in a state of heady disbelief, and it was clear in the expressions around him that each person had involuntarily given over some part of himself to the crowd. They couldn't stop grinning at the novelty of the experience. Chants of 'We're staying here!' and 'We are the people!' rippled through the mass; and when the light from a single camera came on, cheers, catcalls and applause filled the air.

Rosenharte glanced up at the windows around the square and saw astonished faces looking down.

He struggled to the eastern end of the church and decided that the only way to spot Ulrike was to raise himself above the sea of heads. He placed a foot on the moulding of the church's apse and, clasping a bough of the tree, managed to raise himself up to scan the crowd. He reckoned Ulrike must have moved to the flow on Ritterstrasse, which was acting as a safety valve for the Nikolaikirchhof, feeding people towards the open plain of Karl-Marx-Platz. He dropped down and made for the part of the street where the current seemed to be moving quickest.

It was then that he saw Biermeier and his sidekick moving with a steady purpose up Ritterstrasse. He crouched down, waited for them to pass ahead, and slipped in behind them. They had to be following Ulrike too. There was no other explanation.

He lost them almost immediately they reached Karl-Marx-Platz, where a vast number of people were milling about, filling the pedestrian areas and spilling into the roads. A tram bound for Klemmstrasse had been stopped in its tracks. Someone took a photograph of the driver, who was glumly leaning on his controls, while his passengers were cheered and bidden to join in. Way off in the distance, police cars and trucks were parked at random with their lights still on. Night was falling and some kind of operation to muster the forces of the state was underway. Yet everyone seemed oblivious. A loosely defined free territory had been established in the heart of the crowd where it was possible to make an impromptu speech, brandish a slogan that would have been unthinkable a few weeks before. No doubt the undercover Stasi officers were there also, but they were powerless to do anything because of the number of people, and there was nothing in the behaviour of the demonstrators that they could possibly term rowdyism. It was clear that the crowd was trying to get the measure of its own power, probing the defences of the police even if that meant sacrificing people on the fringes.

The light had suddenly faded and as the crowd swelled beneath the tall street lights of the square, Rosenharte reflected that it would be here that the final struggle between the people and Mielke's forces would take place.

A few minutes later he saw the first spout from a water cannon arc chaotically through the air and then train on the people about seventy yards from where he stood. He went forward and saw about half a dozen dog handlers and a line of police with batons and shields. They moved in a pre-planned manoeuvre: each time one end lagged, the other end waited for it to catch up. In front of them people were being skittled over by the jets from three water cannon. The ones that didn't get up fast enough were dragged away behind the explosions of spray and beaten and kicked for good measure.

A roar of indignation arose from the crowd, followed by the chant of 'We're staying here!' They surged forward as if bent on battle, but then a second chant arose: 'No Violence! No Violence.'

Rosenharte swept the scene with his brother's cinematic vision, panning through the spray of the water cannon to the people clustering under the lights and lingering over frames of individual joy and staunchness. At any other time he'd have been content to stand and watch but he had to find Ulrike.

He jogged over to a row of benches just in front of the university building and mounted one. He watched the police line steadily approach the crowd, then stop. His eye was drawn to two men moving from beneath one of the huge streetlights towards a group of women. In the middle was Ulrike, who was gesticulating enthusiastically. Right up until the moment when one of them snatched a sheaf of leaflets from her hand, and the other took her by the arm, she seemed unaware of their presence. The other women protested and one clung to her for a few seconds, but within a very short time they had dragged her from the group and were hurrying her towards a truck parked in the shadows beside the Opera House. Rosenharte jumped from the bench and walked smartly towards them, not knowing what he intended to do, but taking some heart that neither Biermeier nor Zank was anywhere to be seen. He shouted after them with a booming military command which made them stop and look round.

'Leave that woman,' he shouted. 'Let her go immediately!'

'Who says so?' shouted one with lank, black hair.

'I do!' Rosenharte was within a few yards of them now. Ulrike showed no sign of recognition.

'And who are you?'

'Colonel Zank, Main Department Three. You are aware of my presence in the city?'

Both nodded. They were young toughs who thought they knew it all, but Rosenharte could see that at this moment they were not at all sure of themselves.

'And have you any idea what I'm doing here?'

They shook their heads.

'I am acting on the personal orders of the Minister for State Security. So is the major here,' he said, gesturing to Ulrike.

Ulrike shook herself from their grip. 'Colonel, I was told that everyone had been briefed. Weren't the orders passed on?'

'They were, Major, but evidently not to these louts.' He looked at them. 'Your names?'

Neither one said anything.

'Show me your MfS IDs,' he bellowed. 'Now!'

One reached into his back pocket and gave it to him. His name was Pechmann, and he had been in the Stasi for three years. The man with the black hair said his was back at the regional headquarters in another jacket. He smiled sheepishly.

'What is the first rule you're taught during training?' Rosenharte asked. 'Never be without some means of identifying yourself to a fellow officer. The Main Department of Cadres and Training will need to hear of this lapse.' He glanced at Ulrike. 'Major, get back to your work immediately. I will deal with this pair.' Ulrike moved away, but then returned to snatch the leaflets from the man's hand, which Rosenharte thought was pressing her luck.

'Why didn't the major say who she was?' asked one plaintively.

'Operational security,' said Rosenharte. 'Look, there's a lot going on tonight and I'm prepared to accept that the orders and photographs of my officers were not passed on to you. I'm willing to overlook this matter if you don't screw up again. You saw the women she was with?'

Both nodded.

'They're all ours – brought in from Berlin for tonight's operation.'

They nodded again and shuffled. Rosenharte turned and moved with a deliberate walk back to the edge of the crowd. Just as he reached it he heard one of the Stasi shout after him: the penny had evidently dropped, but it was too late. Ulrike and he melted from sight and made their way back to the dense crowds around the Nikolaikirche.

Three hours later they reached Ulrike's home with some people she'd met at the demonstration. They were in a triumphant mood and Ulrike – flushed, with eyes burning – insisted on telling the story of her rescue several times. When another man arrived with news of arrests and hospitals overflowing with people who had been beaten by the police, the mood became subdued.

Rosenharte spoke little until the men drifted off in the early hours, leaving him facing Ulrike over some empty beer bottles and a couple of glasses of vermouth.

'I don't understand you,' he said quietly.

She gave him an odd, startled look.

'After all the warnings you gave me about security,' he continued, 'after all the trouble you've taken to move yourself into a position where you can safely pass information to the West, you mark yourself out at the church and get yourself arrested. If you're going to behave like this, what the hell is the problem with me giving your name to the British?'

'I would have been all right. They let people go after a bit.'

'But Ulrike! You have a responsibility to keep out of their way. All the risks that you and I have taken over the last few weeks will mean nothing if you end up in Hohenschönhausen. I need you to keep a very low profile until I get Konrad out. That's the priority. Okay?'

'You're cross!'

He shook his head. 'Look, I understand how important this is to you, but let's admit that the revolution didn't come this evening. Nothing happened. Your cause was not advanced in the slightest way. Do you remember the talk you gave me in the park, the one about security? Everything you said then was right. We're dependent on each other, and for the next few weeks I want you to remember that.'

She got up and paced around the sitting room, lit up with passion. She spun round and placed both hands on the table. He noticed the veins stand out on the back of her hands and the curious consumptive beauty of her face. 'You saw how many people were out on the streets tonight: twenty or thirty thousand. That's incredible. Nothing like it has been seen for years in the GDR. You can't ask me to leave Leipzig now. We won tonight and next week . . .'

'Next week they will crush you,' he said, turning from her. 'They won't let that happen again, because there is no element of surprise. They know what time your service ends, where people assemble and who the main agitators are. The GDR's anniversary celebrations are over next week. After that the world's back will be turned. The only reason you weren't clubbed down tonight is because Gorbachev is arriving at the end of the week. Next week they won't be so restrained.'

She smiled at him and tilted her head to one side. 'You're really angry, aren't you?'

'No, just very disappointed. I can't believe that you behaved so stupidly. Our lives, my brother's and his family's, depend on us keeping our heads over the next few weeks. If it had been Bier-meier or Zank, you would be under interrogation by now.'

'You mentioned them before. Zank is . . .'

'Counter-intelligence. If Zank and Biermeier are here, we can guarantee they haven't come just to watch you people say your damned prayers. They're here for a reason and I think they're on to us.'

She shook her head. 'If they had had the slightest suspicion about me I'd have been arrested by now.'

Rosenharte looked at her and opened his hands in a gesture of frustration. 'I'll leave early in the morning. I will return once more to Leipzig when I'll hand over my role to professional agents. Is that clear?'

'That means you will give my name to them?'

'Not necessarily. You can meet them without telling them your name.' He got up. 'I need some sleep if I'm to catch the early train.'

'Why take the train when you can use my car?'

'I may be away for several days.'

'I don't use it much. It's an old Wartburg that belonged to my father. He gave it to me some time before he died. It's running okay.'

This was a peace offering of sorts and he accepted it gracefully. He would have to be careful not to break any traffic laws and to avoid the routine checks by the police. That was a risk but a car would make life a lot easier over the next few days.

They went to bed after that, bidding each other good night with abrupt formality. He lay awake thinking about Biermeier and Zank, although it was the former's presence in Leipzig that disturbed him most. Zank might be there on a reasonable pretext – perhaps on a special assignment that followed the meeting in Mielke's office a week ago – but Biermeier and HVA had no business in the city unless it was directly related to him.

He was still awake when she came to his bed and stood looking down at him in the dark.

'What is it?' he asked.

'I want to talk.'

'Go ahead.'

'You have to have faith in me. It will work.'

'It's not that I don't trust you. It's that I don't understand you. Every time I see you, you seem to be a different person. I find you hard to assess.'

'Is that what you do with your women – assess them?'

'You're not one of my women, you're a source. I'm trying to assess you as that.'

'You don't find me attractive?'

'Of course I do, but in the park it was you who said I was only interested in going to bed with you and making you fall in love with me. As it happens, neither statement was right.' At that moment this was true. Over the evening he had consciously tried to extinguish his attraction to her.

She mumbled something he didn't hear. 'You have to speak up,' he said.

'I have more information for you. I forgot to tell you. The Arab will be here for two to three weeks from next Monday. He will stay at the villa and I will see him there. It's all settled. I heard late this afternoon.'

'The information came from your collaborator?'

'From a coded telex to Professor Lomieko.'

'Are you sure?'

'Yes.' She knelt down and cupped his head in her hands. 'Trust me and this *will* work out.' She kissed his eyes and his lips then felt his face with her fingertips. 'It's going to be all right. Believe me.' Then she jumped up and slipped away.

Rosenharte shrugged and shook his head in the dark.

TWENTY-ONE

Sublime No. 2

A dark Skoda saloon kept pace with him as he flogged the Wartburg southwards to Karl-Marx-Stadt. After a while he responded by abruptly accelerating to 100 km per hour and then slowing right down, just as he'd been taught in the MfS training school. The car read his movements well, keeping in touch with him but never getting close enough for Rosenharte to make out the number plate or see the driver's face. At length, without warning, he veered off at the turning to Karl-Marx-Stadt and drove into the city, where he went through an elaborate counter-surveillance measure, doubling back on himself, slipping into parking spaces without using his indicator and slamming on the brakes at the last moment. He wished his car were fitted with a device used by the Stasi in West Berlin, which allowed the brake lights to be switched on manually. It was particularly effective at night, and could throw a surveillance vehicle very easily when the target car appeared to slow down at traffic lights, only to speed away.

He toured through the sad, filthy city for about an hour, stopped and scanned the traffic as he ate lunch, drove a short distance, then bought a cup of coffee and filled the petrol tank on the western outskirts before heading out. He wondered if he had been worrying unnecessarily about the Skoda, but nevertheless going along the small country road towards a town called Zschopau, he repeatedly dived into concealed tracks to see whether anyone was making efforts to keep up with him. Twice he took diversions into villages on the way.

By four o'clock he was satisfied that no other vehicle had replaced the car in his mirror, and made directly for the hamlet beyond Marienberg, where Konrad had sought refuge to bring up his family. He reached Steinhübel, a village of a dozen bleak houses, and began the climb through the pine plantations to Holznau. The first house was Frau Haberl's place on the right, and after passing two smaller houses on the left he let the Wartburg freewheel down a narrow track that glanced off into the pine trees. Within a few seconds he came to a wide, open meadow, which had escaped cultivation during the chaotic management of the district's farms that followed collectivization in the fifties. It was a beautiful place, in summer full of wild flowers and insects. At the far end behind an apple orchard rose a large brick and timber barn with a sharply pitched black roof. To its southern flank a traditional black and white farm house had been added which Konrad had found for himself and Else after agreeing to pay for new windows and doing the repairs to the roof himself.

As Rosenharte bumped down the track, he caught sight of Florian and Christoph with a football, and then, to his surprise, Idris wading carefully in the uncut hay crop, carrying something in the skirts of his robe. The boys stopped playing and looked anxiously at the unfamiliar mustard-coloured car, until Rosenharte shouted and waved from the wheel.

He pulled up behind the barn so the car would not be visible across the fields from Frau Haberl's house, and ran round the side to scoop the boys up in his arms. Their squeals of excitement brought Else to the door. Rosenharte saw her expression light up, her hands reach to her mouth, then her shoulders sag. She had thought he was Konrad. He set the boys down, absorbed her bruised, fearful expression and went to take her in his arms.

'I'm sorry,' she said. 'It was his bag over your shoulder. You just looked so like him. For a moment I was sure he had come back to us.'

'He will come back. It's going to be all right,' he said. 'I promise.'

Idris came round the corner with several kilos of apples in his robe. He put one hand on Rosenharte's shoulder and kissed him three times. This convulsed the boys with giggles.

'What did he say in the letter?' Else asked. 'Can I see it?'

Rosenharte hadn't anticipated this. 'Later, there's much to discuss.'

She shook her head. 'Let me see it, Rudi. I want to read it.'

'Later. Look, I know he's doing well. I have contacts and I have seen him. I'm doing everything I can to bring him home to you.'

'I know, I know.' She was wringing her hands in her apron, fighting back the tears.

Idris moved to her side and craned his neck to look into her face. 'Konrad will come. I know this, Frau Rosenharte. Idris know this.'

She smiled at him and said to Rosenharte, 'Where did you find this wonderful man? He's been so very kind to us.'

Idris looked down at the boys. 'One day Rudi finds me floating down the river and he picks me up and cleans me and gives me the name Idris and I am his friend for ever.' The boys goggled at him and consulted each other on the likelihood of this being true.

'Come on in,' said Else, 'supper is nearly ready.'

Rosenharte lingered for a moment and watched the mist creep over the trees that bordered the meadow, and he prayed that the two British spies would find their way to the rendezvous by four the next morning.

It was agreed that nothing would be mentioned until the boys were asleep. After beer and a risotto made with chicken stock, mushrooms and a mysterious shredded meat that Idris had provided, Else leaned forward and indicated that they should go to the barn so they could speak freely. She wasn't sure whether the place had been bugged while she had been detained.

In the barn she lit a hurricane lamp and they sat on broken chairs surrounded by old pieces of saddlery and the mustiness of centuries of hay. As Rosenharte began to explain the plan to take them across, Idris shook his head incredulously. 'But you have not heard, Rudi? They close border. They close border today.'

'It's true,' said Else. 'Didn't you know?'

'How could I? I've been in the car all day. It has no radio.' He stubbed out the cigarette on the brick floor. 'I'd better find a phone.'

'The only telephone round here is Frau Haberl's.'

'There's no way I can let her hear this,' he said.

Else thought, then clapped her hands together. 'It's Tuesday night. The Haberls go to a Party meeting twenty kilometres away every week on a Tuesday. I suppose you could break in and make your call.' She put her hands up to her mouth and looked over her fingertips.

Ten minutes later Rosenharte parked near the house and walked round it, checking that there was no sign of life inside. Then he slipped his camping knife under two window locks, prised the window open with the blade and climbed inside. The house was very dark, but he groped his way to the front door where Else said the phone rested on a small table. He dialled the number and waited. Nothing happened. He tried three more times, understanding that, like many of the local exchanges, this one was unreliable about connecting outgoing calls. On the sixth time he heard the familiar clicks which prompted the code, and soon after that he was talking to the woman with the English accent. She put him through to Alan Griswald, who was apparently helping out in Harland's absence.

Rosenharte knew enough not to ask for explanations. 'This is Prince. I can't make the delivery as planned,' he said.

'We know there have been problems but it goes ahead anyway. I have a map reference for you. You're to deliver the goods there by seven o'clock. Our mutual friend will meet you and provide transport.'

'I don't have a map with me,' said Rosenharte, cursing himself, but also thanking his luck that Ulrike had lent him the car.

'That's okay. I have instructions.' He gave Rosenharte the name of a village and told him to travel exactly seven kilometres along the road that hugged the winding border with Czechoslovakia. On the right there was a concrete bridge that would be marked in some way. A contact would be waiting nearby. If he was not there, Rosenharte should walk across the bridge and climb straight up the hill. On the other side he would find a small road. The contacts would be waiting there in a Volvo estate car with Austrian plates.

He hung up and stole out of the house.

In the barn he told Else of the new arrangements. Idris's gaze rested on him as he shook a cigarette from the packet and offered it to Else.

'Are you sure you still want to do this?' he asked her.

She bent down to his lighter, shielding it with one hand, then tilted her head backwards as she inhaled. 'I love my home,' she said simply. 'We have found real happiness here, even without money or work for Konrad.'

'I know,' said Rosenharte. 'I know this place means a lot to you both.'

'But I can't stay in a country that did that to my children. You

283

know, they took them in the middle of the night to a place outside Marienberg. They didn't explain why or where we were. Florian asked when they could see us, and the people at the home said they might never set eyes on us again. Can you believe that? "Your parents are criminals," they said. "They deserve to be in prison for what they are doing against the state." And they punished the boys for the slightest thing – for crying even. What state reprimands a child for crying because his parents have been taken away and illegally imprisoned?'

Rosenharte shook his head in disbelief.

'When you got us out, I knew that I could not let that happen again. My first duty is to the boys now.' She stopped and watched her foot, which had been jigging as she talked. 'You see. I'm a bundle of nerves.'

'Where did they hold you?'

'In Dresden for most of the time. They took me to Bautzen for eight days to scare the shit out of me, which it did. I was locked up with criminals – women that you could not believe, Rudi. Monsters, perverts, murderers. Women who are not women.'

'You've done well to keep your sanity,' said Rosenharte quietly. 'You're stronger than you think, Else. You're a brave woman.'

She grimaced to keep her composure. 'I'm not.'

'Konnie would be proud of you.' He put his hand on her knee and she looked up with her soft, grey eyes and he thought how lovely she was.

'Show me his letter, Rudi.'

He shook his head. 'I can't. He wrote it when he was feeling very down. It will do you no good.'

Her shoulders crumpled again. 'But it's the contact I need. I want to touch something he touched.'

'I understand. Really, I do. You will have this letter, but let me try all I can to get him out, Else. Let me do that.'

284

She nodded. She didn't have the will to argue.

'We'd better talk about tomorrow,' he said briskly, 'what you should wear and take with you. We may have to do some walking, so you should keep the luggage to a minimum.'

She replied that she had got everything ready. The boys had a knapsack that they were used to carrying on hikes with Konnie and she was going to take a backpack and a grip with food and drink already packed. 'And Idris has told you that he's coming too?' she said.

Idris dipped his head apologetically. 'I go to Sudan with the money you gave me, Rudi. I go see family and maybe find a wife. It's good time for wife.' Else smiled at his businesslike approach to romance.

'Just like that! You're just taking off?'

'Maybe I come back.'

Rosenharte considered this.

'Let him come,' said Else. 'The boys will think it's an adventure with Idris there. It's important that they aren't frightened tomorrow.'

'What are you going to do when you get over the border?' asked Rosenharte.

'I am going to Prague and I am buying ticket in that city.'

'You'd better take some more money. I will give you two hundred dollars to help with your expenses. Does Vladimir know about this?'

Idris shook his head.

'Besides,' said Else, 'we need someone to carry Konnie's films.' She got up and walked to an ancient barrel, pulled away some sacking and hefted out a sports bag. 'They were buried in the woods,' she said. 'Idris helped me dig them out yesterday.' She eased the bag to the ground. 'This represents Konnie's life's work – all the films that have never been shown publicly.'

Rosenharte got up and looked into the bag. 'I assumed the Stasi had confiscated all this.'

'No, everything is here, and the equipment too.' She took the hurricane lamp to a dusty container once used for animal feed, and told them how Konrad had fitted it with a false bottom and a hidden drawer. She crouched down and, stretching to grasp both ends of the container, pulled hard. Eventually it gave and the drawer came away. Inside was a projector lying on its side, Konrad's old Wollensak Eight camera, a length of cabling and some lenses in black string-pull bags.

'We see film now,' said Idris. 'Yes? We see film now.'

'Why not?' said Rosenharte. 'We've got plenty of time.'

Else shrugged. 'Most of the canisters contain negatives. After a while he couldn't persuade anyone to develop his stuff. But there's one I could show you.' She went to work running the cable to the electricity supply in the house, setting up the projector and unfurling a white cloth, which she hung on the wall of the barn. She chose a canister marked SUBLIME No. 2 and threaded the film through the projector. She spun the spools, unscrewed, checked and wiped the bulb, and turned the machine on.

'There's no soundtrack,' she explained to Idris while adjusting the focus. 'It's a silent film which he wanted a friend to score music for. This never happened, sadly.'

Sublime No. 2 began with the camera moving over a pedestrian concourse, lingering on patches of lichen that grew on the concrete and stone. People seen only from the waist down crossed the camera's field at random, women with shopping bags half full, men with walking sticks, children with bruised knees. Back and forth they went, oblivious of being watched. Rosenharte realized that the subject of the film was not the people or their quaint, disembodied locomotion or the different pairs of legs, but the ground itself. The camera now moved as though sweeping it like a metal detector, probing what lay beneath the space where no shadows seemed to fall. For a few seconds it was diverted to track a dandelion seed bouncing over the concrete, and in the distance some buildings were glimpsed. They could have been in any town in Eastern Germany, but Rosenharte knew with absolute certainty that the film had been shot in Dresden's Altmarkt.

Dusk came and pools of light appeared on the ground. The film cut to a pair of old-fashioned women's shoes and suddenly the washed-out palette of the daylight footage was replaced by luxuriant colour. The camera inched up the woman's legs to a floral patterned dress, also pre-war, and then to a beautifully formed bodice and a head that was turned away. The whole image was lit from above by a streetlight. Behind the woman was a mass of yellow and brown chestnut leaves still clinging to the shoots at the bottom of a large tree. For a moment nothing happened. Then the woman turned to the camera and gazed into the lens. Her lips were very red and slightly parted; her hair was dark and worn curled and bunched in the style of the thirties. It took a few seconds for Rosenharte to see that it was a younger, much slimmer Else wearing a wig or with her hair dyed.

She opened her arms and from each side of the frame a boy appeared and clutched at her legs and skirt. The dark Else smiled. The camera focused on her face. Then the image faded, bleached out by the intense white light that seemed to fall from the lamp above her.

Else returned to the projector as the end of the film snapped round the spool. 'Did you recognize me?' she asked.

'Naturally,' said Rosenharte. 'You looked very beautiful.'

'Yes, most beautiful,' chimed Idris, bringing his hands together with sincerity.

'This was made before the boys were born. It's as though he had a vision of our life.'

'I don't think that's exactly what it's about,' said Rosenharte gently.

'Oh?'

'They aren't your children. And that isn't you. You were playing the part of our natural mother and the boys are Konnie and me. The Square, or somewhere like it, is where he thinks she was killed and buried in the firestorm of 1945. Why is it called Sublime Number Two?'

'I don't know. He never explained.'

The film fascinated Rosenharte because Konnie knew as well as he did that their mother was not at all a warm, beautiful figure. Perhaps he was making the point that in Else he had found a mother as well as a lover. He would ask him about that.

She started packing away the equipment and then suddenly stopped and felt in the pocket of her long cardigan. 'Oh, I almost forgot. The man who came here the other day – the one I told you about. He left this note. The film reminded me of it.' She handed him a piece of lined paper. 'It is addressed to Konnie, but it seems to concern both of you.'

Rosenharte read.

Dear Herr Rosenharte,

For several weeks I and members of my family have been trying to contact you regarding a private matter. My uncle, Franciscek Grycko, was hoping to contact your brother, but died suddenly of a heart attack. I myself have made several attempts to speak with your brother, but have failed and now must return to my home in Poland. I leave my address and my telephone number at the base of this page

*with the hope that we will be in touch in the near future. It is impor-
tant to both of us.*

Leszek Grycko

Rosenharte read it again, then asked Else what it meant.

'He would not tell me,' she replied. 'I thought he was the Stasi playing one of their games so I told him to leave. At first he refused and I became worried that he would do us some harm – it's very remote here and we're vulnerable. He told me that he saw you in Leipzig and that you'd run away from him. He said you didn't respond after he left a letter at the Gemäldegalerie.'

'I haven't received a letter,' said Rosenharte. Sonja hadn't mentioned anything to him about a letter. 'Did he say how he found you?'

She shook her head. 'He had a car . . . I'm sorry, I should have asked him some questions, but I had just got back here and I was concentrating on the boys.'

'It doesn't matter. I've got his number now. I'll call him over the next few days.' He folded the note and slipped it inside his jacket pocket.

The Wartburg's headlights forked through curls of mist that lay about the meadow as they set off down the track. Florian and Christoph had immediately fallen asleep either side of Idris in the back seat, despite the portable radio he held to his ear. Else sat in the front with the food bag on her lap, looking ahead and not speaking. He understood well enough what it meant to be leaving Konrad behind in the GDR and to be closing the door on the home she loved. Yet he thought he'd seen a new resolve in her eyes as they had taken a hasty breakfast in the kitchen. Far from being cowed by the Stasi, as he had initially suspected, she had decided to eliminate all considerations except her children's needs. He touched her on the back of the hand as they reached the road and said, 'So, your journey to freedom begins here.'

'Let's hope so,' she said, without turning to him.

The village of Herresbach lay about twenty-five miles to the southeast of Holznau, but it would take them the best part of an hour to reach it by the exceptionally tortuous road system in the Erzgebirge mountains. Rosenharte was thoroughly familiar with the area and thought he remembered a bridge at the point Griswald had described. As they went, Idris occasionally relayed news from the outside world, in particular from Czechoslovakia where trains were being prepared to take the people from the West German embassy in Prague to the Federal Republic.

'I didn't know you were so interested in the news,' remarked Rosenharte after one of these retold bulletins.

'It's why I speak German so good,' said Idris.

Rosenharte smiled, shook his head and looked in the mirror. 'I hope we see each other again, Idris. I would hate not to have you in my life.'

Idris nodded absently, his attention having already returned to his radio.

Dawn rose on Wednesday 4 October. The valleys below them were filled with mist; to the south was a large pall of brownish smog produced overnight by the lignite-burning power stations on the other side of the border. They passed through four or five villages in which there was no movement whatsoever. Else distracted herself by commenting on the gardens and houses along the way. She reminded him that both sides of her family had been Sudeten Germans who were expelled from their homes in northern Czechoslovakia at the end of 1945. She would be the first member of her family to return to their homeland in forty-four years.

After a long pause, she said, 'It never ends, does it?'

'What?' asked Rosenharte.

'The war: we live with it every day. Konrad, you, me – we live with the consequences as though we've all been cursed. It should end. That's what I think.'

The road rose to a bald summit where there were a few sheep, then plummeted into Herresbach, passing a shop, a church, a yard full of broken-down agricultural machinery and an austere pre-war factory sited beside a roaring torrent. They continued to the bottom of the valley, where the stream meandered through dense pinewoods, and rounded a corner.

Suddenly Rosenharte cursed. Ahead of them were two military trucks parked in a passing place on the right. A detachment of Grenzpolizei – border guards – had evidently just arrived to enforce the new restrictions. His first instinct was to accelerate past them, but then sense prevailed. 'Put the bag on the floor and look as if you are in distress,' he hissed to Else as he slowed to a halt.

He jumped out of the car and hailed them. 'Good morning. Do any of you know where I can find a doctor at this hour? I'm not from these parts.'

'What's the matter?' asked an officer.

'My wife – she's four months pregnant and has complications. We were staying at a friend's house for a few days to try to get some rest but now we've got this crisis we don't know where to go.'

He looked back at the car. Else had laid both hands over her belly, which it had to be said was convincingly large, and was leaning against the window with her eyes closed. Idris had removed the radio from his ear.

The officer walked towards the car. 'Have you tried the village of Herresbach? There may be a doctor there.'

'We've stopped in four separate villages now. We were told that no one can help.'

'Then you'd better go on. You should find what you need in any of the bigger towns ahead – Schwarzenberg, Schneeberg.' He paused. 'Who's the character in the back with the children?'

'He's a professor from the Technical University in Dresden. I work with him.'

'I see,' said the man doubtfully.

'He's more important than he looks,' said Rosenharte with a rather long-suffering look.

Else let out a moan, which was just audible from where they stood.

'You'd better be on your way, friend,' advised the officer. 'Good luck.'

They left the trucks with an impressive spray of gravel and drove on for a further five and a half miles before seeing the bridge on their right. It was blocked to vehicles by a single red and white bar and three large boulders, which had been hauled from the bed of the stream. He drifted to a stop and looked up into the trees. He knew exactly where he was. The border lay just over the hill though the top of it was hidden by the mist that smouldered in the trees from halfway up. He drove on for a hundred yards and then took a lumber track on his left, gunning the Wartburg's little engine to carry them up the dirt slope. He parked behind a stack of timber, hopped out and put on his walking boots and anorak, then folded his coat and stuffed it into his pack. Taking his camping knife, he unscrewed the registration plates and hid them some way off in the undergrowth. The licence and ownership details were placed in the front flap of his anorak for the same reason: if the car was found, he didn't want it to be traced back to Ulrike. Finally, he covered the rear of the car with boughs cut from the trees nearby so it wouldn't be seen from the road.

Before shouldering his own rucksack, he checked Else's and the boy's shoes. They couldn't take their eyes off Idris, who was dressed in a long, tailored prelate's coat, a turban improvised from a piece of striped towel, and trainers. On his back he carried a large grip, which served as a pack, with the long handles acting as straps.

Keeping hidden from the road, they made for the bridge, crossed it and entered a patch of open and very marshy ground at the base of the slope. Rosenharte and Idris carried the boys to a clump of evergreen bushes on the far side and returned to help Else, who was struggling across the tufts of bog grass with the bag of Konrad's films. After redistributing the luggage between himself and Idris, he led them into the dark, silent forest and moved slowly up the hill, along a path more trodden by deer and foxes than by men. Rosenharte brought up the rear while Idris strode out ahead with a boy on each side hanging onto his skirts. It was plain that in all his years in Dresden he had never seen the great, dismal forest of German mythology and now he seemed awed by it, as if something enormously important about Germany had been revealed to him.

The hill was higher than it had seemed from the bridge, and since Else had already broken out in a sweat they sat down on a tree trunk and had another drink. Idris wandered a little way up the path to see how far there was to go, while Rosenharte, encouraged by Else, talked to the boys about their new life in the West and told them that they would never again be taken from their mother in the middle of the night. There was a long journey ahead of them, he said: a funny man with a very red and misshapen nose would drive them in a foreign car. He was English and he talked with an accent that Rosenharte imitated.

Suddenly they spotted Idris sliding and tripping down the path, waving his arms. Rosenharte grabbed the boys by their hands and led them to a spot where the boughs of the pines touched the ground and made them lie down. Else and Idris followed and they all three flattened themselves to the bed of pine needles and waited, panting.

TWENTY-TWO

Escape

It began to rain. At first there were just one or two heavy drops, but within a few minutes a downpour ensued and the mist rolled down the hill, filling the forest. They remained dry under the trees, but visibility was reduced to about forty feet, and they could only just make out the path they'd been walking.

'Did they see you?' Rosenharte whispered.

Idris shook his head.

'How many were there?'

Idris held up four fingers, then made a sign to indicate that they were carrying weapons.

'Grepos?'

He nodded. His eyes were staring out at the forest.

They waited for an hour under the trees. Else pulled her boys to her and held them to keep them warm, because the rain had brought a sudden drop in temperature. Still, the rain was no bad thing: it would cover up their tracks on the hill and wash away the tyre marks on the lumber road. Rosenharte looked at his watch: it was eight fifteen. They were late, but there had been no one to meet them at the bridge, as the American suggested there would, and Rosenharte was sure they'd be on the other side of the border. The mist had lifted a little over the forest and the rain had stopped. He rose to his knees very slowly and crawled out of the shelter to see if there was any movement above them. Idris tugged at his trousers. Rosenharte dropped down. A minute or two passed, during which he heard only the thunder of the stream below. Idris touched his leg again. Rosenharte craned his neck to see him pointing at one of the children's backpacks propped up against the trunk where they had stopped. Anyone coming down the path would see it immediately. He cursed and wriggled forward, but just as he was deciding to get up and save his trousers from the mud ahead of him, he heard the voices coming down the path. It was too late to retreat the few feet back to the others, so he sank to the ground and hugged it for dear life.

There was in fact a party of six guards. Evidently they had been sheltering somewhere on the top of the hill, because their uniforms were barely wet. He could hear what they were saying. One was telling a story about an officer who had been caught on the job at a local farm and been reduced to the ranks and sent to the Polish border. Every time he wanted to emphasize a point, he would turn and his colleagues would stop to listen and chip in with their own comments.

When they reached the bag, one of them spotted it and picked it up. They crowded round and looked inside, but it didn't occur to them that it had been left there recently, still less that the fugitives were within a few feet of them in the undergrowth. The man then flung it high into the trees, where it dangled from a branch by one of the straps. This seemed to amuse them and they continued on their way, laughing.

Rosenharte left it a quarter of an hour before moving again and summoning the others back onto the path. They climbed the next 200 yards quickly, carrying the boys up the steeper parts and helping Else, whose size and lack of fitness was beginning to prove a problem.

Eventually they reached a large rock, from which sprouted a few birch saplings. It was the highest point on the range and they were able to look down into Czechoslovakia, which at that moment was a cauldron of mist broken by the spires of dead pine trees. Else bent over to clutch her knees and asked if they had arrived. Rosenharte told her that there was just one more obstacle which he was going to look at. He urged them to stay hidden behind the rock while he was gone.

He jogged the fifty or so yards and came to a rusty mesh fence topped by three lines of barbed wire. Compared to the defences along the East-West border, this was pretty rudimentary. There were no sensors or automatic guns aimed at body level, and despite seeing the detachment of the guards earlier, he did not think that this section of the border was heavily patrolled. He felt the spring of the mesh and realized it wouldn't take much to dislodge it from the ring fittings on the concrete posts.

A little way up he had noticed a fairly sizeable log, which he now dragged down to the fence. Aiming one end at the point where the mesh was fixed to the fence, he jabbed at the mesh and burst the fitting with little difficulty. He dragged the log to two more posts and repeated the procedure, at the last one shouting for the others to join him. Very soon he had pushed the mesh over with the log so that it lay at an angle of forty-five degrees from the ground. They were able to scramble under the barbed wire and drop down on the other side. When they were all safely over they gave up a little cheer and Rosenharte tousled the boys' hair.

Griswald had said that the road clipped the border about five hundred yards down the slope. If they followed an easterly route they would find it. Rosenharte took his compass from the side pocket of the rucksack and they set off, taking a rather too literal course, which led them first to a little cliff and then across a stream that tumbled over a series of waterfalls into the mist. Eventually

297

they came to the road and quite miraculously found the red Volvo estate parked up in the mist with its lights on.

Inside, the Bird and Robert Harland were sharing a flask of coffee.

Rosenharte knew there would be a difficulty about Idris and there was. Harland got out, shook his hand and explained that Macy Harp was ill with flu. Then he let his eyes run over the figure in the long flowing robes. The Bird articulated his thoughts. 'Who's this? King Melchior? The bloody Lion of Judah?'

Rosenharte made the introductions and explained very quietly that unless they dropped Idris somewhere near Prague they wouldn't hear the new information he'd brought from Kafka.

'I don't mean to be rude, Rosenharte,' said Harland, 'but I'm not fucking around here. I want the information now, or I'll leave your brother's wife and kids on this road. Tell me what you've got and we'll talk about your friend here after that.' He led Rosenharte thirty feet beyond the car. 'Well?' he said.

Rosenharte looked away. He had no option. 'Her name is Ulrike Klaar. She works in the Youth Research Institute in Leipzig. As you know, she's heavily involved in the liberation and peace movement based around the Nikolaikirche. I believe it's only a matter of time before she's arrested for these activities.'

'Right. What do you make of the information? Do you think it's likely she has access to Abu Jamal?'

Rosenharte thought for a moment. 'She says Abu Jamal will be in Leipzig from Monday the ninth onwards. They have kept him out of the country until after the fortieth anniversary is over. He will be staying at the villa in Clara Zetkin Park.'

'How's she getting this information?'

Rosenharte shrugged and lit a cigarette. 'I think she has been his mistress at some point, but I'm not certain. There's a part of this thing that I don't understand. When I asked about certain gaps in her story – certain inconsistencies of behaviour – she answered vaguely and said that everything she had given you so far had proved to be true.'

'She's right but—'

'You think there's some kind of trap?' said Rosenharte.

'That's about the sum of it, yes. Do you like her? I mean do you get a good feeling about her?'

'It's hard to say. I like her, but I don't trust her. There's too much that's unexplained. However, I do believe she's sincere about the peace movement. She has a genuine religious faith, too.'

Harland absorbed this. 'I think we should move. We've got nothing to lose. What about the Annalise side of the operation? Are they buying it?'

'So far, but I saw Colonel Biermeier in Leipzig. It doesn't make sense that a member of the foreign intelligence service was there. I also saw Zank. And that worries me. I mean, maybe one or the other is onto Kafka.'

'And they saw you?'

'No, no.'

'Good. I wonder what the hell's going on.' He stopped and looked back down the road. Idris was playing with the boys while the Bird and Else watched. Harland called out to the Bird. 'Okay, Cuth, you can go ahead!'

'Righty-ho, but I'm afraid I can't do a new passport for King Melchior. He's going to have to sort himself out.'

'That's fine,' Harland called out. 'He wants a lift to somewhere near Prague and that's what he's going to get.'

The Bird lifted the tailgate of the Volvo and started taking pictures of Else, Florian and Christoph against a dark blue cloth that he hung from the car. Harland's eyes returned to Rosenharte.

'I've now given you everything you asked for,' said Rosen-harte. 'It's now time for us to discuss when you're going to bring Konrad out. I've been wondering whether it will be possible to combine it with the Abu Jamal operation.'

'Too complicated,' said Harland briskly. 'They're entirely different kinds of operation.'

'What are you going to do with the Arab?'

Harland ignored the question and looked away. A fine sheen of water from the mist had covered their hair and clothes. Harland brushed his shoulders and shook droplets from his hands. Rosen-harte did not move. 'My brother is currently in the hospital wing, as you know. But that situation is not going to last and they will take him back to the main interrogation centre whether he has recovered or not. We have to move soon or he will be lost.'

'I'll do all I can, but something like this is very out of the ordinary for us. We never have more than ten people in the Berlin Station. It's a minute operation compared to the Stasi. This is a big thing for us, even if we use some help from the Americans.'

'I've found some help. I can get you two good quality passes: a vehicle pass and a docket authorizing the collection of Konrad by the KGB.'

'Jesus, where from?'

'From a friend. Things are unravelling in the GDR. I can get this from the beginning of next week. All you need is a van like the ones they use, a couple of men with good German and a way out of the East. And with the Stasi totally distracted by the demonstrations, it shouldn't be too difficult.'

'But one check and our men are lost and your brother never gets out.'

Rosenharte looked back down the road at Else and Idris. 'That's true,' he said, 'but that's the deal we struck. Anyway, I believe I may be able to get someone to call ahead on the day to say that Konrad is going to be transferred.'

'The Stasi won't fall for that.'

'No one fears the Stasi more than I do, but I've seen them at very close quarters over the last week or so and they are flawed. They are making mistakes. Those people who marched in Leipzig two days ago are not going to be deterred. There is a real sense of revolution in the air and the Stasi are worried. They'll try to put down the demonstrations with force. I'm sure of it. Then we'll see whether the people have it in them to continue.' He paused. 'What I'm saying is that the Stasi are preoccupied by these events.'

'I hear you.'

'Then let us decide on a date.'

'What about the thirteenth or fourteenth next week? We'd move early and aim to get him through the border by mid-morning. Saturday the fourteenth is probably the best for us.'

'Can't you do it any earlier? He could be back in the main inter-rogation centre by then.'

'If he's out of hospital by then, it will be a good sign and besides, if these passes and release forms are as good as you say they are, it won't matter where he is in Hohenschönhausen will it? They'll work just as well if he's in the main interrogation centre.'

Rosenharte had no answer for that.

'Okay, but no later. How will I get them to you?'

'We'll fix a rendezvous in Berlin for the Friday afternoon. You'll call that day using the same system. Don't forget the code changes next week.'

Rosenharte turned to face the car. The boys were looking with great interest at the Bird, who was hunched over something in the back.

'I don't want Else to know anything about this plan,' said Rosenharte. 'She needs all her strength to make her new home.'

Harland nodded. 'Can you make your own way out of the GDR when this is over? We're going to have our hands full with your brother.'

'That will be no problem. I'll take the same route into Hungary.'

'Good.' He paused and looked at Rosenharte. 'There's one more thing I want you to do for us.'

'I have done all you wanted.'

'I know, Rudi, I know.' He put his hands up in an attitude of surrender. 'Can you go back to Leipzig and effect contact between Kafka and our people next weekend? I need you to do this to allay any fears Kafka may have. Will you do that for us?'

Rosenharte nodded. He had to return Ulrike's car in any case.

'Right, we'll fix the meeting for Sunday. You'll find one of the men from the BND whom you met in West Berlin at the main entrance to the park where the Leipzig trade fair is held – the Altes Messegelände. He will be there at five. We want you to walk from the city along Pragerstrasse. That way we will be able to see if you're being followed before you get there. They're the best, these guys. They're already undercover in the city and they will not fail you.'

'Do you need me to bring Kafka there?'

'No. You fix a meeting later. Now that I'm able to give them her name, they can find out exactly who she is and, well, if she's for real.'

Rosenharte turned to the car. 'You still have doubts?'

'Not really, but I am baffled by her.' He kicked the gravel on the road and looked up at three hooded crows that were trying to rise above the mist. 'There's one further thing, Rudi. We've got to keep the Stasi off your back, so we're going to arrange that Annalise makes the final delivery in early November. She will write to you in the usual way and they will intercept the letter. By that time we will have sorted Konrad and the Arab, and we'll just give them some crap that will foul up their computers for a few months.'

Rosenharte turned and walked back to the others. The Bird was wiping the pictures on the spanking new joint British passport for Else and the boys. He showed them the Foreign and Commonwealth Office seal before using it to emboss the newly laminated Polaroid pictures. He gathered them round, flipped through the passport and pointed out the large mauve-coloured visa in the back indicating that they had crossed the border from Austria into Hungary ten days before. Another visa proved the family's legitimate presence in Czechoslovakia.

'You are now indubitably a legal British citizen, madam.' He held the passport up and began to read. 'Her Britannic Majesty's Principal Private Secretary of State for the Foreign and Commonwealth Office requests and requires in the name of Her Majesty . . .'

'For Christ's sake, Cuth,' cut in Harland. 'We've got a long way to go.' He turned and offered his ungloved hand to Rosenharte. 'Good luck, Rudi.'

'Yes, Godspeed old son,' said the Bird, seizing his hand in an iron grip. 'We'll look after this lot for you.'

Rosenharte went to the boys and crouched down. 'Look, keep good care of your mother for me and your father, eh?' They nodded solemnly. 'And I will see you very soon in the West.'

Else kissed him and made him promise to bring Konrad to her. Before he had let her go, Idris had fallen on him and was also kissing him. 'We will see each other again,' said Rosenharte, holding his shoulders. 'I have no doubt of it, my friend.' His eyes watered: he was unused to such a display.

Idris gave him an address in Khartoum, written in English and Arabic, which he produced from inside his coat with a flourish.

Rosenharte shook his hand and palmed the two $100 bills he had ready. With a final kiss to Else, he managed to plant $500 in her coat pocket, which he indicated with a wink.

It was time to go. He turned and was moving quickly up the slope before they had even thought of settling into the Volvo. By the time he heard its engine start and turned to look, the road had vanished in the mist.

He re-crossed the border feeling more bereft than he had for a long time, but a part of him also noted his relief at having one less responsibility. If he could get news of their successful flight to Konrad through the Russian, it would certainly do his morale some good as well. He walked slowly, keeping all his senses attuned to the forest around him.

Having climbed over the border at a different point, just in case the damage to the fence had been discovered, he spent some time fighting his way through a dense area of the forest. It was noon before he hit the path, just at the spot where the backpack hung in the trees. Every twenty feet or so he stopped and listened. About one hundred yards up from the stream he realized that while the car could not be seen from the road, it was clearly visible from this side of the valley. The border guards might easily have spotted it from this point.

Heart pounding, he abandoned all caution and raced down to cross the bridge, then crept through the trees. Having checked that the Wartburg hadn't been immobilized in any way, he went to retrieve the licence plates, screwed them on and pushed the car to a dirt track so he could freewheel down. He jump-started the engine just before the bottom and slipped quietly from the track into the road.

Life was a hell of a lot simpler now. His only purpose was to get Konrad out.

PART THREE

PART THREE

TWENTY-THREE

Termination

Sonja sat down on the bench beside him. 'You should look after yourself, Rudi. One sandwich and a piece of old sausage. No fruit, no protein to speak of. You look shit. What's the matter with you?'

Rosenharte gazed across to the Opera House. It was a beautiful day and he could do without an ambush from Sonja.

'When did you get back?' she asked.

'Wednesday.' He turned to her. 'What the hell have you done to yourself?'

'Oh, this?' she said, fingering a small silver stud that had been inserted just under her lower lip. 'Don't you like it?'

'No.'

She shrugged. 'Well, it's not meant for a man of your generation.'

'My generation doesn't come into it, Sonja. You have a beautiful face. It's a shame to fill it with bits of scrap iron.'

'It's silver. My boyfriend gave it to me.'

'Sebastian?'

'No. Rikki. Rikki's my boyfriend now.'

'What happened to Sebastian? I thought he was the love of your life.'

She shook her head slowly. 'He was too busy for me. I haven't seen him since they let him go and he vanished to Leipzig. He's obsessed with the *events*.'

'Aren't you?'

She shrugged again. 'Yes . . . of course I am.' She hooked one leg under her bottom. She was dressed artlessly – a short denim skirt, scuffed calf-length boots worn against bare legs, and a grey round-neck sweater that he had given her.

'So you got back the evening of the big riot at the Hauptbahnhof?'

'Yes.' He had seen the trains carrying the East Germans from Prague to the West. God knows how many people had tried to board at the station and on the approaches to Dresden. They had been moving at a tantalizingly slow speed, and from the side of the lines, Dresdeners had been able to see the happiness on every face that was bound for the West and freedom. It was too much for them. Some tried to cling to the outside of the carriages, and in one case a man attempted to scramble through the open door of the driver's cab. At the station thousands had been arrested and taken away in trucks. The police used their batons without mercy, but those with serious head injuries declined to receive hospital treatment because they didn't want to be turned in to the authorities.

'You saw it all? Why were you at the Hauptbahnhof? Where were you coming back from?'

'Nowhere. I just happened to be there.'

After the journey from the border he had parked the Wartburg in an old goods yard and paid the man to open up at any time of day or night. He wanted to keep the car out of sight so the Stasi wouldn't make any connections with Ulrike, but he also thought that the Hauptbahnhof was still the best place to lose surveillance when he needed to leave the city.

'You just happened to be there,' she said after examining his face. 'You're a mystery man, Rudi.'

He ate the remains of his sandwich. 'Talking of mystery men,' he said casually, 'do you remember the man who came to see me? You described him as a yokel – a country boy.'

A flicker of worry crossed her eyes. 'Sure. I remember him. He was a Czech or a Pole, I forget which.'

'A Pole,' said Rosenharte. 'I believe he left something for me: a letter?'

'I don't remember. Maybe he left it with one of the other girls.' Her cheeks betrayed a slight flush and she looked away.

'It's okay,' he continued gently. 'I know the pressures. Did you give the letter to the Stasi?'

She nodded. 'They told me that if the man showed his face again that I should call a special number.'

'Do you know what was in the note?'

'Yes, something about your family. It wasn't clear. There was an address and a telephone number at the bottom. Oh yes, I remember now. The man wanted to know something which he could only ask you personally, face to face. That's how he put it.'

'What was the name of the officer you gave it to?'

'Someone from Berlin – a cold bastard called Zank. A real Nazi.'

Rosenharte put his hand on hers. 'Thank you. It's good you told me.'

'I didn't tell them about the phone call you made from the professor's office,' she said, her eyes pleading forgiveness.

'Good, let's keep it that way. And don't tell them that you have spoken to me about this. Act ignorant.' He saw she wanted to say something else. 'What is it?'

'They're going to fire you at the end of today. They had a

meeting of the committee on Monday. They decided then. I've already been told to tell you that you should report to the director's office at five.'

He was only surprised because Biermeier said everything had been squared with the gallery. 'Why? What's their reason?'

She tipped her head to one shoulder. 'You're never here. They say you come and go as you please. They say you drink.'

'Yes, but they know I've been doing something important that I can't talk about. They were warned that I would be away a lot.'

'Zank told the director that you were an undesirable. I heard part of the phone call.'

He got up. 'Well, I'd better make use of this afternoon.'

'What are you going to do with your life?'

'When certain things in my life are resolved, I will write a book I've had in mind for some time. It's come to me very clearly this past week.'

'What's it about?'

He looked up at the side of the Zwinger. 'The pictures that were saved in the war – in other words the collection here and how it has affected the way I see things.' He saw her expression glaze. 'It's not an academic book. It's about the war, and culture in the GDR.'

'Sounds really exciting,' she said unenthusiastically.

He gave her a sideways look, then returned to the gallery where he went to the restoration room in the basement and began to make notes. He could see these works as a private visitor to the gallery, but he would never again have contact with them – the freedom to pore over the paint surface with his magnifying glass and examine the back of the paintings.

At five he presented himself in the committee room to find Professor Lichtenberg at a table, stroking his little grey goatee beard and peering over his glasses. He had always reminded Rosenharte of Walter Ulbricht, the first secretary ousted by Erich Honecker. Three other members of the gallery's committee were also there. Rosenharte smiled pleasantly and sat down on the chair in front of them.

'Certain things have come to our notice, Dr Rosenharte,' said Lichtenberg after clearing his throat.

'Oh? What things?'

'Your repeated absences.'

'But you know that I have been doing work for the Ministry of State Security. It has required me to travel to Berlin and to the West.'

'We were aware of that,' said Lichtenberg, who was evidently rather enjoying the solemnity of the occasion. 'But there are other matters that affect the reputation of this institution and the people who work here. They cannot be overlooked.'

'What are you talking about?'

'Your lectures, in particular the talk you gave at the University of Leipzig ten days ago. Professor Böhme has written to us to complain about your attitude. He said it was very surprising that you had not come to the notice of the authorities given your negative decadent views.'

'It was an aside that caused the offence, one which he wilfully misunderstood. It was nothing to do with the main body of the lecture.'

'Dr Rosenharte, we have *quotations*! He took notes during the lecture. Are we to believe that such a distinguished man invented the whole incident?'

'Believe what you like, but it was a serious lecture that seemed to be received well and was applauded.'

'Applauded by impressionable young people who saw an

important member of the Party humiliated while defending the ideals of Marxism. That is not a state of affairs that any of us will condone.' They all nodded.

'I don't care if you condone it or not. These are my views and I have a right to express them whether they offend a pompous fool like Böhme or not. I invited him to debate the matter, but he was incapable of uttering anything but Party slogans.'

'Better than the decadent nonsense that rots the brains of our youth,' said the woman. Rosenharte seemed to remember that she had something to do with one of Dresden's cultural committees. She was still only in her thirties but had already acquired the prim, desiccated look of the apparatchik. This was the third such woman that he had faced across a table in the last month.

'Free and open discussion of intellectual matters does not rot anyone's brain,' he said, aiming his rage at her. 'Genuine debate is what young people of the GDR have been starved of these past forty years.'

The woman recoiled as though she had been slapped across the face.

'It is not as if this was the only occasion that we've been informed about,' said Lichtenberg, leaning forward and dispatching a sympathetic look in her direction. 'We have a report about the lecture you gave in Trieste. It is said to contain a hidden meaning, an oblique but nonetheless corrosive attack on the criminal justice system of the GDR.'

'You read that paper yourself and approved it.'

Lichtenberg looked flustered. 'I was, perhaps, unaware of your motive . . . blind to the coded message that lay beneath the surface.' He again looked at the woman who was furiously scribbling a note to herself.

'There was no coded message. It is a fact that artists in the late

Renaissance looked about them and recorded the heartlessness of their age in their private drawings.'

'That may be so,' said Lichtenberg, plainly not wishing to be drawn into a debate about art history. 'But these things cannot be ignored. The offence you gave was far too great. We have our reputation to think of. When you give these lectures you represent all of us. You must understand that, Doktor.'

Rosenharte rose and approached the table. Lichtenberg retreated in his chair. 'I represent no one but myself.'

'Exactly – an individualist through and through,' said the woman triumphantly.

'Not an individualist, but an individual. Maybe you don't know the difference.'

Lichtenberg had raised a hand. 'There's little point in continuing this discussion further. The Gemäldegalerie no longer requires your service, Dr Rosenharte. Is that clear enough for you? You will leave at the end of this hearing and remove your personal possessions from your desk.'

'You're throwing me out?'

'Yes, if you want to put it that way, Rosenharte. You must remember that I've the whole gallery to think of. You have done immeasurable damage to its reputation.'

Rosenharte moved to the door, then stopped and turned to them. 'Look around you. Barely a day goes by without a demonstration. People have had enough. The world is changing.'

Lichtenberg put on a hurt expression. 'Why this sudden defiance? These are the views of a rebellious teenager!'

'Why? My brother is in Hohenschönhausen. Maybe you have heard of the place where the Party crushes its opponents. He is being held without trial there and he may be dying. In his life he has never expressed anything remotely as controversial

313

as I have just uttered in this room. That explains my change of attitude.'

The woman shot up. 'I will not listen to this. If he's anything like you, your brother deserves to be in prison.'

'What you need, madam, is a damned good screw,' said Rosenharte. He regretted the profanity, but the effect was truly worth it. It was as though an electric current had passed through her. She sat down and rose again; her hands clenched and unclenched and the blood drained from her face.

He closed the door behind him and went to collect the books from his office and say a few goodbyes to his staff on his way.

There was usually a thin crack of daylight under Rosenharte's office door. In the days when Sonja waited for him he could always tell when she was there by a smudge of shadow on the left. Now as he approached, he saw that his office was occupied. He paused outside the heavy wooden door, then opened it to find Colonel Zank standing at the window with the two men he'd seen with him in Berlin.

'What are you doing in my office?' he demanded.

'Your office?' said Zank. 'Surely it's no longer yours?'

'Until I leave it is.' He moved to take the books from the shelves and began to pile them on his desk.

'I'd like your full attention,' said Zank.

'You've got it,' Rosenharte said, his eyes fixed on the volume about Giorgione.

'We were concerned to ask you some questions about your trip to Trieste.'

Rosenharte turned from the bookshelf. 'What?'

'There're things that do not satisfy us. For instance, how Annalise Schering knew that you were at the restaurant by the canal.'

This threw him. 'Why are you asking this now? Surely the Stasi has got better things to do.'

'We do, that's for sure. But please answer the question.' He folded his arms and let his eyes run over Rosenharte's possessions.

'I don't remember. I think I told someone at the front desk that I was going there. No, wait, they recommended the place and I told them I would be there if anyone called for me.'

'That's odd,' said Zank. 'Because we had two people try the same thing – as an experiment, you understand. They reported that the hotel recommended an entirely different place. On both occasions they said the restaurant on the canal was too expensive. A tourist trap.'

'All I can say is that the man in the red and black jacket told me that it was a fine place. Maybe he got a kickback for sending people there. I remember now that the maître d' in the restaurant asked me how I had heard of the place.'

Zank's lips parted, but there was no hint of a smile. 'I don't believe you,' he said.

'Then don't, but it's the truth.' Rosenharte returned to the bookshelf to control himself.

'We went to the hotel where you stayed with your friend, not your hotel but the Hotel Sistiana.'

'You're obsessed,' said Rosenharte.

'No, just thorough,' said Zank. 'They call it a *bijou* hotel in the guide – small, comfortable and very good service. You know, Rosenharte, many of the staff have been there twenty or more years. It's a family concern.'

'So?'

'We talked to the maids there. Their memories are still quite fresh. After all, it was not long ago. They knew that you had tipped the night porter who brought you food and champagne late that evening. But they were unable to recall you leaving any money for the maid service, which is customary and was certainly expected by them after they had heard how you treated the night porter.'

'That's right. I didn't leave them any money.'

'Exactly, that's why they remember Fräulein Schering's occupation of that room. The other reason is that there were no signs of love. You are a man of the world. I do not have to explain what I am referring to.'

'Sorry, I don't understand.'

'Well, maids, being what they are, tend to speculate on the level of passion enjoyed by a couple from the evidence in the bed. In yours there was none.'

Rosenharte shook his head. 'Is that what you're reduced to – sneaking around looking for semen stains?'

'Don't be frivolous, Rosenharte. This is an important matter.'

'You're trying to frame me to discredit General Schwarzmeer's operation. I will not be used in the internal battles of the ministry. Last time I saw the general – you were not there, of course – he expressed his pleasure with the intelligence from the West. His scientists are looking forward to the next delivery. But there won't be one unless my brother is released, and you're the man who's keeping him there. You'd better be sure of what you're doing, Zank.'

Zank walked to the desk and picked up the top volume of a pile of books and read out its title: 'Art and Illusion by E.H. Gombrich. It might have been written by you, Rosenharte, because art and illusion are your two specialities. The question we have to decide is what is real and what is illusion in your life. I confess I'm beginning to think that most of your life is an illusion.'

'That is not General Schwarzmeer's view and I don't have to remind you that this is his operation.'

'It is, but we at Main Department Three like to keep an eye on things.' He put the book down. 'The man who died on the quay in Trieste was called Franciscek Grycko. Does that mean anything to you?'

'I had no knowledge of him. I've said that before.'

'He was once an operative of the Sluzba Bezpieczeństwa, the Polish state security service.'

'You're joking,' said Rosenharte.

Zank shook his head. 'I never joke. I believe the same man visited this office. Subsequent to his death a person using his name also came here.'

'I heard someone was looking for me here,' said Rosenharte. 'The woman who works for Professor Lichtenberg told me.'

'Ah yes, Sonja. I don't have to tell you what a pleasant girl she is, do I, Rosenharte?'

Rosenharte stared at him.

'We will return to her later, but now I want to ask how Mr Grycko knew that you were going to be in Trieste. What did he want? Evidently this fascination for an obscure art historian continued after his death. Is the second man who came looking for you here related, or merely using Mr Grycko's identity? And how does he fit into the business of Annalise Schering? At the Main Department Three we are trying to make sense of it all, Rosenharte, and we want your help.'

'But I can't help you. If the man had left a note or something I might be able to find out.' He let that hang in the air, but Zank didn't react. 'I've never been to Poland and have no Polish friends. The affair is a mystery to me.'

Zank sucked air through his lips.

'You're trying to make something out of nothing when you know that all I have ever wanted is the release of my brother. I

317

know you're the one who stands in the way of his freedom. You can have me fired from my job. I can deal with that. But if any harm happens to Konrad, you will pay for it.'

Zank gave him a chilling look. 'I am merely doing the best I can to protect the state, Rosenharte. And it appears to me that you're hiding something which may be a danger to the state. I will find out what that is very soon. Let me assure you of that.'

'And for this you hold my brother?'

'Naturally. Who can say how many people are involved in this plot?'

'There is no plot! I am working for General Schwarzmeer, but I will cease to cooperate if my brother is not released.'

There was a knock at the door. Another young Stasi thug beckoned Zank into the corridor and closed the door behind him. Zank reappeared and walked to the window with his hands in his pockets. 'A very pleasant little berth you had to yourself here. You will miss the view over the Zwinger gardens. If only we at the MfS had such delightful circumstances in which to work.' The men nodded. He moved to the door, brushing his upper lip with the edge of his forefinger. 'I must return to Berlin. The rowdies are on the streets again causing trouble for tomorrow's celebrations. What a world we live in, eh?' One of the men opened the door for him. Zank paused and faced Rosenharte. 'Oh yes, it seems you made a call from the director's office two weeks ago – something you were anxious to keep secret. I have learned that it was to a Berlin number but we have experienced difficulties in tracing it. Odd that.'

Rosenharte thought quickly and looked him in the eye. 'I have been told to say nothing about this.'

'Are you saying that the number belongs to the ministry?'

'I cannot say.'

Zank considered him for a moment. 'We will continue this conversation at the earliest opportunity.'

One of the men handed him his raincoat and they left.

Rosenharte slumped in his old chair and stared out of the window. When Zank found out that there was no such number at Normannenstrasse, his suspicions would be confirmed. But he already had enough information to hold and interrogate him. There was no need for him to wait to find out about the telephone number. He could arrest him whenever he wanted. So why didn't he? During the exchange Rosenharte had noticed that instead of pursuing each point about the choice of restaurant, the hotel or the Pole to exhaustion – which was the Stasi's usual nightmarish modus operandi – Zank had merely touched on them. He was putting a marker down, letting Rosenharte know what he knew. Maybe he was also trying to panic him into taking precipitate action.

Two things were clear: Zank hadn't managed to discredit Schwarzmeer's operation, and the Minister of State Security wasn't yet willing to abandon the hope of gaining more information about the NATO system. He sprang up and went to the director's office.

At this time on a Friday very few people were about. He listened at the door for a few seconds then opened it. Sonja was standing by the window. She looked guilty as hell and she had been crying.

'Is he in?' he whispered.

She shook her head.

He went straight in without asking and dialled five numbers – all of them with the prefix for Normannenstrasse. Four of the calls were answered and each time Rosenharte entered a random five-figure code and hung up. Then he dialled Vladimir's number at Angelikastrasse and left a message with a ponderous Russian voice that he needed to speak to someone as a matter of urgency.

Rosenharte hung up and grinned to himself. It might just throw Zank that little bit more if he knew he had dealings with the KGB. He was absolutely certain that Lichtenberg's phone would now be monitored constantly.

He left the office and went over to Sonja. 'You deliberately deceived me,' he said quietly. 'You told them about the original phone call I made here. Was that necessary?'

'I had to.'

'No you didn't. You went out of your way to help them.'

'You used me,' she said.

'Used you? I've never used you, Sonja.'

'You did. You used me.'

He smiled. 'We both know that's not true. There're all sorts of reasons why people help the Stasi. Usually they've been put in a position where they can't do anything else. That I understand. But saying that you did this out of some kind of revenge is . . .'

'Well, maybe I didn't . . . hell, I don't know. I've been confused lately. You're so arrogant and wrapped up in yourself that you never noticed how fond I was of you. I'd have done anything for you, Rudi, anything.'

This was all he needed but he understood: she had felt rejected that last time by the river bank and told Zank out of pique. He sat down on the edge of the desk beside her and took her hand. 'It's okay. You're probably right, but I want you to know that I never felt anything less than the deepest affection for you.' He paused and looked into her eyes. 'How did they make you do it?'

'My mother . . . You know she has arthritis. They promised to get her some new drug.'

Rosenharte nodded. 'Did you tell them anything else?'

She shook her head. 'I don't know anything else.'

'Good.'

'I'm sorry.'

'Just so long as you don't think of yourself as taking revenge on me. You should spare yourself that, Sonja, because it isn't true and it is unworthy of you.'

He didn't have time for this but he waited a few moments before standing and giving her a gentle peck on the cheek. He knew she would tell Zank about the phone calls he'd made. That was good.

He walked straight to Angelikastrasse without bothering to check if he was being followed, and rang the brass bell at the door. Within a few seconds the door had been opened by a thickset man in his early thirties with a small scar on his chin.

He looked across the street and to his right and left. 'Rosenharte?' he said. 'Come in.'

He was shown into a little interview room on the ground floor where the air was stale. A couple of minutes later, Vladimir appeared in a loose-fitting, double-breasted suit and tie.

'I thought you were away in Berlin,' said Rosenharte.

'We're leaving any second. How can I help?'

'They're moving next week. All their people will be in place in Leipzig by Monday evening.'

'The evening of the next demonstration. Who will be there exactly – the British, the Americans – who?'

'I don't know, but I've been told to contact three members of the BND on Sunday evening at the trade fair ground.'

'And you are to take them to Kafka. You were going to tell me her name.'

Rosenharte hesitated. 'How will you use it?'

'Have no fears. The Stasi won't hear of her from us.' He stopped and adjusted his cufflink. 'Maybe you don't know this, Rudi, but in September this year a conference was held in Santa Monica,

California, at the instigation of William Webster, the chief of the CIA. We were there. We have joined with the US in a special task force to fight terrorism. The man leading our side is Major-General Valentin Zvezdenkov, a former chief of counter-terrorism. Also General Sherbak, former deputy chairman of the Second Main Directorate of the KGB, is involved. These are contacts between the East and West at a very high level. You see, it's not just words: the world is changing faster than most of us can comprehend.' He tugged at his suit jacket and briefly checked his reflection in the window. 'If this operation is fighting terrorism, we're not going to disrupt it. So tell me her name.'

'Before I do, I want to know I have your agreement about the passes. The date has been set for a week tomorrow, Saturday the fourteenth October.'

'What is it you want, exactly?'

'A vehicle pass, a release form for Konrad, specifying the KGB's need to question him and two passes for the men whose names I will supply this week.'

It alarmed Rosenharte that Vladimir looked as if he was hearing the request for the first time. But then he said, 'I think we can do this. Saturday the fourteenth. Yes, this should be possible.'

'For delivery in Berlin on Friday the thirteenth?'

'You're not superstitious?' he asked with a mocking smile.

Rosenharte shook his head. Then he gave him Ulrike's name and explained who she was. It troubled him greatly but he had to get Konrad out of prison.

'That's all good,' Vladimir said at length, 'and they're going to take some kind of action next week? I'll want to hear details of that the moment you learn of them. The Stasi have no hint of what's to happen?'

'They're close, but Colonel Zank hasn't made all the connections.

I think they're preoccupied with what's going on. The riots at the station . . .'

'To say nothing about the demonstrations in Berlin. People shouting our president's name on the way from the airport. You should be careful in Leipzig. We think they will use force on Monday. Troops have been ordered to the city. Supplies of blood have been shipped in and specialists in gunshot wounds also. Mielke means business this time.' He gave Rosenharte a curious look and several nods to underline that the information was good. 'If you survive Monday, call me here, at any time. I want to be kept informed of the situation.'

Rosenharte was aware the interview had come to an end.

'May I ask you one thing, as a matter of curiosity?'

'If it's brief. I have to leave.'

'Will President Gorbachev come to Honecker's rescue?'

'How can I know what the president is thinking? Be serious, Rudi.'

Rosenharte then asked a favour of Vladimir. He listened impatiently, glancing at his watch twice before agreeing. One of the men who was staying behind in Dresden would be able to help, he said. This was all he could do.

'Now please go, Dr Rosenharte,' he said, 'and keep in touch.'

All over Dresden that night, groups of youths were gathering to jeer at the Volkspolizei, who responded by running them down and beating them. These were minor scuffles and there was no focal point for these demonstrations, but it was plain that feelings had not dampened after the mass arrests on Wednesday and Thursday. If the people weren't allowed to leave on the trains that crawled westwards through the city, they were going to make life hell for the Vopos. They seemed to have lost their fear: it was as if they wanted to be attacked, to hold up the mirror to the police and show them the reality of the state now celebrating its anniversary. They didn't fight back, but ran shielding their heads, crying out: 'No more violence!'

He saw a young couple, no more than twenty years old, being clubbed viciously over their backs and shoulders by two Vopos in riot gear. He bellowed at them to stop. One policeman looked round, raised the visor on his helmet and shook his baton at Rosenharte. The young man had time to pull his girlfriend free and run off.

On his way home Rosenharte stopped outside an electrical store, where a lone TV set showed the state network's coverage of a youth parade in Berlin. Tens of thousands of kids, indistinguishable from the ones taking on the Vopos at every street corner in Dresden, were marching in the blue and green uniforms of the Freie Deutsche Jugend, along Unter den Linden in the heart of Berlin. The communist leaders looked on benevolently – Erich Honecker, Gorbachev, Ceausescu of Romania, Jaruzelski of Poland, Grosz of Hungary. Honecker appeared to be in a trance. 'He's ill. Look, he's drugged,' said a man who had stopped at the window to watch with him. 'He won't be long for this world.'

'I'll drink to that,' said Rosenharte.

He got home late and sat down with an old bottle of pear liqueur, which was the only alcohol he could find in the flat, and thought about Sonja. Had she tried to give herself to him on the river bank as a kind of apology, or had his rejection been the cause of her betrayal? Either way he couldn't bring himself to dislike her. During their affair she had often given him much joy.

At one o'clock in the morning he turned on the BBC World Service news. There was a short item about the celebrations in Berlin that included a suggestion that the young people had turned it into a pro-Gorbachev demonstration shouting out, 'Perestroika! Gorby help us!' – the same cry that was heard in the crowds kept away from the march by the police. No doubt that accounted for Honecker's parched expression on the podium. A West German radio station gave more time to the troubles in Dresden and on the fringes of the celebrations in Berlin. Next day would come the military parade, free funfairs for Berliners and a summit between Honecker and Gorbachev at the Schloss Niederschönhausen. Almost as an afterthought, the station ran an interview with Gorbachev that had been given at noon that day.

Rosenharte missed the introduction because he was opening the window. Then he heard a reporter ask: 'Do you feel threatened by the situation in Berlin?'

'No,' replied Gorbachev, laughing. 'It's nothing compared to the situation in Moscow. Nothing surprises us any more.'

There was a pause while the interpreter waited for Gorbachev to speak further. 'We are prepared for anything, and we've learned a lot too. For instance, how to initiate and carry out reform programmes and how to defend our policies.' Then he added: 'Danger threatens only those who do not react to life's challenges.'

The West German radio station offered a snappier translation: 'He who comes too late will be punished by life.'

If that wasn't an instruction to Honecker to initiate reform, he didn't know what was. Suddenly Vladimir's imperturbable features appeared in Rosenharte's mind. Everything he had said in the last few weeks was explained.

The world was changing, but would it change fast enough for Konrad?

TWENTY-FOUR

Plans Laid

Next day he packed both his suitcases and the rucksack with everything of importance in his life, for he knew he would not be returning to the flat. He took his luggage down to the hallway at three in the afternoon, and looked outside from the slender window beside the door. Two men in a blue Seat were waiting in the usual place. There were rumours that up to 30,000 would be on the streets in Dresden that day but the Stasi still had men to spare to watch him. He knocked on the door of one of two ground-floor apartments and an eager young face appeared – Willy, the son of the bakery manager. Rosenharte asked if he wanted to earn some money. The boy nodded and in a few seconds he had his jacket on.

He estimated it would take him about five minutes to reach the hostel where Idris had lived. At exactly three forty-five Willy left with the bags and rucksack, then Rosenharte went out and sauntered off in the same direction, apparently unaware of the two pairs of eyes that followed him. Only when he rounded a bend about one hundred yards from his building and heard the car engine start, did he begin to run towards the entrance of the path that led to the hostel. He knew that if the Stasi were doing their job, one would follow him on foot up the path, while the other would drive round the block to meet him at the far end, but he reckoned he had just enough of a head start to beat them whatever they did.

At the last bend he saw the black car with diplomatic plates waiting with its boot open. Beside it stood Willy, looking doubtful. Rosenharte thrust some notes into his hand, slung his luggage into the boot, then slid into the back, regretting his twenty-a-day habit. The car moved off into the sparse Saturday-afternoon traffic, leaving Willy to join a bus queue not far away.

'It's okay, they don't follow,' said the driver. It was the same man who had opened the door to him at Angelikastrasse. Rosenharte nevertheless stayed on the floor until they arrived at the goods yard and pulled up next to the Wartburg. A few minutes later he left Dresden, travelling on the road that exited the city on the south side. From then on he followed a circuitous route to Leipzig to minimize the risk of being stopped in the random police checks that he knew would lie along the main road connecting the two cities.

He drove, glancing in his mirror every minute or so, and in between times weighing up the risk involved in fleeing the Stasi surveillance. Zank would now consider him to be on the run, and infer guilt from his disappearance. If Zank argued his case well, the minister might even abandon the whole Annalise operation and dump the software they had been so desperate to acquire, whatever Schwarzmeer's protestations. And this would not help Konrad. On the other hand, he could not help Konrad if he was followed to Leipzig, particularly as Zank had already shown an interest in something there – exactly what still remained a puzzle to him. The hard fact was that he had to remain free and unobserved for the next seven days if he was to stand any chance of getting Konrad out. His hope during that time was that the swelling revolt would prove a sufficient distraction for the Stasi not to take a decision.

As he went, he listened to his transistor radio, swapping it from the passenger seat to the dashboard to pick up a West German station broadcasting news bulletins every hour. Reports through the afternoon stated that spontaneous demonstrations had flared in Leipzig, Magdeburg, Karl-Marx-Stadt, Halle, Plauen and Potsdam. In Berlin thousands of arrests had been made, and nothing had been missed because so many Western journalists were present to cover Gorbachev's visit and the military parade that morning. TV pictures of the brutal suppression were being shown in the West.

By the time Rosenharte slipped into the suburbs of Leipzig, he was almost convinced that the revolution had begun. The impression soon left him when he saw the half dozen blue and white buses containing hundreds of Volkspolizei parked up in a street not far from Ulrike's place. He circled her block once or twice to make sure nothing untoward awaited him there, then pulled into the bay that lay at right angles to the road and diagonally across from the wisteria gateway. Sitting in the shadows he watched the house for about an hour. At nine he saw a man leave, pause outside the gate to light a cigarette and walk up the pavement in his direction. He passed under a streetlight across from him. He was young and wearing jeans, a sports jacket with the collar turned up and trainers. A few yards on from the light he jogged across the road and Rosenharte got a good look at him. He knew exactly where he had seen him before – at the Nikolaikirche with Biermeier, and then in the square afterwards when the pair of them were making for Karl-Marx-Platz.

He waited half an hour more before leaving the car and making for Ulrike's door. He knocked gently. There was no response. He knocked again and pressed his ear to the door. Nothing moved inside. Then he used an old Stasi trick: putting his nose to the letter flap that had been cut sideways in the door. You could tell a lot from the odour of a house – the smells of recent cooking, fresh cigarette smoke and alcohol. However, nothing but a slightly scented air reached him. He had the sense that behind the door lay a vacuum, a mysterious emptiness he had no hope of explaining. He knocked several times more and called out softly through the letter flap, but the light above him didn't come on.

It hadn't occurred to him that she would be out, and he cursed himself for not taking a phone number where he could have left a message. He'd wait in the car and, if she didn't return, make do with sleeping in the back seat: going to a hotel was out of the question since they would ask to see his identity card and he would then appear on the overnight log given to the local Stasi headquarters.

He walked up the little brick path, which was strewn with a layer of wet leaves. That was odd because the inside of her apartment was so clean and orderly and he felt she was someone who would clear away the leaves. At the gate he nearly ran into a tall young man who loomed from nowhere and then, on seeing Rosenharte, pretended he had got the wrong house.

'Ulrike's not in,' Rosenharte called out to his back. 'Have you got any idea where she is?'

The man turned. 'No.'

'Do you know if she's coming back this evening?' The man looked shifty. Rosenharte realized what he was thinking and introduced himself. 'I was hoping to catch her. It's quite important.'

He took a few paces towards Rosenharte. He was extraordinary-looking. Standing at six feet four, his hair was dyed black and cropped at the sides. On top was a streaked Mohican, which ran front to back like an ancient Greek headdress. His face was long, gaunt and vital and the rims of both ears were clipped with rings and studs.

'You're her friend?' he asked softly. 'A real friend?'

'I'm not a member of the Stasi, if that is what you're asking.'

'Okay, okay, I know you're not Stasi. You don't have the look.' He grinned. 'I'm Kurt – Kurt Blast.'

'That's a good name.'

'That's why I chose it. It's *my* name. You won't find it on any identity card. It's not in the Stasi files. I own this name. The first step to freedom, right?' He looked to his left and right edgily. 'Ulrike, she's in Berlin at the demonstrations.'

'I see,' said Rosenharte.

'You have any cigarettes?' he asked.

Rosenharte felt for his packet and gave him one. 'I don't think we should be talking out here,' he said. 'There're a lot of Vopos about.'

They moved into the gateway and Rosenharte had a chance to examine him. His clothes were even more exotic. A loose leather jacket had been razored and stitched with red cord; his trousers were dark tartan and cut off just below the knee to reveal the longest pair of lace-up boots Rosenharte had ever seen. From his shoulder hung a string of safety pins and feathers.

'Where are you going to stay now?' he asked.

'Probably in the car. It's difficult for me to go to a hotel.'

'Maybe you can stay with me. It's dry and warm and you can pay me a few marks for the night. I'll throw some food your way for a little more money.'

Rosenharte considered this. 'Are you under any kind of surveillance?'

'No. There's no one else there. I play music the whole time – the guitar. They can't hear anything but my amp. Hey, maybe I have a fan base at Stasi headquarters.' The idea amused him.

'But are you watched?'

'No, they had their fun with me a long time back. They don't bother with me now.'

They drove to a strange, mutilated house on the very edge of Leipzig, which had been boarded up and abandoned by the authorities. Inside Kurt Blast had made it remarkably snug. There were two guitars hanging from hooks in the wall, a portable amplifier and neat stacks of records and books, which climbed up the wall in columns.

Kurt Blast turned out to be a rather thoughtful man and a diligent cook. He made Rosenharte a meal of soup and risotto, which they washed down with Marzen, the amber-red beer sold during Oktoberfest in the West. Kurt had an unlimited supply it seemed, and he didn't mind getting gently sloshed in front of Rosenharte. Later Rosenharte bedded down quite comfortably on the L-shaped couch.

Next morning he made arrangements to leave his things there and told Kurt that he was going in search of Ulrike. Overnight he had been gripped by the morbid certainty that she was being interrogated, which is how he explained seeing Biermeier's side-kick outside her home. He had to find out where she was.

He went to her home twice more. Both times he knocked and got no answer but the process took an hour or so each time because he made sure the place wasn't being watched. Before he knew it the day had disappeared and he had to start his walk from Karl-Marx-Platz down Pragerstrasse to the main gates of the trade fair ground. He took his time, stopping at the Friedenspark for ten minutes to read the newspaper, in which several barely veiled warnings were made about the peace demonstration and the likely toll if the people were to push the authorities. Around him there was a sense of siege. Streets had been blocked off and there was evidence that a large contingent of the People's Army was being deployed, just as Vladimir had predicted. Rosenharte even saw men with paratrooper insignia.

He arrived at the gates a little early, walked beyond them, then passed again on the other side of the road. No one was obviously waiting for him, so he stationed himself at the entrance and lit a cigarette. He was there just five minutes before a large truck pulled up and, ignoring Rosenharte, began to reverse into the opening so that it could turn. At the point when it was nearly touching the gates and Rosenharte had to jump out of the way, the door was opened by one of the Germans he'd seen in Griswald's apartment in Berlin, who offered him a hand and pulled him in. Inside, another man was hanging from a strap. The doors banged shut and one of the men guided Rosenharte to a crate and pushed him down. For one wild moment it occurred to him that he had been kidnapped, but then one produced a torch and gave him some black coffee, which had lain too long in a flask and had acquired a metallic taste. Eventually the truck pulled off the road, laboured up a hill then came to a stop. Both doors were opened. Standing in front of a car's headlights were Robert Harland and the short, energetic figure of Macy Harp.

'What the hell are you doing here?' Rosenharte said, jumping down. 'Isn't this too dangerous for you?'

'Things have changed quite a bit,' said Harland, putting out his hand. 'I think we're okay. Look, I have something for you.' He took a picture from his wallet and handed it over. 'That's Else and your two nephews in their new home. They arrived on Thursday morning. They seem to like it a lot.'

'Can I keep this and show it to Konrad?'

'That's why I brought it.'

Rosenharte slipped it into his wallet and looked around. There were eight of them, including Harland and Harp. 'What are you . . . ?' he started.

'We think tomorrow is the ideal time for us.'

'Abu Jamal isn't here.'

Harland turned to Macy Harp and took an envelope from him. 'He's been here all along; at least since last week when our German friends here moved in to do the recce.' He pulled a large black and white photograph from the envelope and gave it to Rosenharte. He held it down to the lights and saw a middle-aged man with a comb-over sitting in a wicker chair. Ulrike was standing a little apart from him, gazing somewhat vacantly towards the camera's lens. The man wore sunglasses. There was a hat and a book in his lap, and a glass of dark liquid on the table beside him. He was smoking a pipe.

'That was taken last week. We've now got a mini-camera in the garden which we can operate remotely,' said Harland. 'It's practically a live feed from the villa.'

'So, how does this concern me? You have all you need.'

'We want you to warn her. To get her out of the villa before we make our move.'

'She's there now? In the villa! I was told she was in Berlin.'

'I guess she conceals her movements from everyone, including you.' He paused and put up his coat collar. Rosenharte did the same. A sharp wind had blown up from the east and was tugging at the leaves on the birch trees around them. 'I'd say from this and other photographs that the Arab is pretty sick. We've observed that he needs medical attention for much of the time. I suppose he gets bored and needs company. It's been quite a reunion. We spotted Lomieko there too.'

Rosenharte shook his head. 'She was quite specific about Abu Jamal not being allowed into the country until the fortieth anniversary was over.'

'Maybe she wanted to keep us at arms' length to allow her to stay in Leipzig; after all, we know that's her priority.'

'It means she'll have to leave, then. Does she know that?'

'We haven't been able to get to her to warn her. That's why we need you. You see we have to move tomorrow night. What can I do?'

'You could wait until the middle of the week at least. Going tomorrow will make it very difficult for her. She will come under suspicion immediately.'

Harland shook his head regretfully. 'There are several international arrest warrants pending on Abu Jamal. Anyway, the GDR are not going to make a fuss, believe me. If they kick up about the snatch, it's as good as admitting their involvement. Once we lift him, they're not going to do anything. They can't.'

'But they'll know you've had help from the inside.'

'It's out of our hands. The American and British governments have to move against Abu Jamal immediately. There's talk of him blowing up the Paris Metro. This man is a serious threat to Western security and I'm afraid that sweeps all other considerations aside, even Kafka's security.'

'What haven't you told me?'

'I've told you everything. It's just that we don't understand how Kafka's been allowed to get away with this and remain a big part of the peace movement. It doesn't add up, unless she has some kind of protection.'

'From whom?'

'From the Stasi; who else?'

Rosenharte guffawed. 'You should hear her views on the Stasi.'

'Still, there's something we're not getting here. I know you feel the same way. We just can't put our fingers on it.'

Macy Harp nodded.

'Why can't you wait until Wednesday or Thursday?' asked Rosenharte.

'Because we're going to deploy the same team to extract your brother. That was your suggestion, and on reflection I thought it a good one, but these men will need time between the two operations. The overriding reason to move now is that the Arab's health is fading: we want to get him out of the country and to a good doctor. Oddly enough, this operation is about preserving his life, not ending it. We have to keep him alive to find out what he has planned – where, when and with whom. There are now several governments waiting on this operation and, quite frankly, we can't let the opportunity provided by tomorrow's demonstration pass. You understand that.'

'So what do you want me to do?'

'Warn her so that she can leave the city, or at least give her the choice.'

Rosenharte laughed bitterly. 'She's not going to leave. You've heard the slogan "We're staying here!" She all but invented it.' He paused. 'Anyway, there are bound to be Stasi guards at the house. Do you imagine they are going to allow me just to walk in and speak to her?'

'There are a couple at the front,' said Harland. 'They watch the house but rarely go inside. Your government has been able to get away with sheltering Abu Jamal for so long that they've become sloppy.'

'I will need help to get into the villa. My house-breaking skills are not what they used to be.'

Harland grinned, as if to say that he didn't know he had a sense of humour. 'No problem: you'll go through the garden. There's minimal risk, I assure you.'

'That I don't believe.' He looked at Macy Harp. 'And are these people to help with my brother?'

Harland nodded. 'We think a team of three: a driver and two men to make the pick-up. Have you any more information on his state of health?'

'No, but I think he's weak.'

'And you say you can supply the passes and the collection docket for the date. What's our story – a transfer?'

'A request for Konrad to be interviewed by the KGB at their Karlshorst headquarters for a twenty-four-hour period.'

'Is this likely? I mean, is this the sort of thing they do?'

'It's rare, but it does happen. When Konrad was in prison last time round, they talked to one of his fellow prisoners twice.'

'And these passes – where are you getting them from?'

'That's my secret. But they're the real thing.'

Harland drew him away and pulled a small bottle of brandy from his coat pocket, flipped the lid and handed it to him, looking through the smoke of his breath.

'You realize that this whole thing is about to come off. We're about to beat the bastards.'

Rosenharte handed the bottle back, feeling the warmth in his stomach. 'Getting Konrad to the West is my definition of victory. I don't care one way or the other about the Arab.'

'What are you going to do after tomorrow? You know you will have to lie low whatever Ulrike decides to do. You could do worse than come here. We'll pack up tomorrow morning and leave. It's all yours.'

'What?'

Harland swept the beam of a torch over a squat single-storey farm building, which Rosenharte had had no sense of. 'The beauty of it is that it is totally surrounded by trees, it's got about three ways in and out. And you can see for miles around. We've used it before and never had any problems. We'll leave the food for you and some other supplies.'

'I don't know where we are.'

'I'll show you a map. That reminds me to tell you where we want to pick you up on Saturday morning as well.'

They went to one of the cars and Macy Harp showed him their position by putting his finger on a spot about twenty kilometres north of Altenberg, the airbase where Rosenharte was convinced they had landed on the way back from Italy. Then he got out a large-scale map of East Berlin, found the place he was looking for and folded it to a manageable size. 'You see the church just off Köpenickerstrasse?' Rosenharte shook his head and Harp handed him his reading glasses. 'You have to be there from six thirty onwards at the back of the church. You got that? Saturday at six thirty,' he said emphatically. 'And no passengers. Okay?'

'How will we leave the GDR?'

'We'd prefer to keep that to ourselves,' said Harland quickly. 'What about the passes? How are you going to get them to us?'

Rosenharte thought. 'There's a train – the Dresden to Berlin service. It stops at six o'clock at Berlin-Schönefeld. That Friday evening I will board the first carriage, carrying a plain white plastic bag, which will contain the passes. At ten past six I'll go to the toilet. I will leave the bag in the towel disposal bin, covered with some newspaper.'

Harland and Harp nodded. 'We need a back-up plan. Trains are cancelled and delayed. There's quite a bit of surveillance at stations – people being asked for their identity cards, and so forth.'

'The newsstand at the Ostbahnhof. I will be there at seven thirty if there is a problem with the train. I will have a copy of *Neues Deutschland*. The passes will be in that. We will have to contrive to make a swap.'

Harland nodded. 'So, let's talk about tomorrow and how you're going to get Kafka out of the villa.'

TWENTY-FIVE

Oratorio

He scaled the wall with help from two BND officers and slipped into the shadows of an overgrown garden that was bordered on three sides by shrubs and clumps of bamboo. He could make out the sliding door at the rear of the villa which led onto a small area of unweeded gravel where there was some garden furniture. If surveillance reports from the previous days were anything to go by, Ulrike would rise early, shower, make a light breakfast and read for about an hour before the Arab stirred from his room and began the painfully slow business of his own toilet. At some stage before he appeared she usually went out onto the patio area. That would be Rosenharte's only chance to speak to her. At eight thirty a nurse arrived to take his temperature, blood pressure and remove a urine sample. Then his doctor looked in and generally stayed for half an hour or so. After that Abu Jamal made one or two phone calls and waited for a Stasi messenger to deliver Arabic newspapers. Lunch was brought to the villa at which point more serious contacts began to drop by. The BND's mini camera in the garden had recorded a number of interesting faces that would come in useful if the West decided to show the extent to which the GDR was involved with one of the world's most dangerous terrorists.

338

Hermann Wuthe, a senior diplomat with several Middle East postings behind him, had been spotted on Saturday afternoon.

He remained for an hour crouching in the bushes with his joints aching, nicotine withdrawal and anxiety nipping at his insides. A glimmer of dawn showed in the east and began to fill the garden with a greyish light. He noticed a movement behind a curtain on the first floor, then Ulrike's face appeared at the window. She was pulling her fingers up through her hair. A few minutes later, wearing jeans and a big mauve sweater, she crossed his line of sight into the kitchen and began to make breakfast for herself. He hesitated, not knowing whether to throw a pebble at the window or wait. But then the sliding door was drawn open with the noise of someone clearing their throat, and she came out. He smelt fresh coffee. When she had reached the furthest extent of the gravel about twenty feet from him, he called out to her softly. She seemed not to hear him, but stepped on to the grass and walked towards him.

'What are you doing here?' she hissed without looking down. 'You must go now!'

He didn't move. 'They're going to take him today, as soon as the villa is clear. You have to leave.'

'Go!' she said. 'You're risking everything.'

She moved a few steps closer, glanced back at the house, then sank down beside him.

'Go back to them now. Tell them this is *my* operation. I'm not leaving until I'm ready.'

'There's nothing you can do to stop them. Please, Ulrike, come now.'

'The Arab isn't even here. He went for treatment at the hospital last night. He won't be back until late morning or early afternoon.'

Rosenharte wondered what else the surveillance team had missed.

'Is this garden patrolled?'

339

'If he's outside, they sometimes put a man with him. But no, not usually.'

'I don't understand why you have to wait for him to return. It's Monday. It would be natural for you to go to work.'

'I'm waiting for information. A contact of mine will visit this afternoon and we'll know whether they plan to use violence tonight. That's much more important than this.'

Rosenharte shifted his weight and looked down at her cup. 'May I have some of that?'

She handed him the cup and watched him while he sipped the delicious black coffee, a supply of which he had no doubt was brought by the Arab for the duration of his visit.

'That's better,' he said, returning the cup. 'Look, Ulrike, forget your contact. We already know they're going to use force. Read the newspapers. There're army trucks everywhere. Paratroopers have been deployed with live ammunition. Everyone knows it. Blood supplies have been increased at the hospital.'

'Don't lecture me about what's going on in *this* city,' she said fiercely. 'This is *my* city. Your British friends are jeopardizing everything. Now go.'

'For Christ's sake, Ulrike, this is an international operation and you're responsible for it. You wanted to stop Abu Jamal. You worked for this intervention and now you can't complain that they have acted on your word.'

She looked away. 'Did you give them my name?'

He said nothing.

'Answer me.'

'Of course. I had to. You know what matters to me is getting my brother out of Hohenschönhausen and sending Else to the West. That was the deal. Remember that you put him there before you get sanctimonious with me.'

She turned to him, her expression furious. Rosenharte wondered why he'd found her attractive. 'You go back and tell them that they move only when I say so. Today is the day. Everything will be won or lost today. Nothing else matters. They must not interfere.' She paused, looked away, then softened her tone. 'Rudi, you and I both know that your brother was put in Hohenschönhausen by the Stasi. That's what we're fighting: imprisonment without trial. The breaking of people's spirits. Taking families from their beds.'

He ignored this. 'I must be able to explain to them why this contact is so important.'

She glanced towards the house. Nothing was moving. 'At the institute where I work there's a professor. He has a relationship with one of the highest members of the Party – Egon Krenz, the man who they say will succeed Honecker. They're close. The professor is driving to Berlin at this very moment to argue that military force will be counterproductive.'

'For God's sake, don't be naïve. If the Party wants to make an example in Leipzig, the views of a provincial academic are not going to overrule Erich Mielke and 80,000 Stasi. He could do it with his own men, if he wanted.'

She put her hand to his knee. 'Listen, the professor has proposed an alternative plan to the Central Committee, which makes concessions. Krenz will pay attention to what he has to say because both men have been involved in youth programmes for so much of their professional lives. They know what they're talking about. And the professor appreciates the level of resistance here.'

'Which will all crumble in the first volley of gunfire. Anyway, what's to stop you learning this information by phone?'

'Here? On this phone? Don't be stupid. My contact must come here in person under an arranged pretext. Thousands and thousands of people depend on this information, though they don't know it. So I repeat, I instigated this operation and I will decide when they move on the Arab.'

He shrugged. 'How will you let us know?'

'I'll leave a white towel on the back of the chair. They can move then and only then. Is that understood?'

He nodded.

'And then Rudi, I will meet you at the church door. There will be places for us. Now go.'

She looked at him for a few seconds then straightened and walked back to the open window, where she shook the dew from her shoes and went inside.

He waited a little while, then crawled back into the shrubs and, using the trunk of a lilac tree, climbed the fence and jumped down.

As he rose to his feet he looked up. Dawn had broken over Leipzig on Monday 9 October. There was moderate cloud cover and a slightly warmer temperature than was usual for the time of year. An ordinary beginning to an ordinary autumn day in the GDR. Leipzigers were starting out for work; smoke was already rising from one or two chimneys and, as he stole across the park, the clank and screech of the trams reached his ears in the still, slightly sulphurous air.

After debriefing Rosenharte, Robert Harland returned to the back of the truck to sit with one member of the BND team. Macy Harp and another West German sat in the front wearing overalls and smoking. They communicated with Harland through a hole punched in the back of the cabin, but mostly they waited in silence listening to the watchers call in from their positions around the park and on the far side of the villa. The enormous police and military build-up going on around the city made it difficult for them to stay in one place. Harland was worried that the city would be sealed off completely in the event of widespread violence and that it would be impossible for them to leave with Abu Jamal.

By three in the afternoon there was still no sign of him and they began to fear that he would remain in hospital overnight. Harland used the scrambled satellite phone to convey his worries in a call that was patched through Government Communications Headquarters in Cheltenham to the German desk of the Secret Intelligence Service in London. On the other end were Mike Costelloe and a man called Apsley from SIS's Middle East Directorate. Both men urged him to sit tight.

'You've gone all the way to the river and you haven't put up your rod yet,' said Apsley.

This brought a snarled comment from Macy Harp up front. 'There's a view in Century House that there's nothing in the world that doesn't benefit from the application of a fishing metaphor.'

The two BND men simply shook their heads.

At four the watchers reported that the villa received a visitor, a young woman in a headscarf and a dark raincoat who approached the two Stasi men at the front and offered her identity card. Harland knew it must be Kafka's contact.

'Kafka's got some bloody balls doing it right under their noses in a Stasi safe house.'

The woman hurried away shortly afterwards. Through the window, Kafka was observed picking up the phone, speaking for a few seconds and replacing the receiver. She then put on her coat and turned off the lights. A minute or two later she was seen on the street outside hurrying towards the centre of Leipzig.

'Fuck, fuck, fuck,' said Macy Harp. 'No white towel; no bleedin' Arab. We might as well go and join their effin' peace demo.'

A second hurried conversation ensued with London, during

which it was decided that the only course was to wait. Mike Costelloe said they had separate reports that hospital beds were being
emptied in the city to cope with a large number of casualties. This
could mean that Abu Jamal would be required to give up his bed.

Harland hung up. It was 4.20 p.m.

The middle part of Rosenharte's day was spent talking to Kurt
Blast and smoking too much for his own good. At noon, after
they'd had several beers, Kurt leapt up and started rifling through
his record collection. He selected a boxed set of J. S. Bach's Christmas Oratorio and showed it to Rosenharte.

'This is appropriate for two reasons,' he said, holding the record
sleeve in his long, slender fingers as though it was a dish of food.
'First of all, it's two hundred and fifty-five years since it was first
performed here in Leipzig. Second – and this is the most important
reason – Bach did not favour either of the two big churches: he
composed the Oratorio for both of them. The first part was played
on Christmas morning in the Nikolaikirche, with a performance at
the Thomaskirche in the afternoon. The second part opened in the
morning of the twenty-sixth of December in the Thomaskirche
and was repeated in the afternoon in the Nikolaikirche.'

'Impressive,' said Rosenharte, wondering anew at the extraordinary man he found himself with.

'Bach alternated between the two churches until January the
sixth, the feast of the Epiphany, when the last part was played in
the Nikolaikirche.' He darted a look at Rosenharte and his eyes
danced with pleasure. 'I see Bach hurrying between the two
churches with his assistants in the dead of winter – snow on the
ground, choirboys sliding along in their surplices, musicians and
singers clutching their wigs with their instruments borne along by
servants in gaiters.'

He stopped, put the first disc on the turntable and bent down to blow some fluff from the needle. 'The Nikolaikirche was really the centre of it all because of course it's the church of Christmas. You know, Saint Nicholas?'

He had a tendency to lecture his audience, which Rosenharte recognized in himself. 'You know a lot about it all,' he said.

'A little. But you see the relevance now! The two churches are to be united this evening. In fact, all the main churches are going to be open so as many people as possible can attend the peace prayers.' He placed the needle on the record and the Oratorio opened with the chorus: *Jauchzet frohlocket, auf, preiset die Tage* – Christians be joyful, praise these days.

They listened to the first two sides before leaving the house and walking briskly to a bus stop. On the way, Rosenharte spotted a phone box and dialled Vladimir's number in Dresden. A Russian answered but it wasn't Vladimir. Without waiting to be put through he said, 'This is Rudi. It's *all* happening in Leipzig this evening. You understand?' and hung up.

They took the bus and arrived outside the hospital on the southeast of the city at 3.30 and headed for the Georgi Ring, the road that encircled the heart of Leipzig. Kurt had done his best to tone down his appearance with a black overcoat that covered the tops of his boots. He had also cut a bleached inch from his Mohican and removed some of the rings from his ears. Yet still he drew some odd looks as they went and it was plain that some of the young soldiers forming up in the side streets wanted to teach him a thing or two about order and self-discipline. Rosenharte suggested they wait until after four o' clock before crossing the ring road and making for the church. They stood at a street corner, where they were joined by a man who had a small transistor radio pressed to his ear. He lowered the set so that they could hear the hourly news bulletin. A declaration had been made by some of the Party's cultural figures, such as the director of the Gewand-haus orchestra, Kurt Masur and a cabaret artist named Bernd Lutz Lange, both of whom it seemed carried weight with Kurt Blast. The presenter read out the joint appeal twice with studied neutrality. 'We are full of concern about the developments in our city, and we are looking for a solution. A free exchange of opinion about the continuation of socialism in our country is needed. This is why the undersigned promise everyone to use all their power and authority to ensure that this dialogue is held in Leipzig and with our government. We urgently call upon you to be careful and thoughtful so that this dialogue can take place.'

It seemed to Rosenharte an awkward statement, hanging with respectful reticence midway between support and the condemna-tion of *Kampfgruppenhundertschaft* – the armed units of the working class that had called for violent suppression in one of the newspapers. Still, it was astonishing that such a thing was being read out on state-controlled radio; unthinkable a few weeks before. He won-dered aloud whether the Party had approached the liberal and well-respected Masur, or if it had been his idea. Kurt Blast said it had to be Masur's suggestion: the Party was too stupid to think of it.

They waited until 4.15 listening to the radio, then began to walk towards the church.

It wasn't just the absence of rush-hour noise – the buses and trams having been taken out of service – or the massive presence of the security forces; there was something profoundly different about Leipzig which Rosenharte likened to a sudden leap in baro-metric pressure, or the peculiar heaviness that silences birds before an electrical storm. The people now making for the churches had evidently taken all their courage in their hands, many leaving fam-ilies without knowing if they would return in a few hours' time.

By far the greater proportion was young, but even so, the act of opposition to the state was a big step. They were sombre, yet also unburdened, because it was clear that something would be settled that night, that an outcome, one way or the other, was imminent.

They reached the church after twice dodging plainclothes Stasi asking for identity cards ahead of them, and struggled through the press of people around the door to find Ulrike standing just inside, gesturing and shrugging to a group of men. Her eyes lit up when she saw him. She continued talking for a few minutes, then broke away, putting her hand to her lips and wishing them all good luck and peace. Not for the first time Rosenharte sensed her ability to switch on a different part of herself.

'It's over,' she said as they hurried up the stairway, her fingers digging into his arm. 'Don't you see? It's coming to an end.'

He said nothing because he didn't believe her. But he smiled a truce and searched her eyes. Had they stormed the villa? Or was the Arab still safe in his hospital bed? She shook her head as though to say that everything he wanted answered would have to wait until later.

They climbed to the first gallery and when they had settled in the beautiful old painted pews she popped her head over the parapet. 'Look, the entire Party membership is down there. They've been here since two thirty. That's why we can't sit there.'

'What's going to happen?' whispered Rosenharte.

She bent towards him, her eyes darting around the congregation in the upper gallery. He could smell her hair.

'My informant says Krenz was persuaded by the argument. They are sure. But there's a rumour that the orders were given out by the Minister for State Security anyway. These may have been countermanded, but we don't know for certain. We do know that the Stasi are all carrying weapons, and that armed reserves are to be held so they can be used at a moment's notice.'

He moved closer so he could speak directly into her ear. 'What about the Arab?'

'He hadn't returned by the time I left, so I guess your friends are just going to have to wait, or postpone the whole thing. But that's not our problem now, is it? We've done what we can. I have led them to him. All I know is that I will never see the inside of that villa again. That part of my life is finished.'

'I'm glad,' he said. She had deceived him about the presence of Abu Jamal in Leipzig and her attendance on him. What else was she concealing? How much could he trust this woman?

All eyes had turned to the front and a sudden calm settled over the congregation as one of two pastors got up, greeted the packed church and began to read. 'Jesus said, "Blessed are the poor," not "Happy are the wealthy." Jesus said, "Love your enemies," not "Down with your opponents." Jesus said, "Many who are now first will be last," and not, "Everything stays the same." '

It seemed a little simple to Rosenharte but it was the essence of the protest. The pleasure of watching the Party officers having to listen easily compensated for any doubts he had about the sentiments. Prayers followed. The appeal for calm from Kurt Masur and the Party was read out. On the second hearing Rosenharte wondered if in fact it contained a coded permission to demonstrate. Perhaps what was happening behind the scenes was a dialogue in which the voice of the people was gradually prevailing. It was on this theme that a preacher named Wendell spoke. 'The reforms will come if we allow the spirit of peace, calm and tolerance to enter us. The spirit of peace must go beyond these walls. Take great care you are not rude to the police officers. Be careful that you don't sing songs or chant slogans that could provoke the authorities.'

It might just work, thought Rosenharte.

*

At 5.10 p.m., one of the watchers on the far side of the villa reported that a car had drawn up and a man in an overcoat had been helped from the front seat. He wore a cap and carried news-papers and a folder under his arm. A nurse accompanied him inside and stayed for about half an hour, during which she made him a sandwich and set it on the table with a glass of milk.

An identification was made in the interval between the man lowering himself heavily to the chair and the nurse walking to the sliding window and drawing the curtains before leaving. He was still wearing his cap and a straggly beard covered his chin, but it looked very much like Mohammed Ubayd, better known to the world's intelligence services as Abu Jamal.

Three clear pictures were taken as he faced the window in those brief seconds and were received on the new portable Apple Mac-intosh that Harland had borrowed from Griswald unused. He attempted to send the pictures via the Inmarsat phone to London, but failed each time. Eventually Mike Costelloe left it to Harland to decide whether they'd got the right man.

'This is the cove we've been watching, for heaven's sake,' said Harp. 'We all know it's him. Let's get on with it.'

Harland rubbed his chin. 'It would suit them down to the ground if we lifted some poor bloody sod they're using as a dou-ble.' He reached for a briefcase where there were two black and white shots of Abu Jamal, and held them alongside the computer screen. The first had been taken in Syria in 1982 and showed him smiling to a female companion as they left a house in the suburbs of Damascus. The more recent picture was snatched by the BND at Lake Balaton in Hungary, where Abu Jamal holidayed with another lady friend while using the name of Mustapha Riffat. This was in 1986 and there were no signs of the kidney and liver complaints for which he had been receiving treatment in Leipzig's university hospital at the time. The man in the villa was puffier around the jowls and had dark rings under his eyes. Yet there was still much in the line of the eyebrows, the shape of the nostrils and, more important, the force of personality betrayed in his eyes, which made Harland call London and tell them Samaritan was going ahead.

At 5.55, Harp and Harland transferred to a dirty cream-coloured Lada saloon while a BND agent named Johann Horst climbed into the driving seat of the truck. Both vehicles rolled to the end of the street without turning on their engines or lights. Ahead of them was the gathering darkness of the oak woods, wedged into the city from the south. Everything seemed clear. Harland listened to the watchers reporting in for the last time. A shadow against the mesh curtains had told them that Abu Jamal was still in the main downstairs room at the table reading. Four of the BND team were in the garden at the rear of the villa. Having fed a tiny microphone into the room through a hole bored in the window, they were now quite sure that no one else was in the house.

Harland nodded to Harp, who flashed his headlight at a truck that moved off ahead of them. Five minutes later Harland said, 'Right, let's get on with it, shall we?'

Because of Abu Jamal's obvious infirmity, Harland had decided that it would be hopeless to try to remove him over the fence and into the park. They would have to enter and leave through the main door, which meant that the most risky part of the operation would take place the moment they arrived in the narrow road in front of the villa.

It took seven minutes to reach the street, at which point Harp cut the engine and turned off his lights. Harland pressed his fingers to the earpiece. Two members of the BND who had been hidden nearby were now approaching the Stasi car parked directly under a streetlight opposite the villa. One bent down and showed his ID card. Harland heard the surly response of the driver in his own earphone. The second BND man approached the passenger side and made a gesture for the man to wind down his window. At this, both men covered their faces and sprayed the inside of the car with aerosol canisters. The gas acted immediately and the Stasi officers slumped forward. Harland knew that the additional dose of flunitrazepam, now being administered by a jab in the arm, meant they wouldn't wake until six the next morning at the very earliest, by which time they would find themselves deep in the countryside with a couple of flat tyres and a bust distributor.

One of the BND men straightened and waved Harland forward, while the other struggled to heft the driver out of his seat and into the back. This accomplished, he got in and drove the car off.

Harland waited for a few seconds before pulling down a ski mask and running to the front door where the other German, now also masked, was trying a series of skeleton keys in the lock. The mechanism succumbed very quickly. By the time he and his German companion had reached the main room, four others were standing round a bemused Abu Jamal who had not had time to move from the table. One of the Germans told him formally that they were executing warrants issued by the French, German and American courts for numerous acts of terrorism, and on the basis of evidence of his plan to carry out further attacks in the West. Abu Jamal looked around the masked faces, astonished. He began to protest in good German that he was an engineer named Halim al Fatah from Egypt. He was in Leipzig legitimately receiving medical treatment and he knew nothing about terrorism. He offered to show them a passport. His head turned from one masked face to another before he let out a stream of indignation – he was too ill to be moved; his guards would be checking any moment; anyone laying hands on him would be arrested and shot as spies. Harland found himself noticing that Abu Jamal dyed his hair and eyebrows and that his lower lip protruded to show a very sick-looking mouth.

He nodded and two of the Germans lifted him up and hustled him out of the front door to the Lada, which Macy Harp had turned round. In a few minutes Abu Jamal would know nothing of his journey through the suburbs to the truck that would take him south. He wouldn't wake until he reached the BND HQ at Munich-Pullach half an hour away, where he'd be given a medical assessment before interrogation.

Harland watched them go, then shut the door. They needed to search the villa. Despite the use of the arrest warrants, there was absolutely no intention by any of the governments to impede the investigations into Abu Jamal's operations by consigning him to a drawn-out judicial process. His life expectancy was too short and the threat too large for this to be considered. But documents could be important, partly to prove the active support of Honecker's regime but mostly because the West needed the vital intelligence to trace Abu Jamal's network before word leaked out that he had been abducted. At best they had forty-eight hours before the news would pass from East Germany to its embassies all over the Middle East.

They moved around the villa sweeping everything of remote interest into a holdall, but they didn't find the cache that Harland and the lead German intelligence officer, Claus Neurath, knew must be there. Twenty minutes into the search, Harland thought back to Abu Jamal's arrival that evening. He was wearing an overcoat that they had forced him to put on before he was bundled into the car. And he was carrying a sheaf of newspapers, which could easily have been used to conceal something. One of the watchers thought he had seen a folder under his arm.

Harland went to the front door, turned and looked at the route that Abu Jamal must have taken into the house. He knew that there had been no time for him to go into another room between being sighted with the nurse at the front of the villa and his appearance in the main room. On the left was a toilet, which contained no conceivable hiding place, and on the right, a little further on, a kind of dresser which was fixed to the wall and included coat pegs, a mirror, a clothes brush that hung from a hook beside the mirror and three drawers at the bottom. Harland searched inside the drawers and felt underneath the dresser but found nothing. He stood up, slipped his hand behind the dresser and pulled up a stiff black plastic wallet. It could have been a free gift from a bank or an insurance company and indeed he noticed the remains of a gold-printed logo on the cover. He withdrew the papers inside and handed them to Neurath, a good Arabic speaker, who whipped through them then clapped him on his back. There couldn't be any doubt about it – they'd found the file that Kafka had spoken of in her first communication with the West: the money file, which proved the extent of Abu Jamal's operation and the range of his contacts in Europe and the Middle East.

This was placed inside the holdall, then they prepared to leave via the sliding door. First Harland went round and switched off the lights in the house. When he returned to the main room he saw Neurath flattened against the wall, making agitated downward motions to silence him. He froze. Someone was at the door. Neurath flashed his head round the corner to look at the entrance and raised two fingers. He had seen their shadows on the frosted glass. Whoever it was had entered and they were now making their way down the corridor. In the half light Harland saw that the BND team were all aiming guns in the direction of the corridor. Before he had time to slip backwards into the doorway that led to the stairs, there was a brief commotion in which the two men were surrounded and pushed to the floor with pistols to the back of their heads. Hardly a voice was raised. Harland glanced down at the man nearest to him, a lean blond in a suit. He recognized him immediately from the files as Colonel Peter Zank of the Main Department for Counter-Intelligence, and cursed under his breath. But he said nothing to Neurath for fear of betraying his English accent. In any case it was clear from the look that darted from the slits in Neurath's ski mask that he knew who Zank was, and moreover he had already decided on precisely the course of action to be taken. Zank and his partner were hauled up, placed on chairs, bound with ropes, gagged and unceremoniously injected with flunitrazepam. Both men were laid sideways on the floor facing away from each other a yard apart. The last lights were extinguished and the party left the villa through the sliding door and stole through the park to a spot where two cars were waiting with a couple of the best drivers in West Germany. The operation had gone well, but Harland wasn't celebrating. Zank's presence in the villa meant he and his department had made the vital connections. Rosenharte and Kafka were in mortal danger and he had no way of contacting them.

He hoped like hell they'd have the sense to leave the city that night.

TWENTY-SIX

The Miracle of Leipzig

Towards the close of the service Rosenharte's gaze drifted across the nave of the church to the galleries on the south side and came to rest on the face of the man he had seen outside Ulrike's home – Colonel Biermeier's swaggering young sidekick. Unlike the rest of the Stasi and the Party membership, he had managed to infiltrate the genuine part of the congregation in the galleries and as before was showing every sign of devotion. Rosenharte scanned the rest of the congregation for Biermeier and Zank, but didn't see them. The light was fading outside and the recesses of the lower gallery were completely in shadow. Maybe they were there or directly below them. He nudged Ulrike and pointed in the man's direction. She touched his thigh and said she'd talk about it later.

A few seconds before the end of the peace prayers, they slid from their seats and went down the stairway so that when the final blessing was over they were at the main entrance before the rest of the congregation. What greeted them as the doors opened was by no means a riotous mass, but rather a sea of faces, many lit in the dusk by candles that people shielded in their hands. Ulrike had told him about this – if the people were holding candles there could be no mistaking their peaceful intentions. A gentle cheer went up. Rosenharte wondered if the crowd sensed that many of the first people to emerge were in fact Party members who had sat stiffly through the service, trying desperately to defuse the sense of moment that filled the aisles. They had failed, and now, as the congregation spilled out into the square, the rush of benevolence made even the grim loyalists smile.

Ulrike took all this in with an ecstatic, slightly manic grin, then linked arms with Rosenharte and Kurt and surged through the crowd towards the other end of the church. Several well-known figures seemed to be making for the same spot. Ulrike nodded and called out to them. She seemed to know everyone of any importance there. When they reached what appeared to be the head of the march, she withdrew her arms and told Rosenharte and Kurt that she was joining the people at the front. They should walk just behind her so they didn't lose touch. The demonstration moved off northwards from the Karl-Marx-Platz towards Leipzig's main station. At a high point in the road Rosenharte and Kurt turned to see the huge swell of people behind them. They had no way of estimating the numbers, but guessed there were anything between 70,000 and 100,000 Leipzigers on the streets. As before, the overwhelming majority were under thirty years of age. Some of them shouted, 'We're staying here!' and 'Join us now!' as they passed onlookers and buildings where the lights were on, but once the crowd was moving, things settled down. It seemed the people had decided that the best way of making their point to the formations of helmeted riot troops and soldiers glimpsed along the way was to pass them in silence.

The aim was to march round the four sides of the Georgi Ring without being stopped – and so achieve the symbolic encirclement of the city. Along the first leg, which took them through a wide canyon of bleak apartment and office blocks, Ulrike broke away from the front rank and came back to them. She pointed to the top of the church that they were passing on the right, and said that a cameraman had hidden in the clock tower to record the demonstration. By the following day the film would be broadcast in the West. She didn't want her face on every TV screen.

'What are you going to do afterwards?' asked Rosenharte.

'Celebrate,' she said, as though he was being stupid.

He bent down to her. 'But if they've removed our friend, life is going to become very difficult for you.'

'I don't see why. If they've done it well, no one will know where he's gone.'

'The man's sick. They'll know that he hasn't just left town on a whim. You have to hide.'

'We'll see.' Her expression was so exultant that he wondered whether she was absorbing anything he said. For his part, he knew that he wasn't going to remain in the city. He would ask her if he could borrow the car until Thursday, by which time he would be making his way to Berlin to meet up with Vladimir and Harland again. He touched her on the shoulder. 'Ulrike, you have to pay attention. I saw one of the Stasi men come from your house. The same man was in the Nikolaikirche. Maybe he was bugging the place. Maybe he's tailing you.'

'Not everything is as it seems,' she said.

This irritated him. 'Look, I know this man! I saw him with a colonel in the foreign intelligence service – Biermeier. I told you about him. I saw him last Monday with Zank, here in Leipzig! This is no coincidence.'

She took his hand and looked at it then let her eyes travel up to his face, where she held his gaze with a strange expression. 'When you arrived at the Nikolaikirche I told you that everything was over. If the foreigners managed to take our friend, which I imagine they did, then it *is* over. My life of deceit is over. And with this demonstration,' she gestured at the crowd with her free hand, 'everything changes. Where are the police and the Stasi now? Nowhere. Things have changed for good tonight.'

'Don't talk too soon. We have a long way to go and they may arrest people as they make their way home. Violence is still a possibility.'

'No,' she said firmly. 'That's not going to happen now. The people up in front have had assurances there will be no violence. They have talked to the Vopos and the Party leadership. That's what they've been telling me. The professor was right. Krenz – or someone – overruled the Minister for State Security. Don't you see? We've won.'

'But that doesn't mean you're safe. When they find the Arab missing, they'll know you had something to do with it. That's why Zank has been in Leipzig. He's on to something, I'm sure of it. And this other man – Biermeier's associate – he's here for a reason too.'

'In which case you're also in danger.'

'Exactly. And I need to remain free to get Konrad out.'

'So your solution is?'

'We hide. I know a place.'

The progress of the march had been slowing and now it came to an abrupt halt alongside a piece of hideous futuristic architecture known as the Tin Box, which had been built a few years before as a symbol of progress. The crowd had shunted into them from behind and she was pressed close. Her fine hair shimmered in the breeze and he smelled her scent. She looked up into his eyes, gently shook her head and mouthed, 'I'm staying here.'

'Then I will go without you.'

'If that's what you want to do. But you must stay tonight and drink to our victory and remember every minute for when you return to Dresden. Your city will have its own moment. We have set the pattern.'

'I won't be returning. My schedule doesn't allow it. Anyway, they fired me from the gallery on Friday.'

'You told me you had some kind of protection.'

'What protection was that?' he asked.

'You said someone squared the director of the gallery so you could be absent for long periods.'

'I didn't tell you that.'

'You did.'

He shook his head. 'How did you know?'

She ignored him and pointed to a couple in front of them. 'I'm seeing so many people I know tonight. Over there is Max Klein, who is an evolutionary biologist. He was prevented from research-ing inheritance because the Party does not permit studies that suggest traits such as intelligence are passed from generation to generation. So he does simple research into mice at his home. His wife Sarah is a research psychologist, but because her husband's work was banned she failed to get the university post she wanted. At the front there's a woman whose son refused to do military service. He was locked up for eighteen months and came out of Bautzen with a nervous breakdown. My friend Kurt is a brilliant lyricist but he may not have his songs performed in public. And you see the guy he's talking to?' Rosenharte craned his neck and saw a small man in leather with a shaved head and two thin side-burns. 'That's Ebbe – he's a graphic artist who works as a plasterer because he once drew a rude cartoon of Chernenko. Those little old monsters – Honecker and Mielke – have been sitting on our heads for too long. Tonight is the beginning of the end for them.'

'Ulrike,' he said firmly, 'I didn't tell you that I had any kind of protection at the gallery.'

'I'm sure you did. But if you didn't, I must have imagined it,' she said nonchalantly.

They were on the move again, and were now passing under some trees on the approach to the Runde Ecke, or round corner – the regional headquarters of the Stasi. To their left was the extension built in 1985 to help accommodate the 8,000 MfS officers who worked in Leipzig, a number he now realized was probably larger than the entire domestic and foreign intelligence services of the United Kingdom. The Stasi's doors were closed, but lights blazed from nearly every window in all five storeys, and units of soldiers and uniformed Stasi lined both sides of the wedge-shaped fortress. When Rosenharte and Ulrike passed the entrance and read the silver-on-black nameplate – *Bezirksverwaltung für Staatssicherheit: Leipzig* – they glanced up four storeys to a penthouse office that had a rounded balustrade. A man in uniform gazed down at the dark tide of marchers. People whispered that it was Lieutenant-General Manfred Hummitzsch, the local Stasi chief, but of course it was impossible to tell.

The rest of the march passed in a pleasant blur for Rosenharte. He relished the sudden affection that had sprung up between strangers all around them. The people had taken control of their city for a few blissful hours and had proved that this could be done without a single window being broken.

Near the end of the route Rosenharte began to observe the general mood in the faces of the conscripts who had been drafted in to protect public buildings and on the younger members of the Volkspolizei, some of whom looked longingly at the marchers. Almost no force was used that evening, though late at night as people were beginning to disperse, Rosenharte did see a half-hearted baton charge, which netted a man in a wheelchair and a woman who had been pushing him.

Some time after midnight they said good night to Kurt. Rosenharte told him he would collect his things and the car in the morning. They each hugged him and then set off for Ulrike's place. She put her hand through his arm and placed her other hand on top. She looked up at him occasionally and smiled but they did not speak of the Arab, of Konrad or of Else's escape over the border; nor of the British spies, or of Zank, Biermeier and his sidekick. Rosenharte was too exhausted and, anyway, the extraordinary events – the miracle – of that night in Leipzig when the regime rolled over and let the people have their way practically occluded everything else.

They reached the wisteria gateway and walked through the dark to her door. As she placed the key in the lock she said to him, 'I haven't ever seen you smile. Not properly.'

'That's nonsense. I do smile.'

'You don't; you grin. You have a very attractive grin, and you use it well when you're talking to people or giving one of your highbrow lectures. But you don't smile, Rudi. You're always holding something in reserve.'

'You could say that about everyone.'

She wrinkled her nose. 'Not the way you do.'

She pushed the door and listened to the empty apartment, then put her face to the draught of stale air that came to them.

He coughed. 'I'm beginning to think you had the same training as me.'

'You're right. I did.'

He said nothing. Her admissions always came at the most unexpected moments.

'But like you, I didn't fit.'

'You're telling me you were in the Stasi?'

She turned to him with a look of amusement. 'Who do you

think gave me all this training in languages? My father was in the diplomatic service, for goodness' sake. I thought you had put all that together. It wasn't so difficult.'

Rosenharte shrugged and said he hadn't.

'Maybe you're not the sharpest knife in the drawer after all.'

They went inside. She switched on a table lamp and went to her little kitchen to find a drink and some glasses and returned clanking a bottle of red wine and two large bottles of beer. Rosenharte stood where he was in the centre of the room, suddenly aware of the fatigue in his back and legs. She opened the wine and came to rest her head on his chest, handing him a glass in the same movement. He took a mouthful. 'I do smile,' he said plaintively.

'You don't. In all the time I've known you, I haven't seen you smile naturally – I mean with your eyes.'

'You've only known me a few weeks.'

'Known you, yes,' she murmured into the material of his coat.

He moved back – regretfully, for he loved the feeling of her hair on his face. 'What do you mean?'

'Nothing,' she said and rolled her head across his chest.

'You must have meant something.'

'Tomorrow, Rudi, we'll talk tomorrow.' She kissed him on the chin and moved to his mouth to stroke his lips with hers. He felt her smile.

'Are you trying to tell me you're still working for them?'

'No, I don't work for them, though I may have been guilty of letting them think that I was.' She paused, put the glass to her lips. 'When I said we knew who the informer was, that was true, Rudi. You see, it was me. I was the Stasi informer for this group. That's how we were able to plan so much without them knowing.'

'Jesus, your life's so complicated.'

'I offered to help them and they leapt at the chance. Naturally,

I didn't go to the Runde Ecke one morning and say, "I am Ulrike Klaar and I want to spy on my friends." I let people know indirectly that I was concerned by the developments I was seeing in the research for the institute, and soon enough they asked me to become an IM, even gave me money for it. The arrangement allowed me the freedom to follow my faith and sometimes to gain a sense of their plans. It has all worked very well because I was able to protect my friends.'

'And the Arab?'

'I was already on their trusted list because of him. But of course he couldn't provide me with the pretext to go to church, to mix with the people I wanted to see and talk to.'

'But you just said you didn't fit into the Stasi.'

'I didn't. I lasted just three years before I was thrown out. That was a long time ago.'

'Why?' He felt her stiffen in his arms.

'I had a baby . . . a baby who died. But I wasn't married and, well, I wasn't in love with the father and anyway he wanted nothing to do with it. They told me to get rid of it, but I refused and they got rid of me. Those old bastards disapprove of anyone having a sexual relationship that has not first been designated as a means to the state's ends. And a fatherless child, well, forget it.' Her head remained on his chest and she spoke without looking at him in the deliberate voice of the confessional.

'Did you sleep with the Arab?'

She inhaled deeply. 'Yes, twice in two years but . . . you know . . . he wasn't up to it. There was no actual consummation. The reason he was in Leipzig was that Misha Lomieko had got him treatment at the hospital, and by the time he started coming here and I became his regular companion, he was so debilitated from the years of drinking and cocaine and chewing ghat, a habit he picked up in Yemen, that he didn't function as a man. He liked my company: I speak his language and understand Arab men. I even like ghat. He helped me in many ways, getting extra food and alcohol for my friends and special stuff from abroad. There were a thousand small benefits to me, and a kind of protection.' She stopped and looked at him. He noticed the flecks of light brown in her eyes. 'But that's all over now.'

'It may not be,' he said. 'If he's been taken tonight, they'll come after you. You're an obvious suspect. How else would the West know where and when to find him?'

'You said all that before. If they've done it intelligently, no one will know where he's gone. Momo – that's my name for him – is a free agent. He comes and goes as he pleases. Only Misha knew his movements. So we may have more time than you think.'

He slipped his hands under her shirt and tried to engage her eyes while feeling the suppleness of her back. 'Ulrike, you're in danger. They know who you are and where you live. Why was Biermeier's man here? That means something to you, surely?'

She put her finger to his lips. 'Nothing's going to happen tonight. They won't check on him until morning. Look, it's simple. I will telephone the number he uses to see if I get an answer. Then we'll know.'

'And you'll come with me then?'

She dug him in the ribs playfully. 'Surely it's you who will be coming with me, unless you've bought another car?'

She dragged him to his feet and began to kiss his neck. 'Take me to bed,' she whispered. 'Take me to bed before I pass out.'

He cupped her face in his hands and looked into her eyes. 'What happened to the woman who stood in the park and accused me of wanting the double victory of your body and your love? Where's she gone? That was quite a talking-to you gave me.' She pulled away reproachfully. 'You see,' he continued, 'I find it very hard to know which person I'm dealing with – the hard, calculating former agent, or the woman who laughs so endearingly at the idea of the Stasi arresting a bunch of respectable members of an orchestra instead of unlicensed street musicians.'

'Well, it was funny,' she said.

'That's not the point. You change so often that I wonder if you have multiple personalities. Seeing you this morning at the villa and then later at the church was like meeting two completely different people.'

'Perhaps you're confusing personality with behaviour,' she said sharply. 'Anyway, let me assure you that you're with the real me now. *This is me.*' She stepped away from him and held out her arms as though she was showing him a new dress.

'How can I tell? I feel there's so much that you're keeping from me. You're impenetrable.'

'Try me,' she said lasciviously.

'I didn't mean that.'

'Ah! You nearly smiled, Rudi.' She poured more wine for herself, Rosenharte having drunk only a little.

'Why Kafka? Why did you choose the name Kafka?' he asked.

She nodded as though to say she understood that he needed to take his time. 'Because he predicted the world we live in today: the secrecy, the men who ruin a person's life with rumours and lies, the mysterious persecutions and executions, the senselessness of it all. He got it exactly right.' She paused. 'Drink with me, Rudi, to the end of the lying old crows and the beginning of us.'

He retrieved his glass from the table and raised it. 'To the most puzzling person that I've ever met.'

She shook her hair vigorously. 'I just know what I think about things. And this – you and me – is right.' She looked up to the ceiling. ' "Life's splendour forever lies in wait about each one of us in all its fullness, but veiled from view, deep down, invisible, far off. It is there, though, not hostile, not reluctant, not deaf. If you summon it by the right word, by its right name, it will come." That's Mister K at his best. I am summoning life's splendour now, Rudi. And you are part of it.'

'I'm flattered.' He held his pack of cigarettes out to her. She shook her head, but presented her mouth for a puff after he'd lit one for himself. He was struggling to get his bearings with her, to find the right language. In the end he didn't manage to rise above banality. 'I could love you. Maybe I already do. But I want to love you – us to love each other – properly. No secrets. You were right about me when you said those things in the park. I'm going to be fifty soon. It's time for me to stop making mistakes.'

She put down her glass and came to him. Soon she was pulling off his clothes as well as her own. She led them half-dressed to her bedroom. The bed was pushed into the far corner and was covered in a rough white cloth. She turned and pulled her shirt off in one motion, which made her hair shimmer with static. Without seeming to notice she undid her bra and removed it. 'Hey, look, you're smiling!' she exclaimed. 'Is my body really that funny?'

He moved to her and held her lightly above her waist. 'No, it's beautiful. I'm smiling at your static. I've never seen anyone with their own electricity supply before.'

'Yes, but you smiled, Rudi, and you look a different person when you smile. I love that.' She clasped her hands together and looked up. 'Wasn't tonight wonderful? Can you believe what we witnessed? It was a miracle, wasn't it?'

He nodded.

He undressed, sat down on the bed and watched her draw the curtains and switch on a lamp that was covered with a piece of red cloth. She slipped off her jeans and pants and stood before him to let his eyes run over her body, then approached and guided his head to her breasts. It was a natural movement, barely sexual, and Rosenharte was aware of something he hadn't felt for a very long time. He was pleased to find how present he was and how very much he needed her. He held her away from him, thinking that a beautiful woman in the flesh never tallied with any mental image he had or the paintings he knew so well in the Gemäldegalerie. Her body was astonishingly white and slender, though not as fragile as he had believed when she had joined him in bed the week before. She gazed down at him, pleased with the effect she was having. He began to kiss her, his hands not exploring, but rather gauging the warmth and shape of her ordinary mortal form. It moved him like no other experience with a woman, made him love humanity and its vulnerability. He said something of this and she mocked him for being the aesthete, told him that he didn't have to articulate every absurd thought that came into his head; nevertheless it seemed to please her and she touched his face and dragged the backs of her fingers under his eyes and along his hairline.

'Look at me, Rudi, and clear your mind.'

She parted her legs to straddle his thighs. 'This is different, isn't it?' she whispered and he nodded in reply. At some point she moved forward a little and let her head drop to his shoulders. Then he lifted her on to him.

TWENTY-SEVEN

Flight

Rosenharte woke with a start, aware that someone was in the room. A man was calling Ulrike's name and fumbling his way to her bed in the dark. He lifted his head from the pillow, cursing that he hadn't made Ulrike leave the night before. Then she stirred and sat bolt upright.

'Who . . . ? What do you want?' she hissed back.

'You must leave,' said the voice. '*Raus, raus.* You have to get up and leave if you don't want us all shot.'

She climbed over Rosenharte, taking a sheet with her, and approached the outline of the man.

'Who's with you?' the voice demanded. 'Have you got someone there? For Christ's sake, we haven't time for this.' Rosenharte was struggling to process what he was hearing because he was now sure that Biermeier was in the room. But instead of arresting them, he was warning them of an impending danger. The light came on. Biermeier was standing in the middle of the room in a trenchcoat streaked with rain. 'Couldn't you wait?' he said when he saw Rosenharte. 'Look, if he's found here, we'll all be shot. Come on, girl, get your damned clothes on.'

'Tell me what's happened,' said Ulrike, calmly picking up her jeans.

'The Arab's gone. Zank has been found unconscious in the safe house by the park. He was drugged and tied up. He's still out of it, but when he comes round all hell will break loose. We're in the shit, unless you get your pretty little arse out of Leipzig and go into hiding.'

'What was he doing at the villa?' she asked.

'I don't know, but the fact that he *was* there and someone tied up and drugged him means that he's made discoveries that we never thought he would.' He picked up her shirt and threw it at her. 'That's enough talk. You've got to get out of here. Make for the border and don't get caught.' He turned to the bed. 'Rosenharte, you too. You got your sister-in-law out, now you leave the GDR and make sure Ulrike goes with you.'

He began to protest about Konrad.

'Forget your damned brother. You must go.' He was tearing round the room, throwing any article of clothing he could find at them. His knobbly face was white with fear and there was no doubt that he had been drinking. He stopped as if noticing the gun in his hand for the first time. 'If I had any sense I'd put a bullet in your head now. That way I'd know you couldn't talk. But I'm giving you this chance because you're with Ulrike.' He moved to the door and spoke directly to her. 'There's no surveillance outside, but there will be soon. Leave by the window at the back where I came in. If I don't see you leave in five minutes, I will come back and kill you both.'

He vanished into the dark of the passageway. A couple of seconds later they heard him pulling open the window in the sitting room. Ulrike started to stuff a rucksack with her possessions, while Rosenharte went to retrieve his coat and pullover from the sitting-room floor.

'The car's at Kurt's place,' he called out.

'That's good. There can be no danger of them following us from here. Go to the kitchen, put as much food as you can find in the shopping bag. Pasta, eggs, oil, candles – anything. We'll need it if we're going to stay hidden.'

He tipped the cardboard box where she kept most of her provisions into a big red and white striped canvas bag and added a skillet, a larger pan, torch, cups, knives, a loaf of bread that was on the side table and all the alcohol he could find.

Ulrike appeared in the kitchen carrying the sheets from her bed and placed them in a plastic bowl. While the taps ran she went to fetch the ashtray and glasses from the sitting room. Rosenharte understood that she was eliminating all trace of his being there. She glanced round her sitting room one more time before she turned the lights off, heaved the rucksack through the window and jumped down into the garden. Rosenharte followed with the bag. Then she turned round, wiped the mud Biermeier had left on the windowsill with the cuff of her jacket, and pressed the window shut.

Not far from the house they came to an opening onto the road that ran parallel to her street. She told Rosenharte to wait while she fetched the car, took the keys from him, put her hood up and left him with the bags in the cover of some laurel bushes. He lit a cigarette and began to consider the implications of Biermeier's appearance in the apartment. Clearly Biermeier was involved with Ulrike in passing the intelligence about Abu Jamal to the West. His presence right from the start of this affair meant that he had not merely sanctioned it but was one of the prime movers. Rosenharte thought back to the hotel in Trieste and realized that while checking the microphone and transmitter he had sabotaged it. That's why no one had heard the Pole blurt out the name in the last moments of his life. It was broken before he even entered the sea because Biermeier had thought Rosenharte would give everything away in the first encounter with Annalise's substitute.

How much more of the last few weeks could be explained by his involvement? Was he working with the British? How did the two Poles fit in? Was he going it alone, or was Schwarzmeer involved as well?

In the centre of this mystery was Ulrike. Even in the most tender and open moments of their lovemaking the night before, he understood she was still holding back. At one moment she'd looked into his eyes with the strangest dread, as though she'd seen the precipice they were walking towards but could not – or would not – warn him. Now he understood why Biermeier's man had been outside her home and how she knew that the gallery in Dresden had been squared about his absences. Biermeier had clearly told her about the arrangement with the head of the gallery before it was overturned by Zank. This meant that she was privy to the smallest details of the operation, and that argued for a very close involvement indeed.

He could now see the pattern of Zank's suspicions. Everywhere Biermeier went Zank followed, checking on the hotel in Trieste, accompanying him to the meeting with Mielke in Normannenstrasse, tracking his movements in Leipzig. He remembered the world-weary look that Biermeier had risked at Normannenstrasse, then the next morning his barely concealed disgust as they left the Hohenschönhausen compound. Perhaps some kind of struggle was going on in the Stasi between the forces of crude decency as represented by Biermeier, and Zank's unwavering zealotry. He knew from his own time that a few officers retained an honour of sorts and did not regard the oath of allegiance to the Ministry of State Security as a holy text. Biermeier, though an oaf capable of palming someone else's money, might be one of the few who, when confronted with the evil of Abu Jamal's plans, decided to do something about it. Whatever he felt personally about the man, he couldn't help but admire his courage and his planning. Yet the fact was that Biermeier and Ulrike had used him and Konrad ruthlessly. If Zank really began to see all the connections, it would put Konrad in terrible danger.

He waited nearly three-quarters of an hour under the dripping laurels and was beginning to wonder whether she would return, when the little beige Wartburg trundled into the opening with its wipers working furiously.

She flung open the passenger door and yelled, 'I had to get your stuff from Kurt's apartment. It took for ever to wake him.' He slung their bags in the back and climbed in.

'Where're we going?' she asked.

'Got a map?'

She pulled an old dog-eared fold-out from beneath the driving seat and handed it to him. The scale was too small to find the farmhouse, but he had a pretty good sense of where it was. 'Go southwest. Take minor roads.'

'Are you sure this place is going to be safe?'

'Nowhere is safe, but if we keep moving and have reasonable luck we should be all right.' He examined her, and decided to wait until they got out of Leipzig to ask her the questions he so desperately needed answered. He pulled his radio from his bag to listen to the news on a West German station. The Leipzig demonstration was the lead item, yet the explanation of why the army had not been used against the marchers was very confused. One report had Egon Krenz flying into the city, while another cited a renegade officer from the people's army who had refused to order his troops to shoot. The GDR had, it seemed, decided to make a virtue of the restraint when it was clear that neither their own troops nor the Russians were prepared to fire on unarmed civilians attending prayers for peace.

They listened to the rest of the news from a world that seemed very far away. A man named David Dinkins was favourite to become the first black mayor of New York; the killing of military bandsmen by the IRA in England two weeks before was said to presage a new rash of attacks; and the Soviet news agency Tass reported that UFOs had been seen hovering over Russian soil for the third time that month.

'So now we know where Gorbachev comes from,' Ulrike said. Her eyes left the road for a second. 'I guess you want an explanation?'

'Don't bother,' he said sharply, 'unless you're going to tell me the truth about everything.'

'I couldn't tell you about Biermeier before. It would've been too dangerous for him.'

'For him, yes. But what about my brother? You didn't think that you had an obligation to keep me informed about everything so I could make my own decisions?'

'What good would that have done? You would've reacted differently to Biermeier if you'd known his involvement with me. Zank would have spotted it in your eyes. As it was, you were hostile and contemptuous of him. That was what we needed.'

'How long has this been going on, this private operation to expose the Stasi's use of Abu Jamal? Was it Biermeier's idea?'

She nodded. 'Nearly two years now – for as long as he's had medical treatment in Leipzig. Biermeier got me the job. He had put someone close to Misha and he needed someone next to Abu Jamal.'

'Biermeier set you up as Abu Jamal's mistress in Leipzig?'

'Pretty much, though what I told you last night was true. He's incapable of physical love. There's no desire for anything except destruction. He wants to leave his mark on the world by causing many, many deaths. The Party had no idea what he was doing – the extent of what he and Misha planned, although it was the Party's machinery, *their* money, *their* inspiration, that enabled him. Biermeier wrote one memorandum to Schwarzmeer and got nowhere. He was told it wasn't his business and that he was exaggerating the extent of the Arab's ambitions. So he decided to get evidence that no one could doubt by spying on Misha and Abu Jamal. At first he had no idea of sending this information to the West – you know Biermeier; he'd rather cut off his hand than help the capitalists. When he got the evidence he fed it into the information chain and managed to make it seem as though someone else was making the allegations. He's very shrewd. That's why he's lasted so long. But still nothing happened. There was no response whatsoever. That was in the spring. So he – no, *we* – decided that there was only one way of stopping the Arab. In May we began to plan how we could do that.'

'What was the point of Misha's use of Abu Jamal? Why did the GDR want to cause this devastation and chaos? No other communist state has planned anything like this.'

'That's an interesting question. I thought about it a lot because, well, I'm socialist and I couldn't understand why a socialist regime could get involved with such a man. In the end I came to the conclusion that it has something to do with our technological inferiority, a certainty that the West is leaping ahead and we're being left behind. The kind of operations the Arab put in place would certainly have caused a grave crisis, particularly as the attacks were planned so closely together. Oddly enough I think it betrays a sense of panic in the leadership.'

374

'Maybe. When did you think of using me?'

'Later. Early June.' She offered her mouth to him to take a puff of his cigarette. He held it up to her and she exhaled, then began to cough.

'You should have someone look at your chest. It doesn't sound great.'

'I told you: it's the pollution. Anyway, we wanted someone who could visit Leipzig legitimately. Biermeier did some research after I suggested you and discovered you had a very interesting past.'

'You mean he went into my Stasi files?'

'He didn't manage to pull all of them. Just the one that said you had been in the HVA. The rest are in some ultra-secret section. We wondered why that was.'

Rosenharte flicked the cigarette out of the window. 'So you must have known about Konrad; you knew I had a brother they'd imprisoned once before?'

She shook her head. 'Only when he was arrested.'

He laughed bitterly and looked away. 'You lied to me about that, too. You said the first you had heard of him was when someone wondered if the filmmaker Konrad Rosenharte was my brother. You told me a deliberate lie. What vanity!'

'Vanity?'

'Yes, my vanity! Here was I thinking that you had chosen me because you liked the look of me. Actually, I'm glad that that wasn't true because it would make me feel doubly bad about Konnie.'

Her hands tightened round the wheel. 'Rudi, I want you to know that I'm truly sorry. I wish I could do something to change what's happened. I feel very, very bad about it.'

Rosenharte wasn't listening. He saw his brother's drained, lifeless features in the hospital wing at Hohenschönhausen – the image that had imprinted itself on his mind as he looked back when he left the room. There were just four days before they would enter the prison with Vladimir's fake documentation, and for the thousandth time he prayed Konnie would hang on till then.

Ulrike knew what he was thinking. 'I'll do anything I can to help you now,' she said.

In the cold light of day he knew that he could not trust her with the plan. Now that they were on the run, with Zank not far behind, the less she knew the better. He couldn't risk her falling into Zank's hands with that knowledge. He changed the subject. 'The two Poles – where do they fit in?'

'We didn't know who they were. The man in Trieste very nearly spoiled all our plans. We couldn't work it out.'

'You saw the second man, the tall one outside that cafe. Had you ever seen him before?'

'No, never.'

'Did you know he was Polish then?'

'No, I just wondered who was showing such interest in you. And then you denied all knowledge of him.'

There was only one other solution that Rosenharte could think of. The Poles were somehow connected to Vladimir. Though Vladimir insisted he knew nothing of the operation in Trieste, Rosenharte was now inclined to disbelieve him. The more he thought about Vladimir, the more bizarre his motives seemed. The little homily he'd delivered on the cooperation between East and West on terrorism didn't quite explain why the KGB had looked the other way as the West had taken Abu Jamal. All he appeared to be concerned about was knowing the details of the plan so he could report them to his superiors. A wild idea suddenly occurred to him.

'Is Biermeier working for the KGB?'

She looked genuinely startled. 'He doesn't like the Russians any more than the Americans. His father was killed by them in the defence of Berlin.'

'And you're sure he's told you everything?'

'Yes. The whole point, the whole brilliance of Biermeier's plan was to get the West to do all the dirty work for him. There would be no need to involve the Russians.'

They had travelled about twenty miles under the wide Saxony sky and had passed several military trucks going in the same direction, but now there was almost no traffic on the road. The flat, featureless countryside seemed already resigned to winter. About thirty miles from Leipzig they filled up with petrol and bought a couple of cups of black coffee from a man with a drooping Gallic moustache who, seeing their Leipzig number plate, was curious to hear news from the city. No, Ulrike replied: with all the rumours of violence they had kept well away from the demonstrations. The man congratulated them for their good sense. There were too many troublemakers in the country and it would be a good thing if they were all put on trains and sent out of the GDR.

'The old solution,' said Rosenharte, without the man noticing the edge in his voice.

He took the wheel and after criss-crossing the countryside and trying several tracks, they found a turning which he thought looked promising because recent tyre ruts had been left by a large truck. He pushed the Wartburg gingerly into an area of scrub, birch trees and wild cherry. Several rabbits shot across their path and Ulrike cried out when she saw the white hindquarters of a deer flash in the undergrowth. The track ahead of them rose gradually to a hillock surrounded by trees. They swung right, then left, and glimpsed part of a wooden roof, at which point he pulled up and turned the car round so that it faced the direction they had just come. They got out and approached the top of the mound through the trees, stopping to listen several times before reaching a plateau of dead grass in front of a farmhouse. A wooden fence enclosed this space, and at the southern end there was a rusty iron gate, hanging into the yard on one hinge. By the tyre marks and flattened grass they saw that several vehicles had been there. Rosenharte turned through three-quarters of a circle to look at the roads leading to the farmhouse. They came from four directions, one from a large beech forest that bordered the estate to the south-west. The important point was that each route was hidden from the others. If they kept watch, they would stand a very good chance of escape were they to be cornered there.

The house itself was in worse repair than Rosenharte remembered from his night visit. The windows were rotten and the roof looked near collapse in one or two places. They entered by slipping the latch with his camping knife. There were signs not just of the recent occupation by Harland's team, but one which predated it. Someone had lived there up until a year or two before, judging by the old packets of food on the shelves which had clearly been disturbed by mice. They unpacked their food and a few other items from the car, then concealed them in some bushes just off the road that led into the beech forest. No rain had fallen in this part of the country and Rosenharte suggested they make a meal in the open rather than use the stove inside the house. That way he could keep an eye on the amount of smoke they were producing. He made a fire using dry kindling found at the side of the house and they sat on an old bench together, sharing a bottle of beer and devouring the contents of several cans, which they heated in the pans. Rosenharte dispersed the smoke by fanning it with a piece of board.

He knew very well that Ulrike was still hiding a lot from him, but unless this had a direct relevance to Konrad, he wasn't interested. The only thing that mattered now was collecting the documents from Vladimir, getting to Berlin and handing them over to the British. He touched her on the shoulder, then took her chin in his hand to turn her face towards him.

'I find myself in an odd position,' he told her. 'I've fallen for someone who's lied to me about the most important thing in my life.' He stopped and looked into her eyes, trying to plumb the depths of her deceit. 'Lie to me again on this, Ulrike, and I will not answer for my actions. If there's anything you know that is relevant to Konrad, I want to hear it now.'

She shook her head and said there was nothing more. A minute or two of silence followed and then she pointed to a small pink bird that had shot up from the scrub below the hillock and perched at the top of a clump of hazel nearby.

'A male rosefinch,' he said. 'It will fly all the way across the Ukraine and Iran to India in the next few weeks.'

'You're migrating the other way.'

'I want you to come with me.'

'One day, maybe, when there are no travel restrictions. But I am staying here. I want to see it through. Last night was just the beginning. We have to keep up the pressure.'

'But Ulrike, you're on the run. Not for a petty transgression, but for spying. That's a mandatory death sentence. Spies don't even get a court appearance. After they've beaten you and got everything they want they kill you. The last thing you'll feel is the barrel of the gun behind your ear. A fraction of a second later a bullet enters your brain. Then they burn your body and dispose of the ashes down the drain. You're eliminated, no longer even reviled by the state.'

'Don't, Rudi.'

'For you, a trusted informant and sometime member of the

Stasi, they will reserve the most savage treatment. Because you haven't just betrayed the GDR but the state within a state – the Ministry for State Security.'

She was agitated and her cheeks were flushed. 'You don't seem to understand what happened last night. It's the beginning of the end. People will demonstrate all over the GDR because it's not just in Leipzig that they hate the system. There are groups springing up in every city. We have contacts with them.'

'If that's true, there's all the more reason for you to keep yourself safe until Honecker goes. But that could be months – maybe years. Come with me to the West when I take Konrad out. You'll be welcomed as a hero now that they've got the Arab. That means they'll find you an apartment and a job and give you money. They are already housing Else and the kids.' He took out his wallet and showed her the picture that Harland had given him.

'The sons look like you,' she said.

'That's hardly surprising. Konrad and I are identical. Well, we *were* identical. He's lost weight and he looks older than I do now. But we'll get him the best treatment and see if we can't restore him to what he was.' He was aware of the emotion in his voice and glanced away.

It began to spot with rain. They went inside the farmhouse and drank beer at the table, looking through the open door at the rain and talking with a familiarity that surprised both of them.

Later Rosenharte noticed some gas cylinders in the corner of the kitchen, looked for an appliance to go with them, but found nothing. He fiddled with an old cast-iron stove to see if he could get it burning when night fell and the smoke would not be seen. Both kept an eye on the tracks and the road across the fields to the north of them. Very little traffic passed on this road, and in the fields there was no sign of activity. They were alone and could remain undetected for the next few days. He knew he'd have to break cover to make phone calls to Vladimir and Harland, but for the present there was no need to move. When the sun came out to give them a warm autumn afternoon, they sat out front and he whittled the end of a piece of hazel wood into a crude-looking bird, which he gave her.

Their farmhouse was still supplied with electricity, but the light fittings had been stolen, along with the mattress from the bed, the sinks and lavatories. Even the taps had been taken and the pipes sealed. But outside water sputtered from a faucet and using this they made a meal of pasta with a sauce of cheese and mushrooms that she'd dried and preserved in an old tin. They drank one of the two bottles of wine they had and toasted recent events. She sat down on their makeshift bed, which mostly consisted of Rosenharte's sleeping bag and some clothes, and began to undress in the light from the open mouth of the stove. Rosenharte watched her, then did likewise and kneeled and held her, seeing again the look of wonder mixed with uncertainty in her eyes.

They slept until midnight when they both awoke to the sound of a phone – not the bell they were used to, but an electronic trill that was coming from beneath the stairs. Rosenharte pulled on his trousers and went with the torch to investigate. He found a bulky white telephone inside a cupboard under the stairway, picked up the handset and listened.

'Is that Prince?'

'Yes.' Rosenharte recognized Harland's voice.

'Glad you found the set. The news is very good. The package proved more than we expected. We're very pleased. Everything's set for Friday. Owing to the high-grade information we now have we want to make sure Kafka comes with you. It's no longer safe for anyone connected to this business to remain *in situ*. During the removal we were disturbed by certain parties and we now believe the situation's extremely volatile. You understand what I'm saying? Kafka must come with you.'

'We know about the problem. That's why we're here.'

'Glad you've taken action. Our feeling is that everything's blown. The parties who disturbed us will understand all the implications. They'll work it back and put things together.'

'Understood.'

'So we'll see you at the place you specified on the day you specified. If you don't show, we'll take it that it's off.'

'Agreed,' said Rosenharte.

'Pass on our congratulations and thanks to Kafka.'

Before he hung up, Rosenharte asked whether they could use the phone, and if so what codes they should use to dial a number in the GDR. After giving him some basic instructions and the codes Harland said, 'It's not advisable for domestic calls. But use it if there's no other means available. Keep your calls short, and don't use the phone continuously at the same location unless you're about to move. We'd like the set back, so if it's humanly possible bring it with you to our meeting. Otherwise leave it where you found it and we'll have it picked up at some stage.'

Rosenharte replaced the handset and wrote down the codes on the back of his hand.

TWENTY-EIGHT

A Call to Poland

They rose early next day, stiff, cold and snapping at each other. Both yearned for a bath. Rosenharte hadn't shaved for two days and dark gingery stubble was showing on his chin. He made a drink of beef stock for Ulrike, who perched on the table to escape the draughts, blowing steam from her cup.

'You make the call, then we should go,' she said.

'The phone has a battery so we can use it wherever we like.'

'Why don't you do it before we go? It'll save you having to set it up again.'

'Whatever you say,' he said testily and went out for a cigarette.

He returned five minutes later. 'You can't stay in the GDR. That's what Harland said last night. You have to come with me.'

She gave him a trapped look and put down the cup. 'All these years I've worked and planned, lied and risked my freedom for what is happening. I have to be here.'

'Let's see what you think after a day or two of living rough.'

'Don't be stupid. This isn't about my comfort.' She swivelled on her bottom to look away from him and out at the still grey landscape that seemed to have been laid down with strokes of watercolour wash.

'If you stay I can give you money, which will make things easier for you,' he said after a few minutes. 'Maybe there's a reason you want to stay that I don't understand, but I think you should come. And that's the last I'll say on the matter.'

After a silence she held out a hand. 'Rudi – I'm sorry. I can be a bitch in the morning.'

He nodded.

They waited until ten to make the call to Poland. After rehearsing the procedure and reading the letter that had been left with Else by the second Pole, he dialled the number and got through the first time. A male voice answered. Rosenharte asked if this was Leszek Grycko.

A Polish voice recognized the name and produced what sounded like a stream of instructions.

'Do you speak any German? This is Rudi Rosenharte. Ro—sen—harte.'

The receiver was put down, then a few seconds later it was snatched up, this time by a young woman with a high, panicky voice who was desperate to make herself understood, but she too spoke no German. Rosenharte raised his eyes to the ceiling and said, 'Later, I will call later.' He hung up.

'It's odd that he left this number where no one speaks German. I guess it's not important, but it does interest me that these two men have made such efforts to contact Konrad and me. When Zank questioned me in my office he said that the one who died in Trieste was part of the Polish secret service. Do you think Biermeier has anything to do with this? Could they have been working for him without you knowing?'

'No, he feared that that man would ruin the whole operation in Trieste. The other members of the Stasi team, who weren't in all this, wanted to pull out after his death because there was too much they didn't understand about it.'

'Franciscek Grycko died of a heart attack.'

'It will all be clear soon, no doubt.' She started picking up things from the floor and packing them into the two bags they had brought from the car. Rosenharte returned to the phone and dialled Vladimir's number as instructed, using a code as though he was phoning from outside the country. Vladimir picked up and simply said, 'Yes?'

'It's me – Rudi. Did you get my message that everything was happening on Monday night? It all went as planned.'

'Yes,' he said warily.

'Everything is set for the date we discussed. Do you have the papers I requested?'

'What kind of telephone are you using? It sounds different.'

Rosenharte read off the name Inmarsat.

'We shouldn't speak long on this phone.'

'Have you got the material I asked for?'

Vladimir hesitated. 'There may be a problem. Call me later on an ordinary telephone. I can't speak now.'

'What sort of problem?'

'I can't say because I don't know.'

'But we *are* going ahead. Everything's in place your end?'

'Not now. Call me later.' There was a click as he hung up.

Rosenharte replaced the receiver feeling troubled, but he decided to put Vladimir's manner down to routine cautiousness. He unplugged the phone from the electricity supply and followed the cables to the back of the house where a small dish had been erected. This he removed, then he coiled the wire and went to place the phone on top of the large bags. Ulrike was staring out of the window.

'What's the matter?' he asked.

'I don't remember more than a couple of cars passing on that stretch of road yesterday, but I've just seen a van and three cars pass in the last minute.' She motioned him over. 'And is that a vehicle parked by those trees, or am I seeing things in the mist?'

Rosenharte thought he made out the canopy of a truck but couldn't be sure. 'Come on, let's get out of here.'

Just as he was about to pick up one of the bags an idea came to him. He ran over to the stove and stoked the open front with the remains of the floorboards he'd broken for heat in the middle of the night. Using a poker he levered the plate from the top and exposed the fire below. He rammed one gas cylinder down the opening and balanced the other across a metal lip on the front of the stove, so that the flames licked one side.

They rushed to the back of the farmhouse and forced open a door into a thicket of bramble and hazel. He went first and turned and pushed backwards so she could follow. The car lay about two hundred yards away and they would have to cross one of the tracks leading up to the farmhouse. Ulrike got snagged by the brambles several times and Rosenharte had to turn and slash at the tentacles with his knife. Once they got through the worst of it he left her and snaked through the bushes towards the track. There he waited and listened. All was clear. He beckoned to her and they dived across the track and plunged in to some dead bracken.

They heard a vehicle moving slowly down the track.

Rosenharte cursed and shoved her head down into the grass. 'Don't move until I say,' he hissed.

He glimpsed the car – a black saloon with four men inside – and began to crawl through the trees on his elbows, each step of the way placing the bag with the phone in front of him. He reached the firm ground where he'd parked the Wartburg, slipped the catch on the boot, inched it open and placed the phone dish inside.

Two more journeys to fetch the bags followed, then he led Ulrike to the car.

They were hidden from the house but close enough to hear the men talking in the still morning air. One was speaking into a radio. Evidently they were waiting for further instructions before entering the farmhouse. He looked at Ulrike's fearful expression and touched her cheek with his fingertips to calm her. She gave him a tight little smile. A minute or two later they heard more vehicles approaching from different directions. He crab-walked to the driver's side, reached to the door handle and, still crouching, worked the action to see if he could open it without making a noise. There was a click followed by a metallic yawn from the hinge. He froze, one hand holding the door, the other splayed on the ground. Ulrike grimaced and shut her eyes.

But no one had heard. The other vehicles were pulling up at the bottom of the hillock and the sound of doors banging reached them. He beckoned her, indicating she should climb across into the passenger seat, then followed and gently pulled the door to.

He pulled out the choke and put his hand to the ignition key. At this precise moment two almighty bangs occurred in quick succession, which seemed to shake everything around them. The explosions reverberated in the woods and birds scattered from all around them into the sky. He started the engine and pumped the accelerator a little, but rather than lunging forward, he nosed the car into the track, letting the wheels roll down into the tyre ruts with almost no sound.

Then he hit the accelerator and they shot forward. 'Are they following?'

'I can't see anything except the smoke.'

'Well at least it means they can't see us.'

In a few seconds they reached the golden cover of the great

beech forest and were going like the blazes along a well-made road littered with beechnuts that snapped and popped as they ran over them. One or two mushroom hunters were out, but they saw no one for the next twenty minutes as they headed for somewhere that Rosenharte knew would be the very last place the Stasi would search for them.

TWENTY-NINE

A New Traitor

Harland took no part in the interrogation of Abu Jamal. A team from London was flown in to the military base sixty miles from the BND headquarters at Munich-Pullach. As well as the SIS and BND officers, the CIA had conjured a dozen anti-terrorism and Middle East specialists to comb through the documents taken from the villa. But he noted with satisfaction that what had generally been dismissed as his hare-brained operation in Trieste had already produced important results.

Two men had been picked up, one in Vienna and the other in Italy, and now that the identities of Abu Jamal's main contacts were known, the embassies of six nations had been alerted across the Middle East to pay special attention to the comings and goings at East German missions, and to the movement of known Stasi operatives. Harland's stock was high in London and he had received a note from the Chief of SIS congratulating him on his 'superb effort' in neutralizing Abu Jamal. The celebrations, however, were muted. The Arab no longer represented a threat, but the size, sophistication and ambitions of his network did give cause for alarm, particularly as so little of it was picked up on Western intelligence radar. The more important lesson, defined by Costelloe in an instant piece of analysis, was that Misha Lomieko and the East Germans had inspired the terrorists with techniques and a boldness of vision that was utterly new. This knowledge had escaped into the ether for ever.

Feeling triumphant but also rather superfluous, Harland went to seek out Alan Griswald, whom he hadn't seen since he got back from Leipzig. He found him in a corridor of one of the low wooden buildings reading *Small Boat* magazine, clutching the perennial Styrofoam cup of coffee. 'Hey Bobby, that was a wonderful operation. Just beautiful. You must be feeling pretty pleased with yourself.'

Harland nodded his appreciation.

'Is he talking yet?'

'Not much, but we got his address book, a fake passport or two and, most important, papers relating to the bank accounts. It's all there. Have you seen him yet?'

'No, but that's part of the reason why I came – and to get my laptop.'

'Oh, didn't I mention that we left it in the truck?' said Harland.

Griswald nodded, signalling that he knew his leg was being pulled. 'Right, Bobby.'

'I'll give it you before you return to Berlin. Let's go and see the Arab being questioned. There's an observation window we can use.'

Abu Jamal faced his three interrogators calmly, hands folded on the table in front of him, answering in a soft, amenable voice. He was wearing a black corduroy cap and behaving as though he was about to leave, glancing at the place on his wrist where an expensive watch had been. His line was to deny all knowledge of the man named Abu Jamal, saying he had never heard of the name, still less Mohammed Ubayd. It was all a grotesque case of mistaken identity for which the West would pay dearly. Every ten minutes or so he demanded that he should be taken back to East Germany.

'He's playing for time,' said Harland as they watched through the one-way mirror. 'He doesn't know we've got his little cache of secrets, so he thinks he's giving the East Germans as much time as possible to retrieve the stuff from the villa and alert their people abroad.'

'Maybe,' said Griswald, 'but who's to say they knew everything he was up to? We think that even Misha didn't have the full story. That's what makes Abu Jamal such a helluva big catch.'

'What makes you say that Misha didn't have the full story?'

'It's not my theory but the Russians'. We've had formal contact with them on this – more than the usual back channel. There was a suspicion that they might develop things when we first received information from them. They were aware of the situation and had a very good estimate of Abu Jamal's plans. And get this – they knew when and where you were going to snatch him. They were right up to speed and didn't inform the Stasi. So we took that as a sign of their good faith and had our little talk yesterday.'

'And . . . ?' Harland knew Griswald enough to know that there was more to come.

'And you're going to take me to the finest restaurant in London if—'

'Agreed – wherever you want.'

'Well, we think that your man Rosenharte told them everything.'

'That makes sense,' said Harland. 'He's managed to get some passes in Hohenschönhausen for Saturday morning which only the Russians could supply. So he did a deal. That was very smart of him.'

'Once a spy . . .'

'Always an untrustworthy bastard,' said Harland.

'There's a KGB man in Dresden who he's been talking to, and you're right – they're helping him.'

'How do you know this? Did the Russians tell you?'

'Unlike you, Bobby, we made an intelligent guess.'

'You want that laptop back, Al? Because you're talking as though you don't.' He looked at Griswald. 'What's going on?'

'There's been some pretty high-level contact with the Soviets on terrorism for a couple of months now. You see, for a good part of the last fifteen years we've been pushing the idea that every bad thing that came out of the Mid East was the Soviets' fault. They're kind of pissed about the reputation they've gotten. Under Gorbachev they decided to show they're whiter than white. They're really helping now.'

They took one more look at the Arab hunched at the table and left the airless space for the corridor.

'Let's take a walk, Bobby. I need to see the daylight.'

They left through a door where a couple of armed US military policemen stood guard. Griswald nodded to them. 'It's all right if we go out here for a couple of minutes?'

'Sure thing, Mr Griswald,' said one.

'You're known here?'

'We occasionally have business we want to do away from you people. No offence, but we all have our secrets. However, because you are who you are, Bobby, and I like you, I'm going to tell you something interesting.'

'What?'

Griswald stopped and thrust his hands in the pockets of his jacket.

'The other side have got someone in here. A senior BND officer is reporting straight to Schwarzmeer.'

'Jesus, which one?'

'The woman sitting in on the interrogation, Doctor Lisl Voss.'

'Their chief analyst! Christ!'

'Indeed.'

'Do they know?'

'We just told them. That's really why I came here, Bobby, not to look at your chubby British cheeks.'

'Do they know what we plan for Saturday?'

'No, we don't think so.'

'Does she know that Kafka and Prince are still in the East?'

'Well, that's very much the immediately relevant point. And that's why I'm telling you *entre nous*. I'd hate to see you end up in Hohenschönhausen just as you really got the wind in your sails, Bobby. The BND don't know what you're planning in Berlin, so there's no real risk with the woman Voss. But you can use her to your advantage and gain a little extra security perhaps.'

'How?'

'Bobby! Tell me you're not losing it.' Griswald enjoyed having Harland wriggling on the end of his line. He grinned. 'It's simple: we let her know that the two people responsible for the operation against Abu Jamal are being brought to the West at this very moment. That way the Stasi will stop looking for them.' He looked at Harland with the odd, open-mouthed expression he had when he was being serious. 'And make no mistake, when Zank found you at the villa it was a racing certainty that he would put it all together. He knows Kafka and Prince are in this thing. He would understand that it was all one operation.'

'You're saying that he knows all that bullshit in Trieste with Annalise and the extraction of Abu Jamal are one and the same thing? How can he make that leap?'

'Believe me, he has. The Stasi know the disks are baloney and that they've been had.' He put his hand on Harland's shoulder. 'Still, it was fun while it lasted, wasn't it? You're riding high and you've got permission to go to Berlin to get Konrad Rosenharte.

Don't screw up and get caught. We don't want to have to swap you for Abu Jamal.'

Harland looked across a helicopter pad to a stand of pine trees. 'So let me get this straight. Lisl Voss is passing them everything we're learning here. Jesus! Everything?'

'Fortunately she has been involved in just one part of the interrogation, and then only as an observer so that she's able to make her report to the German Chancellor. She doesn't know about the documents you found and she's ignorant of the means and methods used in this exfiltration. So you see there's a real good opportunity to mislead the GDR in a number of ways while the West Germans build their case against her with phone taps and the usual surveillance. It's a gift.'

'So who's going to do this?'

'You are. When they break for lunch, you join them and casually let it be known that Rosenharte and Kafka are about to arrive safely in the West. Don't use any names. Just say that things have worked out perfectly. She'll be wetting herself to make the call to her controller to tell the Stasi that the Arab isn't talking. At the same time she will pass on your information that Rosenharte and Kafka are out.'

'You don't think this will jeopardize the brother's situation in Hohenschönhausen?'

'Look, I can't tell you how they're gonna react, but I do know that you can help your operation immeasurably by doing this. The Stasi are in chaos with all these demonstrations. They'll be thankful that the Arab isn't talking and that they've got time to get their act together and distance themselves from any fallout.'

'How long are the West Germans going to let Dr Voss run?'

'That's up to them. But they gotta get the evidence to make criminal charges stick. So my guess is that they'll wait for a week or two.' He stopped and punched Harland on the arm. 'Off you go, sport. I'm going to catch my ride to Berlin.'

'Thanks.'

'Think nothing of it.'

'What about the computer?'

'Bring it with you Sunday. Remember, brunch at my place.'

'See you then.'

'And Bobby, you stay safe.'

Harland went inside.

By the time he got to the debriefing room, the assembled intelligence officers were already having sandwiches and coffee. The head of the BND team, a man named Heinz Wittich, introduced Harland to Voss as the mastermind of operation Samaritan. Harland smiled modestly and said that the German component deserved just as much praise for its professionalism.

Dr Voss, a brunette with a neat little bun and a handsome, straightforward face, regarded him with pleasure. 'We know the British culture dictates modesty at all times, but really, you should accept our praise, Herr Harland. It's a wonderful thing you've done.' Voss was good. He wondered how long she had been working for the Stasi and what had led her into the clutches of Schwarzmeer. It had to be ideological conviction because it was plain she wasn't some lovesick secretary with nothing to do in the evenings. Voss was an attractive and self-possessed pro, a career spy who had probably been put in place by the Stasi in the sixties or seventies.

Harland poured himself some coffee and complimented her on her suit, a well-cut grey tweed. She thanked him.

'I have to confess,' he said, 'that we're very pleased about the latest development. I can report that the pair who helped us on the other side are on their way out.'

Heinz Wittich gave him a wintry smile. Clearly he had just been informed about Voss's treachery. He was willing Harland not to say any more with a steady gaze that no intelligence officer could mistake.

Harland ignored him. 'They had a few close scrapes but it's all worked out fine. I'm going back to Berlin this afternoon for the celebration.'

'You deserve it,' said Voss with matronly indulgence.

Harland drank his coffee. 'Thank you. In fact I've already shared a couple of brandies with my friend Alan Griswald.'

At the mention of Griswald's name, a shadow of understanding passed through Wittich's eyes. 'I wish we had some beer here to toast you for a magnificent job,' he said.

'And to absent friends,' said Harland. 'In particular to a diligent young colonel in Main Department Three. Where would we be without him, eh?'

'I'm afraid I do not know to whom you refer,' said Wittich, playing it beautifully.

'Sorry, I can't enlighten you further, Heinz,' said Harland. Everyone knew he was referring to Zank. 'I've already said more than I should.'

'You're among friends here,' said Wittich.

'Yes, but even in these hopeful times we must maintain operational security.'

'Quite so,' said Dr Lisl Voss, with not the slightest hint that she had registered the significance of what had been said.

Rosenharte watched the blackbird furiously wipe its beak on the side of a branch, then straighten and sing for a few brief moments before dropping into the air.

They were in the car waiting for the dark. Ulrike watched him watching the bird. 'When did you become interested in birds?' she asked.

'When we were boys, I suppose, but it wasn't until I was in my forties that I really came to love them – their defiance of gravity, the mystery of migration and their sudden reappearance in the spring, as if they've been hiding all through the winter in the forests. They fascinate me. They're not part of this earth.'

'You said when *we were* boys, as though you did all your thinking with your brother.'

'I suppose that's right. My interests were Konrad's, and vice versa. Up until we were eighteen there were very few things that we didn't experience together; nothing, in fact, because we had no secrets, no privacy. That's why we had such an advantage over the other kids; we pooled everything, shared our knowledge.'

'Like having another self.'

'Yes.'

'But you must have had arguments, like all children?'

'We did, but intellectually Konrad always beat me and when I won, well, he would usually make me feel so guilty that I would concede in the end.' He smiled and reached for his cigarettes on the dashboard.

'Should we be going? It's nearly dark.'

They had already passed through the village once and had noticed that the public phone by the church was not overlooked by any houses. They parked on the far side of the church and Rosenharte approached the booth via an alley without street lighting. He dialled the number and was told to wait. After a little while he began to worry whether he would have enough money. Eventually Vladimir came on the line.

'I'm using a public phone,' said Rosenharte.

'Good, that's good. Thank you.' His voice was different. Hesitant.

'So is everything arranged as we agreed?'

'There is a problem,' said Vladimir.

'What kind of problem?'

'I was hoping that you'd learn before I spoke to you, but I see now that there was no way you could know.'

'What? What's the problem?'

'I'm sorry to be the one to break this to you, but your brother has died. He died of natural causes – a heart attack – the day after you saw him.'

Rosenharte couldn't react.

'Rudi, are you there?'

He was staring at the outline of the church steeple, doing all he could to remain on his feet.

'Yes, I'm here,' he said slowly.

'They kept it from you because they wanted you to work for them,' continued Vladimir in his factual monotone. 'They needed the third delivery. It seems that he died after composing that letter to you. I'm afraid he never saw your letter to him. Rudi, I can imagine what you're feeling, but you must listen to the rest of what I have to say. They plan to use this against you. They know you're on the run and they will use—'

'How?' he heard himself say. 'What can they do?'

'They plan to say that you killed your brother in order to marry his wife. That way they can use your picture in the newspapers and encourage people to turn you in. They're very angry about what happened in Leipzig, more so at being fooled by these disks. Take my word for it you have to cross the border tonight. You must leave.'

Some part of Rosenharte understood that Vladimir needed him to run. If he was caught, there was no doubt that he would eventually reveal Vladimir's knowledge of his plan to spring

Konrad. That could end the Russian's career. But given his exposure, Vladimir's tone was not unsympathetic.

'Have you understood what I've told you?'

'Yes.' He fought to keep his voice normal. 'What happened to his body? Where did they bury him?' This was suddenly very important.

Vladimir coughed. 'Rudi, I'm afraid they cremated your brother a few days later. It's said that they tried to contact his wife, but that she'd already fled to the West. I have no reason to disbelieve this.'

Rosenharte's rational part was functioning, like a wounded animal still running on adrenaline. 'So, there's no proof that he was killed by them?'

'Ultimately, no. But I believe my source on this. He's always been reliable.' He stopped. 'I'm sorry for you. Truly, you have my deepest sympathy.'

Rosenharte muttered something and Vladimir said goodbye; the constriction in his throat was audible. The line went dead. He sank to a squatting position still holding the receiver, then he let go of himself completely, falling against the inside of the booth. He had no sense of anything other than the unimaginable void that had opened in him and also, he felt acutely, beside him. The presence existing alongside him that he had known all his life had gone, and with it the context of his being. His parameters had suddenly and catastrophically disappeared. He didn't know where he was nor why he was there.

It began to rain, a thin, mountain drizzle, and his gaze came to rest on the halo of light around a solitary street lamp about fifty yards down the road. He could not see any reason for rising and running to some cover, but Ulrike was now in front of him, pulling both his arms, insisting that he stand. 'What's the matter?' she kept on asking. 'What happened to you?'

He stood and found a strange, autonomous calm. 'Konrad's dead. They killed him one way or the other – by design or neglect, I don't know which. Vladimir's just told me.'

'Oh, my poor love.' She cradled his head against her chest. He submitted, but it was a very short time before he straightened, pulled away from her and went to the iron gate of the churchyard to stand by himself.

THIRTY

Family Photographs

He got drunk on the bottle of Goldi she had put in the back of the car, and spoke without stopping because it meant he didn't have to think. The talk was automatic, a free association of tales from his boyhood about school, their hideout on the lake, the first girls who came their way and were dated and kissed by the twins with the farcical interchangeability of a play by Shakespeare. He even laughed in the hour or so it took to travel to the place where he knew they would never be found, a place he now also had an urgent need to see. Ulrike followed his directions, occasionally glancing at him with concern, but mostly concentrating on the roads which were awash from the autumn storm.

At length they found the gateway he was looking for and he was able to get his bearings. Rather than forcing the padlock, he told her to go back down the road and turn into a lane about four miles on. He did not remember the actual lane, but he knew that it must be there. Very soon they came to a much more imposing gateway with massive stone gargoyles that had all been decapitated. This was also barred to them with coils of barbed wire and two or three boulders that had been dropped in the way. He remembered that a little way along there was another entrance to what once had been the estate farm.

Rather doubtfully, Ulrike crept along the lane until they saw some abandoned farm buildings in the headlights. They took another right and proceeded up an overgrown driveway where the car kept slewing right and left because the wheels found no grip on the grass. Four or five hundred yards from the farm buildings they burst from the cover of the dripping trees and came to a mesh fence. Stapled to one of the posts was a notice that read 'Verboten – Ministerium für Staatssicherheit'.

'Where the hell are we?' she asked Rosenharte as he almost fell out of the car. He did not answer, but ran to the fence and started working with a blind fury at the post immediately in front of them, rocking it back and forth until he felt the wood give beneath the soil. The wire came away easily and he rolled it back.

'Where are we?' she repeated.

He got back into the car. 'Go straight ahead and stop asking so many damned questions.'

'Rudi, I have every right to know where you're taking me,' she said reasonably.

'Pull up there,' he said as they reached the façade of the great ruined house. 'Over there by the wall.'

Ulrike looked up at the baroque profile looming over them. 'What *is* this place?'

He didn't answer, but got out and started removing all the bags from the car.

'Rudi!' she said, placing a hand on his arm to stop him. 'Tell me where we are.'

'Schloss Clausnitz. The ancestral home of my family that was stolen by the Stasi. It's also Schwarzmeer's private country retreat. But he stays way over on the other side of the estate.'

'We can't stay here!'

'We can,' he said, wresting his arm free. 'It's mine now.'

'For goodness' sake, Rudi. Calm down. We need to think about this. It's crazy.'

He was aware of his unreason, but could not stop himself. He rushed to the stairs with the two bags and quickly broke in through the French windows with his knife. Ulrike followed him into the dusty blackness.

'Where are we going to sleep?' she asked.

'There must be fifty rooms in this place. It shouldn't be too difficult to find somewhere warm and dry.'

'But why are we here?'

'Because this is where we came from. This is my home. Konrad's home.'

'Forty-five years ago it was your home,' she said softly. 'It's no longer yours. There's nothing of your life here.'

He looked at her in the beam of his torch. 'I thought of coming here yesterday, because they won't look for us here. There's nothing around here except the forest: no villages, just a few houses. And Schwarzmeer won't be here. He'll be far too busy defending his rear in Berlin.'

'What happened to the farm we passed? Aren't there people still living in it?'

He saw that she was trying to calm him down. 'Who knows? Probably screwed up like everything else during collectivization. You know, I had an idea to tell Konrad about this place. He didn't know about it. I thought it would entertain him to come back here and make one of his strange little films.' He paused. 'It's where we come from! For all I know we were conceived here, early in 1939, just on the eve of war.'

The beam from the torch skidded along the floor as he stumbled from room to room with the bottle of brandy. He paused in the dining room, where there was nothing but a pile of floorboards and a jumble of rags, then in a reception room, which he seemed to remember was used in the mornings by women dressed stiffly in suits of dark green and grey. They came upon the double staircase, which still had a semblance of grandeur like the stairway of an ocean liner, though it was much older and palpably better made. He flashed the torch across the ceiling where there was an eighteenth-century mural of a winged archer that had been left untouched by the troops who had been briefly billeted in all the great houses of southern Germany after May 1945. Around the walls, the old mirrors had been vandalized and bits of glass hung from the plaster frames and flashed in his beam.

'We used to play here,' he said, his hand sweeping wildly across the stairway. 'There were pictures along here. I remember dogs were everywhere: terriers, German shepherds, dachshunds and an English spaniel. The place was alive with guests, the extended family and servants and they all came through this part of the house. It was like a rail terminus.'

They turned to the entrance, where someone had attempted to prise the marble from the floor but had succeeded only in breaking it.

'And here was the front door where we lined up to watch our parents arrive – us in uniform, no doubt.'

'Who was your father?'

'I thought Biermeier had seen my file and told you everything.'

'Not everything. I knew they were Nazis and that there were some remarks in your records about it. But he didn't tell me much.'

'What did he tell you?'

'Oh, I don't know – that your father was a general and that both your parents died at the end of the war.'

'My father, Manfred von Huth, was in the SS,' he said savagely. 'He was certainly a war criminal. He became a Brigadeführer und General of the Thirty-second Panzergrenadierdivision "30 Januar". History does not relate how he died. Maybe he was shot on Hitler's orders. The Stasi have a theory that he was killed by his own troops. Who knows? My mother was a von Clausnitz. This place belonged to her family. She died in the Dresden firestorm.'

'And that's when the Rosenhartes took you in?'

He took a swig of brandy but didn't answer her. 'Damn it,' he said at length. 'Konnie should have seen this place. He would have told me what it explains about us, the things inside us that we got from our parents here. He had very good instincts, you know; he didn't need to be told something, he didn't need it written down. He understood because of his humane intelligence.' He repeated the phrase several times and then threw the remains of the brandy to the back of his throat. This made him retch. Still coughing, he staggered down the corridor to find a kitchen, pantry, larder, storage and laundry rooms. All of them bore the signs of abuse and sudden evacuation. He explored every room on the ground floor, wildly throwing open doors, looking in and moving on. Ulrike did all she could to keep up as he roamed through the house, cursing the ghosts of the von Clausnitz family.

In the end she said it would be best if she left him alone while she found somewhere for them to sleep. She touched him before leaving and said: 'Be careful with yourself, Rudi.' He brushed her away and went up a back stairway to find he knew not what: his parents' bedroom? A boudoir where the repellent Nazi she-wolf retired? A nursery perhaps – his home for the first years of his life with Konnie. He had no idea what he was searching for, but as he went he was conscious that he was mapping the extent of his loss. It was a matter of seeing how much of him survived the unthinkable absence at his side. Yet by and by there were deeper truths that he probed. The possibility occurred to him that he had not done as much as he could for Konrad after his release from jail, so preoccupied was he by his own needs, his own safety. There were, he knew, shameful occasions when he should have helped him but did not. He could, for instance, have made an appointment in his name to see the dentist and then encouraged Konnie to go in his place: no one would have been the wiser. But it hadn't occurred to him and of course Konrad never complained, never asked anything of him. That was because Konrad understood he was the stronger of the two and yet he loved him nonetheless; loved him despite the weakness and selfishness.

He had arrived in a room at the front of the house which had four windows, inlaid mirrors on two sides and the remains of a small chandelier that dangled from the ceiling. The thought came to him that the house was just too large to have been completely wrecked after the war – this room, for instance, would take very little to restore. He lowered himself onto a wooden window seat, a low rhomboid-shaped box that had once been upholstered and was still stuck with padding and horse-hair.

The clouds had lifted and the night had become lighter. The near-full moon sent a beam to the floor, which flickered like a movie screen from the silent era as the clouds ran across the sky. He took out Konrad's letter, unfolded it carefully and read it. The first tears of his grief soon hit the paper and he hurriedly wiped them away so there would be no stain. What he had taken as a product of his brother's despair he now realized was noble resignation, the stoicism of a great man who had been martyred by the state's leaden vindictiveness. Konrad had had the courage to know that he was dying and to make his peace. He did not complain about his lot, but used the opportunity to pass his love to his children and wife and to give Rosenharte the sacred duty of their care. It was so typical of him that he allowed no word of regret or anger to intrude on this priority, typical of his humane intelligence.

Rosenharte sat with his head in his hands and wept for his brother's incorruptibility. Very slowly it was Konrad's loss rather than his own that assumed its rightful place in his mind. Konrad had lost everything, from the sight of his children and the comfort of his wife to the hopes of his own creative impulse. Against this, Rosenharte had merely lost his twin – his closest relationship by far and the person he had relied on and sought approval from all his life. But he hadn't suffered like Konrad and he hadn't lost his life.

He stayed there for several hours. His rage began to pass, although he was no less stricken. He moved from the window to escape a draught and slid to the floor so his back rested against the seat. He smoked several cigarettes there, lining up the extinct butts on the floorboards in front of him. At some point he noticed that part of the front of the seat and the top lifted up. He turned his torch into the space and saw a lot of documents. It took only a moment to discover that they were the personal papers of Isobel von Huth. They were not, however, very revealing, merely the kind of thing you'd expect to find in the bureau of an upper-class woman. There were bills from her dressmaker, old invitations, the 1937 membership of an equestrian club, correspondence from lawyers about a property in Berlin, meaningless keepsakes and scores of personal letters all written in elegant early twentieth-century script. These also had a rather businesslike air and they mostly concerned arrangements and meetings. One bore the address and insignia of the National Socialist Party headquarters in Berlin, yet the only matter discussed on the single sheet was the purchase of a gelding named Schnurgerade.

He looked through it all with a sense that Isobel von Huth was a rather dull woman. There was little sign of life, even in the black pocket diaries that she had kept from 1933 onwards, each one of which bore a small silver Swastika on the cover. No doubt one day he might be able to piece together a life, but faced with the loss of Konrad, his interest in the person who had given birth to them seemed suddenly academic. She had not counted in their lives, and now there was simply no reason to resurrect her from the punctilious world of the German aristocracy.

He was thumbing through the 1938 diary absently when he realized that several small snaps had dropped between his legs. There were five in all, three of an elderly man with a walrus moustache, and two of a woman with a horse. He assumed that this must be his mother, Isobel von Huth, though he found no spark of recognition in himself, and even though it was the first image he had ever seen of her he felt nothing stir in his heart. In both poses she stood with her legs set apart in a slightly masculine stance, her fists turned back on a slender, belted waist. Her breeches were perfectly pressed, her riding boots polished to a metallic sheen and the light military-style shirt betrayed no bust to speak of. It was her expression that interested Rosenharte. Her gaze had settled on something in the far distance in conscious mimicry of the images of the time that showed heroic German youth looking into the future of the Fatherland. He flipped over one of the pictures. An ink inscription read, 'Myself and Schnurgerade, September 1939' and he muttered aloud that it was a damned good thing she had died. He couldn't imagine such a woman adapting to life under the communists.

He slipped the pictures into the little flap pocket at the back of the diary and put it into his coat. Then he got up, rubbed his buttocks and legs into life and made his way along the vast corridors to the main staircase, feeling the true weight of his grief.

He found Ulrike sitting in the kitchen lit by two candles,

reading a piece of newspaper from the thirties. She gave him an enquiring look as he came in.

'It's okay,' he said wearily. 'I've blown out. It's over. Gone. I won't shout any more.'

'Come, sit. I've made us a meal.'

He nodded. Part of his problem now was knowing how to be with her. The grief was like shame. He found it very hard to look into her eyes.

They sat silently in the nest she had made from the clothes and his sleeping bag, eating a little sausage. 'I've been reading this old newspaper from the Nazi era,' she said. 'It's like opening a door into another world. There's nothing like a newspaper for doing that, is there? You see their attitudes and the things they took for granted in every line. Even the advertisements tell you something.'

'I had a similar experience upstairs.' He pulled out the diary and handed her the photographs. 'That's my mother.'

'Good Lord. She doesn't look a bit like you. She has a peevish little mouth and her eyes are set too close together and have no humour.'

She looked at the inscription on the back and he saw something pass through her eyes.

'What're you thinking?'

She examined him for a moment, then returned the photographs to their place in the diary. 'It's dated September 1939 – the month war was declared by the British.' She paused. 'And you found them in this diary from 1938?'

'Yes,' he said, not really concentrating.

'Then perhaps she got the date wrong on the back of the photograph.'

'Maybe,' he said. It didn't seem to matter one way or the other. She was dead, like her son.

THIRTY-ONE

Limbo

At dawn Rosenharte slipped from Ulrike's cold embrace and went to urinate from a window. He looked out over the courtyard, feeling the effects of the brandy behind his eyes and at the base of his skull, and cursed himself, not quite remembering why he had sunk the majority of the bottle of Goldi. Two or three minutes of being his usual hung-over self elapsed before Konrad's death hit him and his hands began to shake uncontrollably. He revolved from the window and slumped against the wall, trying to disentangle the events of the previous day – the phone call to Vladimir, the furious search of the house, finding the jumbled cache of his mother's letters and photographs.

What stopped him from complete collapse was the sound of a voice echoing round the walls of the courtyard outside. A man was musing about the presence of the car. He nudged Ulrike with his foot. 'Get up, we've got company,' he said roughly, as though it was her fault.

She leapt from the bed and followed him into a passage that led from the kitchen to the dining room. Rosenharte crept to the window. The car was still there but no one was in sight.

'Maybe you imagined it,' she whispered.

'No, no, there're fresh footprints in the grass. They're not ours because it was still raining when we left the car. Those were made this morning.'

'We'd better leave.' As she said this, they heard a dog scampering along the main corridor outside the dining room. Then came a voice ordering it to heel. There was nowhere for them to hide, and a second or two later a man appeared at the door of the dining room.

'Hey, this is state property. You're in a restricted area: authorized personnel only. We don't allow vagrants here.'

'Good morning,' said Rosenharte. 'Sir, let me assure you we aren't vagrants.'

The man held a stick, which he lowered at the sound of Rosenharte's measured tone.

'Then what're you doing here?'

'You want the honest answer? I am looking over my ancestral home. This belonged to my mother's family – von Clausnitz. So you could say I've every right to be here.'

The man entered the unforgiving light of the dining room and examined them. He looked to be in his seventies, and was wearing an old traditional leather jacket with horn buttons, corduroy breeches and brown leather boots that fastened with a strap just below the knee. His eyes were a watery blue and the skin of his face was weathered, but still stretched tightly across a Slavic bone structure.

'This is all owned by the state now. The Clausnitz name counts for nothing here. It's the name of a place, not of a family.' He looked at him shrewdly. 'Besides, you can't be a von Clausnitz.'

'I'm not,' he said. 'I was originally given my father's name – von Huth. I am the son of Manfred von Huth.'

'If you are who you say you are, and you're not just some vagabond, then worse luck for you. The man was a Nazi, a butcher.'

'Indeed sir, but we cannot choose our parents.'

'That's true,' said the man, melting a little.

'Have you known the place long?'

'All my life, but I was away from the beginning of the war until 1950, a prisoner in Russia.' He spat on the floor. 'Six years in a hole that wasn't fit for pigs.'

Rosenharte nodded. 'I'm trying to do a little research. You know how it is when you get to middle age: you want things explained. You want to try and understand your past.' He pulled out the picture of Isobel von Huth. 'This is my mother. Did you by any chance know her?'

The man peered at the photograph, but it was plain that he couldn't see properly. He shook his head. 'Yes, yes, I remember her. Her heart was as cold as a winter's night. I used to work on the estate before joining up in 1938. She was stuck up, if you know what I mean. Never said hello or gave anyone the time of day.' He looked up at Rosenharte. 'And you're her boy? You don't look like her.'

Rosenharte shrugged. 'Perhaps that's a good thing. Did you know a woman named Marie Theresa? She worked here during the war. She adopted me and my brother in 1945 and became our legal mother.'

The man shook his head. 'I got just two weeks' home leave during the entire war, and let me tell you I had better things to do than come up here to the house. I saw what went on on the battlefield and I knew that some of the people who were responsible for that carnage were dining in luxury in this very room.' He looked around them and spat again.

'So you're the caretaker now?'

'I keep an eye on things for them. I feed the fish in the lake, see that the hunting is right when he comes out here in the winter. I have a couple of lads to help when I need it.'

'Is there anyone here now?'

'No, they won't be here until November.'

'There are some houses at the other end of the estate. Are they occupied?'

'How do you know about those houses? This place is secret.'

'I was the guest of General Schwarzmeer a month back. We had some business here, but I didn't realize until the end of my time that we were in Schloss Clausnitz. I wanted to come back and take a look in my own time.' As he said this he felt in his coat.

'That doesn't seem very convincing. Are you a friend of his?'

'No, I couldn't honestly claim to be that,' said Rosenharte, hoping that he had judged the man right. 'To be frank, I am no friend of the Stasi. They were responsible for my brother's death two weeks ago and I cannot forgive them. I'm here to settle some things in my mind.'

'First you say you are the general's guest, now you say the Stasi killed your brother. To me those two things don't add up.'

'Both are true.' Rosenharte moved towards him. 'Look, we want to stay here a few days. Would that be all right? No one has to know we're here.'

The man looked doubtful.

'I can make it worth your while,' he said, pulling out a hundred dollars.

'I'm not interested in money. I can't be bought.' He stamped his stick on the ground and a terrier shot round the corner to do an excited turn in front of Rosenharte and Ulrike.

'He likes you,' said the man, his tone softening again.

'We probably smell pretty awful,' said Ulrike, bending down to play with the dog. 'Both of us could do with a shower.' She paused and looked up at him with a luminous smile. 'Can we level with you, Herr . . .'

'Flammensbeck – Joachim Flammensbeck. Go ahead.'

'Herr Flammensbeck, we need to stay here for some time. My friend has just received the terrible news about his brother and he needs peace and quiet. We'll pay any money you need, or nothing, according to your wishes. We appeal to your good nature to allow us to remain here out of sight for a little while.'

'What've you done?'

'Demonstrated for peace, liberty and democracy. That's all. We were part of that march in Leipzig and things became difficult for us there. We need to lie low for a bit.'

He looked at Rosenharte. 'So all that stuff you just told me about being Manfred von Huth's son was a lie?'

'No, it was the complete and utter truth,' said Rosenharte. 'Do you have sympathy for the marchers? You've probably heard that they're demonstrating all over Germany now. Do you think they have a case?'

Flammensbeck blew out his cheeks and exhaled. He seemed to be weighing something. Eventually he addressed them both. 'By the spring of 1945 I was in a prisoner of war camp in the east – we didn't know where. I was lucky to be alive because they shot many of us when we surrendered. Then one day in April it was announced that the Führer had committed suicide. We were stunned, but after a bit we fell to asking each other what it had all been about. So much death and destruction. Millions dead. And each one of us with innocent blood on our hands. What was it all about? No one could say. Then one in our group answered that it was about nothing. There was no point to it, no hidden meaning. Nothing! We'd been had. The German people had been fooled by a lot of gangsters, by men like your father.' Rosenharte nodded and looked down at the dog. 'The same question came to me the other day. What is this all about? This socialism? This supposed equality? There's no equality in the GDR. I see how they live here with their women and their caviar and rare wines. I know what Schwarzmeer uses this place for. The Party bosses come here and they screw like goats and drink themselves into oblivion. So, what's it all about? I'll tell you – we've been had again. Another gang of criminals has been taking us for a ride.'

Rosenharte nodded grimly. After forty years it was all so simple, so easily reduced.

'So we can stay here?' asked Ulrike.

'Yes, but you must hide the car and if they catch you, we've never spoken. I have never seen you.' He put out his hand, palm turned down, and took the money without changing his expression. 'Do I have your agreement on that?'

They both nodded.

'Are there guards at the Stasi compound?' asked Rosenharte.

'An idiot named Dürrlich who thinks he's my boss. He comes in once a day. But he's drunk most of the time and when I need him out of the way I give him some of my homemade slivovitz and he stays in bed. He's away in Berlin filling in as Schwarzmeer's driver.'

'Some driver,' said Ulrike, smiling.

'Let's hope he puts the general into a wall!' His eyes twinkled and he called the dog to come to him. 'Move the car and I'll go and mend the fence you broke last night. If you had looked a little longer you would have found an unlocked gate.' He left shaking his head.

Later they made their way across the Clausnitz estate to Schwarzmeer's hideout in the forest. In all it was about two miles from the house and if Rosenharte hadn't had some idea of the way they'd never have found the cluster of dachas hidden in the beech trees.

'Why did you want to come here?' she said as they watched for signs of life at a distance of a hundred yards.

'It's the one place we can make a phone call without being eavesdropped.' He was aware of her flinching at the harshness of his tone. A lot had fallen into place overnight, though he hadn't had time to articulate it to himself other than knowing that she was as much responsible for Konrad's death as the Stasi. He found that he felt little more than a distant contempt for her.

There was no problem gaining entry into Schwarzmeer's house. He used a hoe with a broken handle, which had been left propped against the veranda, to lever the doors apart and burst the lock.

He went straight to the phone and, remembering the code for that week, dialled Harland. As he spoke he could hear the sounds of an office in the background. A woman was complaining about a broken coffee machine.

Harland came on the line. 'Konrad is dead,' said Rosenharte, barely believing what he was saying. 'The operation is off.'

There was a pause. 'You're certain?'

'Yes, it happened when I was in Berlin that day. They kept it from me because they wanted me to continue working for them.'

'Jesus, I'm sorry. How did you learn?'

'The Russians told me. They have sources.'

'Please,' said Harland sharply. 'Be careful not to use any names or specific details from now on. This call may be intercepted.'

'I'm not using the satellite phone. We were nearly caught yesterday because of it. This phone is safe.'

'Be as vague as you can.'

'You need to tell Else what's happened,' said Rosenharte urgently. 'You have to tell Else and the boys. Do you understand? That's what you owe me. You must go to them.'

'Of course,' Harland replied.

'It's not going to be easy. She'll go to pieces. She has suffered from depression herself and she'll find this very hard to bear. Tell her that he died peacefully in his sleep. Try to make it easier for her. And say that I will come as soon as I can.'

'Of course. But you should leave now. There's no reason for you to stay. Cross the border now and bring your friend. I'll have someone meet you at the same spot as before.'

Rosenharte's eyes had come to rest on the cane chair that Schwarzmeer had occupied while he was questioned by the team from Normannenstrasse. 'No,' he said quietly. 'I am staying here. I am staying here until this thing is over. It's what Konrad would have wanted.'

'Surely what your brother would have wanted is for you to look after his family in their new home,' Harland retorted. 'They need you. You've done everything you can there.'

Rosenharte looked at Ulrike. 'No, we're staying here.' She smiled at him and nodded.

'It's understandable that you feel as you do. But don't give them another victory, Rudi. They won with your brother. Don't let them win with you. Nothing is certain. They're not beaten yet.'

'We're staying here,' he said heavily. Ulrike saw he was about to collapse and rushed to catch him. He pushed her away and then rolled into the chair.

She picked up the receiver, which had fallen to the floor. He heard her say: 'It's not possible for your friend to travel. You understand. He's taken it very badly . . . yes . . . We'll call again . . . yes . . . goodbye.'

She put the phone down, crouched in front of him and held his hand.

'Get away from me,' he mumbled.

For the next thirteen days Rosenharte moved in his private limbo of guilt and anger, knowing little of what was going on around him. He drank Flammensbeck's sweet and deadly home brew and once or twice he used a powdered sleeping draught which the old man had acquired from a friend with cancer of the prostate. He roamed Schloss Clausnitz, by turns raving and silent. He was vaguely aware of Ulrike always there a few paces behind him, watching that he did no harm to himself. On the Saturday after they had received news about Konrad, he climbed up on the roof in the light of the full moon of that night and was deliberating whether to throw himself from a gable into the courtyard. Ulrike talked him away from the edge and then knocked him out with a blow to the back of the head with a piece of wood. He woke up God knows when, naked and wet from the flannel bath she'd given him to clean the blood away. He yelled at her and called her a lying bitch then saw the shock and hurt in her face and muttered an apology. She said she understood.

It was odd how much he heard his brother's voice during these days and nights. 'Don't let them see you cry,' and, 'Come along, it isn't that bad. You have everything to live for.' The voice was as clear as if Konrad was in the room with him, and he couldn't help replying. For some reason, the Konrad he saw in his head was not the wreck in Hohenschönhausen, but the boy of thirteen or fourteen, the age when the gifts of mind and body began to reveal themselves. He grasped that he was merely remembering Konnie, yet the stream of images was so delightful and absorbing that he didn't want to disturb the flow. Between his naps in front of the range, which had been fired up after Flammensbeck knocked a couple of pipes into place in the flue, he sat thinking and remembering, almost living his childhood again.

Flammensbeck seemed to be there a lot with his dog, which had formed an obsession with Rosenharte and would sit for hours looking at him with its head cocked to one side. His master's only comment was to refer to *die Kriegsneurose* – the shellshock he'd seen as a young man – before turning away to talk to Ulrike with a pipe in his hand.

When they were alone he sat watching Ulrike, searching her face for signs of the personality that he had so badly misjudged. He remembered the fake smiles where only the lower half of her face moved, the steady gaze she produced when lying and the effortless diversions in her conversation. A spy through and through, and yet he could not entirely expel the warmer feelings he had for her, and he recognized that he would not have survived these past weeks without her.

On 18 October, a Wednesday, they were listening to a radio discussion touched off by a statement published a couple of weeks back in *Neues Deutschland* by Erich Honecker. A Western station commented that the article was an overture to the people inspired by reformist voices such as Egon Krenz and Gunther Schabowski, a senior figure who'd once edited *Neues Deutschland*, and suggested that there was some kind of struggle going on in the Central Committee. A few minutes later there was an announcement. Erich Honecker had resigned for reasons of health and had been replaced by Egon Krenz. The man who had organized the building of the Berlin Wall and ruled the GDR for the eighteen years since replacing Walter Ulbricht, was gone.

The miracle had occurred but it was another five days before he began to feel himself again. Ulrike begged him to accompany her to Leipzig for what promised to be the biggest Monday demonstration, but she had to be content with reports from friends about the 300,000 who had gathered in Karl-Marx-Platz on a warm evening. The following Wednesday she stood in front of him and said: 'Okay, that's it. Enough! You need some good country air.

We should go to the lake. Really, it's a wonderful day. Makes you happy to be alive.'

They left by the French windows and made for the far end of the lake where they came to a jetty hidden in some reeds. He walked to the end and looked across to a couple of coots bobbing like bath toys in the choppy waters on the far side. The air was sharp and invigorating. Ulrike had turned towards the house rising from the swirl of dead grass and brambles. 'I agree with old Flammensbeck: this place has some kind of magic, despite its history.'

After a silence in which she asked if he was okay, he said, 'I'm thinking about *your* history. I am thinking that your story has never stacked up. Too many coincidences. Too many gaps. Too many lies. Why did you choose me, Ulrike? What's behind it all? Are you still working for them?'

'Rudi,' she implored. 'You're still not yourself. Of course I'm not working for them. You know that.'

'Oh, but I am myself, which is why I'm asking these questions.' He whipped round and moved the five or six paces to the bottom of the jetty and grabbed her. Then he slapped her, pulling the force of the blow at the last moment. 'Tell me the truth,' he said savagely.

She did not react, but stood with her face turned in the direction of the blow. 'I never took you for a man who hits women,' she said eventually.

'I'm not,' he said. 'I need the truth, Ulrike. No more lies. You put Konrad in prison – you and Biermeier.'

She pulled herself from his grip and looked up at him. Her cheek was red, but there were no tears. 'Before I tell you everything, I want you to know that I love you more than I have ever loved a living soul. I hope you'll still feel something because I cannot stop loving you now.'

'All love is conditional. Mine is dependent on the truth.'

She asked for a cigarette. Then she walked to the end of the jetty and began to speak without looking at him. 'Okay, I'll tell you. I graduated top from the language course at Humboldt University and was immediately taken up by the Stasi, just as you were. You see my father was well connected and he wanted this for me because he thought it was the best way I could serve the GDR. After training I was sent to Brussels undercover – false papers, references, everything.' She glanced at him over her shoulder. 'That's when I first set eyes on you. I was just twenty-four years old.'

'You! You in Brussels!'

'Yes, as a translator.'

'Like Annalise Schering!'

'Yes,' she paused. 'I knew her.'

His mouth formed the first syllable of several questions before he managed to say, 'How did you know her?'

'By that I mean I knew the second Annalise, the one who took the place of the first. I still do, Rudi. I know Jessie. Do you understand what I'm saying?'

He remembered the strange remark Jessie had made in the café just before he crossed over to the East with the disks. She seemed to be telling him to pass on her regards to Ulrike. If he hadn't immediately had to face the Stasi on the other side of the Wall and then fallen ill he would probably have thought more about it.

'I was her contact at NATO. I passed the stuff back to Biermeier, who was the case officer. This was after you'd left, but I do remember seeing you twice.' She smiled briefly. 'You were something to see, Rudi – a most beautiful man.'

Rosenharte brushed this aside. 'Surely you're not suggesting that you fixed this whole thing up to get to know me?'

'No, of course not. A lot of it was Biermeier's idea.'

'Biermeier! You would have needed Jessie's cooperation. How the hell did he get that?'

'He didn't need her help. Don't you see? The letters to you came from British Intelligence, not her.'

'But somewhere along the way she must have been involved.'

'He got word to her.'

'I don't believe you. She used to be a full-time employee of British Intelligence. You don't find such people in the London phone book, even after they've left.'

'She's a member of the British Campaign for Nuclear Disarmament. The Stasi keep an eye on such people. In fact, the Stasi had close relations with one or two of the movement's members in the UK. It proved no problem to discover her address and telephone number, and then it was simply a matter of Biermeier contacting her.'

'But why would she trust an oaf like Biermeier?'

'Because she trusted me. You see, I knew that she wasn't the real Annalise Schering. Do you understand what I'm telling you? I knew, and I told no one in Brussels and no one on our side. You know why? Because we were both convinced members of the peace movement. That was our first loyalty. Jessie declared her feelings to me. She was worried by the rumours of the deployment of Cruise missiles in Western Europe and when that happened she supported the thousands of women at Greenham Common, the US base in England.'

'The person I met in Trieste and Berlin is not the sort to get involved with a lot of well-meaning women who make an exhibition of themselves.'

Ulrike's eyes flared. 'Is that what you thought when you saw one hundred thousand people march for peace in Leipzig? Were they making an exhibition of themselves?'

He said nothing.

'She felt the women at Greenham Common had found the only sensible answer. I shared her belief utterly. At the time I wasn't a prisoner of the GDR's propaganda machine: I read the free press in Europe and I could make up my own mind about such things. It was this issue that forged our friendship. We had our own secret pact.' The breeze made her hair shimmer. He couldn't help but be stirred by her beauty and bitterly regretted slapping her.

'What was she telling the East? Why was she so valued?

'Annalise was the truth channel. Everything she told us was true, but at that stage only I had guessed she was being used to tell the Soviet bloc the real intentions of the West.'

'You're not telling me she just blurted this out to you. There'd be no purpose in telling you a secret that so much of Western diplomatic planning relied on. The risk was far too great.'

'She didn't. I discovered it for myself.'

He shook his head. The thing still seemed highly improbable, another tier of lies. 'She isn't the sort of person to make mistakes.'

'But she did. At the end of 1980 she gave me an advance copy of NATO's annual communiqué and I realized that she could not have acquired the sensitive sections about the arms race *without* official help. I didn't say anything. Then the following February she went on holiday for ten days in the Caribbean and came back with a glorious suntan. On her wedding finger there was a band of white skin. She had worn an engagement ring during her holiday. I knew then she was hiding another part of her life, because she had never worn a ring on that finger in my presence. I told her I knew and – to cut a long story short – she implored me to allow the truth channel to continue. And why not? It served the interests of peace. That was our shared priority.'

'The Stasi must have suspected something.'

'No, the British and Americans did a good job. Everything she passed to us was good material, so there was no reason to question her motives. They were pleased with what they could pass on to the Soviet Union.'

'And Biermeier? When did he get into the picture?'

'Much later. By '86 I'd told him everything. At that time I was back in Leipzig and out of the Stasi. The baby – all that had happened by then. Biermeier was working on the Middle East, keeping an eye on the various Arab factions in the GDR and relating it to the information we were receiving from abroad. That's how he got to hear about Lomieko and Abu Jamal's plans, though Misha always kept him in the dark.'

'Who did he think was sanctioning this stuff?'

'Schwarzmeer and his predecessor, maybe Erich Mielke too. Biermeier never knew who was running things. That's why he arranged for me to get the job of looking after Abu Jamal; he had to find out what they were planning on GDR soil. It fitted in well with my other work in youth research and I had clearance, though I was still in disgrace for my *immoral behaviour*. But Biermeier argued that only a woman of loose morals would be prepared to befriend the Arab and so I got the job.' She stopped. 'Look, the only way we could get this information out was through an intermediary like you. We had to improvise as we went along. It wasn't any great plan to punish you or put your brother in Hohenschön-hausen. We both thought that you'd be perfect. The fact that you'd never told them about the death of the first Annalise would mean that you'd have to go along with it.'

'And you call this an improvisation? Look what happened! Konrad lost his life. Else and the boys lost a husband and a father. That's what your improvisation did. Konrad would be alive today if it hadn't been for you.'

'I know, I know. I understand how bitter you must feel. A lot of what you say is true.'

'Understanding's not good enough. That doesn't help Else or me.'

She nodded and looked down. He never knew with her: these signals of remorse seemed genuine but how could he believe her? 'And Biermeier was put in charge of the operation in Trieste because . . .'

'Because he knew her. He could verify that she was the same woman who had been their number one agent in NATO. Remember she had very little contact with the Stasi. She kept her distance and would only see a few handlers: me, Biermeier and a man code-named François.'

'The gardener at NATO headquarters who was arrested?'

'Exactly.'

'Were the British involved?' he asked. 'Did they understand any of this?'

'Of course not. They didn't need to know about the collaboration between Annalise and me. It would have served no purpose whatsoever. Anyway, our plan meant that Annalise didn't have to do anything except what they asked her to do.'

'And who was the person you first used to take your message to British intelligence from Leipzig? Was that Annalise, too?'

'No, a friend of hers called Mary Scott — she's in CND and a Christian. Biermeier had the material inserted in her luggage before she crossed into West Berlin. It was all very simple.' She screwed up her face against the light and looked at him. It was an expression he found very endearing, though he held himself back. 'Rudi, I know there are things that you can't forgive, but you must believe me when I say that if I'd known what would happen to your family, we would have found another way of getting the information out.'

They were silent for a few minutes.

'You're in touch with Biermeier?' he said, focusing on a grebe that had surfaced near the coots.

'Yes, I've spoken to him several times since we've been here.'

'He can help me find Zank.'

'Zank's under investigation,' she said. 'Biermeier doesn't know what happened, but two weeks ago Zank disappeared on sick leave. He has been questioned several times. You don't have to bother with Zank any more. Zank's finished.'

Rosenharte shook his head. Zank wasn't finished.

THIRTY-TWO

Stasi Storehouse

That afternoon they dug out the car, which had sunk into a boggy patch near a spring where they'd hidden it, and took the long route around the lake to Schwarzmeer's compound. They knew Dürrlich was still in Berlin because that morning he had sent word to Flammensbeck telling him to carry out some running repairs to a light and a broken cistern. When he pulled up outside the shelter where he'd been questioned and beaten in the middle of the night, he saw that it had been disguised to look like an aircraft hangar. The half-barrel shape was covered with soil and grassed over. Beech saplings sprouted from the roof.

'The old man said there's enough stuff in here to equip a small army,' he said to Ulrike.

She nodded.

He placed the crowbar Flammensbeck had given him to the first of two padlocks, jerked upwards and the lock fitting burst from the door. For the caretaker's sake it needed to look like a break-in.

Cool air, laden with the smell of oil and earth, rushed towards them. Rosenharte threw a light switch and they both exclaimed at the same moment. When he had been interrogated there with the beam of a single light shining in his face, he'd had little sense of what was in the store, but now they saw a hoard of equipment and luxury goods – bio-hazard suits, hoses, ropes, coils of wire, rubber boots, new tyres were jumbled up with boxes containing tape decks, cameras, video recorders, electric kettles and steam irons. 'What could the Stasi want with half a dozen steam irons?' asked Ulrike.

Rosenharte thought. 'To stop anyone else having them.'

Deep in the interior of the shelter was a cage illuminated by a naked bulb, which contained a dozen wine racks, two televisions, several shortwave radio sets and a case of shotguns, hunting rifles and pistols which hung from their trigger guards on hooks.

Ulrike hunted round for a paint sprayer and the tins of paint Flammensbeck said were there, while Rosenharte approached the cage and rattled its side. 'It'd be good to drink some of the bastard's wine,' he said. 'I'll take a few bottles for this evening.'

'Come on, Rudi, keep your mind on the job. We shouldn't stay here long.'

He didn't pay any attention to this and started attacking the locks on the cage with the crowbar. When he failed to make any impression on them he resorted to a long spiked pole, which he drove with some relish into the hinges. After a few blows they gave way and he went along the wine racks, picking up bottles randomly and examining them against the light. Many of the labels had disintegrated, but he saw enough to understand that this was a very fine collection of wine from before the war. The earliest bottle of Cognac came from 1928 and the Armagnac 1924. He called out to Ulrike: 'This must all have belonged to my family. There's no way a Stasi officer, even Schwarzmeer, could lay his hands on this. It would go for tens of thousands of Deutschmarks at auction in the West.'

'You don't need that,' Ulrike said despairingly.

'Nonsense,' he said, gathering up several bottles of French wine and some vintage champagne. 'Besides, it's rightfully mine.'

He placed the drink in the car, returned to the gun case and smashed the glass, selecting a SIG-Sauer pistol and a box of two dozen 9 mm shells. He put these in his pockets and returned to her.

'You don't need a gun,' she said.

'I'll tell you when I want advice at every turn.'

She looked as if he had slapped her again. 'Really, you don't have to be so unpleasant. Look, Rudi, we don't have to be lovers but can't we be friends?'

'Friends! Men and women are never friends. They want too much from each other to be friends. They fall in love or they make alliances, but they're never friends.'

'That's simply not true. I have male friends.'

'I don't believe you. I've had countless relationships with women that didn't end in bed and they never lasted because basically women are as interested in sex and finding a mate as men are supposed to be.'

Her arms fell down to hit the tops of her thighs in a gesture of irritation. 'No wonder you didn't stay married long,' she said and picked up the spray gun.

'Ah well, there you have the advantage over me; I haven't yet had the pleasure of reading your Stasi file.'

He could see that that had hurt her but she said nothing and turned to finish the job of painting the car. He unscrewed the number plates and replaced them with a pair from a pile just inside the door. They worked in silence for about half an hour before removing the masking tape and scraping at the missprays. Eventually they stood back and looked at the matt black Wartburg.

'You can be a real bastard when you want,' she said without looking at him.

'Maybe it's the Nazi in me.'

She shook her head, dropped the spray gun and walked into the woods. He didn't see her for several hours.

That evening after Flammensbeck left she pulled a chair in front of Rosenharte. He was mildly drunk and the fury had left him.

She held out her hands to touch his. 'I need to go back to Leipzig,' she said, 'back to my old life.'

'You'll be arrested.'

She shook her head. 'No, Rudi. I won't be. Things have changed; Biermeier told me Zank's under investigation himself. Since Zank was found in the villa he hasn't been seen in Normannenstrasse. By some miracle all this seems to have reflected badly on Zank.'

'But there is still a risk.'

Slowly she shook her head. 'That stuff you said about relationships when we were painting the car makes me, well, doubt who you are. You made yourself out to be a misogynist.'

'Perhaps I am. Perhaps it's because I have been disappointed.'

'Or perhaps *you* were disappointing,' she said quickly. 'Perhaps *you* didn't give enough and expected too much. Have you thought of that, Rudi?'

'I was thinking about the deception I've encountered recently. There was a woman I knew in Dresden. We had an affair, and after it was over she ended up informing on me. She used the friendship to gain leverage with the Stasi.'

'That was the Stasi's fault, not hers. We all make compromises in this shitty system. Look at me and the Arab! These things have to be done to survive.'

'And what you did to me, the way you lied to me about your involvement . . . I mean how can I trust you after that?'

'You don't have to trust me. You can go your own way, although

430

I hope you don't. I think we had something that . . . it could last. And . . .' She stopped and looked up at him. 'And, well, I feel I must say this, Rudi. You need to become a whole person without your brother. I know you worshipped him and plainly he was a remarkable human being but you make him out to be a saint and that can't be true. He had faults too. You know that. Tell me what his faults were, Rudi.'

Rosenharte didn't like being pressed on this but the wine – he had never tasted the like – and the look of candid appeal in her eyes had mellowed him. He put the glass down and shifted in his chair to look at a distant corner of the room. 'Well, he could sometimes be rather strait-laced, a bit of a pedant. He always knew he was right. But that was because he was right most of the time.'

'Not the most humble person, then.'

'Oh, he could show humility in the face of great art or intellectual achievement but he could also be very dismissive and he had a bad temper.' He shook his head and smiled. 'It was terrible. I saw him lose it just three or four times but it was unforgettable.'

'And you don't lose yours?'

He shook his head. 'I lose control – as you've seen – but I don't have a temper. I always wondered where it came from.'

'Which of you was born first?' she asked.

'I don't know. We don't have that sort of detail about our birth. But we both agreed that Konrad must have been. He used to be slightly taller, too.' He picked up his glass again. 'You should have some of this and stop trying to analyse me. It's Château Margaux 1928.'

She nodded appreciatively, then fixed him with a look of appraisal. 'You see we all have faults and secrets and shoddy episodes in our lives. Me? It's not the spying and the deceit that I regret but the loss of my baby.'

'You had an abortion?'

'As good as. I was ill. I didn't look after myself and I kept on work-ing in a temporary post I'd got myself. I had been told by the doctor that I needed to take things easy because there were complications. Then I had a miscarriage. At the time I thought it was a good thing and didn't regret my behaviour, but I do now – bitterly.' She looked at him intently for a few seconds. 'You see, now that he's gone, you have to become a complete person so you can stand on your own. You're clever and funny and kind, but you have to go on without comparing yourself to your brother.' She paused again. 'And by the way, you should stop thinking about yourself. Call his wife, comfort her and her sons instead of wallowing in your own grief. Do it now.'

'Enough of the lecture. I'll do it tomorrow.'

'Why not now?'

'Because it's late and I need to think what to say: to offer her some hope.'

'Hope? There's no hope. Just say that you're going to be there with her. Forget this obsession with Zank. Men like Zank aren't worth your time. Zank means nothing.'

He leaned forward to touch her face, but she avoided his hand. 'I'm dreadfully sorry about what happened out at the lake,' he said. 'It's just that I can't stand not knowing where I am with you. You've deceived me so much. You've lied and lied and lied.'

'No, I dissembled. It was necessary by our lights and of course we had no idea that Konrad would die in prison. How could we?'

'I accept that and I want to apologize.'

'Okay, but forget Zank.'

'I can't. Konrad died primarily because of him. Zank must pay for that.'

'You're going to try to shoot him with that gun? You're not the type. You're an intellectual, an aesthete: you know that killing him will only harm you. And what would Konrad think? He would say you're behaving like a child. Imagine his disdain if you shot Zank. He'd say you've lost your mind.'

'Maybe I have.'

'No, Rudi, you're just very, very sad. And that won't be cured by killing Zank.'

He shook his head, got up and made for another open bottle – a Cos d'Estournel from 1934. Having rinsed his glass he poured a fraction, held it to the candle and marvelled at the amber glow at the edge before giving some to Ulrike. They sat in silence drinking and listening to the pine kindling wood snap in the fire. Eventually he set down his glass and leaned forward to peer under her brow. Her eyes avoided his but he took her chin and turned her face to him. Then he kissed her rather tentatively, just grazing her unmoistened lips with his. Her face was almost totally in shadow but he could see the whites of her eyes and the deliberation that was going on in them. She pulled away to read his intent, and after a few seconds seemed to settle something and offered her cheek. He brushed his lips across the patch of down in front of her ear and she murmured her pleasure. Again she looked into his eyes. 'You know, the thing with the gun is very childish.'

He shrugged. 'That's enough from you,' he said. 'Anyway, I need to take something from Schwarzmeer.'

'You already have – the wine.'

'No, that's my inheritance. The gun is Schwarzmeer's.'

She shook her head but smiled and began to kiss him with increasing urgency. He stood and she started to fumble at his trousers but he picked her up and carried her to the bed they'd surrounded with old boards and doors to defend them against the vicious draughts that whistled round the building. He let her down on the odd assortment of sheets and sleeping bags. Her eyes no longer searched his for reassurance, but held them with pure

433

animal need. He undressed her slowly, removing bits of his own clothes too, and turned her on to her stomach to run his hands over her back. She clawed the bedding and her body arched as he began to kiss the backs of her thighs and buttocks, his lips moving inch by inch to her centre. When she could stand it no longer she turned on her side and held his face to her and began to move rhythmically over his lips until she came with a shudder. He entered her and they lay almost motionless, watching the pleasure in each other's eyes. Then he shifted on top of her and she came for the second time, holding on to his head until finally she pulled his face into the fine brush of her electrified hair.

'The axe to my frozen sea,' she whispered eventually, stroking his back.

Next morning he saw her standing in a huge old bath, bending down with a pail to scoop up the warm water they'd heated on the range. Things were easy between them now. As she emptied the pail over her the light from the mottled glass of the bathroom windows fell across her slim white body. He watched her do this several times before she caught him smiling and flung some water in his direction. 'What is it?'

'It's just that I saw a painting in my mind – the picture Rembrandt did of his wife Saskia in that exact pose. You know the one?'

'No.' She stepped out of the bath and wrapped herself in the length of sheet they used as a towel. 'I know the exact moment when I completely fell for you. It was when you looked at that bird by the phone box and talked about your brother. When was it for you?' she asked rather earnestly.

'I felt something in the cafe that first day but resisted it.'

'What!' She came over and pinched him on the leg. 'God, I love you. I have never meant it like this before and it feels so wonderful to be able to say it without the usual doubts and qualifications. I'm like a teenager. I'm weak with pleasure when I watch you.'

He took her hands and held them. 'I can only say this: that I've never loved a woman like I love you. In fact I barely credited the existence of such a state. I am . . .' He searched for the right words. 'Your raging glory, your conviction and tenacity, your brilliant, eccentric courage and your beautiful, beautiful body which leaves me helpless with desire. You simply overwhelm me, Ulrike.'

She held his hand and stroked it with pleasure shining in her eyes. 'This is too much,' she said.

'The hibernation is ending,' he said.

Later he walked to Schwarzmeer's house and broke in again. He dialled Harland and was put through to Else very quickly. They spoke for fifteen minutes, which included some long, painful silences. He did not tell her about the cremation, because he judged she wasn't up to hearing about the East German state's final indignity to her husband. He would have to break it to her later that there was no body for her to weep over, no place where Konrad lay. He read her Konrad's letter – the letter that he'd wept over so many times in previous days – and apologized for not giving it to her before. She listened in silence, and when he came to the end, said that Konrad never wrote anything that better caught his nobility and generosity. She told him Harland had been to see them three days in a row and had set up a bank account for her. She had been in touch with Idris and was arranging for him to get a visitor's visa. He was so good with Christoph and Florian that she wanted him to stay for a few weeks and help them settle down. He said goodbye and told her he would be with her as soon as circumstances allowed, an odd phrase that she didn't question because she was too busy telling him to be careful.

He lit a cigarette and thought guiltily how much he could do with a drink. He looked down at the chair where he'd collapsed and put the idea to the back of his mind. It was too early and he was too damned old to go on behaving like this. In a few weeks he was going to be fifty.

He picked up the phone again and dialled the number on the piece of paper that had fallen from his pocket with Konrad's letter – the number that had been left with Else by the Pole.

'It's Dr Rudi Rosenharte,' he said when the call was answered.

'This is good,' said a man in German. 'I need to meet you or your brother about a most important matter.'

Rosenharte drew breath. 'My brother is dead.' There was a silence at the other end. 'Hello? Are you there? My brother died nearly four weeks ago.'

'I'm very sorry to hear that news. It's tragic – very shocking.'

'Well, can *I* help you?'

'This is a delicate matter . . . er . . . I must talk to you in person. I cannot speak of these things over the telephone. It concerns your natural mother.'

'My natural mother? Why would you want to talk about her . . .' He stopped and crouched down. The top of a man's head had passed the window at the far end of the house. 'I can't talk now,' he whispered.

'It's very important I speak to you, for your sake as well as mine.'

'Not now,' Rosenharte hissed and replaced the receiver.

He took the gun from his pocket, slipped the safety catch and checked the clip, then crawled noiselessly to one of the windows and looked out. He guessed the man had come from the direction of the storehouse, in which case he would know that someone had been there. He waited in silence, then heard a noise to his left. Whoever it was would soon notice the broken door latch and investigate. Inwardly cursing his own stupidity, he got up and moved on to the veranda, where he perched on the edge of one of the cane chairs. A second or two later a large man wandered round the corner of the house. He had a beer gut, a powerful, slow-moving gait and rather mean, unintelligent eyes. This was clearly Dürrlich, back from his spell of driving Schwarzmeer in Berlin.

'Good morning,' said Rosenharte cheerily. 'I don't think we've had the pleasure.'

Dürrlich did a comic double-take. 'Who the fuck are you?'

'I might ask you the same question.'

'I have a right to be here. You don't.'

'Don't be so sure about that. And anyway I've got a gun and will have no compunction in blowing your head off.'

This didn't seem to affect the man. He moved to the bottom of the steps and placed his hands on his hips. He was breathless and sweating from his walk.

'I mean it,' said Rosenharte calmly. 'To kill you would not be an unpleasant way to start the day.'

The man absorbed this. 'What have I done to you? You're on the property of the Ministerium für Staatssicherheit. This is part of a restricted zone. Maximum penalty ten years for trespassing. It's you who is in the wrong.' He paused and squinted at Rosenharte. 'I know you. You were the man they brought here in September. They kept you locked up in one of the guest houses.'

'That just shows me how stupid you are, doesn't it? I mean, if you wanted to get away with your life this fine morning you wouldn't say you knew who I was.' He rose and approached him with a two-handed aim. 'You have a choice: you can die or co-operate with me. Which is it to be?'

'There are other officers here. You won't get away with this.'

'Call them. We can have a party.' Rosenharte waved the gun towards the storehouse.

The man said nothing.

'You people are all washed up. You'll be out of a job soon. You might as well do as I say and save your wretched life. Now, start walking to the storehouse carrying this above you.' He moved a heavy oak dining-room chair to the edge of the veranda, which Dürrlich reluctantly hoisted over his head.

When they got inside, Rosenharte made him sit down on the chair with his back to the cage. 'Burgundy or Bordeaux? Ah no, I've got just the thing for you. There's a very fine brandy here.' He picked up a bottle, knocked the top off with a clean swipe against the cage door and handed it to Dürrlich. 'No glass, I'm afraid, so you're going to have to watch that you don't cut yourself.'

Dürrlich began to drink. When he had emptied the brandy, Rosenharte gave him a bottle of wine and then some port, but Dürrlich was already looking pretty pale. Rosenharte waited a further forty-five minutes before he slumped back in his chair, dribbling and groaning. He made him drink a little more port, then bound his hands and feet and tied him securely to the cage. 'If I was a less charitable man, I'd gag you,' he said. 'But I believe you're going to need your mouth in the coming hours.'

Dürrlich shook his head. 'Please . . . no . . .'

'By the time you come to, I'll be over the border. I'm saying goodbye to this apology for a country. So you can forget any idea of following me.' He pushed the door shut and began to walk to the Schloss.

It took no more than fifteen minutes to load the Wartburg and say their goodbyes to Flammensbeck, who told them of a place they could stay with a friend of his called Krahl in the mountains. He said he'd discover Dürrlich towards evening on the pretence of doing the repairs that had been ordered. Before getting into the car, Ulrike hugged him and kissed him on both cheeks. The old fellow's eyes watered up. He had enjoyed having them there more than he could say. It had been the best time he'd had in years, he said.

THIRTY-THREE

A Battle Won

They spent the next few days touring the sites of his boyhood – the house that once belonged to the Rosenharte family, the school and sports ground where the Rosenharte boys starred and finally Konrad's last home, which had an air of deserted melancholy now. They camped, hid out in barns and one night stayed with Flammensbeck's friend Krahl, who asked no questions when he was presented with two bottles of vintage Burgundy and a flagon of Flammensbeck's slivovitz. As well as explaining his past to Ulrike, the trip served to fix Rosenharte's position for himself after Konrad's death. He knew that he was saying goodbye to it all because he'd decided to go to Else in the West.

They were sitting at the top of a valley on a Sunday afternoon when Rosenharte turned and touched her cheek with the back of his hand. 'Marry me and come with me,' he said suddenly. 'We can get over the border no problem.'

'I can't.'

'Which are you saying *can't* to?'

'Coming with you.'

'But you will marry me?'

She nodded. 'Of course, Rudi; of course I will.' She was smiling but also matter of fact about it. 'But I *must* attend the demonstration tomorrow. I've missed too much of what's been going on. This is my destiny, to stay in Leipzig and see it through.'

He put his hand on her shoulder and craned his head to see her eyes. 'Most of the time a person's destiny is what they choose. But if you choose to go to Leipzig I'll come too and march for one last time. Then I want you to think about leaving with me. Because this – us, you and me – is your destiny now.'

She was watching some geese that were moving nervously across the field below them with a sheepdog running and crouching behind them. 'I'll think about it,' she said.

'Going to Leipzig now is a big risk.'

She pursed her lips and turned to him with utterly resolute eyes. 'There isn't a risk. And even if there is, I have to be there. Look, I'll phone Biermeier.'

'His phone will be tapped.'

'I doubt that, but I won't speak. I'll just see if he answers. If he does, we'll know it's okay. He'll know it's me.'

Later she dialled the number in Berlin twice and let it ring three times before hanging up. On the third occasion she beckoned Rosenharte to place his ear to the receiver. They both heard Biermeier say 'Hurensohn' – sonofabitch – before hanging up.

'Good. *Hurensohn* is our code for all's clear. We're going to Leipzig tomorrow.' She paused. 'Well, I'm going. I don't know about you.'

'Of course I'll come,' said Rosenharte.

They stayed that night in a shack above the high, still waters of the lake where Konrad and he had spent so much time flat on their bellies looking at the sticklebacks in summer, and in winter fooling with classmates on an ice slide. It was without question the place he loved most, for it was here that his mind had first become attuned to nature, a passion that down the years had become the counterpoint to his scholarship, urging him to solitude and contemplation.

They made a fire outside the shack, put their backs to its wooden side and covered themselves in rugs and the sleeping bag. The lake seemed to hold light well into the night and above them one or two stars shone through the cold winter haze, which had settled on the mountains at dusk. Rosenharte thought of some lines that he had consciously committed to memory when he was a young man and haltingly spoke them in their original English. 'These beauteous forms, through the long absence, have not been to me as is a landscape to a blind man's eye: But oft, in the lonely rooms and 'mid the din of towns and cities, I have owed to them in hours of weariness, sensations sweet.'

Ulrike watched him with a curious expression. 'Who wrote that?'

'William Wordsworth. It expresses what I feel about this place.'

'Do you admire the English?'

'They killed my mother with their bombs, though that was probably a merciful release for her, Konrad and me. And they must share some of the responsibility for my brother's death. I always liked the idea of the English but not the pleasure they take in their own amateurishness. As Konrad said, they are the only Europeans content to be ignorant.'

Soon afterwards, Ulrike fell asleep propped up against him. He stayed awake for a long time, moving carefully so as not to disturb her when he took a swig from the last bottle of Schwarzmeer's wine or lit a cigarette. Then he too slept.

They left early next day and found a phone. Ulrike called several friends and when she returned to the car she could barely contain herself. The leadership was in a state of paralysis and didn't know how to respond to the popular movement or to the country's worsening economic problems. That very day Democratic Awakening was to constitute itself as a political party, and although the Stasi was trying to mould the revolution by infiltrating new political groups, no one was taking any notice of them. There was almost no evidence of them in daily life in Leipzig. Across East Germany the people were in a state of constant and open defiance of the authorities: demonstrations on the Leipzig model were occurring in every major city. And they were peaceful. Not one example of vandalism had been reported. There was no violence.

'The beast isn't slaughtered yet,' said Rosenharte. 'I mean it; we have to be careful tonight.'

'How are they going to find me in a hundred thousand people?'

'Still, they may be looking, so I think we should stay apart.'

In Leipzig, Rosenharte parked a few streets north of her place and went straight to the Nikolaikirche. When they arrived in the huge crowd outside the church she squeezed his hand and reached up to him, and whispered in his ear that everything that she had dreamt of had come true. She looked at him for a fleeting second with the myopic intimacy of their lovemaking, lifted his hand and placed it to her lips before turning to go into the church.

Rosenharte hung around in the crowd uneasily. He raised the collar of his coat and avoided eye contact with the people around him. At the end of the service the congregation poured into the crowd with a surge of joy. He moved quickly to fall in behind the group of people surrounding Ulrike and followed them to the rally in Karl-Marx-Platz. Nothing could prepare him for the size of the crowd. There were three or four times the numbers of 9 October. Yet the atmosphere was far less charged by the fear of official violence. The citizens of Leipzig had laid title to the square named after the father of socialism: they owned their city, not just for the heady hours of the Monday demonstrations, but for all time. Rosenharte began to feel the battle had been won. He relaxed and fell into conversation with a man next to him, who explained that change had even been noticed in the security forces: young Vopos were refusing to police the demonstrations and desertions from the armed forces were said to be in the hundreds.

Through the evening he never lost sight of Ulrike as she threaded through the crowds greeting old friends, hugging and kissing the companions with whom she had fought the long campaign at the Nikolaikirche. At about ten the crowd began to thin. The people had made their point, and they would do so again, pushing their numbers towards the critical mass necessary for permanent change. But their feet were tired, the working week was ahead of them and, whatever the joy of Leipzig's new fellowship, they needed their sleep.

Rosenharte tapped Ulrike on the shoulder and said it was time for them to be going. 'We should leave the city too,' he said.

'No,' she replied firmly. 'After so long on the road I need my own bed. It will be fine. They would have picked up Biermeier if they suspected anything.'

They walked briskly from the city centre, heads bent against the sharp breeze, talking excitedly about the things they'd seen that night. As they entered her street she slipped her hand in his hip pocket for warmth then withdrew it and looked down.

'What's this? Ah, the picture of your mother.' She handed it to him. 'I wanted to ask you a question about that picture.'

'Oh, what?'

'Why don't we talk about it when we get inside? It's probably nothing. I'll go ahead and make sure everything's okay. If the outside light is on you'll know the coast is clear. Okay?'

'What about the picture? What were you going to say?'

She stopped. 'It says September 1939. That can't be right.'

'Why?'

'Well, look at her, Rudi! She's as thin as a rake. Yet you were born three months after that picture was taken. She should have been five or six months pregnant with boy twins that September but she looks like she's just won a slimming contest.'

'It's dated wrongly. I found it in a diary for 1938.'

'You're probably right, but what mother makes a mistake like that?' She smiled. 'Wait a few minutes then follow me.'

He watched her go, slightly puzzled, and felt for his cigarettes and lighter. He saw her disappear into the wisteria gateway then he began to move slowly up the road. He was less than fifty yards from the entrance when a car moved from the bay that he had used to observe her building and drifted to the kerb on his side of the road. Rosenharte flung the cigarette away and backed into the shadows, his heart pounding. He reached for the gun and fumbled with the safety catch. A man got out and held the back door open as a chauffeur would do. Then two men emerged from the gateway with Ulrike between them. No more than a few seconds elapsed before she was bundled into the back seat and the three men climbed in, but during that time Rosenharte registered that Ulrike did not look his way and that the man who opened the door was Colonel Zank. He raised the gun and aimed, but knew he couldn't fire. He might hit Ulrike and the sound of the shots would certainly bring a response from Zank's men. He would be outgunned and killed or taken prisoner. Neither would help her, and that was why she didn't cry out for his help.

THIRTY-FOUR

Dark Energy

Vladimir turned from the window and dropped the phone onto its cradle. Rosenharte hadn't understood a word he'd said, and Vladimir's manner and inflection gave nothing away. After a moment's deliberation in which he moved a few things around his desk, Vladimir looked him straight in the eye. 'She's been taken to Hohenschönhausen. Biermeier also. They're being held in isolation and neither has any idea of the other's presence there.'

Rosenharte lowered his eyes then raised them to Vladimir, conscious that his chin was thrust forward. Even now, as the new premier Egon Krenz returned empty-handed from his summit with Gorbachev in Moscow to face a bankrupt economy, as millions demonstrated and the border with Czechoslovakia reopened to placate them, the dark energy at the heart of the state did not wane.

'And . . . she's sick,' said Vladimir. His steady gaze betrayed no feeling. 'Some kind of respiratory infection. My source says pleurisy or bronchitis. Something she's had for a while, possibly?' Rosenharte thought of the dry little cough she'd developed while they were on the run and the almost translucent pallor he had noticed that first day.

'Is there anything you can do?' he asked.

The Russian grimaced. 'You must understand that I compromise myself every time I talk to you. I can't make these decisions to interfere in the affairs of a sovereign state, not from the regional KGB headquarters and on a salary of eighteen hundred East German marks. What happens if you get caught and tell them about our conversations?'

'I'm not going to get caught.'

'But they're watching for you. You saw how difficult it was to get you in here. The Stasi is still one of the most efficient secret services in the world. You're mistaken if you think you're going to walk into Hohenschönhausen and rescue your girlfriend. It's not in my interest to facilitate your arrest and interrogation.' He stopped and softened his tone. 'Abu Jamal has been dealt with; Misha has been effectively neutralized because he has no network to operate through. You achieved what you set out to do: you should leave the country. The borders with Hungary are open again.' Rosenharte began to shake his head, but Vladimir ignored him. 'If you go, you can help your friend by using the Western media and publicizing what she and Biermeier did to save people's lives. The Stasi don't like high-profile prisoners because they've got to look after them.' He smiled and offered Rosenharte a chunky silver cigarette case engraved with the initials VVP.

'I'm not going to lose anyone else to that place,' said Rosenharte quietly. 'I won't let her die there like Konrad. I can't let that happen. One way or another I'm going in to get her, so it's in your interest that I do this with the minimum of risk. It's very important to you that I don't get caught, isn't it, Volodya?' He intentionally deployed the nickname he'd heard the other Russians use when he entered Number Four Angelikastrasse that afternoon in the boot of a car.

Vladimir shook his head and sat down. 'That's a form of blackmail. I won't accept it, Rudi.' He paused and handled the cigarette case, evidently getting some satisfaction from it. 'In our game we always need a return on risk. I can't help you unless I'm able to show my superiors there's a substantial advantage.'

'I've told you everything. I have nothing more to give.'

'The man Harland – could you get him here?' Vladimir picked up a pen and swivelled his chair to look out over the dismal view of East Dresden in the rain.

'Why here?'

'It doesn't matter. Bring him here and I'll help you. Tell him that there's something in it for both of us. And for the Americans too.'

'I must give them an explanation.'

The Russian contemplated the pen, which he held between the tips of his index fingers, then looked over his shoulder and gave him a silent shake of the head. 'No,' he said at length. 'No explanation.'

'They will think it's some kind of trap.'

'They won't. They know how much help we gave them on the Arab.'

'You did?'

'Yes, we helped in the early stages. Ulrike Klaar's first information to the West was confirmed by my service in the Yemen. Tell them there's something else that we can cooperate on. Something very big.'

Two possibilities occurred to Rosenharte. Either Vladimir was acting outside his authority or he was a more important player than he had let on. Perhaps the Dresden HQ was a kind of cover, concealing a more top-flight KGB operation than the down-at-heel offices would suggest. Perhaps Vladimir had no boss and was running things himself.

'Okay. You provide the passes for myself and one other man and the release documentation in Ulrike's name, and I will get them here for you. What about Biermeier?'

'Don't tell me you're in love with Biermeier too.'

'He has a family. He has taken more risks than anyone. He's a brave man and doesn't deserve to be shot in the back of the head.'

'It's less easy to rescue Biermeier. They'll vent the very worst of their fury on him. He may already have been executed. After all, my information about him being alive is a couple of days old.' He got up and walked round the desk. 'You don't owe him anything. He was in the business. He knew the risks. Forget Biermeier. I'll get the Stasi ID for you, but beyond that you're on your own. You'll need to arrange transport and at least one other man, probably two.' He raised his finger close to Rosenharte's face. 'But I'm afraid you will have nothing from me until they are here. You understand these are the wishes of my superiors. Why don't you make the call now?'

'I have to tell them something. I have to offer an incentive.'

Vladimir's eyes slipped to a filing cabinet in the corner of the room. 'Tell them that things are falling apart here, much more than anyone in the West appreciates. New travel laws will soon be discussed by the Central Committee and people are going to flood out of the country. Our estimates put the figure at two hundred thousand for this year alone. If they relax the travel restrictions the country is finished. But the profits of chaos are going to be very large indeed. Phone them now and tell them that.'

Rosenharte tried to read his expression. What the hell did he mean?

'There's the phone; use it,' said Vladimir.

'I should spend some time thinking how to get them here. I've probably only got one chance at this.' He made as though to leave, then thought better of it. 'Are we talking about something you're going to offer them? Something from the Stasi?'

'Yes and no. I'll show them how to get it for themselves, but they're going to have to pay for it. A very large sum of money.'

Rosenharte was now beginning to understand the strength of his position. Vladimir hadn't agreed to speak to him because of Ulrike, but because he wanted him to act as an intermediary.

'What about our exit – can you help with that?'

'Ask the British.'

He nodded and sat back in his chair. 'There's one other thing,' he said. 'Members of the Polish secret service have been trying to contact me for the last two months. With Konrad and now Ulrike being arrested I haven't had time to discover why. Can you find out who they are and what they want? The Stasi were interested in them. They may have something on them.'

Vladimir smiled. 'We already have some information. The man who followed you to Trieste was formerly in the Polish secret service – Franciscek Grycko. The younger one, Leszek, is also in our business, though a less formidable operative.'

'What reason did you have for looking into this?'

'Because Zank was interested. Your friend at the museum, Sonja, was very helpful. We wanted to know who these Poles were and what they wanted from you.'

'And what did you find out?'

'Certain things have come to our notice. The first man was a fifty-eight-year-old veteran. A tough character who had had a very hard life. He entered the camps as a ten-year-old, survived and became one of the Polish secret service's best operatives. He used his contacts to find out that you were going to be in Trieste. He had someone in Schwarzmeer's office we think, but we're not sure. By the same means he had also requested, and has seen, some of the files on you. We know that.'

'How could you know that?'

Vladimir looked at him with his poker face and shrugged.

'I was left a number by the younger one and I called him,' said

Rosenharte. 'I was disturbed while making the call so we didn't speak for long. The man said he wanted to talk about my natural mother.'

'And that aroused your interest?'

'Obviously.' Rosenharte was unwilling to share the glimmer of an idea that had come to him on waking that day. 'And I understood that whatever he wanted to say must have been important for this other man, Franciscek, to travel to Trieste when he was so ill.'

'You're convinced that he died of natural causes and that he wasn't murdered?'

'Yes, for the simple reason that no one had a motive to poison him. No one knew who he was. He just appeared out of the blue. His breath stank of chemicals, but maybe that can be explained by the use of drugs to control his condition.' He paused. 'What's interesting is that the second man seemed to have this urge to contact either Konrad or me. He followed me all the way to Leipzig, then went out to Konrad's home and left a note there with a telephone number.'

'The behaviour would suggest a desperate rather than sinister motive,' said Vladimir.

Rosenharte nodded.

'Well, you have the number, so phone him.'

'I'd like you to make some enquiries on my behalf. You've got contacts, influence. Find out about them. Besides, I don't know where I'm going to be. I can't plan anything until I've got Ulrike out.' He withdrew the note Else had given him and handed it to Vladimir before he could protest. Vladimir took it, shaking his head, and copied down the number.

'I'm not promising anything,' he said.

'I understand,' said Rosenharte, 'but thank you.'

Vladimir handed it back to him. 'You haven't let me down so

far, and besides I'm beginning to like you. However, I won't help with those passes unless I see Robert Harland.'

'I'll call later about the venue of the meeting and about my own operation at Hohenschönhausen. I need time to carry out a recce, so whatever I might feel on a personal level about the need for haste I won't make my move until next week.'

'That's sensible. You're talking like an intelligence officer. I hope it means you appreciate the need for caution and good judgement. You know that if they catch you they'll shoot you straight away. Those disks you got from the West were a Trojan horse; they screwed up the mainframe in Normannenstrasse and now they are having to rebuild it. That's your fault and the Stasi know it. If they arrest you they won't even bother with interrogation. They'll torture you and shoot you before the day's out. It won't be a pleasant death.'

Rosenharte felt his neck and back go cold. The Stasi had Biermeier in custody and Biermeier was responsible for setting up the deal that brought the disks to East Germany. It wouldn't take a genius to piece the whole thing together linking Ulrike, Biermeier and himself in a network of betrayal. Zank had probably put most of the pieces in place back in Leipzig. Yet Rosenharte disagreed with Vladimir about the summary executions. From what Konrad had told him the dark energy required everything to be in order, the plot to be recorded in laborious detail, the suspects wrung dry and their motives made explicit. Ulrike was therefore faced with the terrible prospect of having to hold out on Zank in order to remain alive.

Vladimir's eyes settled on Rosenharte as though he could see into his mind. Rosenharte looked away. 'I need to know where she's being held,' he said. 'What room, what floor? Also the times of her interrogations and the numbers of men involved. Anything that might be of use to me.'

'Phone Harland now and I will see what I can do,' Vladimir said, revolving his watch and glancing at the time.

'One more thing,' said Rosenharte. 'They will want to know who they're dealing with. I want your real name.'

'I told you,' said the Russian. 'Major Vladimir Ilyich Ussayamov.'

'Then why does your cigarette case bear different initials — VVP?'

'That is observant of you. I did not know you could read our Cyrillic script.'

'I know the alphabet. That's all.'

'VVP was a friend of my father's who died in Leningrad. When my father died I inherited it.'

'And the medallion, awarded to VVP for judo?'

He smiled to indicate that he was not prepared to discuss the matter further. 'Make the call, Dr Rosenharte.'

Alan Griswald nursed a cup of coffee and examined Harland over his reading glasses. 'I can't go. Langley won't allow it. And nor should you consider it, particularly if you haven't got any kind of diplomatic cover. Does London know?'

Harland stroked his chin.

'Is that a yes or a no?'

'I've got cover as a TV journalist and accreditation for the whole of next week. There's a demonstration tomorrow in Alexanderplatz, Berlin — the biggest yet. London is anxious to know what the hell's going on in East Germany so I said I would go and find out. What's the problem if I have a word with the Sovs' man in Dresden? I mean, they did help us on Abu Jamal. Without their material we'd never have taken Kafka seriously. Besides, we want to find out what they plan to do. They've got four hundred thousand men in the East. Are they going to stay put in their barracks or are they going to oil up the tank tracks and do another Prague? It's important we know.'

'Then send one of your people – someone who wasn't involved in taking the Arab. Their counter-intelligence people are all over this thing. Kafka's under arrest and her main collaborator is in the slammer too. What's to be gained by you going over as an illegal? If London thinks you can pull this one off, Bobby, they've got a collective case of cranial-rectal penetration.'

'What?'

'They've got their heads up their asses. They're nuts and so are you.'

'But we owe Rosenharte.'

Griswald's finger had begun to wag at him before he finished. 'No, Bobby, No! No! No! The man had his chance to leave and he didn't take it. There's still time for him to go but he won't because of his girlfriend. If they've got this Abelard and Héloise thing going, that's not your responsibility.'

'Yes, but the brother's dead and Zank is doing his demonic worst with Kafka and Biermeier. I need to look into this.'

'For fuck's sake, don't be a patsy. We got what we wanted and you did very, very well. Don't tell me you're going over to help them.'

'If I can, I will.'

'No, go and hear what the man says but don't get near that damned jail. You're not a knight in fucking armour, Bobby. You're an intelligence officer with responsibilities.'

'But what if the Sovs really have something to offer us?'

'That's a different matter. The Soviets look after themselves. Never forget that. This guy in Dresden, he's small time. What can he offer?'

'Access,' replied Harland more testily than he meant to. 'Access to the Stasi files. Things are unravelling there. Rosenharte actually put the guy on to me while we were speaking. It's clear he's been involved in some way. He knew a lot about the Arab, and he lives in the same city as Misha. Anyway, things are changing minute by minute over there and I want to hear what he's got to say.'

Griswald put down his coffee cup and looked round Harland's office with the ill-concealed embarrassment of a wealthy relation.

'We're having it done up,' said Harland. 'Work starts next week. I got it through after the Arab started coughing his entire network.'

'You mean to say that the SIS station chief has to risk his life apprehending a terrorist on communist soil before Her Majesty's government agrees to a simple paint job?'

'The painter has to be flown in from London. We're very security conscious. No locals are allowed in there unless cleared.'

'Nothing is simple in our business. And this idea of yours is crazy. Don't do it.'

Harland looked at his friend. 'It could be big. I just have this feeling. I know something's going to happen.'

Griswald sank in his chair and regarded him indulgently. 'Well, you were right about the Arab, right to follow your nose on Kafka. So maybe you've got something going here. Maybe . . .' He got up and held out his hand in an oddly final gesture. 'If you really do find the pot of gold at the end of the communist rainbow and manage not to get arrested, cut me in, Bobby.'

'Of course,' said Harland, looking down at his new press pass and the passport in the name of Philip Liversedge. 'But only after I've taken my share of the profits of chaos.'

Rosenharte drove through the night to Leipzig. There had been just one more item in the papers about him, which stated that he was believed to have fled the country. He didn't know whether to take this as a sign that the Stasi had given up looking for him, or that Zank had planted the story in order to lull him into making a mistake.

He arrived at 2.30 a.m. and parked a little distance from Kurt Blast's place, then went to hammer on his door with one fist. In his left hand he held the pistol in case Zank's men were waiting for him on the other side. He heard a scuffling behind the door and saw an eye pushed up against the hole bored into the wood. 'Who's there?' came Blast's voice.

Rosenharte asked to be let in and told him that he was alone.

Blast deliberated a few seconds, then began to draw back several locks and turned a key.

'I need your help, Kurt,' said Rosenharte before the door was closed behind him. 'Ulrike's in prison and I'm going to try to get her out.'

'Which one?' asked Blast, rubbing one eye with his knuckle and looking at the gun with the other.

'Hohenschönhausen.'

'Shit. That's not good.' He was beginning to wake up. 'I wondered what had happened to her. She disappeared nearly three weeks ago.'

'We were together most of that time. They took her when she came back for the Monday demonstration. They were waiting for her.'

'Shit – Hohenschönhausen. Poor woman. It nearly fucked my head for good.'

'You were in there? You didn't tell me that!'

'For about three weeks before I got six months for writing a song about the People's Army. I told you about it.'

'No, you just said you'd had some trouble.'

'I didn't know where the fuck I was. They don't tell you. I

455

could have been in Siberia for all I knew. It was so damned cold at night. The only people I saw were my two interrogators. They drilled holes in my brain then pissed in them. It took me two years to shake off the depression. That's when I took my new name. You see, Kurt Blast never went to Hohenschönhausen or Bautzen. But Hans-Joseph Huch did.'

'So will Kurt Blast help me?' asked Rosenharte.

'What do you want me to do?'

'I want you to drive us in and out of there. I'll do the rest. I am getting some forged release papers: ID cards. I will need you to give me a photograph of yourself as you were.'

'And what happens if they don't believe them? What do we do then? We're locked inside Hohenschönhausen facing a sentence of twenty years' hard labour – or worse. Rudi, I can't do that time. I couldn't even do a week in that place. You're asking too much of me.' He perched on a box that was covered with a piece of red cloth, and began to divide the tobacco from the cigarette Rosenharte had given him into two papers. Having made two roll-ups, he lit one and lodged the other behind his ear.

'You've been in Hohenschönhausen so you know the layout.'

Kurt didn't reply, but went over to the turntable with the cigarette stuck to his lower lip and selected a record. He straightened and waited without moving until he heard the first bars of Beethoven's Archduke Trio.

'I don't remember much about the Central Preventive Prison for Political Prisoners.' He spoke the title of Hohenschönhausen deliberately. 'Every floor looks the same. Every room looks the same. Every light fitting, stool, chair and desk is placed in the same position in every room. The place has a kind of infinity about it – endlessly repeated shapes and people and objects. It's like a nightmarish film or something. What I'm saying is that the fact that I've been an inmate makes no difference to you. I was taken there at night and I left at night. I saw no one except a man in the van bay and he turned his face from me as I was brought out. It was like something out of Kafka.'

Rosenharte gave a grim smile at the irony of Ulrike's chosen code name. 'You know that Ulrike is a very, very courageous woman,' he said quietly.

'What did she do?'

'I can't tell you until I know you've signed up for this.' He paused. 'Look, Kurt, I wouldn't ask you if there was someone else I could go to. But there isn't. I know I can rely on you in a difficult situation.'

'What if we do manage to get her out? What then?'

'I'm going to take her to the West. You can come too. You make a new life for yourself: Kurt Blast the writer and recording artist. Exploit all that talent you've got.'

He got up and stretched. Rosenharte noted his rangy rock-star delicateness, and wondered if there was a reason for there being no evidence of a girl in Kurt Blast's life.

'Okay, I'll do it,' he said suddenly. 'But I hope my nerves don't pack up when we're inside. Have you got another gun? I'd rather shoot myself than be arrested.'

'No, but I think we can get one.'

'Then I guess I'm in. I love that woman almost as much as you do – but not in the same way, of course,' he added with an embarrassed glance at Rosenharte. 'She's helped me many times over the last two years. She kept me fed when I was broke; kept me sane when I was depressed. You know what they do to political prisoners inside that place?'

Rosenharte put up his hand. 'My brother was in there. He died there and they burnt his body and now they accuse me of his murder. I know what they're capable of.'

He nodded. 'They dismantled me, took my personality apart. I didn't know who I was, what I thought about things when I came out of Bautzen, and that was because they had softened me up at Hohenschönhausen. Ulrike put me together again. No shrinks, nothing like that. Just Ulrike talking and being natural and funny. I owe her my sanity – probably my life.'

They left an hour later and travelled southeast to the Clausnitz estate. He roused Flammensbeck and told him about Ulrike. The old man's jaw set firm and he insisted on accompanying them to the shelter. They broke the outside locks with little difficulty, then smashed the new hinges on the cage and the boards that had been ineffectually nailed to the front of the gun case. Rosenharte took three handguns and filled his pockets with ammunition.

'You look as though you're planning some kind of battle,' said Kurt.

'No, but two guns each with a lot of shells means we can fight our way out, if needs be.'

'Jesus.'

'You know how to handle one of these things?'

'I did my military service. In fact I was the best in my regiment with an AKS74. They even wanted to make me a Grepo and put me on the Berlin Wall to shoot escapers, so then I found I couldn't hit the target.'

'Right, we'd better be going,' said Rosenharte. The fifth day of Ulrike's ordeal had begun.

That Saturday – 4 November – was marked by protests in Halle, Magdeburg, Leipzig, Plauen, Potsdam, Karl-Marx-Stadt and Rostock. In Berlin half a million people stood in Alexanderplatz to hear speeches by the leaders of the new political movements, while the Stasi's surveillance cameras, fixed permanently at every point ostensibly to monitor traffic, impotently swept the multitude. In Dresden the surveillance was not as intense, but nevertheless Rosenharte and Kurt Blast weren't tempted to leave Idris's snug cabin by the River Elbe and join the city's largest demonstration. Instead they dug in for the weekend with a supply of firewood, drink and groceries bought that day with Rosenharte's dollars, and took turns to cook on the efficient little stove. When one slept the other sat in the armchair with a gun in his lap.

On Monday morning they ventured out to buy some more conventional clothes for Kurt and to get him a haircut. Then they went to have their photographs taken. Rosenharte waited for the pictures to be developed reading *Neues Deutschland* and nearly gagged on the statement of the deputy director of the Stasi, Rudi Mittig, who said: 'The total surveillance state, the ubiquitous spy system, exists only in the imagination of the Western media.'

The more important news was carried in a smaller item that referred to the resignation of the Minister of State Security Erich Mielke, which explained why Mittig was making public statements. Rosenharte hoped that the absence of Mielke and the general turmoil would mean that summary executions would be less likely.

On the other hand, sensing an end of his power, Zank might well choose to use it in one final act of revenge.

THIRTY-FIVE

The Prison Walls

Rosenharte left Kurt in the car and moved towards the entrance of the old stockyard building 600 yards up the track from Neustadt station. Night had not quite fallen, but inside the huge shed it was utterly dark. He hesitated at the entrance. A murmur of voices reached him from the far end of the building and someone was swinging a storm lantern so that shadows dashed across the floor.

He withdrew his gun, but kept the torch switched off and began to walk towards the light.

Someone called out. It was Vladimir. 'Is that you, Rudi?'

He didn't answer, letting his eyes become accustomed to the dark. Then he started moving towards the light.

Eventually he made out four men, including Harland. He called to them.

'Well, come over here then,' said Vladimir, clinking a bottle and a glass in the light of the lantern. 'Your friends are here and we've had a very useful conversation. I imagine you could use a drink.' Harland said hello in that non-committal English way. The Bird nodded affably. Vladimir gestured to the other man, who filled a shot glass with vodka and handed it to him.

'Here's to better times,' said Vladimir turning to Harland, 'and to the conclusion of our business.'

'To you, Dr Rosenharte,' said Harland. 'It's good to see you're safe. But I wish you'd left when I told you.'

Rosenharte held the glass to his lips. As the impresario of this meeting he was annoyed to have been cut out of their conversation. 'And to the freedom of Ulrike Klaar,' he said fiercely.

'Indeed,' said Harland. 'And I gather you're receiving help from Vladimir Vladimirovich in exchange for arranging this meeting?' Harland and Vladimir seemed to be on remarkably good terms and it irked a little.

'Not yet,' replied Rosenharte.

'I'm a man of my word,' said Vladimir quietly. 'You'll have everything by this evening.'

'But I will need transport from Berlin to the West and some medication.'

Harland coughed. 'I'll see what we can do, but it's not going to be easy at such short notice. Make contact in the usual way and we'll fix a rendezvous.'

'May I know what you've been talking about?' he asked.

'This business only concerns us,' said Vladimir, 'but we thank you for bringing us together.'

Harland nodded.

'As long as you keep your word about Ulrike, I don't mind. Is there any news on the other thing I asked you to look into?'

Vladimir nodded. 'I have a colleague based in Warsaw who's making enquiries. We are to speak tomorrow morning. You can telephone me and I'll tell you the results. I'll be in Berlin for the next few days, but the message will get through.'

'The same applies to me,' said Harland. 'I'll be at the Berolina Hotel under the name of Philip Liversedge. But follow the old procedure and you'll get me – eventually.' He showed Rosenharte his press pass so he could see how the name was spelt. At the same time he slipped something into Rosenharte's pocket, a movement that even Vladimir's trained eyes did not spot.

Five hours after the meeting, Rosenharte and Kurt Blast left Dresden for East Berlin with a form requiring the presence of Ulrike Klaar at KGB headquarters in Berlin-Karlshorst on 8 November at 5.00 p.m., a docket from Department XIV – the Penal and Interrogations section at Normannenstrasse – which authorized the transfer of the prisoner and was countersigned by the director of the Stasi unit responsible for liaison with the KGB. Also in their possession were two Stasi photograph ID cards in the names of Bernhard Müller and Werner Globke.

They were well rested after the weekend and content to go through Monday night without sleep. By six in the morning of 7 November they slipped into the southern part of the district of Lichtenberg. Rosenharte parked the car beside a chapel on Münsterlandstrasse, some distance from the huge Stasi complex north of Frankfurter Allee. Before leaving the car he turned to Kurt, who looked unrecognizably normal in a plain sweater and an open-neck shirt. 'Okay, so you are now Werner Globke,' said Rosenharte. 'You have nine years' service in the Stasi. You walk with a discreet swagger. You know where you're going and what you want: you never seem hesitant or unsure. You have no reason to hang around the corners of Normannenstrasse and you never look at the cameras. You are at home in this area but you never pass down the same street twice, or move to circle the headquarters. Leave an hour or two between passing into the cameras' field. Remember, different cameras are watched by the same team over an eight-hour period. If you're approached on the street, don't show your ID straight away. Play it cool, a little arrogant maybe. Don't make any notes or gaze at anything or anyone too intently. Remember what you can without looking too hard at the white trucks. My experience is that they never go directly to the prison, but follow any number of longer routes to the Hohenschönhausen district. It's a very short ride as the crow flies, but the truck I went in took fifteen to twenty minutes. We need to isolate one of these routes for tomorrow and pick a good interception point. That's our only purpose today. Don't get distracted, and if you think you're being followed, get the hell out of the area. If you feel it's not safe to meet me here at seven this evening, I'll look for you in the Ostbahnhof. Wait outside the station and I'll cruise by at nine. If you still think you're being watched, rub your chin when you see the car. Leave the rest to me after that.'

'Okay professor, what do I do if you don't show tonight? What happens then?'

'That's up to you, Kurt.'

'You mean you expect me to get her out on my own?'

'I don't. That is too much to ask of anyone. Make your way back to Leipzig and take this. It's the five hundred dollars that the Englishman gave me last night. It's British guilt money because they aren't helping on this operation.' Kurt tried to give the money back. 'No, take it – I have plenty.' He paused and looked ahead of him. 'You can also take one of the guns, if you want. I don't advise that you use it: I plan to go unarmed. Later when we go in we'll both be armed.'

Kurt nodded.

'Okay, Officer Werner Globke, it's seven o'clock. Go and get yourself some breakfast. I'll see you in twelve hours' time.'

Rosenharte watched him turn his collar up and walk past the chapel with his head bowed to the damp west wind. A few minutes later he locked the car and walked away in the opposite direction to take a deserted street north towards an area called Hellersdorf. He turned left on Landsberger Allee and found somewhere to get a bite, just south of the Hohenschönhausen district. The place was empty. He ordered tea, bread and cheese and read a paper until a group of five men entered. He was aware that even at this distance from Normannenstrasse they were likely to be Stasi officers, employed in the various covert buildings surrounding the prison complex. He left almost immediately, keeping his face turned from them, and went to wait at a discreet distance from the cafe.

His memory of the exact position of the prison was vague. Naturally, it never appeared on any map and even during his brief period attached to the Main Directorate, he had never been to the prison or the buildings near it. However, when Biermeier had picked him up after seeing his brother for the last time he had noted that the car turned onto Konrad-Wolf-Strasse.

By now it was 7.40 a.m. The group of men exited the cafe with their lunch boxes and newspapers and proceeded along Frankfurter Allee. They turned right on Genslerstrasse, a dismal street, which he knew must lead to the prison, and in the distance he glimpsed a red and white road barrier. He moved on to the intersection with Konrad-Wolf-Strasse where he waited, smoking a cigarette, reading the paper and occasionally glancing at the traffic. A man asked him for a light and another stopped and gave him several enquiring glances. Only a member of Stasi would do such a thing. Rosenharte smiled and volunteered that he had been stood up.

'At this time of day?' asked the man.

'I sometimes walk my daughter to school from here,' said Rosenharte. 'Her mother and I are divorced.'

'Ah well, there you go,' said the man as though he richly deserved to be left standing there on this dank Berlin morning.

Rosenharte said goodbye to the man's back and noted how easily his mind had regressed to the adept young Stasi trainee. The guile and the lies came as second nature now.

He walked around the area for about two hours, seeing just one of the Stasi trucks. This emerged from a side street on Frankfurter Allee and took the long way round to the prison, avoiding Genslerstrasse. He saw it turn right off Frankfurter Allee and then, having doubled back, reappear some minutes later to cross Konrad-Wolf-Strasse and head for the prison.

Through the day he moved in and out of the area but by the end of the afternoon he had learned that whatever routes the Stasi trucks took in the early stages of their journey to the prison they almost always approached it by crossing Konrad-Wolf-Strasse. This last stretch offered several possibilities for interception, but he would wait until he had consulted Kurt before settling on a plan. All that remained now was to study the routine followed by the prison transports as they neared the gates of Hohenschönhausen. He waited until he saw a truck appear on Frankfurter Allee, then walked rapidly up Genslerstrasse, where he encountered a barrier across the road manned by two plainclothes Stasi. He was now entering the closed area. He offered his ID and said he was late for a meeting. The men raised the barrier without examining the card. Rosenharte kept to the left of the street, so he could study the prison on his right without seeming to do so. The first corner watchtower came into view. He hurried on under a line of young lime trees, passing a green and white office block on his left and the main entrance to the prison on his right. The walls were no more than twenty feet high, but ten feet of wire added to them on the inside of the prison. Several cameras were trained along the perimeter, but they did not rotate to follow him. Just as he reached the end of the compound, the white truck appeared from the direction of Konrad-Wolf-Strasse and took several turns round the block to enter the prison unseen from a street that ran east and west. He dared not approach closer to see what happened when the truck reached the gate. However, he was pretty sure from his own experience a few weeks before that the truck had pulled up at the gate at the side of the prison and waited for it to roll back.

It was now 5.30 p.m. The longer he stayed in the prison's vicinity, the more likely he was to attract interest. He turned towards Konrad-Wolf-Strasse. He had gone fifty yards when a Skoda tore across a stretch of old cobblestones towards him. He looked up and instantly saw Kurt in the back seat on his side. A man was holding onto him by the scruff of the neck. Kurt's gaze skated across Rosenharte without recognition as the car sped towards the main entrance. Rosenharte did not turn but just kept walking towards the barrier that lay a hundred yards up the road.

THIRTY-SIX

Larsen Trap

Some twelve hours after Rosenharte's call to Harland in the middle of the night, the Bird materialized at the Ostbahnhof – the main station in East Berlin. Rosenharte had said little on the phone except that the trainee was detained elsewhere and that he would need a replacement in order to load the goods. The pick-up would be made at the station any time after midday.

When he spotted the British agent striding through the crowds in a long leather jerkin without sleeves, the like of which he was sure had never been seen on German soil, he hastened towards him and greeted him like an old friend. The Bird responded with similarly dramatic signals of affection, but they didn't speak until they had climbed into the Wartburg.

'Where's Harland?' Rosenharte asked in English. 'I thought he would be coming.'

'He sends his apologies,' said the Englishman, stroking his nose. 'But we really can't have the chief of Berlin Station breaking into prisons at the moment. But if you need a spare pair of hands I'm ready and willing.'

'Can you drive a truck?'

'Of course. Where is it?'

'We have to hijack it first. I know the routes.'

'Jesus, when are you hoping to do this?'

'In the next two hours.'

'Got any kind of weapon?'

Rosenharte turned round and lifted the back seat to show the guns and boxes of ammunition.

'Right, well that's something, I suppose.' The Bird looked to the front and sniffed. 'What's the plan after you've got her out?'

'Harland gave me these when we were in Dresden.' He showed him two dark-blue British passports, complete with East German entry visas dated the week before and laminated strips that peeled back so that the picture could be fixed underneath. A note clipped to one had told him to heat the strips briefly in the steam from a kettle. 'I don't have a photo of Ulrike, and I need another passport for my friend Kurt Blast. He was the one arrested yesterday.'

The Englishman's head whipped round. 'Will he talk?'

'No, I don't think so. I'm his only chance of rescue.'

The Bird nodded. 'But you admit there's a possibility that they could know your whole plan, such as it is?'

'Yes, but I must try – Kafka won't last much longer in that place. We all owe her. You too.'

The Bird considered this. 'All right, I'm in but it's against all my better instincts. We'll leave this car near the prison. At the first sign of trouble we'll have to ram or shoot our way out.'

Rosenharte nodded.

'Afterwards we'll all go our separate ways. This isn't a flaming package tour, you know. You've got your passports. You make your own way out of this apology for a country. Right, I think we'd better get a move on.'

'Don't you speak *any* German?' asked Rosenharte.

'No, I'm like most Englishmen: I can order from a menu and

ask for a lavatory quite convincingly, but beyond that I'm rather at sea.'

He started the car and pulled out into the traffic on Mühlen-strasse. 'Doesn't your service require languages?'

'Yes, but they chose to overlook my cloth ear because of my other skills.'

'And those are?'

'Oh, you know – duffing up people, driving cars, releasing the odd hostage, backgammon, explosives, weaponry. The usual things.'

Rosenharte nodded and offered him a cigarette. 'Why are you called the Bird?'

'I would have thought you'd got that by now, but maybe even your English doesn't stretch that far. My name – Avocet – is a type of bird. A wader, I believe, with a long beak for sifting through the mud. That's me,' he said, stroking his crooked nose.

'Ah, yes. Your name in German is *Säbelschnäbler*.'

'Never had much time for birds myself – except driven grouse, of course. And the odd woodcock.'

They parked about a mile from the prison in Friedrichsfelde and, after ripping one of Rosenharte's shirts into several lengths of cloth, they shared the four guns between them. They took the U-bahn four stops to Mollendorf and walked the rest of the way to Hohenschönhausen. The Bird was evidently unaffected by his proximity to the heart of darkness, yet for all his extraordinarily vivid Englishness, he did somehow manage to blend into his sur-roundings more than Rosenharte would ever have imagined. He walked with a stoop, didn't look anyone in the eye and contrived with a rather depressed demeanour to appear much older than a man in his late thirties.

They reached the spot that Rosenharte had chosen, a narrow

right-angle bend, where the trucks slowed to a walking pace. It wasn't overlooked by any of the houses in the area. The only problem was that it was just three hundred yards from Konrad-Wolf-Strasse and, therefore, many hundreds of Stasi officers.

'We've got no option,' the Bird murmured with his hand in front of his mouth. 'How many Stasi do we expect on board?'

'Two, maybe three if they've got a guard in the back.'

He explained his plan and they split up to wait at different positions around the right-angle bend. Rosenharte took up a position beside a wooden fence and watched the gradual incline that the truck would climb before reaching the bend. The area seemed to be almost uninhabited and not for the first time in these last few weeks Rosenharte had the sense of expiration around him. The traffic on the arterial roads seemed muted, the factory chimneys in the south dribbled smoke into the sickly air and, as the night rushed from the east, the houses and apartments began to leak feeble lights into the dreary evening of the exhausted, hunched city. Rosenharte did his best to think of other things, but as the hands of his watch moved past five o'clock – the hour when the forged release documentation came into effect – his stomach knotted with anxiety.

Near seven the Englishman appeared from nowhere, offered him some whisky from a hip flask and asked whether he thought there would be any more trucks passing that night. The Bird snorted a laugh. 'We don't want to hold up some bloody bread van in the dark, do we now?'

Rosenharte replied that they had nothing to lose by waiting and the Bird again melted into the darkness on the other side of the street.

It was just past nine when the lights swung into the road from Frankfurter Allee and the truck began to grind up the gentle slope.

Rosenharte threw away his cigarette and called out to the Bird.

The vehicle was almost upon them when he saw him lope at great speed from the shadows and jump up to the driver's door at the point where the truck was moving at its slowest. Rosenharte drew his gun and ran to the passenger side, reached up and wrenched it open to find no one there. All he saw was the astonished face of the driver as the Bird hauled him out on the other side. The truck was still moving. Rosenharte dived for the gearstick, but the driver's foot had left the accelerator and the vehicle juddered forward with a series of complaints from the engine and then stalled. He scrambled through the cab, turning off the lights on the way. 'Where're the keys for the back?' he demanded. The driver's head turned towards him. 'Tell us and we won't kill you.'

'There's no one in the back!' he protested.

'Then why are you going to the prison?'

'To leave the vehicle there for tomorrow morning. They need it first thing. That's all I know.'

'Why?'

He looked down at the barrel pressed into his chest. 'I don't *know*! I'm just a driver. I don't know anything.'

'Where're the keys to the back?'

The man pointed to a hook above the driver's door. Rosenharte reached up and then got out of the cab. They frog-marched him round to the right side of the truck, unlocked the door and placed him in one of the open cells. The Bird gagged him with one of the strips of cloth, turned him and tied his hands behind his back, running the cloth through the bar on the side of the cubicle.

'Now you listen to me,' said Rosenharte. 'Any sound out of you and you'll die. Keep quiet for the next two hours and you'll remain unharmed. Is that understood?'

The man nodded and they slammed the door on him.

'I'll drive into the prison,' Rosenharte said. 'I know the way and I may need to speak to the guards. Then you drive us out. Is that okay with you?'

'Righty-ho,' said the Bird enthusiastically. 'Let's go and get your friends.'

The truck was cumbersome and slow, and only as he neared the prison gates did Rosenharte understand that he had to pump the brakes to make them respond. The gate inched back and he let the truck shoot forward into the garage space, but managed to stop before hitting the second door that led into the compound.

A man came down a short flight of metal steps. 'Hey, what's going on? We're not expecting any more deliveries.'

'This isn't a delivery,' said Rosenharte. 'This is a collection.' He waved the papers at him. The Bird got out and nodded to him.

'You'd better come to the office. We don't know about any collection.'

'This is a *special* collection. Anyway, weren't you expecting a truck to be left here for morning? There's another on the way.'

'Identity card,' said the guard, putting out his hand and turning to take the steps. He glanced at it and handed it back before opening the door. 'Well, what are you waiting for? We have to sort this out now.'

Rosenharte looked nonplussed. 'Yes, we're in a hurry too. We're four hours late. The prisoner was meant to be at Karlshorst at five.' He followed him into an office where there was a table, a bank of four black and white TV monitors, which showed murky impressions of the perimeter wall, two telephones and a single desk light. On the wall was a notice board and a complicated three-tiered diagram of cells and interrogation rooms but – naturally – no names of prisoners were attached to the numbered cells. The records and cell number of each inmate would be kept in the main administration block at the centre of the compound.

The man ran his finger down a list then looked at the forged papers. 'I have no record of this.'

'You mean to say that the prisoner isn't ready for immediate transport? That's ridiculous.'

'Of course not; she's not on the list.' He opened the palm of his left hand displaying a line of warts.

'This is bad,' said Rosenharte testily. 'Very bad. Have her brought down here immediately.'

The man's hand went to the telephone. The Bird darted a warning look to Rosenharte, but it was too late; the man had begun speaking. He listened for a second or two and put the phone down. 'She's still in interrogation. That means you'll have to wait.'

Rosenharte leaned forward confidentially. 'Colonel Zank is being as diligent as ever, eh? You'd better take us to the interrogation room. This is a matter of national security.' He drew the man aside. 'My companion is from the KGB. He is their chief interrogator and he has come to take delivery of the prisoner. Let's not waste any more time.'

The man nodded, picked up the phone again and barked an order. Very shortly a younger man appeared in an ill-fitting dark suit. 'Take these men to the interrogation wing. Forty-two A.'

He beckoned them down a flight of five steps and out into the U-shaped courtyard formed by the interrogation cell blocks. They walked diagonally across the yard to a door on the eastern wing. The buildings that had seemed so expressive of the police state's dull efficiency when he saw Konrad that last time, appeared brooding, much larger and more sinister at night. Behind the net curtains in one or two windows lights burned bright, indicating that no effort was being spared to break the few souls still being questioned at that hour. The Bird gave him an encouraging nod behind the man's back as he worked at the door lock. They entered and looked up a stairwell that was barred all the way up to the top floor to prevent prisoners jumping to their deaths. They climbed to the second floor and turned left, were taken through an iron gate and walked past twenty or so identical doorways. Lights on above some indicated the room was occupied, but apart from the squelch of the guard's rubber soles on the patterned lino there was no sound in the airless gloom of the passage. The guard stopped and looked up at the number, then pulled a heavy, padded door open to reveal a second door. He knocked. 'Do not interrupt us!' came a muffled command from within.

The Bird drew a gun and put it to the prison guard's head.

Rosenharte leaned forward and whispered, 'Open the door or he will shoot you now.'

The man put a key in the lock, turned it and pushed against the door with his body. A pneumatic sigh came from the hinge. The Bird flung the man into the room and stepped inside, moving the gun between the three interrogators. 'Move and I'll fucking kill the lot of you.' It was said in the unrepentant tones of the English upper class.

Rosenharte looked down. Ulrike was crouching, bare feet on the floor, torso wobbling, grimacing like a child trying to hold a pose, her face streaked with tears that shone in the single desk light trained on her. She did not look up when they came in and clearly had not absorbed their arrival. He rushed to her and lifted her in his arms. 'It's okay,' he said. 'We've come to take you away from here. It's okay – I'm here, my love.' She looked at him with the same incomprehension as Konrad had – that same disbelief that Hohenschönhausen would suffer any intrusion or trespass from the reasonable, humane world outside. There were bruises round her eyes and her neck was ringed with a chain of love bites – strangle marks.

The Bird glanced round. 'Here, give her one of these.' He passed a blister pack to Rosenharte. 'It's a painkiller and light opiate. There's some water over by that fucker with the red tie. And then give her one of these. It will keep her awake.'

Ulrike took the pills, gulped at the glass and put it down. She stood kneading the blood into one foot by rubbing it with the other, shaking the numbness from her hands. Rosenharte quickly took in the standard hell of a Hohenschönhausen interrogation room. There was a T-shaped desk, partly in pale-blue formica, three chairs, a low stool for the prisoner, a safe, a console for the recording equipment and phones, and a desk light designed around an upright bracket that allowed the shade to be swivelled to the horizontal, as it was now. In the lino, curtains and wallpaper, the Stasi had striven for a bureaucratic norm. 'What shall we do with these fucking bully boys?' asked the Bird. He turned to them. 'Treating a woman like that! You're a bloody disgrace, d'yer hear? A bloody disgrace.' He jabbed the gun at each of them in turn.

Rosenharte left her side and went over to the lead interrogator at the head of the table, pulled his head back by his hair and put the gun to his ear. 'You people killed my brother. I told Zank I'd hold you responsible; now I'm here to keep that promise.' There was no question in his mind that he was going to kill this man. He must pay for allowing Konrad to die and burning his body like a piece of trash.

Ulrike said, 'Don't, Rudi. This isn't you! Konrad wouldn't want this.' She put her hand to her forehead and waited a few seconds. She looked dreadfully pale. 'He's not worth the trouble it will cause your conscience.'

He looked down at the man's moist, puffy skin. The other interrogators and the guard who had brought them had imperceptibly moved away, believing that he was about to pull the trigger.

Instead he raised the gun and let it come down very hard just above the man's ear. He fell forward with blood seeping from a deep, curved gash, still conscious.

'Where's Kurt?' Rosenharte demanded.

'They've got Kurt?' said Ulrike, her voice rising.

'They picked him up yesterday on the street outside. He was in on this with me. Where is he, you bastard? And where's Biermeier?'

'Biermeier's dead,' she said. 'They killed him – shot him last week. Zank showed me his body.'

Rosenharte turned to the man he had hit. 'Is that what you did with Konrad – put a bullet into the back of his head? Is that what you did, you filthy piece of scum?' But by now he was watching himself at a distance, perhaps with Konrad's eyes. He knew Ulrike was right: this wasn't him. He leaned forward with the fingers of one hand splayed on the table. 'Where's Kurt?' he said to the back of the man's head. 'Is he in the U-boats? Is that where Zank put him?' He glanced up and caught the expression on the face of the guard, which told him he'd guessed right. He leaned forward to the senior interrogator. 'Then you'd better come with us and let him out.'

Rosenharte felt in his pocket and handed Ulrike the other gun. 'You may have to use this; it could be our only way out of here. Okay?' She stuffed it into her pocket and hobbled to the door, where her shoes were. She leaned on Rosenharte while putting them on.

The Bird took the keys from the guard then began to rip the wires from the base of the console. With one hand he hauled the chief interrogator towards the door and, having deposited him in Rosenharte's charge in the passage, tucked the gun into his waistband and went back inside. Holding a hand over his nose and mouth, he sprayed the room with an aerosol canister. Rosenharte saw the three remaining men slump to the desk and floor before both doors were shut and locked.

'We won't be hearing much from them for a while,' he said, taking the interrogator in an arm lock. 'Right, you bloody toe-rag, show us where these U-boats are.'

Outside in the yard nothing stirred as they made their way towards the van bay. Eventually they would have to pass through the office to reach the truck, but this wasn't their immediate problem. The entrance to the U-boat cells lay across from the office and van bay, and they would have to pass through an area that could be observed from the watchtower some way off on Genslerstrasse. Rosenharte led the way around the corner of the old brick kitchen block, hugging the wall. Ulrike clutched his hand while the Bird followed with his arm hooked round the man's neck. In the shadows of the old Nazi kitchen they could make out the steps sunk like a well on the side of the building. When they came to the bottom the Bird said, 'Now get them to open up, you little cunt.'

The interrogator pressed a bell and announced himself through an intercom. Immediately the door was pulled open and Rosenharte sprang inside with Ulrike behind him. One man, almost a caricature of the medieval jailer, was inside. He had protruding, expressionless eyes, a vast stomach and two or three days' worth of stubble. He staggered backwards. On a table beneath a lone naked light was a pair of reading glasses, a newspaper, a large bottle of beer and a cigarette smouldering in an ashtray. Though the air was rank with mustiness and urine, Rosenharte could see no evidence of the cells. He moved to a low door below the spine of the building and told him to unlock it and lead them to Kurt. A look of awkwardness came into the man's eyes. He glanced at the interrogator. 'This facility hasn't been used for years. He's the only one here – just for the night, you understand.'

'Take us to him,' said Rosenharte very quietly, before ducking to get through the doorway.

They followed the beam of the guard's torch as it dodged along a narrow brick passageway. Overhead a number of pipes shuddered and made a dull clanking noise, but little else moved in the thick dankness of the U-boats. It was easy to imagine that they were submerged a mile beneath the ocean, locked in an isolation tank. The man stopped outside a door painted the same light blue-grey as the prison gates and turned a key in the lock, which allowed him to draw a bar across the surface of the door and tug it open. There was no light or sound in the void beyond. Rosenharte snatched the torch and, pushing the guard aside, went in. Kurt was propped against a stone ledge. His arms and legs were bound up in a kind of canvas jacket so that he could not stand, lie or sit. He was wet through and deathly cold. Rosenharte tried to undo the ties but realized he'd need more than one pair of hands. He picked him up and helped him into the passageway, knocking his head on the low ceiling several times in the process, and told the guard to undo the jacket. This he did, shaking his head with a look of theatrical remorse, as though he was as shocked as they were. The interrogator stared down without feeling.

'Did you order this?' demanded Rosenharte.

'No, he's not my prisoner.'

'Colonel Zank?'

The man seemed to nod.

At length Ulrike helped Kurt to his feet. He stood naked and white in the light of the torch. He managed a smile, but was mostly taken up with trying to control the shaking in his arms and legs.

'You,' she said, waving the gun at the interrogator. 'Take off your jacket and trousers and shoes and give them to my friend here – and that nice sweater too. Move it.' Rosenharte saw real anger in her eyes, and fleetingly noted that although she had been treated badly too, and over a much longer period, she had no pity for herself. Kurt was her only concern.

The interrogator undressed, dabbing at the cut on his head. Then Rosenharte pushed him into the cell, consigned the fat guard to the neighbouring hole and locked both doors behind them.

Kurt could feel nothing in his feet and they had to help him up the passageway. When they got into the light at the entrance to the U-boats they saw that he had been beaten very severely. There were welts on his forehead and chin, and he was bruised on his back, feet and legs. The sharp pain he experienced on the in-breath suggested that at least one rib was broken on his left side. They sat him down at the guard's table and gave him pills to swallow with the remainder of the beer. Ulrike held his shoulders and kissed the top of his head.

Eventually he rose and stretched his arms, but he was still unable to put any weight on his feet.

'You two bring him,' said the Bird, moving to the door. 'I'll go ahead and get the truck started and the gate opened up. Don't worry about the guard. I'll sort him out. Leave it two minutes, then come.'

He disappeared through the doorway and shot up the steps. A minute passed before they moved into the dark space outside the door and began to help Kurt take the steps one by one. As they reached the open, Rosenharte heard some movement off to the left. He let go of Kurt and turned round to see a group of three men running towards them in the shadow of the kitchen block. He raised his gun and took aim.

Two men with pistols emerged into the light, with Colonel Zank following. He was smiling and slightly out of breath. 'Put down your weapons. You cannot escape.' Ulrike had moved away from Kurt and levelled her gun at Zank.

'We may be outnumbered,' she said, 'but you'll die with us.'

'You're a pacifist,' said Zank teasingly. 'You only take punishment; you don't hand it out.' He looked at Rosenharte. 'You should have seen what I did to her; I began to wonder if she got off on it . . . But then perhaps you would know about that better than I.'

'There's no question you will die,' said Rosenharte.

Zank laughed. 'You're interested in birds, aren't you, Rosenharte?'

'Birds! What the hell are you talking about?'

'Little Ulrike told me that you were interested in birds. Perhaps you know about the Larsen trap?' He moved towards them, one hand in his pocket, the other holding a standard-issue handgun. 'Do you know about the Larsen trap?'

'No.' He moved a pace backwards to keep the other men in view.

'It's a new invention from Sweden that traps magpies. You first catch one magpie and you put it in a cage with several compartments. Then you set the cage out in the open and the trapped bird – aptly named the caller – summons other magpies which enter the trap one by one.' He pointed first to Ulrike with his gun then turned it to Kurt and Rosenharte. 'One, two, three. Soon you've trapped all the magpies in the locality – and all from one bird singing its little head off.' He stopped. 'I knew you would come, Rosenharte. I left Colonel Biermeier free because I knew she would call him. And I was sure that a vain romantic like you wouldn't leave her.'

Rosenharte moved closer so that his gun pointed at the middle of Zank's forehead. 'Your world is over – the little traps you set for people, your power to destroy good men like my brother and Kurt. Your obvious delight in tormenting a beautiful and brave woman. You're a sick bastard, Zank, but more important you're the past, a leftover from the time when this disgusting place was built.' He gestured with his left hand at the Nazi kitchen block to divert attention away from the Bird, who had slipped without a sound from the office above the van bay and had rolled a clutch of round objects behind the men. 'And that's why you're going to let us walk out of here.'

Zank was saying that once caught, magpies never left the trap, when three small explosions occurred behind him, causing his two companions to reel backwards and start shooting wildly in the direction of the Genslerstrasse watchtower. Rosenharte was ahead of the game because he had at least expected something to happen, though he couldn't have predicted the blinding flash of the stun grenades or the clap of localized thunder that was now occupying the greater part of his consciousness. He spun round and saw that Kurt and Ulrike had fallen to the ground. As he moved to haul them up, he was aware of the Bird rushing at Zank's men, hitting them with terrifying force, one in the throat and the other in the small of his back. It appeared an almost preordained sequence as he recoiled, crouched, slid to the left, then rose behind Zank to hook an arm around his neck and place a gun beneath his chin. He waved to Rosenharte and shouted for them to make for the truck. As they scrambled into the office and passed the unconscious gatekeeper, he saw the Bird backing towards them with Zank held like a child's soft toy in one long, powerful arm. With his left hand he chucked two more objects into the compound, then delivered a single blow to the crown of Zank's head. Zank crumpled at the base of the steps.

A few seconds later they were all three crowded into the front of the truck. The Bird revved the engine and reversed furiously out of the bay, clipping the edge of the electronic door that some remote hand had ordered to close. The vehicle spun round and they caught a glimpse of dense white smoke leaking over the prison walls.

'Well, what now?' said the Bird with a lunatic grin. 'Know anywhere you three can put up for the evening?'

THIRTY-SEVEN

A Magnificent Blunder

'Where are they?' demanded Harland.

'Somewhere in Prenzlauer Berg. They're being sheltered by political friends of Kafka.'

'You know the address?'

'Not exactly,' said the Bird.

They were standing in the car park near the three-storey building that housed the endless deliberations of the Central Committee of the Socialist Unity Party. Theoretically Harland was there to cover the meetings as a member of the press corps, but it had just been announced that news of the day's proceedings would be given at a conference held at the new International Press Centre. When the Bird's call came through it had been the best rendezvous he could think of.

'Why didn't you get the address?'

'Because we had to split up. Half the bloody Stasi were pursuing us at one point. We did pretty well to get away in that little car.'

'Anyone hurt?'

'The lad's not in great shape, but he's got guts and he'll pull through.'

'But you don't know where they are. That's the point, isn't it? I could do without this today. I'm meeting the Russian and I still haven't heard from Griswald. Why the hell didn't you take them over last night? You had everything you needed.'

'Keep your shirt on, Bobby.' The Bird shook his head in annoyance. 'Look, this little unofficial op of yours resulted in springing two bods from Hohenschönhausen. I believe that's a Cold War first. It should be written up with a dramatic flourish in the annals of Century House by one of those pert little numbers in Records. Come on, Bobby, we did well. We couldn't go last night because Rosenharte and Kafka wouldn't leave the other man. Besides, we still need a picture of her for her passport.'

Harland made an apologetic nod. Cuth was right: he had done magnificently.

'You seem out of sorts, Bobby. Is there anything I can do?'

'No, I've got a lot on, that's all. And those bloody idiots in London just won't free the funds we need. We're on the threshold of the greatest intelligence coup in the history of the Cold War, and they're still scratching their heads wondering about flaming cost-benefits. This could save millions on the budget. Literally millions. To say nothing of increasing security tenfold.'

'It's that good, is it?'

'Better. It's so good you and I could retire and leave the running of the Intelligence Services to Jamie Jay.'

The Bird smiled. 'A likely outcome, I'm sure. What happened to the young sprog, anyway? I rather liked him.'

'As a matter of fact he's temping at the Stadium for a few weeks. I think they got tired of his boundless enthusiasm in the Gulf so I said I'd happily use up his excess energy. He appeared at the tail end of last week, listening to language tapes. He'll bring the passport over this afternoon.'

'So we just wait for the call from Rosenharte?'

'Yep, then you arrange the reception committee the other side. Get Kafka and the other chap any treatment they need. Put Rosenharte in a hotel. And we'll follow up from there in a few days. Rosenharte will want to go see his sister-in-law. There's all that to fix. But that's Jay's job.'

The Bird was smoking a rare cigarette and had begun to pace in a circle. 'So let me guess: you're buying something from the Russians. Right, Bobby? That could only be information.' He paused and considered this. 'Jesus, what a bloody merry-go-round we're in. Buying intel from one lot of Commies about another lot of Commies. We live in interesting times, Bobby. Interesting times. How good is this info?'

'Sorry, Cuth. I can't tell you, certainly not here. But you'll be the first to know if we get the go-ahead. We're getting a sample delivery this afternoon.'

'That sounds familiar. Are you sure they aren't having you on? I mean it doesn't take an IQ higher than the average biscuit's to see they might well be playing a return match for your little jape with the disks. One lot of false information in exchange for another lot.'

'I think not.'

'Where are you going to get this free sample?'

'At the conference this afternoon.'

'Well, I hope there'll be a suitable number of unwashed scribes in the room, otherwise you'll stick out like the Pope's prick.'

'There will be,' said Harland. 'This is a big day. The Council of Ministers is going to discuss the new travel regulations and the GDR economy. Actually, I've picked up a lot of useful stuff this week. For one thing, Mielke's still very much in the saddle at Normannenstrasse, even though he's resigned.'

The Bird's attention had wandered. 'Look, old cock, I need some breakfast and a kip. I'll be in touch later.'

They said goodbye. Harland's gaze followed the remarkable figure of Cuthbert Avocet as he passed unnoticed through the news crews assembled outside the building to film the uniformed members of the Stasi, the Grenzpolizei and People's Army as they arrived for the first session of the day. He reflected that whatever happened during the panicky deliberations of Egon Krenz's government, the Bird's exploits in Hohenschönhausen would provide far better copy than any journalist would find for himself that day.

Ulrike's friends, Katya and Fritzi Rundstedt, were two mathematicians who lived on the top floor of a once gracious nineteenth-century building in Prenzlauer Berg which still bore the scars of Allied bombs and Russian shells. It stood on a gentle rise, and from the fifth floor you could follow the line of the Berlin Wall from the north, observe the bulge as it swooped round the old ceremonial and administrative centre of the city captured by the Soviet forces in 1945 and continued its jagged path southwards towards Schulzendorf. Rosenharte spent some time with Fritzi early on the morning of Thursday 9 November, watching the light and shade play across the free part of the city, picking out the crossing points and a corner of the Brandenburg Gate. They turned from the window with empty coffee cups and looked down at Kurt and Ulrike, who were still asleep on the floor in the adjacent room. Fritzi nodded benignly and they stole away to the kitchen.

During the night Katya Rundstedt, a quiet woman with short grey hair and watchful eyes, had become worried about Kurt and phoned a doctor friend at the local hospital. Half an hour later he appeared to treat the fugitives without the slightest qualm. In Kurt's case, he diagnosed two fractured ribs on the left side, together with several broken bones in his right foot, which had apparently been slammed in a cell door. Ulrike needed rest. The shock of nine days' interrogation had buried itself deep inside her and he told Rosenharte that he mustn't imagine she'd recovered just because she was showing such concern for Kurt. 'It's the beginning of the process of denial,' he said, regarding him sternly over wire spectacles that made him look like Gustav Mahler. 'You see, it's difficult for someone who has such a positive view of her fellow human beings to accept that they are capable of such behaviour. It may shake her faith in those around her. I have helped several people who were in Bautzen and I believe that she risks depression and a possible breakdown if she doesn't acknowledge her own suffering.'

'You speak as though you know her.'

'Yes, she's been active in the same circles as me and my wife. We're members of the same church. Your friend is a woman of rare spirit and very special qualities, Dr Rosenharte, but I'm sure you already know that.'

Rosenharte had nodded and found himself suddenly overwhelmed by the thought of how close he'd come to losing her, and how much he wanted to look after her.

At midday a photographer, another contact of the Rundstedts, came to take passport pictures of Ulrike and Kurt. Both were made up by Katya with foundation to cover their bruises and injuries. The photographer returned at two with the pictures and Rosenharte was able to fix Ulrike's into the passport of Birgit Miller. Now all that remained was for the British courier to turn up with Kurt's passport.

At four he went to a phone box and dialled in the code for the second time that day, to be told that the man had crossed the border and was on his way to the meeting place arranged by the Bird in a park near Greifswalderstrasse station. The courier knew what Rosenharte looked like and would find him.

It was a five-minute walk. Rosenharte went, promising himself this would be the very last clandestine meeting of his life. He was sick of the whole ridiculous business of subterfuge and spying.

He chose a bench under a lime tree that had not quite yet shed all its leaves, and read a book he'd borrowed from the Rundstedt apartment. Some ten minutes later he was approached by a young man in a stone-washed denim jacket, scuffed suede ankle boots and black jeans. He sat down and asked for a light with an excruciating English accent. It was then that Rosenharte recognized the young man who had pulled him out of the gulf of Trieste.

'You can speak English. No one's going to overhear,' he said, weary of hearing the British butcher his language.

'Did I introduce myself before? I forget. I'm Jamie Jay of Her Majesty's et cetera, et cetera, and I've just put the passport in your pocket. So, we'll expect you when we see you. Cross by Checkpoint Charlie any time after six. We'll see you coming and have an ambulance ready for your friends. Everything is organized for you. Hotels, money, so on.'

Rosenharte studied the avid, healthy young face beside him. 'Why are you in this business? Couldn't you find anything else to do?'

'King and country, and all that stuff,' said Jay simply.

'Patriotism? It seems an odd way to show it.'

'Yes, I suppose so.'

Rosenharte nodded. 'There's one other thing. The Pole – the man who died in Trieste. Do you believe he was killed?'

'At first we thought he had been, but we checked his hotel and found several different types of pills for heart and liver disease. He was a very sick man, it seems: he looked much older than he was and, well, we gather he liked a drop more than was good for him.'

'He was an alcoholic?'

"Fraid so.'

'Grycko was what age? Fifty-eight or fifty-nine?'

'Thereabouts.'

'Can you tell me anything more about him?'

'We didn't bother to learn more after we realized he wasn't relevant to the operation in hand.' He paused and flashed a bright, uncomplicated grin, then clasped his knees. 'If there's nothing else, I'd better be getting along, sir.' He rose. 'It's good to see you have come through all this in one piece. Many congratulations.'

Rosenharte acknowledged this, thinking that in truth half of him was still missing.

He returned to the Rundstedts' building. He was let in by a neighbour with an impressive spreading moustache who said: 'There's trouble. The Stasi have traced the car to a street nearby. Two of them are here now.'

'Where are my friends?'

'They're fine. We have decided to detain the Stasi while you make your way from here.'

'What do you mean?'

'Well, we are having words with them – putting them right about certain things that we in this building feel strongly about. It seemed a good opportunity to act. We've locked them in the cellar and your friend Fritzi is plying them with a cheap brandy and giving them a piece of his mind.'

Rosenharte realized that Zank must have worked out they were using number plates stolen from Schwarzmeer's retreat in the country, and put out a general alert for the missing pair. 'Okay, we'd better leave.'

'Not all at the same time,' said the neighbour. 'Leave one by one and meet up somewhere. Your friend has been given some crutches. We'll help him reach his destination.'

Rosenharte thanked the man and tore up the staircase, the noise of his pounding feet reverberating through the tired old building.

Harland filed into the press conference at 5.45 p.m. with members of both the Western and communist media. Already twenty or so TV crews had set up, and about a hundred journalists were in the room. There were still seats free but he took up a position at the side of the room, just behind one of two banks of cameras trained on the dais. The air of expectation was palpable. This would be the first time that a member of the Politburo had taken part in a news conference broadcast live to the people of the GDR. Once Gunther Schabowski, a former newspaper editor whom Krenz had appointed to handle the media, was sitting against the willow-green satin backdrop Harland knew he'd be at the mercy of the press in a way that a career communist could not possibly appreciate. Even a former newspaper editor wouldn't see the perils ahead.

For Harland the only thing that mattered was picking up the documents from Vladimir, but he was interested in Schabowski. MI6 had reports that suggested that the East Berlin Party chief was one of the key figures in the putsch that ousted Erich Honecker, and it had recently been established that at an earlier Politburo meeting Schabowski openly challenged Erich Mielke on the numbers of people working for the Stasi. London wanted to know whether this indicated real political muscle or recklessness.

Schabowski entered in a grey checked suit and striped tie and threaded a route through the journalists and cameramen. He had the face of a battle-hardened army sergeant, which betrayed some of his Slav origins. Just as he arrived, Harland spotted Vladimir standing on the far side of the room, merged most effectively in the media throng. Their eyes met for a second or two and looked through each other. Harland turned to the dais. There was time enough for Vladimir to make the delivery.

Schabowski began to speak about the 'intensive discussion' at the Central Committee. The new proposal on travel regulations was being dealt with and it was understood that Krenz would confront his colleagues with the bleak facts of the East German economy, after Gorbachev's refusal to come to the country's aid. Schabowski's manner was more ponderous than Harland expected and unease communicated itself to the three apparatchiks on the dais with him. Perhaps they had a dim sense that they were riding a machine without knowing where the brakes were.

Harland checked on Vladimir several times, then at 6.30 p.m. noticed that he'd left his position. Next thing he knew the Russian was sidling up to him with a folder of holiday brochures in his hand. He tipped his head to the rear of the room.

'We hear they all got away last night,' he said when they reached the back wall. 'All except the man who was executed last week. A very good result for you.'

'Yes, it was and thank you for your help.'

'It's nothing. This is the first delivery.' He spoke from the side of his mouth. 'There are details of cases you know about so your side will realize that what we're offering is very, very important information. The crown jewels, as you say.'

'What cases?' asked Harland, his gaze returning to the figure of Schabowski. From this vantage point he seemed tired and beaten down.

'You've got everything you need on Abu Jamal and Misha. In other words, the documentary proof of the GDR's official involvement. We've added in some other cases that have interested MI6 and Langley in the past. Oh yes, and there's one other file in there.'

He paused long enough for Harland to turn and raise his eyebrows. 'It's Rosenharte's personal file.'

'Good, that'll be a useful way of verifying the material.'

'It's more than a means of authentication, as you'll see. You should give it to him at the earliest opportunity, then telephone me.'

'What do you mean?'

'Not here. We can't talk about that here.' He slipped the file into Harland's left hand and then turned his attention to a question from Riccardo Ehrman, an Italian journalist from the ANSA agency who had arrived late and was perched strategically on the ledge below and to the right of Schabowski.

Schabowski seemed nettled by the Italian's point, which had referred to mistakes in the release of the draft travel law a few days before. 'No, I don't think so,' he was saying. 'We know about this tendency in the population, this need of the population to travel or leave the GDR. Today, as far as I know a recommendation of the Council of Ministers has been taken up. We have highlighted that passage from the draft travel law which regulates so-called permanent emigration. Therefore we have decided to adopt a regulation which enables every citizen of the GDR to leave the country by means of GDR border crossings.'

Harland began to say something but Vladimir put up his hand. 'Listen.'

'When does that take effect?' someone called out from the middle of the room. Schabowski either didn't hear or was playing for time. 'Is that effective immediately?' another reporter asked.

'Well, comrades,' said Schabowski, 'it was communicated to me that the press release had been distributed today. You should all have it in your possession.'

Vladimir had begun to shake his head.

'What's going on?' asked Harland.

Schabowski had put on his spectacles and was now reading from notes. 'Trips abroad may be applied for without meeting preconditions. Permission will be given forthwith. Permanent emigration may take place at all border crossings from the East to West Germany.'

'When does it take effect?' came the call again.

'As far as I know, immediately,' Schabowski replied.

Vladimir turned to Harland, shaking his head. 'The man's an idiot. There was a press embargo on this until tomorrow morning.'

Harland had been so focused on when and how he was going to get the documents to West Berlin that he had not seen the significance of Schabowski's statement.

'He hasn't mentioned passports or visas,' said Vladimir. 'The Central Committee has revised the travel laws so that people apply for *visas* without preconditions. But it still means they have to have a passport to leave. Don't you see? Most East Germans don't have a passport. He screwed up because he didn't mention that they still must have a passport.'

Schabowski now seemed to have an idea of the gaffe he'd made. Someone asked whether crossing from East Germany to West Germany included crossings in West Berlin. Schabowski put on his glasses and consulted the handwritten notes in front of him. Then he looked up and, failing to see the significance of the question, murmured that a crossing into West Germany of course included a crossing into West Berlin. He added that he was not completely up to date because he had only just been handed the information before coming in.

For about a minute or so a rather studious-looking journalist in the middle of the room had been on his feet, waiting to gain Schabowski's attention. His name was Daniel Johnson, a young

Englishman whom Harland recognised. 'Herr Schabowski, what will happen to the Berlin Wall now?'

The room was suddenly electrified. It was the question on everyone's mind. Schabowksi sat back, then seemed to sink in his chair. He toyed with his reading glasses and seemed to be trying to give the impression that he was in control of the situation. Yet he could not escape the logic of the young man's question. If people could travel whenever they wanted without preconditions from that moment on, what indeed was the point of the Wall? After a pause, Schabowski noted that the time was seven o'clock and that this was the last question he would deal with. 'What will happen to the Berlin Wall?' he mused. 'Some information has already been provided regarding travel activities . . . the question of the permeability of the Wall from our side does not yet or exclusively answer the question of the purpose of this . . . let me say . . . *the fortified national border of the GDR.*'

With this baffling statement the press conference ended and the reporters surged forward to gain clarification from the dais. Vladimir shrugged his astonishment and then glanced at Harland. 'We'll speak. I'd better let my people know that Gunther Schabowski has singlehandedly torn down the Berlin Wall.'

'They already know,' said Harland. 'It's on TV.'

Harland went into the hall where there was a TV on and made a call on Alan Griswald's mobile phone to Griswald in West Berlin and left a message. 'The deal's on and by the way, the Wall is coming down. At least that's what Gunther Schabowski's saying. Turn on your TV. I'll be at Checkpoint Charlie by nine.'

Then he called London, where it was now 6.25 p.m. Mike Costelloe had already left Century House. Harland told the European desk the news and asked them to get Costelloe to call him.

Five minutes later the mobile rang. 'This isn't a secure line but I have got good news,' said Harland.

'Is it true what the East Germans have been saying?' asked Costelloe. 'There's a news flash from Associated Press being put out.'

'I heard it with my own ears,' said Harland, watching Johnson talking animatedly with his colleagues.

'Well, they must put out a clarification soon. I can't believe they'll let that stand. What's got into them?'

'Search me,' said Harland, 'but look, our main business has gone very well. I will call again in a couple of hours. Where will you be?'

'At Langan's Brasserie,' said Costelloe, a smile audible in his voice. 'I think you'll relish the piquancy of the occasion. We're entertaining our German clients and they have their chief analyst with them.'

'You mean Lisl . . .'

'Exactly,' he paused. 'I'll look forward to bringing that particular party up to date with the events. Look, I've got to go now.'

Harland wished he could see the consternation spread over Dr Lisl Voss's face as the news came through. 'Hold on. Don't go,' he said. 'The TV news is on. You can hear what the East Germans are saying.'

He held the phone to the set as the rather prim but attractive newscaster went straight into an item about Schabowski's statement. 'He announced a resolution by the Council of Ministers regarding a new travel rule. Effective immediately, private trips abroad may be applied for without specifying a particular reason.'

Harland put the phone to his ear. 'See what I mean? They're not talking about passports or visas.'

'Jesus, it's soon going to be too late for them to claw that back,' observed Costelloe. Harland knew he was already composing his line for the Joint Intelligence Committee the following morning. 'Keep me in touch. And well done on the other thing. It sounds very exciting.'

'But we'll need to have a decision on the money by tomorrow morning. I can't put them off any longer.'

'Message understood,' said Costelloe.

He hung up, wondering if he had been too indiscreet on an open line, but then he reflected that the permeability of the fortified border increased every day without Schabowski's help. However good the East Germans were, there was little they could do to track cellular phone calls. But the Wall was still there and for the moment he needed to know whether Rosenharte and Kafka and their friend had crossed over. He dialled a number in West Berlin and waited.

THIRTY-EIGHT

The Gate

They were driven one by one from Prenzlauer Berg to a neglected courtyard off the Hackescher Markt, near Alexanderplatz. Then they were shown to an apartment belonging to a violinist named Hubert, an excitable man with tufts of black hair above his ears and a wandering right eye. Moments after Rosenharte arrived in the musician's tiny flat he received word that Colonel Zank was now questioning everyone in the Rundstedts' block. This worried Rosenharte and Ulrike. Both knew that the Stasi would consult records held in Normannenstrasse and draw up lists of known contacts of the Rundstedt family and their neighbours. They excelled at this kind of rapid triangulation and sooner or later Hubert would show up on that list. More troubling was the certainty that Zank knew they hadn't already left East Berlin and that they would be attempting a crossing with false credentials in the very near future. Every border post would now be on alert and in possession of the picture of Rosenharte used in the press and the photographs of Kurt and Ulrike taken in Hohenschönhausen.

At 7.20 p.m. Rosenharte used Hubert's phone to call Robert Harland. A woman answered and said that everyone dealing with the operation was out. She would urgently try to get in touch with Harland.

'How are we expected to come across?' asked Rosenharte, almost at the end of his tether.

'Haven't you heard?' she asked.

'What?'

'All travel restrictions have been lifted. The news has just come through. There was an announcement by Gunther Schabowski just before seven – twenty minutes ago.'

'But we still have to go through checkpoints. They'll be looking for us.'

'If you're near a TV, turn it on,' said the woman. 'The situation's very fluid. Call again in an hour's time. In the meantime, I will contact Mr Harland.'

Rosenharte returned to the others. 'Something's happened. No one knows what's going on. There's been an announcement about the travel laws.' He turned to Hubert. 'Have you got a TV?'

He removed a white cloth to reveal a TV set in the corner of the room and retuned it from the West German station to an East German state channel. At seven thirty the blue logo of the *Aktuelle Kamera* show appeared, and after a prologue about the Central Committee meeting, they heard the words: 'Immediately effective, private trips abroad may be applied for without specifying a particular reason.'

Ulrike rose. 'What does it mean? Can anyone travel at any time? It can't be true.'

They continued to watch, but no further explanation was offered. Hubert rang round his friends. They had all seen it, but were confused as to what the government had actually said. Some had heard rumours that people were beginning to gather at four of the main checkpoints – at Bornholmerstrasse railway bridge to the north of the city centre, Invalidenstrasse to the west of them, and at Checkpoint Charlie and Sonnenallee to the south. They were showing up with nothing more than their identity cards and demanding to be allowed through.

It was now 8.45. Rosenharte called the British again, but got no further information. Hubert's phone rang several times. Brisk, incredulous exchanges took place. The consensus among his friends seemed to be that people should mass on the border and so increase pressure on the authorities to raise the barriers. At Bornholmerstrasse, the crossing closest to a large residential area, thousands had already gathered. Then at 9.15 they learned from another call that the Stasi officer in charge of passport control at Bornholmerstrasse was easing the pressure by allowing a trickle of the most troublesome East Berliners to pass into the West with nothing more than a stamp on their identity cards. 'Without passports,' shouted Hubert before making arrangements with friends to go to Bornholmerstrasse. 'You must come too,' he said. 'We'll all go.'

'Do you have transport?' asked Rosenharte. 'Kurt won't make it that far.'

Hubert shook his head.

'I can walk,' said Kurt.

Rosenharte shook his head. 'No, we'll head for Checkpoint Charlie. It's the closest.'

Hubert snatched up a coat, but just as he was about to leave they heard shouts from the yard below. A man was calling up to Hubert that four Stasi cars had pulled up in Rosenthalerstrasse and were preparing to enter the obscure little courtyard.

They crashed down the rickety stairway. At the bottom Hubert slipped into a doorway near the courtyard's entrance, while a friend who had acted as lookout led them to a dark opening at the far end of the yard, then left them. They were hidden a minute or two before Zank appeared in the courtyard and started to organize half a dozen men to search the buildings. There seemed to be some reluctance among them, and when Zank vanished into Hubert's stairway, two of them remained in the yard grumbling. The whole operation came to an end when Zank appeared, brandishing one of the crutches that Kurt had left in Hubert's apartment because he'd move more easily with one.

'We missed them,' he shouted to the others. 'They've only just left – the coffee pot's still warm. They'll be making for the Wall. We'll search the area west of here.'

They waited a few minutes then left the yard, hurried through the area just to the south of the Hackescher Markt and made for the cold, friendless heart of the old city where the museums and churches of a more graceful age stood dark and brooding. Rosenharte's plan was to keep to the smaller streets until they hit Friedrichstrasse, the north-south axis that sliced across the centre until it reached Zimmerstrasse, where it was itself cut in two by the border. At this intersection was Checkpoint Charlie. Rosenharte and Ulrike knew every inch of the way for they were within spitting distance of Humboldt University. Even with Kurt hobbling along beside them Rosenharte thought it wouldn't take them more than twenty or thirty minutes to reach the border.

Having crossed the Spree, he decided it would be safer if they walked along Unter den Linden, the wide boulevard running east-west to the Brandenburg Gate. They took the right-hand side, passing the Hungarian cultural centre and the Atrium cafe. At the building containing the Polish centre they retreated to the shadows of a shopping precinct as a police car cruised by. Kurt leaned on his crutch like a war veteran and smoked a cigarette. He was slightly drunk on Hubert's plum brandy, which had dulled the pain in his foot.

Ulrike slipped her hand into Rosenharte's. 'It's so near and yet so far,' she said. And then as an afterthought: 'Whoever thought of dividing a city like this? It's so bizarre when you see the reality of it.'

Plenty of people were milling around now. Many East Germans were making their way to Checkpoint Charlie and among them were some West Germans who had crossed over and were intent on a party. A young man came up to them and asked where he could get a beer at this hour. He told them his name was Benedict and that he'd just walked straight through Checkpoint Charlie from the West without anyone asking for his papers or stopping him. 'There are more people on the western side than on the eastern. We're waiting for you. But I have come to rouse you lazy communists so we can pull down this Wall together.'

'You're drunk,' said Ulrike with a broad grin.

'And why not, on a night like this?' asked Benedict good-naturedly. 'It's the duty of every decent Berliner to be drunk on a night like this. You see, my friends, this thing, the thing that is happening around us is now official: Hans J. Friederichs, no less, has just been on his television show *Tagesthemen* to say that the Wall is wide open. That's what he said. The Wall is wide open. So, come along and help me get your comrades out of their beds.'

Rosenharte placed a hand on his shoulder. 'If you don't mind, Herr Benedict, we three have come a long way for this. We've been waiting all our lives for this moment, so we'd very much like to go and see it all for ourselves. But we may need your help because there are people pursuing us.'

'The Stasi?' said Benedict excitedly. That was the difference with Westerners. They had no fear because they didn't understand the reality of the Stasi. 'I'll bring my friends over here. We'll all go together to the Brandenburg Gate. People have climbed on top of the Wall.'

He whistled to a group across the street. Soon six eager students had joined them and they headed for the intersection with

Friedrichstrasse where they paused in a darkened part on the north side of the street. It was with a grim lack of surprise that Rosenharte spotted Zank standing like a sentinel about seventy yards away on the other side of Unter den Linden. He was scanning the crowds that were making their way to Checkpoint Charlie down Friedrichstrasse. As far as he could tell, there were now just a couple of men with him. Their body language betrayed shiftiness and a certain bewilderment rather than menace. But nonetheless Rosenharte was convinced that he, Ulrike and Kurt had become a kind of symbol to Zank and the waning powers of the dark energy. If they could be prevented from crossing the Wall, the Wall would not fall.

He consulted Benedict. Three of the young students agreed to set up a diversion while the remainder of the party would crowd round and convey them across the intersection, then to the Brandenburg Gate. Rosenharte knew this was their only hope. With their new British passports they could pose as Western revellers, and if arrested they stood a very good chance of being ejected into the West.

The diversion worked well. Rosenharte saw the three young men approach Zank and begin to caper around him with a bottle, slapping his back and insisting he pose for a picture with them. He had to call for his men to get rid of them but his attention was drawn long enough for them to have moved out of sight and begin the final walk towards the Brandenburg Gate.

Cut off from the East by the barriers and in the West by the most massive and impassable stretch of the entire Berlin Wall, the Brandenburg now stood stark against the white haze of TV lights hurriedly set up on the other side. The dark hero of the Cold War, so remote to the people of both Germanys for so long, was now illuminated like an opera set. The few guards visible from the East moved between the six Doric columns like stagehands.

Rosenharte was now aware of a gentle murmur in the air, the rise and fall of the crowd's voice, which resembled nothing so much as the sea breaking on a distant shoreline. As they got closer, the constituent parts of the sound separated into cheers, cat-calls, song, laughter, the thud of a drum and a loudhailer.

They covered the open ground between the end of the Boulevard and the Gate feeling desperately exposed. Rosenharte put his arm round Ulrike and glanced back several times but Zank was nowhere to be seen. They came to a low metal fence, which ran from one side of the street to the other. Though a relatively simple affair without the barbed wire, alarms and automatic guns that could be found along the rest of the Berlin Wall, this barrier had effectively denied Easterners contact with their own landmark since August 1961. It was easily climbed and after Kurt was lifted over they pushed on across another stretch of tarmac. Now they could see that the Wall was lined with people silhouetted against the TV lights. A thousand people or more had taken Gunther Schabowski's faltering announcement to its ultimate conclusion. Some were even dropping down from the lit world of the free West into the shade of the death zone immediately in front of the Gate. Ulrike stopped and gasped at the sight and raised her hands to her mouth.

Rosenharte put his arm round her shoulder and spoke into her ear. 'It's amazing, but let's get over the other side.'

'They've been using water hoses,' shouted Benedict enthusiastically, pointing to pools of water on the other side of the gate. 'Let's go and join the party.'

Until now they had attracted little interest from the Grepos who were all turned to face the West, but when they got to within fifty yards of the Gate, two dozen troops appeared from the guard houses either side of them, formed up and shouted for them to go back.

'Shit, they don't seem too pleased to see us,' said Benedict. He called out to them. 'Lads, come and join the party. We'll have a drink and we can find you some good West Berliner girls.'

Rosenharte turned to Ulrike and Kurt. 'What we have to do now is seem as drunk as Benedict and his friends. Remember, we're from the West. We've come through Checkpoint Charlie and we're on our way back to the West. Okay?' Kurt nodded. 'Remember that you're British subjects. Act with an air of entitlement.' He winked at them.

Benedict turned to them. 'Well, are we going?'

Rosenharte nodded. They passed through the unblinking line of guards without one of them raising his gun. 'You,' a young officer shouted at Kurt, 'what's the matter with your leg?'

'Some bastard slammed it in the door,' Kurt replied, and hobbled on.

Halfway under the Gate, an officer ran to them holding up his hands. What were they doing there? Where had they come from? Benedict became their spokesman again. 'We're exercising our right ashhh citizens of free Berlin to walk under shish monument of peace.' He was perhaps slurring his words more than was necessary. 'Shish emblem of peace was built by Friedrich Wilhelm II exactly two hundred years ago. You know that the maiden driving the four horses on top of this pile of beautiful neo-classical shit is carrying an olive branch? A shymbol of peacsh. Not an Iron Cross as she did for Nazis, but an *olive branch*. Do you hear me, shir? That'sh why we're here – to toast peace on the anniversary of the conshtruction.' He gave a rather drunken bow at the end of this speech.

The officer lost patience. 'You'd better get back to the other side or there'll be trouble for you damned Western agitators.' With this he hurried back to the line of troops, ordering them to move forward to the fence to prevent further encroachments from the East. But he was too late for Benedict's friends, who had just crashed through their cordon.

They emerged on the other side of the Brandenburg and found themselves not in the death zone, but a playground. A man performed a stunt on a bicycle. People wandered around, chatting up the guards, swigging from beer and champagne bottles and kissing and hugging each other randomly, without the slightest sense of their trespass. Suddenly about thirty of them formed a chain and began to dance in a huge circle. A painting by Goya depicting exactly the same insane joy flashed into Rosenharte's mind. To his astonished ears came the sound of a nursery rhyme.

> 'On the wall, lying in wait, sits a tiny little bug.
> Take a look at the tiny little, the tiny little bug . . .
>   take a look . . .
> On the Wall, on the wall, lying in wait . . .'

The Berlin Wall was falling to the sound of a children's song; the death strip had been irrevocably breached and demystified. The spell was broken.

Ulrike clutched Rosenharte's arm and shouted above the roar of the unseen crowd on the West side. 'My God, are we seeing this? Is this really happening? I can't believe it.'

Rosenharte turned from the jubilant faces and looked up at the Gate where the shadows of the people on the top of the Wall were projected like a huge Chinese lantern show. He would never know what made him look down and through the columns. Perhaps it was his habit of remembering a scene by consciously imprinting the image in his mind. At any rate, just in the eastern lee of the gate he saw Zank gesticulating to the officer who had stopped them a few moments before. He took Ulrike by the arm and rounded up Kurt and Benedict. 'We've got to get out of here. Come on.'

Benedict was too far gone to pay any attention. He shook his head. 'You go,' he shouted. 'I'm shtaying here.'

They hurried into the shadow of the Wall, which now seemed every bit as forbidding as a cliff face. Rosenharte crouched with his back against the Wall and cupped his hands in front of his knees. 'You get up first,' he shouted to Ulrike. 'Then help Kurt.'

She placed one foot in his hands and he hoisted her bird-weight with little difficulty to a height of about nine feet. The hands of the people on top came down to meet hers and she was pulled the last few feet. He passed Kurt's stick to her and then crouched again. From the corner of his eye, he saw Zank with the officer coming towards them. The officer seemed hesitant and was making gestures of hopelessness. 'Okay, let's get you up there,' he shouted. Kurt placed his left foot in Rosenharte's hands. Rosenharte lifted him four or five feet then turned and, placing one hand against Kurt's rump, pushed upwards. Kurt yelled as his ribcage connected with the concrete and his injured foot pawed the surface trying to get some hold. Eventually strong arms hoisted him to a point where he could scramble over the edge.

Rosenharte turned round, panting. Zank was within a few feet. 'You must arrest this man,' he was shouting to the officer. 'This man is an enemy of the state – a spy. Arrest him now. Or I will.'

'You have no authority here,' the officer told Zank, before turning to Rosenharte. 'Who are you?'

He proffered the passport. 'I'm a British citizen. It's my first time in East Germany.'

'Nonsense. This man is a spy. He's a traitor to the state. He must be arrested.' Spittle flew from Zank's mouth.

This all seemed very much beside the point to the Grepo officer and he threw out his hands in despair. 'I leave it to you.'

Then someone on top of the wall aimed the beam of a powerful flashlight at Zank. At the same time Kurt started up a chant of 'Sta-si! Sta-si! Sta-si!' Soon hundreds on this section of the Wall had joined in. Zank put up his hands to shield his eyes from the light, and his arm reached for something in his breast pocket, but then he seemed to think better of it and backed away a little, his gaze never leaving Rosenharte. 'You think you've won,' he shouted. 'But you haven't.'

Rosenharte moved a few paces towards him, at which point the baying of the crowd became deafening.

He gestured upwards at the crowd. 'These people have won, but I haven't. I lost my brother – remember? If I had obeyed my instincts last night, I'd have killed you there and then in Hohenschönhausen. That's where you deserved to die, you piece of shit.' He was right up close to him now. He could smell his breath and see the hatred in his eyes. 'But you'll live to see everything you believe in crumble; everything that your cowardly, brutal, limited being has worked for will disappear. That's good enough revenge for me.'

He didn't wait to hear Zank's retort, but turned and ran to the Wall and, using one foot to power himself upwards, he stretched and found the hands reaching down to grab hold of his arms. There was a moment when it seemed as if he would slip back into the death zone, but two of Benedict's friends gave him a mighty shove from below and he clambered up and rolled over the edge just as he had done on the sea wall in Trieste all those weeks ago. Then he was on top, dusting himself off and looking down at the sea of happy faces on the other side.

Ulrike's eyes were filling with tears. 'Is this true?' she asked. 'There's never been a moment in history like this. Are we dreaming?'

He shook his head very slowly and bent to kiss her.

THIRTY-NINE

The Cafe Adler

An hour later they approached Checkpoint Charlie from the western side. The only part of the crossing that remained visible was the little cabin set up in the middle of Friedrichstrasse by the Americans. Across the white line, painted by a young East German officer named Hagen Koch twenty-eight years before, was a vast crowd of young people who had filled all but one of the three lanes leading to the passport and customs control of the GDR. They had swarmed over the first pillboxes in the East and were now standing on or hanging from anything to get a better view of the people coming through from the parallel universe on the other side.

The East Berliners making the trip in the middle of the night were no longer just the pushy, the foolhardy or the young. Entire families were coming over, and they were bringing their babies in pushchairs, their dogs and their elderly relatives. Strangers hugged each other, lovers kissed as they crossed the line and some people simply looked up and cried to the heavens in disbelief, tears of joy welling in their eyes. Few of them took the time to consider the accumulation of accident, daring and political will that had brought the crowds from both sides of the Wall to overrun all seven crossing points by midnight on 9 November. And that, perhaps, made the evening seem all the more miraculous.

Watching these scenes with Kurt and Ulrike, Rosenharte found it very hard to absorb what he was seeing. Shaking his head he followed Kurt and Ulrike into the Cafe Adler. Robert Harland was sitting at the corner table by the window on Zimmerstrasse. Opposite him were the Bird and Jamie Jay. All three wore the standard expressions of the night's incredulity.

They ordered champagne and brandy chasers on the British government and made toasts to Berlin, freedom and, in the case of the three Germans at the table, to a united Germany. Harland told them the story of Schabowski's gaffe, and how it had taken the journalists a few minutes to realize what he had said.

'Was it planned?' asked Kurt, through Ulrike. 'Surely, he knew what he was doing – an experienced Party official like that?'

'Who knows, who knows,' said Harland, 'but here we are in a new world. The things that mattered on November the ninth don't even figure on November tenth.' He looked at his watch. 'We're twenty minutes into a new day and a new era. What's happened tonight is irrevocable. Without the Wall, there's no East Germany, at least not one that will function as a viable state. The game is up.'

For a further half-hour they sat huddled round the table, but then Ulrike's cough and Kurt's obvious discomfort made Harland insist that they go and get the medical attention that had been arranged. He rose to his feet, but not to usher them from Cafe Adler. The Bird and Jamie Jay stood also. 'I would like to offer you three a toast – to your indomitability, your courage and endurance. What you did is very important and will remain so, even in this new era of ours.'

Rosenharte looked at his two companions. 'I know I speak for us all when I thank you each for your role in getting us out. Without your help, Mr Avocet, my friends here would still be in Hohenschönhausen. We thank you from the bottom of our hearts for this deliverance.' The Bird's utterly English features began to redden from the neck up. 'Before this extraordinary night is over, I want us to toast Ulrike, one of the true founders of the revolution. She is one of those who have made tonight possible.' He raised his glass to her. The others followed suit.

'You two had better be off before we're all in tears,' said Harland briskly. 'I want to have a word with Rudi in private, if that's all right with him.'

Rosenharte nodded.

When they were alone, they ordered more brandy and smoked a cigarette each. Harland delved into a plastic bag, withdrew a folder and placed it on the table.

'This is your Stasi file,' he said quietly. 'I acquired it this evening from the Russian. I thought I was being given it as a means of checking some information that they've supplied to us, but he made it plain that his motive in handing it over was principally his concern and liking for you.' He pushed the file across the table but left his hand on top of it. 'Before you read it, I must warn you that there are a number of shocks in here – things that you may not want to know about. Things that will change your life.'

Rosenharte looked into Harland's grey eyes and placed a hand on the file.

'Are you sure?' asked Harland.

He nodded. 'It's my life and I think perhaps I should know about it before my fiftieth birthday.'

Harland coughed. 'That's what I mean. This file will tell you that you already *are* fifty, Rudi. Do you understand me?'

He took the folder and opened it. There were thirty loose leaves held by two metal clips. His eyes skimmed the first page. There could be no mistaking the file's authenticity. The spacing and indents, the coding, dating and filing information all written at the top right corner of the page were exactly how he had been taught to lay out a report in spy school.

'Naturally, I haven't read all of it yet,' said Harland. 'But I think it's perhaps best to start at the back. The last sheet will set everything in context.'

Rosenharte glanced at him then turned to the back.

It was a letter from the Dresden Bezirksverwaltung für Staatssicherheit – the Stasi headquarters in Dresden – to Normannenstrasse HQ. It was dated May 1953.

We have made extensive inquiries into the two young men known as Rudolf and Konrad Rosenharte and have found that there are good reasons for taking no further action on the request from the Polish authorities for investigation and repatriation were these inquiries to be fruitful. Even taking into consideration their likely actual age, both young men have attained an exceptionally high academic standard, which is matched by their physical prowess. There is no telling what they may achieve for the state in future years. Since the war they have been brought up in a good socialist home. Their adoptive parents Marie Theresa and Hermann Rosenharte have no history of sympathy with the fascists. They are robust working-class stock, ideologically staunch and active in the Party's cause. Frau Rosenharte's residual Catholic belief does not seem to have unduly affected the boys. On the question of their time in the household of the fascist general and his wife – Isobel and Manfred von Huth – we believe it is safe to conclude that there has been no negative influence of any sort in the formation of the personalities of the twins or of their political consciences.

We recommend a course of action which suggests to the Polish authorities

- *that the two young babies were killed in 1945. Isobel von Huth died in the Dresden bombings and it would be quite reasonable to expect her to have taken the children on the visit to Dresden in February 1945.*
- *or that we have been unable to trace the children on the information supplied.*

A note was added in ink that the latter course had been followed. This was initialled FH, but the original memorandum was unsigned.

Rosenharte turned over the sheet and found a copy of a letter that had been sent at a later date. Clipped to this on the reverse side were two small brown snaps of identical babies dated 'November 1938'.

'I would say you were about six months by then, wouldn't you?' said Harland carefully.

Rosenharte hardly knew how to react. Then he blurted, 'I knew it. Both of us felt this from the earliest age. We knew we couldn't have been born to that woman. And we always thought that Marie Theresa suspected something but had never told us.'

He took out the picture from his hip pocket and flattened it on the table. 'This is Isobel von Huth. Ulrike noticed that the photograph was taken in September 1939, when of course she should have been six months pregnant. But she's not. I thought it must have been a mistake in the dating. The man Grycko – this is what he was going to tell me in Trieste, wasn't it? He must have been some kind of relation, or closely associated with our family there.'

'Yes, I think that's plain,' said Harland. 'Maybe later you should talk to the Russian. He knows more about this than I do. After all, I've only had the file for the last five hours.'

Rosenharte returned to the papers and began to read the letter that had been sent by a Monsieur Michel Modroux from Red

Cross headquarters in Geneva on 3 December 1956 to the Foreign Ministry in Berlin.

We again communicate with you on the matter of two twin boys taken from the Kusimiak family home near Bochia, Poland. Ryszard and Konstantyn Kusimiak were kidnapped in November 1939 by German officers working for the Germanization programme, known as Lebensborn. They were the only children of Dr Michal Kusimiak and his wife Urszula, both academics at the university of Krakow. After the execution of their father and the imprisonment of their mother, it has been ascertained that the boys were taken by the Brown Sisters to Lodz concentration camp where they were inspected by Nazi authorities and assessed as racially valuable. Soon afterwards they were moved to a Lebensborn home and given new names. It is likely that these included the first one or two letters of their original first names – that is to say K or KO, R and RI (there being no German name that starts with RY). Documents in the Ministry of Interior in Warsaw suggest that the Kusimiak boys were not, as was usually the case, split up. Instead they were found a home with a senior ranking Nazi, almost certainly a member of Heinrich Himmler's SS. There is no record of their ultimate destination. It is hoped by the Red Cross, therefore, after several approaches from the Polish government and two formal requests from this organization, that the time and energy will now be found to research this case in the archives that are known to exist in the GDR. Extensive inquiries have been carried out in the Federal Republic of Germany but there is no evidence of the Kusimiak boys living in the West. It is the conclusion of the Polish authorities, as they have already informed you, that they were settled in what is now the GDR and that there is every chance that they survived the war. We would urge you to expedite this matter with all means at your disposal.

Attached to this was a carbon copy of the reply from the Foreign Ministry, which was dated 8 May 1957 – five months later. It ran:

At your request, a third investigation was undertaken and we again report that no match was found between the description provided and the records preserved by the government of the GDR for precisely this kind of humane research. As the Red Cross must appreciate more than any other organization, the criminal fascists stole many children in Eastern Europe and when these young persons resisted Nazification they were often liquidated. We regret that we cannot help and must now insist that this matter is closed.

Rosenharte put down the file. 'You know what Lebensborn means in English?'

'Spring of life,' replied Harland.

'They knew the whole time! Those bastards in the Stasi knew the whole time that we had been taken from Poland. And if the Polish were making inquiries, it means that a part of the family survived the war. We have relatives. They denied us contact with our own flesh and blood.'

'Do you think your adoptive mother . . . did Frau Rosenharte know?'

Rosenharte shook his head. 'She may have had her suspicions, but she only went to work at Schloss Clausnitz very late in the war so she wouldn't necessarily have known. She was a good woman and a very good mother. It wasn't in her nature to deceive.' He stopped. He was quite simply stunned by the documents. 'I can't get over the fact that we weren't told. They used our Nazi parentage to make us feel that we each had something to be ashamed of and that we owed the state, when the very opposite was true.'

'They kept you for your talents,' said Harland, 'and it explains why you were allowed to join the Stasi in the first place. No one with an SS general as a father would have been allowed to join the HVA.'

'What else is in here?'

'The documents are divided into two sections. The first are copies of the records of your time as a Stasi officer – reports on your progress, your training at the Main Directorate and your success or otherwise as an illegal abroad. The second section is devoted to your life in Dresden after you were allowed to leave the service. It's clear they did everything they could to keep tabs on you because of your knowledge of the inner workings of the MfS. There were any number of IMs working on your case: colleagues, friends. It would seem that they turned most of your girlfriends and your ex-wife. Of course the majority is tittle-tattle.' He stopped and looked across at Rosenharte. 'But there's one significant thing that you should know, and this will be a shock to you.'

'What? Tell me now.'

Harland regarded him steadily but said nothing. Outside, the noise of the crowd rose with each new surge of East Germans coming over; inside the Adler there was a celebration going on like no other. But for Rosenharte the events of the night – indeed of the last two months – had suddenly receded to a great distance. He may have been sitting beneath the Adler's glass ceiling, in which all the joy of the world was reflected, but he was locked in his private capsule of time and space with the British spy. Before him was a shabby, well-thumbed folder which contained more information about his life than he had ever possessed himself. The Stasi had owned the objective truth of his existence, and of Konrad's. They had hoarded that truth and used it to mould and manipulate their lives. It occurred to him that reading the file was an act of repossession for both him and Konrad.

'Tell me what I should expect in here.'

Harland took the file and flipped through the pages, moistening his index finger as he went. Then he turned it round with his finger pressing down on a page. 'It seems that your brother was recruited as an IM specifically for the purpose of watching you. I'm sorry, Rudi. I didn't want you to see this.'

Rosenharte began to read the account of a meeting with Konrad that had taken place in Bautzen. His handler was an officer named Lange, and it seemed they met every six weeks or so at various safe houses in the Dresden area. Rosenharte counted notes on twenty-two secret meetings. He knew that he had to read it all now. There was no possibility of leaving this until later, or skimming it as he would the other material.

The first pages included observations about Konrad – his diligence, nimbleness of mind and generally helpful demeanour. After his experience in Bautzen, the Stasi had high hopes of making him an important source, not only on his brother. There were members of the intelligentsia that they wished to target; creative types, hostile negative elements, decadent subversives that they wanted to know more about. In order to make certain of Konrad's cooperation they regularly implied that he could be sent back to prison and they offered medical help and dentistry as incentives, though it seemed these never materialized.

Konrad had told them about a long walk they had taken together in the hills. Rosenharte remembered the conversation as though it were yesterday because they had come close to falling out about religion and the unworkability of socialism. Konrad was agnostic, Rudi a lazy atheist. Konrad was a convinced socialist; Rudi was a sceptic. The account of the conversation, however, presented an entirely different picture. Konrad had evidently allowed Lange to draw him out on his brother's inner convictions, and these Konrad had portrayed as a polar opposite of his actual sentiments. Where Rudi had been doubtful about the likely success of a socialist state, he was reported as being cautiously optimistic. When he asserted that he would have nothing to do with the Party, Konrad had surmised that he was lacking in confidence, having failed the state so catastrophically during his foreign service. He pretended not to know about the business in Brussels, but his handler filled in the details and concluded that Rudi Rosenharte was discreet about his time in the Stasi.

As he read on, Rosenharte began to smile. According to a reluctantly disloyal Konrad, he, Rudi, was guilt-ridden, politically naïve, mean with his money, depressed, self-absorbed, selfish, and had difficulty in forming permanent relationships with women, most of which were the opposite of Rosenharte's actual characteristics. Here and there were grains of truthful observation and reports of incidents that had taken place, but the total picture was false. He let the file slip to the table and summoned the image of Konrad in the late spring of that year sitting in a rickety chair, watching his sons playing in the hay meadow. He remembered his expression as being curiously detached at the time. And when he'd asked if there was something the matter, he had turned to him with the odd look that seemed to suggest Rudi's trespass. Now he understood: that gentle mind was planning each step of his brother's protection – a lonely course which required sacrifice and patience and was plotted alongside his own oblique defiance of the state.

Harland waited for him to speak.

'He used them,' said Rosenharte. 'He told them a whole pack of lies about me. He made fools of them and helped protect me.' He paused. 'It's a tragedy that he did not live to see all this tonight. He would have been amazed and a very shrewd interpreter of what has happened.'

Harland nodded. 'I know there's always a diminishing return with the third cognac, but I think you're going to need it.'

Rosenharte wondered at the tension around Harland's eyes. Surely tonight of all nights a British spy could relax. But he seemed on edge and distracted. He asked why.

'Everything's changed. I may lose the deal I set up with the Russian. Five hours ago it looked pretty sweet, but then this happened and, well, it seems that the Americans are going to step in with their money and gather up everything I was working to get hold of.'

'Does it matter? After all, you achieved the arrest of Abu Jamal. You got Konrad's family out. And without your strange friend, Cuth Avocet, I would never have managed to release Ulrike and Kurt.'

Harland pursed his lips. 'You're right. But my pride is offended. I wanted to pull it off. Still, when history takes over we all have to stand aside.'

He signalled for another round. When it came he said: 'My instructions from London specifically require me not to tell you the thing that I believe you ought to know.' He stopped, swirled the brandy in front of his nose and glanced out of the window. 'However, while watching you go through that file and seeing you read about yourself and Konrad, it struck me that tonight I also have a duty to the truth.' There was another agonized pause during which he took a cigarette from Rosenharte. 'In our line of work, things necessarily remain hidden. Deception and subterfuge are allowed to stand as the truth; the lie becomes the record, if you like. On this occasion, I don't want that to happen.'

Rosenharte shrugged. He was suddenly exhausted. He needed time to himself.

Then Harland said, 'Annalise Schering never died. There was no suicide.'

Rosenharte felt himself stiffen. He slammed down his glass, almost breaking it, and looked away. 'No! She was dead. I saw her.'

'But you didn't *touch* her.' He paused. 'You left immediately. We had people in the apartment. The moment you went in there we arranged for the doorbell to go and the phone to ring. You saw our little tableau with Annalise in the ice-cold bath and panicked, just as we hoped you would.'

'Why? It doesn't make sense.'

'She wasn't up to dealing with you. She wasn't sharp enough and she wanted out. We didn't know how you'd react. When you didn't immediately tell your people that she was dead and that you had in effect failed, we knew we could use you. We got the police involved and put a deal to you. Then we made sure they got rid of you by using the second Annalise to feed some bad stuff back to the Stasi about your drinking and your lack of discretion as an agent. I think they did a pretty good job on you. Well, you already know that.'

Rosenharte was still dumbfounded. 'But the risk! I might have told the Stasi at any time.'

'There was no risk whatsoever. The only person who was exposed was you. The longer the operation went on, the more important Annalise Schering became to us, the Stasi and of course the Russians. You've got to remember it was the only method of telling your side what we actually intended without them putting it through the usual filters of suspicion. *Because* she was a traitor they trusted her.'

He opened his hands to invite reaction. Rosenharte shook his head and said nothing.

'You have every right to be angry about this,' said Harland, pushing the tip of his cigarette around the ashtray. 'I know how much that little stunt affected your life, but then . . . but then you have to appreciate that to us you were just another communist spy, a Romeo sent to the West to steal our secrets and threaten our security.' He paused and revolved the watch on his wrist. Rosenharte had never seen him so unsettled. 'Look on the bright side, Rudi; at least you have no death on your conscience. The real Annalise Schering has grown plump and happy and is living in the English shires with three teenage children.'

Rosenharte shook his head. He could have sprung his own shock on Harland by telling him how Ulrike and the second Annalise had bonded and worked together in the cause of peace for so long. But that was their secret and it wouldn't serve any purpose to reveal that a young Stasi translator had seen through MI6's great subterfuge. He rose from the table and threw back his brandy. 'That was another time – an age ago.' He stretched and then stubbed out his cigarette. 'Right now, Mr Harland, I need some sleep.'

'You're not angry?'

'In some ways, yes. But remember I was able to leave the Stasi and devote my life to the study of art. Where would I be now without your spy games?'

FOURTY

The Bridge

On Saturday 11 November, some thirty-six hours after the Wall fell, Rosenharte got up early in the hotel, showered and dressed with more than usual care, putting on a tie and the trousers of a dark-grey suit that he'd bought with Ulrike the day before on the Kurfurstendamm. Then he sat at the desk overlooking the Tiergarten, made some calls and read the notes he'd made while on the phone to Leszek Grycko late the previous evening. After about an hour Ulrike came in from the adjoining bedroom, still wearing the hotel bathrobe.

'How're you feeling?' he asked.

'Not great. It's unnatural to sleep for twelve hours.'

'You've woken from a long hibernation,' he said and touched the faint crease made on her cheek by the pillow. 'We all have.' He paused and gazed at her. 'You know the problem with a love like this?'

'No.'

'It renders me speechless. I can't begin to express what I feel.'

'You're doing just fine,' she said, nuzzling him. 'Just fine. Have you talked to Kurt?'

'Yes, he says he'll have the cast on for five or six weeks. The ribs are going to have to heal themselves. He'll be out tomorrow or the next day.'

'And Else?'

'They'll all be here by early evening.'

'Explain this to me,' she said, pointing at the crude family tree he had made while she slept.

He placed his finger by the name of Dr Michal Kusimiak. 'This is my father. He was a graduate of the Cieszyn Business School and a protégé of a man named Dr L. Fabanczyk. He left the school in thirty-six and went to teach politics at the University of Krakow where he became a committed Marxist. There he met my mother, Urszula Solanka, who was a nineteen-year-old student of literature. They were married almost immediately and on 5 July 1938 she gave birth to me and Konrad. We were named Ryszard and Konstantyn after our grandfathers.

'Come the war my parents went into hiding at the Kusimiak family estates near the city of Bochia. They were hunted down. My father was summarily executed on 7 November at the age of thirty-one; Urszula was sent to Ravensbrück then Auschwitz. We were taken to Lodz, then very soon afterwards to the von Huths at Schloss Clausnitz. We were there by the first Christmas of the war. The only things we had from our previous life were the first letters of our names. That apparently was common practice and allowed some of the stolen children to be traced after the war.'

He moved his finger to the name Luiza Solanka. 'This is my mother's older sister. She married a man named Grycko at the age of eighteen and had one son, Franciscek, who was born in 1930. She and her husband both perished in the camps, but their boy somehow survived and emerged at the end of the war, a hardened adult aged about fifteen. This was the man who died in my arms in Trieste.'

'Your first cousin!'

He shuddered. 'That's one of the things that I can't really absorb. The fact that he came so close to telling me all this.' He paused and remembered the man on Molo IV in Trieste and his own disgust. 'After university and military service Franciscek joined the Polish Foreign Intelligence Service. He rose quickly and in due course began to make representations through his government and the Red Cross about the lost Kusimiak children. But it was useless. You see, about two hundred thousand Polish children were kidnapped in the Germanization programme. Only thirty thousand were ever found and returned to their natural parents. By the time Grycko got into any position of influence the child tracing operation in Heidelberg had long been terminated. It seems that Franciscek couldn't let go of this thing, and when he retired from the service because of ill health he devoted all his energies to tracking us. It was he who made the breakthrough by finding a contact in Schwarzmeer's office. When he died, his son Leszek seemed to have inherited the cause. He was the man who followed me to Leipzig that day when we first met, and then he went all the way out to Konrad's home.'

'The Russian said he was in the service too. Is that right?'

'He's a technical officer with little field experience.'

She rose from the arm of his chair, yawned luxuriously and went to fill her cup from the pot on the room-service trolley. 'Who told you he had a contact in Schwarzmeer's office?'

'The Russian.'

'Both the Gryckos were certainly well informed. For one to find you in Trieste and the other to run you to ground in Leipzig indicates a huge amount of advanced knowledge.'

'I see what you mean, but I guess the Stasi were always watching me and Konrad, so it was just a matter of tapping into that source of information.'

She returned to him and kissed the top of his head. 'How odd this must feel to you – seeing a life that was yours but that you haven't lived.'

'You could argue that if we hadn't been taken by the Nazis there would be no life at all. We might have died with the others in the camps.' He lit a cigarette and blew the smoke away from her.

'You have to give that up, what with my bronchitis and your advanced age.' She smiled impishly and pecked him on the cheek. 'Still, I suppose you won't have to go through the usual pain of becoming fifty because you did that last year.'

'I'm sticking to my old birthday,' he said testily. 'Look, shouldn't you be getting ready? Harland will be here soon.'

'Are you nervous?' she said, leaving him for the bathroom.

'Yes . . . and no. I don't know what I feel. I don't know what I *should* feel.'

She hesitated by the door. 'Kusimiak – I like that sound. It's vaguely Russian or Cossack. Will you change your name?'

'I have no idea.' Then he said: 'Probably not. I owe something to the Rosenhartes, and actually I like being German. I feel German and I don't want to be anything else.'

It was a glorious autumn day, brilliant and animated with joy in every quarter of the free enclave of West Berlin. Upwards of a million came from the East that morning to receive their welcome money from the West German government and to spend it on clothes, books and every sort of cheap appliance. It was striking to Rosenharte how much food was bought that day, particularly *Südfrüchte* – the bananas and oranges and mangos that were commonplace in the West and so rare in the GDR. The rush of joy of the first hours had now been replaced by huge questions and a sense of unbridgeable inequality. It was not that the Easterners wanted to reverse the events of the last two days, but seeing the wealth of the West and the goods in the stores for themselves was a different order of experience to watching them illicitly on West German TV from behind the impenetrable barrier of the Berlin Wall.

'What are they going to do?' asked Ulrike as they waited for Harland at the entrance to the hotel. 'How are they going to make this work?'

'Not our problem,' said Rosenharte. 'Not today. And anyway, for the moment it's enough that this has happened.'

As they drove southeast to Wannsee, Harland told them that the first sections of the Wall had been winched out of place at Potsdamerplatz to make a new crossing and that the Russian cellist Mstislav Rostropovic had played for the crowds streaming through another opening. He also mentioned there were rumours that in the GDR the Stasi was already beginning to destroy its most sensitive files, burning them and pulping them in machines designed to make animal feed.

Rosenharte murmured interest in these bits of news, but said little as they went.

They had reached Königstrasse, the long, straight drive that cuts across Wannsee and ends at the Glienicke Bridge. They could hardly believe the clarity of that afternoon: the sunlight streaming through the trees, the steady shower of golden birch and beech leaves. Ulrike clasped his right hand between hers and once or twice lifted it to her lips.

They parked about a hundred yards from the bridge and all got out. 'Why here?' she asked.

'This is the only crossing point controlled by the Russians,' said Harland. 'Maybe Vladimir is making some kind of point.'

'Vladimir is the KGB spy from Dresden?' Ulrike asked Rosenharte.

'Yes,' he said, looking across the bridge. 'Major Vladimir Ilyich Ussayamov.'

'His name isn't Ussayamov,' said Harland. 'It's Putin. Lieutenant-Colonel Vladimir Vladimirovich Putin.'

Rosenharte shrugged.

'Do you want me to come?' Ulrike asked him.

He shook his head, turned and began to walk towards the old iron bridge over the Havel Lake that marked the border between the city of Berlin and the state of Brandenburg, between the territories of West and East. He walked with his gaze fastened on the Soviet flag on the far side of the bridge and to distract himself, tried to remember the name of the Russian spy who had been swapped on the bridge for the U2 pilot Gary Powers nearly three decades before. Of course. Colonel Rudolf Abel was the name of the Soviet spy and they passed each other on the bridge without saying a word.

He reached the bridge and moved to a stone parapet on the right where there were fewer people. No one, least of all Rosenharte in his rather uncertain state of mind, could fail to be moved by the scene. Westerners stood clapping as each little Trabant car passed over the line at the centre of the bridge. Pedestrians hugged and kissed with a total lack of reserve. Red roses were flung at the cars and pedestrians and once or twice the women from the East stooped to pick them from the road and pressed them to their hearts.

Harland had followed and now passed him on the other side of the bridge. They nodded to each other. Rosenharte watched him with mild interest as he moved along the southern walkway and came to a halt by a figure who was leaning over the railings, looking down on the evenly rippled, sparkling waters of the Havel. The figure straightened, controlled a wisp of blond hair and they shook hands. It was Vladimir. Harland gestured in Rosenharte's direction. Vladimir stepped into the centre of the road, put his hand to his forehead and then held it high above him in a kind of salute. Rosenharte returned the wave but didn't move from his spot.

Then a dark-green helicopter with US markings, a Huey polished like a limousine, came to hover over his side of the bridge, so low that Rosenharte could make out the faces of the men clinging to the straps in the open door. He assumed that they were watching the crowds stream over the bridge, but then he saw Alan Griswald's face appear at the door for a fleeting second. The helicopter had come to observe the conversation between Harland and Vladimir, presumably with their knowledge. The intelligence business never rested.

The Huey remained there for several minutes, the throb of the rotor drowning the applause and cheers, yet also adding a compelling pulse to the reunion of two peoples. Then the note of its engine changed. It began to rise, sending a powerful downdraft onto the bridge, which tore at people's clothes and flattened their hair and caused them to cry out with the sudden artless gaiety of people at a funfair. For a split second each person's defences fell away and they looked around and caught each other's eyes and glimpsed each other's souls.

It was in the afterglow of this moment that Rosenharte spotted Leszek Grycko on the other side of the road. The tall young Pole saw him and waved back with a broad grin, but a van came to a halt between them and they both bobbed up and down, waving. The van moved forward. Beside Leszek stood an elderly woman in a well-cut woollen suit who was looking at him with intense curiosity. She brushed away a strand of dark-grey hair that had come loose from her bun, nodded, then seemed to smile at him.

Until that moment, Rosenharte had had all sorts of complicated doubts and explanations why this couldn't be true, but now he was absolutely certain. For his entire life he had seen precisely the same expression of clever, restrained interest in Konrad's face. Here it was again in Urszula Kusimiak – his natural mother.

She waited for him to cross. Then, as he approached, she held out both her hands. He took them and she absorbed the face of the child she had lost exactly fifty years before.

'I'm sorry,' he said. 'I'm sorry I couldn't bring Konnie with me.' She nodded and shook her head and the corners of her mouth trembled with emotion. But her eyes remained composed, watching him with growing love. 'I wish he could have met you.' He suddenly thought of *Sublime No. 2*, the film Else had shown him. 'But I'm sure he knew instinctively of your existence. I believe he was aware of you in some deep part of himself.'

She put her head to one side. In precise and deliberate German she said: 'We've both lost so much these past years. But now this long hiatus has ended. I have found you and I've gained two grandchildren. That is more than I expected; more than I could have ever hoped for.'

'You speak German. I was thinking it would be the final irony if we weren't able to communicate.'

'I learned in the camps in order to survive. I knew also that I would need it to find you after the war.' She stopped. 'And now I have.'

From the corner of his eye, he saw Ulrike approach. He turned. 'This is my friend Ulrike – the woman I hope to make my wife.' He was aware that he was blushing.

Ulrike was shaking her head and pointing towards the bridge. They all turned. Standing in the middle of the Glienicke Bridge, oblivious of the traffic and of Harland and Vladimir, was Colonel

Zank. Rosenharte's hand moved automatically to the pocket where he kept the gun that he'd meant to dispose of on the way.

Ulrike put her hand up. 'He's not coming; he's watching, Rudi. Leave him.'

Urszula Kusimiak seemed to know exactly what was going on. 'I suspect he is one of the few people who cannot cross the Glienicke Bridge today.'

'You're right,' said Rosenharte, noticing that Harland had left Vladimir and approached Zank from behind. Now he was saying something and patting his own pocket to indicate that Zank shouldn't try anything. Zank looked away.

Then Urszula Kusimiak took her lost son's arm and they turned to walk the gentle incline away from the bridge, leaving Colonel Zank trapped behind the forcefield that was once the Iron Curtain.

AUTHOR'S NOTE

East Germany was the only member of the communist bloc to disappear as a state. A decade and a half after the Wall came down and the process of German unification began, most people would be hard pressed to trace the border between East and West Germany on a map. The very idea of two Germanies, of an Iron Curtain slicing across Europe, seems astonishing today, especially to those born after 1975. And nothing was more bizarre during that era of division than the arrangements in West Berlin, a free enclave 100 miles inside communist territory, unswervingly guaranteed by the Western allies but surrounded by the watchtowers, barbed wire and concrete of the Berlin Wall.

We have forgotten East Germany's baleful presence at the centre of Europe, the tragic power of the Wall and also perhaps what it meant when on Thursday 9 November 1989 East Germans massed at the border crossings and West Germans climbed onto the Wall in front of the Brandenburg Gate to demand its destruction. Few who were there will ever again experience the surge of joy and optimism of those hours. Or the incredulity. For even after one million East Germans demonstrated against their government in Alexanderplatz, no one would have dared to predict that within a week those same people would be shopping in West Berlin.

It seemed a miracle then but it's easy today to see how events combined to destroy the GDR and spark the fall of communism across Eastern Europe. In the Soviet Union Mikhail Gorbachev's introduction of the policies of *Glasnost* (freedom of expression) and *Perestroika* (restructuring) came with a new realism about the failure of the Marxist economies. Put simply, they were broke. East Germany, which unlike West Germany had little coal or steel of its own, survived into the eighties on cheap oil from the USSR and by exporting agricultural and industrial machinery at bargain-basement prices to the West. But Russia could no longer afford to subsidize the GDR, and the emerging Tigers of southeast Asia were producing far better machinery at even lower prices. Erich Honecker's East German government seemed incapable of responding to the mounting crisis other than by resisting the reforms of the Soviet Union. To the old men in Berlin the unthinkable had happened: the mother ship of Marxism had veered wildly off course, leaving them to continue the socialist struggle.

There were other straws in the wind. In Hungary a new regime had removed the barbed-wire border with Austria in May of that year and in September the Hungarian foreign minister announced that East German tourists would not be prevented from crossing to the West. At the same time the communist government of Czechoslovakia seemed powerless to halt the flood of East Germans coming over the border and claiming asylum at the West German Embassy in Prague. Much the same was happening in Poland. Those not intent on fleeing the country were bent on change. '*Wir sind hier,*' they shouted through September and October – we're staying here. Diverse groups – punks and skinheads, greens, peace campaigners and those who simply desired political reform, free expression and unrestricted travel – came together around the thriving evangelical churches of the East, particularly the Nikolai-kirche in Leipzig. As the Monday evening demonstrations swelled with crowds chanting the simple but unprecedented self-assertion, *Wir sind das Volk* – we are the people – Honecker seemed incapable of acting. It's interesting to speculate what might have been if a younger generation of hardliners had succeeded at the beginning of the decade. Honecker was seventy-four and had undergone an operation that summer, Willi Stoph, Chairman of the Council of Ministers, was seventy-five, Erich Mielke, the head of the Stasi, was eighty-one. The other members of the Politburo were mostly over sixty-five. In the face of such orderly and disciplined defiance of the state they simply froze.

Yet it is also true that China and Russia had been ruled for long periods by ruthless old men and in China that summer between 800 and 1,200 demonstrators had been killed in Tiananmen Square. So it is important to understand that while the conditions seem favourable to us today, the German uprising was not ordained to succeed. The reality was that the protesters who met outside the Nikolaikirche in Leipzig every Monday evening might have been crushed by the Stasi at any step along the way, just like the students in Beijing. It's still largely a mystery why the orders to suppress the demonstrations with all necessary force on 9 October were never carried out, though of course former leaders and members of the security forces have since tried to take credit for defying the high command in Berlin.

We have also forgotten the curious nature of the East German state. Besides its fanatical pursuit of sporting glory, the obsessive militarism and religious faith in science and technology, the GDR possessed the most formidable intelligence services the world has ever seen. A population of just over 17,000,000 was served – if that's the right word – by 81,000 intelligence officers belonging to the Ministerium für Staatssicherheit – or Stasi for short. There was very little in a person's life that the Stasi could not reach. Some estimates put the number of informers at 1,500,000, which meant that every sixth or seventh adult was working for the Stasi by making regular reports on colleagues, friends and sometimes even lovers and relations.

Run from a vast complex in Normannenstrasse, Berlin, the Stasi was a state within a state. It had its own football team, prisons, special shops selling foreign luxuries, holiday resorts, hospitals, sports centres and every sort of surveillance facility. Large and well-equipped regional offices were in every city. In Leipzig, where part of my story is set, thousands of pieces of mail were opened every day, over 1,000 telephones were tapped, and 2,000 officers were charged with penetrating and monitoring every possible group and organization. Their efforts were augmented by as many as 5,000 IMs- Inoffizielle Mitarbeiters, or unofficial collaborators – who were debriefed by Stasi controllers in some seventy safe houses around the city. In numbers this effort in Leipzig far exceeded the joint operations of Britain's Security Service (MI5) and Secret Intelligence Service (MI6).

The dismal paranoia of Erich Mielke's organization is hard to imagine today. Suffice to say that even school children's essays were examined for signs of political dissent at home, and in museums in Leipzig and Berlin you can still view the sealed preserving jars containing cloth impregnated with the personal smells of targeted dissidents. It has never been clear what use this archive was put to, but there is no better symbol of the Stasi's powers of intrusion and absurdist obsession. The special equipment they made for themselves has a comic ingenuity about it: the cameras hidden in briefcases, petrol cans or the headlight of a Trabant car; a bugged watering can, which lay unregarded in one of the garden allotments outside

Leipzig to catch anyone being disloyal as they tended their vegetables. The Stasi officers took delight in these gadgets and were in love with the shoddy business of spying on ordinary human beings who represented no threat to the state whatsoever. The breaking of spirits in Hohenschönhausen interrogation centre and at Bautzen prison, the persecution by rumour and lie, the destruction of relationships and careers, the crushing of individual creativity and talent, the tireless search for 'hostile negative elements' were all done in the name of security. East Germany was a truly dreadful place to live if you objected to the regime, or showed anything but craven loyalty to the state. Looking at the relatively crude surveillance apparatus sixteen years on, one wonders what the Stasi would have done with today's technology – our tiny radio tracking devices, biometric identification, number recognition systems and the rapid processing power of surveillance computers. One thing's for certain: the reformers in Leipzig would have had a much harder time of it.

The GDR may have disappeared along with the Berlin Wall, the institutionalized vindictiveness and the slogans calling for ever greater sacrifice, yet East Germany is still very much in evidence today. You can walk around the soulless housing complexes in Dresden and Leipzig, visit Hohenschönhausen and Erich Mielke's office in Berlin – now both museums – or in the forests of the south happen upon the huge secret installations of the Cold War, long ago abandoned by the Soviet army. The fabric of East Germany is still pretty much intact and, naturally, the people are there with their memories of one of the most efficient dictatorships of modern times.

I have tried as far as possible to thread my story through the actual timeline of events that occurred between the beginning of September and the weekend of 11-12 November 1989. The dates for the closing of borders with Czechoslovakia, the transport of Eastern refugees to West Germany, the time and routes of demonstrations in Leipzig, and the sequence of events in Berlin on 9 November are all, I hope, accurate. I have also taken care to use the exact words spoken by Gorbachev on 6 October, by the priests officiating at the Nikolaikirche in Leipzig and by the people who took part in the crucial press conference held by Gunther Schabowski in East Berlin on 9 November. Extracts from broadcasts on both sides of the Wall that night are also word for word.

Although this is clearly a work of fiction, some real people are portrayed. Erich Mielke, the head of the Stasi, makes a cameo appearance. I hope that I have done him justice. Lt Colonel Vladimir Putin was at the time of the action a KGB officer stationed in Dresden. His duties included spying on the city's Technical University and after the Wall fell he was indeed responsible for rescuing certain sensitive files from the Stasi's Dresden headquarters. But of course his role in this plot is entirely made up. My character Colonel Otto Biermeier is very loosely based on Colonel Rainer Wiegand, a courageous member of the Stasi's counter-espionage directorate who revealed details of East Germany's active collaboration with Middle Eastern terrorists to the West. In 1996 Wiegand was due to be the star witness in the trial of the perpetrators of the bombing of La Belle discotheque in West Berlin, when his car crashed in mysterious circumstances in Portugal killing both himself and his wife. It is assumed that he was murdered.

How much the Eastern Bloc had to do with the Middle Eastern terrorism of the seventies and eighties is still largely unknown. The CIA successfully managed to attribute much of the responsibility for support of Arab terrorists to the Soviet Union. Now it appears the Russians were relatively innocent in the matter. The same was not true of the East Germans, who had a relationship with the late Abu Nidal and sheltered terrorists from Lebanon, Libya and Yemen. It is true that before the Wall came down Russia and America had begun to cooperate at a high level on Middle Eastern terrorism.

The characters of Mike Costelloe and Lisl Voss are based on real people. When news of the Wall coming down hit London on 9 November 1989 both were attending an informal dinner held at Langan's Brasserie for the West German intelligence service, prior to a briefing by Germans of the British Joint Intelligence Committee. The West German traitor on whom I have modelled Lisl Voss insisted that the fall of the Wall would not entail the end of the GDR.

There was never anyone remotely resembling Dr Rudi Rosenharte working at the Dresden Gemäldegalerie during the eighties. Rosenharte's background was inspired by an account of the Nazis' *Lebensborn* programme in Caroline Moorehead's excellent study of the Red Cross, *Dunant's Dream* (HarperCollins).

Finally, Schloss Clausnitz – the grand country house where Rudi and Konrad Rosenharte were taken as babies at the beginning of the war – is based brick for brick on Schloss Basedow, a huge pile in the Mecklenburg-Vorpommern region. I have moved it to the beech forests of southern Saxony.

Henry Porter
London, 2004

ACKNOWLEDGEMENTS

Thanks are due to Pamela Merrit, who read the manuscript and gave me unstinting encouragement, and to Jane Wood, my editor at Orion, Tif Loehnis of Janklow and Nesbitt, and Sophie Hutton-Squire, who all contributed greatly to *Brandenburg*'s final form. My research trips to East Germany would have been far less easy, pleasant and effective without the help of Birgit Kubisch. I thank Christopher Hilton, author of the definitive history of the Berlin Wall (*The Wall, the People's Story* – Sutton) for his introduction to her. Finally, I offer my gratitude to my wife Liz Elliot, who put up with the agonies of another book being written in her home, and to Lina Dias for all her support.

Scores of books have been written on the GDR and fall of the Wall. These are some of the best. *The Rise and Fall of the German Democratic Republic 1945-1990* by Mike Dennis (Longman), *The Fall of the GDR* by David Childs (Longman), *The Stasi: the East German Intelligence and Security Service* by D. Childs and R. Popplewell (Macmillan), *The Stasi: Myth and Reality* by Mike Dennis (Longman), *The Stasi Files* by Antony Glees (Free Press), *Anatomy of a Dictatorship: Inside the GDR 1949-1989* by Mary Fulbrook (Oxford), *Keine Gewalt!*, a photographic record compiled by Norbert Heber and Johannes Lehmann (Verbum), *Beyond the Wall: The Lost World of East Germany* by Simon Marsden and Duncan McLaren (Little, Brown), and finally the hypnotizing *Memoirs of a Spymaster: the Man Who Waged a Secret War Against the West* by Markus Wolf with Anne McElvoy (Pimlico).